This novel is dedicated to the memory of my good friend, mentor, and editor, George M. Coleman, executive editor at G. P. Putnam's Sons. From the very beginning of my writing career, whenever I needed a guiding hand around all the land mines in the publishing world, he was always there.

The greatest gift God could give us is to put the soul of George Coleman into another person and let his charm, excitement, and thirst for life bless us once again. I hope to meet that lucky person someday.

This novel is also dedicated to the men and women of the Aircrew Life-Support Section, 31st Fighter Wing, Aviano Air Base, Italy, for their hard work in training and equipping U.S. Air Force F-16 pilot Captain Scott O'Grady, which helped him to survive being shot down over Bosnia and to successfully escape the clutches of the Bosnian Serb army in June of 1995. Mission after mission, year after year, they pack the 'chutes, charge the bottles, check the straps, and change the batteries as if they will be the ones who'll strap on that jet. Thanks for bringing a crewdog home safely.

continued...

NIGHT OF THE HAWK

The exciting final flight of the "Old Dog"—a shattering mission into Lithuania, where the Soviets' past could launch a terrifying future...

"Dale Brown brings us the gripping conclusion of the saga that began so memorably with *Flight of the Old Dog*. A masterful mix of high technology and *human* courage."
—W.E.B. Griffin

SKY MASTERS

The incredible story of America's newest B-2 bomber, engaged in a blistering battle of oil, honor, and global power...

"*Sky Masters* is a knockout!"
—Clive Cussler

"A gripping military thriller . . . Brown brings combat and technology together in an explosive tale as timely as this morning's news."
—W.E.B. Griffin

HAMMERHEADS

The U.S. government creates an all-new drug-defense agency, armed with the ultimate high-tech weaponry. The war against drugs will never be the same...

"Classic . . . His most exciting techno-thriller!"
—*Publishers Weekly*

"Whiz-bang technology and muscular, damn-the-torpedoes strategy."
—*Kirkus Reviews*

DAY OF THE CHEETAH

The shattering story of a Soviet hijacking of America's most advanced fighter plane—and the greatest high-tech chase of all time...

"Quite a ride . . . Terrific. Authentic and gripping!"
—*New York Times*

"Breathtaking dogfights . . . Exhilarating high-tech adventure."
—*Library Journal*

SILVER TOWER

A Soviet invasion of the Middle East sparks a grueling counterattack from America's newest laser defense system...

"Riveting, action-packed . . . a fast-paced thriller that is impossible to put down!"
—*UPI*

"Intriguing political projections . . . Tense high-tech dogfights."
—*Publishers Weekly*

"High-tech, high-thrills . . . a slam-bang finale!"
—*Kirkus Reviews*

FLIGHT OF THE OLD DOG

Dale Brown's riveting debut novel. A battle-scarred bomber is renovated with modern hardware to fight the Soviets' devastating new technology...

"A superbly crafted adventure . . . Exciting!"
—W.E.B. Griffin

"Brown kept me glued to the chair . . . a shattering climax. A terrific flying yarn!"
—Stephen Coonts

SHADOWS
OF STEEL

DALE BROWN

BERKLEY BOOKS, NEW YORK

SHADOWS OF STEEL

A Berkley Book / published by arrangement with
Target Direct Productions, Inc.

PRINTING HISTORY
G.P. Putnam's Sons edition / July 1996
Berkley edition / May 1997

The Putnam Berkley World Wide Web site address is
http://www.berkley.com

ISBN: 0-425-15716-4

BERKLEY®
Berkley Books are published by The Berkley Publishing Group, 200 Madison Avenue, New York, New York 10016.
BERKLEY and the "B" design
are trademarks belonging to Berkley Publishing Corporation.

PRINTED IN THE UNITED STATES OF AMERICA

10 9 8 7 6 5

ACKNOWLEDGMENTS

Thanks to my good friend Lieutenant General Don Aldridge, USAF (retired), former vice commander of the Strategic Air Command, for giving me the inspiration for this story and for again providing me with many valuable insights into the behind-the-scenes world of strategic air power.

Thanks to General J. Michael Loh, commander of USAF Air Combat Command, Langley AFB, Virginia, for his invaluable assistance in gathering information about the deployment of heavy bombers, and particularly his help with learning about the B-2A Spirit stealth bomber. Thanks also to Colonel Mike Gallagher, Captain Steve Solmonson, and Major Barbara Carr, Public Affairs Office, Headquarters, USAF Air Combat Command, Langley AFB, Virginia, for their assistance.

Thanks to Brigadier General Ron Marcotte, commander of the 509th Bomb Wing, Whiteman AFB, Missouri, the first home of the B-2A Spirit stealth bomber, and Colonel William Fraser, vice commander, for their help, their time, and especially their special insights into the new world of long-range bomber operations. Meeting officers like them and visiting a modern, hard-charging base like Whiteman were a very special privilege and treat for me.

I also want to thank Captain Bill Harrison, 509th BMW Public Affairs; Colonel Greg Power, 509th Operations Group commander; Lieutenant Colonel Fred Strain, 509th Operational Support Squadron commander; my old B-52 buddy Lieutenant Colonel Rick Sorenson, Operations Plans Team chief; fellow ex-FB-111 crewdog Lieutenant Colonel Tony Imondi, chief B-2A instructor pilot; Lieutenant Colonel Dick Newton, 393rd Bomb Squadron commander; Major Steve Tippetts, Captain Buzz Barrett, and my old fellow FB-111 crewdog Major Jim Whitney of the 393rd Bomb Squadron "Tigers"; and all the others I met and who offered ideas and answered questions during a spectacular visit to the 509th Bomb Wing and the incredible B-2A Spirit stealth bomber. It was good to see old friends so successful in the world's most sophisticated combat warplane.

Thanks to Major Emerson Pittman, chief of public affairs, secretary of the Air Force Public Affairs—Western Region, for his help in gathering information for this story.

A major source of historical, political, and military information on various countries around the world on which I relied was *Defense and Foreign Affairs Handbook* (London: International Media Corp., Ltd., 1994). Thanks also to the many members all over the world of SOC.CULT.IRAN (SCI) newsgroup on the Internet for their invaluable help and ideas.

Thanks to Neil Nyren, publisher and editor-in-chief at G. P. Putnam's Sons, for his valuable help with the manuscript—within sixty seconds of my first meeting with him, this man helped me over a particularly rough spot in the manuscript! I'm lucky to have him with me.

AUTHOR'S NOTES

Any similarities in this novel to any person, living or dead, are purely coincidental and entirely the product of the author's imagination.

My faithful readers will note that this story takes place after *Day of the Cheetah*. I hope you welcome back our old friends as much as I enjoyed bringing them back for you.

Your comments are welcome! Please e-mail your thoughts to me at Reader Mail@Megafortress.com, or visit my Web site at http://www.Megafortress.com.

REAL-WORLD
NEWS EXCERPTS

DEFENSE & FOREIGN AFFAIRS STRATEGIC POLICY, OCT 31, 1994 (reprinted with permission)— . . . In mid-September, Tehran concluded that a clash over the islands in the Strait of Hormuz—Abu Musa and the Tumbs—was inevitable. This assessment was based on intelligence from Saudi Arabia and the GCC (Gulf Cooperation Council) and was reflected in the intensification of Iran's military preparations and exercises in the Gulf. By late September (1994), Tehran was actively preparing for a possible military confrontation with the Persian Gulf states over the islands. Tehran believes that by demonstrating its strong and uncompromising position over the Gulf issues, it will be able to influence such countries as Egypt and Iraq to recognize Iran's unique position in the hub of Islam.

**IRAN SAYS WESTERN TROOP BUILDUP POSES THREAT TO SE-
CURITY (OCT 20, 1994/0600 GMT)—NICOSIA—REUTERS—**
Iran's Intelligence (Internal Security) Minister Ali Fallahiyan
said on Wednesday night the presence of Western forces in
the Gulf was a threat to Iran's security.

He said Iran should be vigilant and prepared ''for any
eventuality,'' the official Iranian news agency IRNA reported.

It quoted Fallahiyan as saying that the ''presence of alien
forces and their movements in Iran's immediate vicinity
needed vigilance and full preparation for any eventuality.'' He
blasted United States policy in the Gulf region and urged oil-
rich Gulf Arab states to end their alliance with Washington.

The official news agency IRNA said the English-language
Tehran Times and Iran News attacked the United States in
editorials marking the November 4 seizure of the U.S. embassy in Tehran after the Islamic revolution in 1979.

Addressing neighboring Gulf Arab states, it said: ''Now
you are the victims of U.S. exploitation and usurpation carried out in more subtle ways to deprive you of your wealth.''

It urged them to oppose the presence of U.S. forces in the
region. ''Let the shout of 'Death to America' ring loud in
the desert as a clear expression of your opposition to any
pretext of a 'Desert Storm,' which we all know was just a
game of cards the CIA played to justify their presence in the
region.''

**IRAN USES STYX TECHNOLOGY IN CRUISE-MISSILE DEVEL-
OPMENT (NOV 17, 1994/FI) 11/17/94 FLIGHT INTERNA-
TIONAL**—Iran is developing a range of ballistic missiles, and
a cruise missile derived from the Russian SSN-2 Styx anti-
ship missile, according to German intelligence documents
obtained by Flight International.

Tehran has access to Styx technology via the Silkworm,
the 80-km (45-nm)-range Chinese-built version of the Styx.
Iran took delivery of its first Silkworms in 1986 and the

missiles are deployed on the Strait of Hormuz at the entrance to the Gulf waters.

Four Silkworm launch emplacements have been built on the mid-gulf island of Abu Musa, where administration is shared by Iran and the Arab emirate state of Sharjah.

The documents say that Tehran is also involved in the development of a solid-fueled missile and in the development of enhanced-performance Scud ballistic-missile systems. . . .

ARBITRATION REJECTED IN UAE ISLANDS ROW (DEC 23/1221 GMT) 12/23/94 TEHRAN (DEC 22)—BLOOMBERG—Iran spurned a call from its Arab neighbors to accept international arbitration in its dispute with the United Arab Emirates over three islands in the Persian Gulf.

The Iranian Foreign Ministry said bilateral talks with the UAE were the only way to resolve the row which has soured relations between non-Arab Iran and the six states of the Gulf Cooperation Council (GCC).

GCC leaders, ending a summit in Bahrain last night, called on the Iranian government to let the International Court of Justice decide who owns the islands of Abu Musa and the Greater and Lesser Tumbs.

Iran, which controls the islands, said it will never give them up to the UAE. Raising the issue of territorial disputes posed a threat to the security of the Persian Gulf and served the interests of foreign powers in the region, the Foreign Ministry statement, carried on Tehran Radio, said.

AEROSPACE DAILY—01/19/95—Defense Intelligence Agency Director Lt. Gen. James R. Clapper, Jr. . . . said Iran is in the midst of rebuilding its military capability. . . . Clapper said Iran has been spending between $1 billion and $2 billion a year on arms, and has focused on missiles and weapons of mass destruction and some "limited growth" in conventional capabilities. Some of the systems Iran is acquiring, such as Russian Kilo submarines and anti-ship cruise

missiles, "could complicate operations in and around" the Persian Gulf, he added.

GULF STATES AGREE TO BOLSTER CAPABILITIES (JAN 27/ JDW) 01/27/95—JANE'S DEFENSE WEEKLY (JAN 21)—

Leaders of the Gulf Cooperation Council have agreed at their annual meeting to bolster their defense structure, possibly by purchasing three to four airborne warning and control aircraft.

The six-nation alliance, comprising Saudi Arabia, the United Arab Emirates, Kuwait, Oman, Qatar and Bahrain, said in Bahrain last month it would develop a "unified strategy" that could "act swiftly and decisively" to counter any threat to any member.

That includes bolstering the GCC's 6,000-man rapid-deployment force, known as Peninsula Shield and based at Hafr al-Batin in northern Saudi Arabia, to 25,000 men.

The GCC's move to bolster defenses came as Iran is reported to be building anti-ship missile sites and other fortifications on three disputed islands in the southern Gulf. Abu Musa, Greater Tumb and Lesser Tumb are being transformed into military arsenals, claims the UAE.

IRAN DEPLOYS HAWK MISSILES TO GULF ISLANDS— SHALIKASHVILI 03/08/95—

Iran has placed Hawk antiaircraft missiles on islands at the entrance to the Persian Gulf, Gen. John Shalikashvili, chairman of the Joint Chiefs of Staff, said Feb. 28.

"We spotted them putting missiles onto launchers, which they haven't done before," he told a meeting of reporters, according to wire reports.

U.S. reconnaissance has also spotted the Iranians moving artillery into forward positions on its islands in the Strait of Hormuz, he said.

"All of that could lead me to lots of conclusions. One of them is that they want to have the capability to interdict the traffic in the Strait of Hormuz.'' The U.S. is carefully monitoring the situation, he added. While Iraq is considered the biggest military threat in the Persian Gulf, Iran could become the region's major power toward the end of the century, Shalikashvili said.

ARMS BUILDUP MAY THREATEN GULF OIL—PERRY (MAR 22/ 0951 GMT) 03/22/95—ABU DHABI—REUTERS—Iran has moved 8,000 troops, chemical weapons and anti-ship missiles to islands at the mouth of the Gulf in a buildup that could threaten oil shipping, U.S. Defense Secretary William Perry said on Wednesday.

Perry, on a weeklong Gulf trip, hammered home a warning that he has made in moderate states in the region that Iran might one day try to control the flow of half the world's oil using a recent buildup on islands in the Strait of Hormuz.

''This involves almost 8,000 military personnel moved to those islands. It involves anti-ship missiles, air defense missiles, chemical weapons,'' Perry told a news conference in Manama, capital of Bahrain.

''It can only be regarded as a potential threat to shipping in the area,'' he added, charging publicly for the first time that Iran had stationed chemical weapons on the islands, some of which are claimed by the United Arab Emirates (UAE).

Perry did not name the islands but the Pentagon has previously identified one as Abu Musa.

NAVY FACES EXTENDED RANGE OF IRANIAN MiG-29S—NAVY NEWS & UNDERSEA TECHNOLOGY (NVTE)—08/21/95—A major new headache for Central Command and Navy battle groups in the Arabian Sea has emerged with Iran's development of in-flight refueling probes for its MiG-29s, intelligence community sources confirm.

... The Iranian air force possesses four tanker versions of the Boeing 707, roughly comparable to the U.S. Air Force

KC-135, which was based on the never-built civilian Boeing 717.

. . . The U.S. analysts look to the roughly 2,100-nautical-mile distance from Iran to Diego Garcia in the Indian Ocean. With in-flight refueling, Diego Garcia would come within the range of the Iranian MiG-29s. . . . Thus, the aircraft could be used to disrupt U.S. air supply lines in the event of future conflict in the Persian Gulf. Additionally, although the MiG-29 is heavily geared to air-to-air combat, one analyst said "there is some evidence" that the Iranians are working on adapting the aircraft to carry the air-to-surface version of the French Exocet anti-ship missile.

In this case, he noted, the U.S. Maritime Prepositioning Squadron based at Diego Garcia would be at risk.

. . . The possibility of such legal Iranian harassment of U.S. battle groups concerns several analysts, who observe that because of the *Vincennes*'s (CG 49) shoot-down of an Iranian airliner in 1988, U.S. forces would be reluctant to attack in the face of Iranian provocations.

At press time, U.S. Central Command officials had not responded to Navy News' requests for comment on the MiG-29 development.

B-2 Bomber Fight Brewing on Capitol Hill, Phillips Business Information 01/19/95. By Kerry Gildea— . . . Rep. Ron Dellums (D-Calif.), ranking member on the House National Security Committee who has staunchly opposed additional B-2s, attended a closed National Security Committee briefing on military intelligence operations yesterday, said he learned of no changes in the world threat situation that would demand additional weapons systems or increased defense spending.

"I absolutely do not think there is anything we see presently in the world that would justify 20 more B-2s," Dellums remarked. "Where are you going to fly them? Where is the threat?"

PROLOGUE

The attackers were first spotted on radar only twenty miles from Abu Musa Island; by the time the chief of the air defense radar unit issued the air defense alert notification, they were seventeen miles out. Because this was the morning of Revolution Day in Iran, only a skeleton crew was on duty at the Islamic Republic Pasdaran-i-Engelab Revolutionary Guards air squadron base, and the pre-Revolution Day celebrations had ended only a few hours carlier—response time, therefore, was very slow, and the attackers were within missile range long before the Islamic Republic Air Force F-5E Tiger II fighter crews could reach their planes. The order to commit the Pasdaran's British-built Rapier antiaircraft missiles and ZSU-23/4 antiaircraft artillery units was issued far too late.

Four three-ship flights of British Aerospace Hawk light attack jets streaked in at treetop level, launched laser-guided Hellfire missiles on the six known Iranian air defense sites, then dropped laser-guided incendiary bombs and cluster munitions on the island's small airfield. One unknown Rapier site launched a missile and destroyed one Hawk, but two trailing Hawks flying in the "cleanup" spot scoured the area with cluster bombs where they saw the Rapier lift off, receiving a very satisfying secondary explosion as one of the unlaunched missiles exploded in its launcher. The cluster bombs also hit the U.S.-built F-5E fighters on the ramp, destroying both and damaging two hangars where another F-5E was parked, the control tower, and some sections of taxiways. One adjacent empty hangar was left untouched.

The second punch arrived just a few moments later. Four flights of four SA-342 Gazelle and SA-332 Super Puma attack helicopters swooped over the island, firing laser-guided Hellfire missiles and AS-12 wire-guided missiles from as far away as two miles—well out of range of the few Pasdaran soldiers who were firing blindly into the sky with handguns and rifles at any aircraft noise they heard. Each attack was quick—launch on the move, no hovering in one place. The next two flights did the same, swooping in and destroying targets; then the first two waves came in again to kill any targets they'd missed on their first pass, followed by the second two flights making a second pass.

The attacks were fast and chillingly accurate. In just a few minutes, the attackers had claimed the prizes for which they had come looking: six Iranian HY-2 Silkworm and four SS-22 Sunburn antiship cruise-missile launch sites, several Rapier antiaircraft missile batteries, and a handful of antiaircraft artillery sites, plus their associated munitions storage and command-control buildings. All were either destroyed or severely damaged. The Silkworm and Sunburn missiles had been devastating long-range weapons, capable of destroying the largest supertankers or cargo vessels passing through the Persian Gulf—their presence on Abu Musa Island, close to the heavily traveled international sea lanes, had been protested by many nations for several years. Other missile attacks had claimed a large portion of the island's small port facilities, including the heavy-lift cranes, long-boat docks, and desalinization and petroleum-handling facilities.

But the big prize, the real target, had also been destroyed: two Rodong surface-to-surface missile emplacements. The

Rodong was a long-range missile that had been jointly developed by North Korea, China, and Iran, and could carry a high-explosive, chemical, biological, or even nuclear warhead. From Abu Musa Island, the missile had had sufficient range to strike and attack targets in Kuwait, Bahrain, Qatar, the United Arab Emirates, Oman, and most of the oil fields in eastern Saudi Arabia—about two-thirds of the oil fields in the Persian Gulf region.

The Hawk, Gazelle, and Super Puma crews were incredibly accurate, almost prescient. A building that supplied power to the communications and military base facilities was destroyed by two missiles, but a virtually identical building just a few yards away that supplied power to the housing units was left untouched. A semi-underground Silkworm missile bunker with a fully operational Silkworm inside got a Hellfire through its front door, yet an adjacent empty bunker undergoing refurbishment but identical in every other respect was left undamaged. Although nearly half a billion dollars of weapons, equipment, buildings, and other infrastructure were damaged or destroyed, out of the more than two thousand men stationed on the island, only five unlucky Pasdaran soldiers, plus the F-5E pilots and their crew chiefs, lost their lives, and only a handful more were injured.

From the nearby air defense base at Bandar Abbas on the mainland, just 100 miles to the northeast, Islamic Republic Air Force MiG-29 fighters were scrambled almost immediately, but the attackers had hit their targets and were retreating south toward the Trucial Coast and the United Arab Emirates long before the Iranian fighters arrived. The MiGs tried to pursue, but Omani and UAE air defense fighters quickly surrounded and outnumbered them and chased them out of UAE airspace.

• • •

As the surviving Pasdaran troops scrambled out of their barracks and began to deal with the devastation of their island fortress, five black-suited two-man commando teams silently picked up their gear, made their way to the shoreline of the one-square-mile island, clicked a tiny wrist-mounted code transceiver, then slipped into the warm waters of the eastern Persian Gulf after their leader cleared them to withdraw.

Before departing, one member of the lead commando team took a last scan around the area, not toward the military structures this time but northeast, toward the Strait of Hormuz. Peering through the suitcase-sized telescopic device he and his partner had been operating, he soon found what he had been searching for. "Man, there's that mutha," he said half-aloud to his partner. "That's what we should've laid a beam on." He centered a set of crosshairs on the target, reached down, and simulated squeezing a trigger. "Blub blub blub, one carrier turned into a sub. Bye-bye, *Ayatollah* baby. . . ."

"Get your ass in gear, Leopard," his partner growled under his breath. In seconds they had packed up and were out of sight under the calm waves of the Persian Gulf.

The object of the young commando's attention was cruising six miles northeast of the island. It was an aircraft carrier, the largest warship in the entire Persian Gulf—and it was flying an Iranian flag. It was the *Ayatollah Ruhollah Khomeini*, flagship of the Islamic Republic of Iran's new blue-water naval fleet. Once the Russian aircraft carrier *Varyag*, and now the joint property of Iran and the People's Republic of China's Liberation Army Navy, the carrier dwarfed all but the largest supertankers plying the Gulf. Not yet operational and used only for training, its officers and crew had only been able to look on helplessly as the missile batteries on Abu Musa Island exploded into the night.

Leopard and his partner, along with the rest of the commando teams, followed tiny wristwatch-sized locator beacons to small Swimmer Delivery Vehicles anchored to the muddy bottom, and four divers climbed aboard each SDV. There they changed air tanks for filled ones, and followed their watertight compasses south and west to the marshaling point, where all five SDVs rendezvoused. They traveled southwest together, surfacing for a few seconds in random intervals to get a fix from their GPS satellite navigation receiver. An hour later, still submerged, air tanks just a few minutes from exhaustion, they motored up to the hull of a large vessel, and hammered a code onto it. A large section of the port center side of the hull opened, and one by one, the five SDVs motored inside, surfaced inside the chamber, then hooked onto cranes that hoisted them out of the water onto the deck, where the crewmen disembarked.

Each two-man team handed up their scuba gear and personal weapons to the deck crews, along with forty-pound, suitcase-sized devices. These were their AN/PAQ-3 MULE (Modular Universal Laser Equipment) portable telescopic laser illuminators. Tuned to a predetermined frequency and set on a target up to a mile away using electronic low-light telescopes, each invisible laser beam had reflected off its target and then been received by an airborne sensor, thus "illuminating" the proper target and allowing the missiles to home in and destroy the target with pinpoint accuracy. Although each aircrewman had been well familiar with the area and could have found most of the targets without help, the commando teams had known precisely which buildings were important and which were not, and had made each shot fired by the attack aircraft count. Not one precious shot had been wasted—one missile, one kill.

A thin, non-military-looking gray-haired man in civilian clothes greeted the crewmen as they emerged from the SDV, shaking their hands and giving each of the exhausted, shivering men a cup of soup and a thick towel with which to warm up and dry off. Tired as they were, however, the commandos were still excited, chatting about the mission, congratulating one another. Finally, the last two men emerged from their SDVs, turned in their equipment, and met up with the civilian. One man was tall, white, and powerfully built, with cold, fiery blue eyes; the other was slightly shorter, black, and much leaner, his eyes dark and dancing. The tall man moved silently, with slow, easy grace, while the lean man was animated.

"Man, what a ride!" he exclaimed loudly. He quickly stepped down the line of commandos in the dock area, giving each of them a slap on the back or shoulder, then returned to do the same to his partner. The men quietly acknowledged his congratulations, but did not return the enthusiasm—in fact, they looked at him with wary, almost hostile expressions. The cold shoulders didn't seem to dampen the young commander's exuberance, though. "It was great, man, awesome!" he exclaimed. "How'd we do, Paul? We kick ass or what?"

Retired Air Force colonel Paul White, operations commander of the top-secret U.S. Intelligence Support Agency team code-named Madcap Magician, nodded reluctantly. Both he and the tall commando had noticed the looks from the men, but did not mention it. "You kicked ass, all right, Hal," he replied.

And he was right, they had. In an unprecedented act of regional military cooperation, the Intelligence Support Agency, a cover-action organization of the CIA, had just teamed up with the seven Arab member nations of the Gulf Cooperation Council's military arm, called Peninsula Shield, to attack a disputed Iranian military position in the Persian Gulf. It was the first time in White's memory that the CIA had actively supported an Arab military mission, albeit secretly. Sure, these guys were happy—their mission had gone off without a hitch, a potential enemy had been crippled, and the good-will they had built by joining with their Arab friends might last for many years.

White's team had been the spearhead of the attack. Most Arab countries had little or no air-combat experience, especially at night. White's job had been to guide the Arab pilots and gunners to their targets accurately enough so that key targets could be destroyed quickly and efficiently, with minimum loss of life on either side. It had been important for Peninsula Shield to score a major victory in its first military mission, especially against one of the very nations that it and the Gulf Cooperation Council had been formed to defend against—the Islamic Republic of Iran. Of course, White's *other* mission had been to see to the safe return of his commandos and the security of his vessel.

"Ten divers out, ten divers back, and this rust bucket is

still afloat,'' Chris Wohl, the tall man, said in a low, slow voice. ''*That's* a success.''

''Damn straight!'' Hal Briggs crowed. ''So let's celebrate! Let's—''

Just then, another of the commandos walked up to the three Americans. Briggs stopped abruptly, and his face went limp and dazed, as if he had just been shot full of painkillers. The commando was much shorter than Briggs, but was just as wiry and powerful—and she filled out a Mustang suit much better than he. Her name was Riza Behrouzi, and she was the commander of the Peninsula Shield security team. A Peninsula Shield commando had gone along with every Madcap Magician commando to assist and to secure the area while the targets were lazed. ''All Peninsula Shield operatives present and well,'' Behrouzi reported. ''On behalf of the nations of the Gulf Cooperative Council, I wish to thank you all for your help.''

White was about to accept her thanks, but Briggs interjected: ''It was our pleasure, Major Behrouzi . . .''

''Riza, please,'' Behrouzi said to Briggs. Wohl and White got the impression they had instantly been forgotten. ''I know it is against your rules to give us your real names, but I have no such restrictions—about names, or about this.'' She stepped closer to Briggs and gave him a full kiss on the lips. ''Thank you.''

''It was nothing . . . Riza,'' Briggs said, apparently having difficulty catching his breath.

''Okay, Leopard,'' Wohl said irritably. ''You want to celebrate, go ahead—*after* you clean and stow your gear, conduct the post-mission briefing, see to it that your men are fed, and prepare your reports for the National Security Agency and the Director of Central Intelligence. And I believe you have the morning watch, so you better get some sleep. And since you're within eight hours of your watch, you're off the sauce. Other than that, you can celebrate all you want.''

''Gee, Mondo, thanks,'' Briggs said dejectedly. ''You're a real party animal.''

"I would be happy to assist you, Leopard," Behrouzi said. "We shall conduct the briefing and see to our men together."

"I like the sound of that," Briggs said, instantly perking up. "I tell ya, Riza," he said as they headed out, "I had that Iranian carrier in my sights for a sec out there. It might've taken the entire UAE air force full of Hellfires, but I woulda loved to see that big bad boy roll over and die." He may have just returned from two hours of scuba diving and six hours of crawling on his belly, but he sounded as hyper as before the day started.

"Leave it to Briggs," Wohl said. "Ten thousand miles from home, in the middle of the Persian Gulf, and he still manages to find the pretty girls." Catching no response, he looked at White. "Everything OK, sir?"

"Yeah, fine," White replied noncommittally. "Ah . . . Briggs didn't really laze that Iranian carrier, did he?"

"No. He's cocky and a smart-ass, but he's a good troop," Wohl said. "He's not stupid enough to ignore orders, no matter how easy the target of opportunity might be. The carrier's safe. It launched a few choppers, but none of its fighters and no missiles. Intel was right—the fighters and weapon systems aren't operational on that thing yet. Still can't believe Iran has got an aircraft carrier. We're gonna hear from that thing one of these days, I know it."

"The guys don't exactly seem enthusiastic about Hal," White observed. "In fact, they're pretty much ignoring him. . . ."

"It's tough for a team that's been together for so long to accept a brand-new commanding officer right away," Wohl said. "This is Briggs's first mission with the team—"

"Second—you're forgetting the Luger rescue mission in Lithuania . . ."

"On which Briggs just happened to be one of the passengers, along with McLanahan and Ormack," Wohl said. "It turned out that Briggs was better prepared, very close to *our* standards. But he wasn't one of us, and he sure as hell wasn't our leader . . ."

"But he is now."

Wohl stopped and glared at White, then shrugged. "Hey, I was never the real commander of the ops group of Madcap Magician," he said. "You asked me to be reassigned to you because you needed a commanding officer, and I accepted because I was tired of pushing papers at Parris Island. It was only a temporary billet—"

"That lasted three years," White said. "The men bonded to you right away. You brought them together like no one else could."

"Because I knew all these guys—I trained them all, even Briggs," Wohl said. "We're all Marines first—except Briggs, of course—then ISA operatives . . ."

"So Briggs being ex-Army and ex-Air Force, he's not going to fit in . . . ?"

"Depends on him," Wohl replied. "He's got a much different style than me—emotional, energetic, touchy-feely. Briggs rewards guys for good performance and 'counsels' them when it's poor—I *expect* good performance and loudly kick ass if I get anything but. And he's an officer, too, a young field-grade officer at that—younger than some of the guys on the team—and after all the years I've spent bad-mouthing officers in general and field-grade officers in particular, he's got a tough road ahead.

"He's a good troop, but a good commanding officer . . . ? Too early to tell. The guys aren't sure how to respond to him yet, that's all. Whether he succeeds is totally up to him. They're the best—whether or not he can lead them is the question only he can answer."

White nodded absently. Wohl studied him for a moment, then asked, "If everything's so OK, Colonel, why the hang-dog look?"

"Because I've had some reservations about this operation from the start," White said. "We just kicked over a big hornet's nest out there tonight, Chris—and we did it on Iran's Revolution Day, their Fourth of July."

"Shit, I didn't know that," Wohl said. "I thought it was in November sometime, when they took over the embassy in '79."

"No, it's today—and I should've known that. I never would've recommended executing this mission on that date," White said.

"Obviously the GCC knew what day it was."

"Which you know will make this attack sting even more in Tehran," White said. "And it'll be the U.S. that takes the brunt of Iran's anger. We keep on saying this was a GCC action, but you know damn well that Peninsula Shield isn't going to be leading the fight when the Iranians retaliate for this."

"How do you know they're going to retaliate?"

White looked at him grimly. "Because Iran has been preparing for exactly this attack for years, ever since the end of the Iran-Iraq War. We just justified all the billions of dollars they've been spending on modern weapons for the past six years. They aren't going to rest until someone—until *everyone*—is punished for what happened today. . . ."

TEHRAN, IRAN
THIRTY MINUTES AFTER THE ATTACK ON ABU MUSA ISLAND

General Hesarak al-Kan Buzhazi was supreme commander of the Islamic Republic's Armed Forces and commander of the Revolutionary Guards—and this was the first time in his career that he had ever been admitted to the residence of the leader of the Islamic Revolution, the Ayatollah Ali Hoseini Khamenei. And to tell the truth, he was scared. But as scared as he was to be in the presence of a man who, like Ruhollah Khomeini before him, could by a single word muster the lives and souls of a quarter of a billion Shi'ite Muslims to his side, it was even more exciting to consider the simultaneous disaster and opportunity that had befallen him that morning. This was one opportunity that could not be missed.

Buzhazi bowed deeply when shown into his presence, and kept his head bowed until the Faqih spoke. The door was closed behind them. "Your Eminence, thank you for this audience."

"Some disturbing news has reached me this morning, General," Khamenei said quietly. "Allah has told me of a great threat to the Republic. Tell me what has happened."

Buzhazi raised his head and stood solemnly, his hands respectfully clasped in front of him as if standing at an altar or at prayers. Khamenei was in his late sixties. While his predecessor, the Imam Khomeini, had been tall, gaunt, and ethereal, Khamenei was short, with a round face, a short, bushy dark beard, and large horn-rimmed glasses, which gave him a scholarly, professional, quick-witted appearance. This man before him was the nominal Faqih, the font of jurisprudence of the Islamic Republic and the ultimate law-maker, whose word could overrule the Parliament and any cleric, any lawyer, any scholar in the Twelver house; he was also the named Marja Ala, the Supreme Leader and spiritual head of the Shi'ite Muslim sect and the keeper of the will of the twelfth Imam, who was hidden from the world and would soon return to call the faithful to Allah's bosom for all time.

But for all that, he was a man, not a saint or a prophet. Buzhazi had known Ali Hoseini Khamenei when he had been nothing but an ambitious, backstabbing know-nothing fire-brand from a wealthy pro-Shah cargo shipping family from Bandar-Anzalt on Iran's Caspian coast. Little more than a spoiled rich kid back then, Khamenei had wanted to impress his friends and rebel against his parents by joining up with the wild, shrill-voiced fundamentalist Shi'ite cleric named Ruhollah Khomeini. He had joined the Khomeini revolution because it was cool and tough to do so, not because he'd had any particular holy vision like Khomeini, but as time went on, he became deeply committed to Khomeini's theo-cratic ideas. Khamenei held many high positions in government service—soldier, first commander of the Revolutionary Guards, even president of the republic. Now he was the Su-preme Leader. But he was still just a man. Buzhazi had seen this holy man angry, and sad, and drunk, and just plain stupid.

Buzhazi knew a lot more about Khamenei's shadowy past. Khamenei was a well-trained soldier as well as an accomplished politician, and throughout his rise through the ranks of power, he'd left a lot of bodies in his wake. Iran was nearly being overrun by Iraq at the beginning of the nine-year War of Retribution; when the president, Abolhassan Bani-Sadr, accused the then-commander of the Pasdaran, Khamenei, of not doing his job and failing the country, suddenly the Ayatollah Khomeini dismissed Bani-Sadr. When a rival politician, Muhammad Ali Rajai, was elected President in 1981, he and his Prime Minister were mysteriously killed in a bomb blast in the Cabinet room—Khamenei somehow survived. Time after time, Ali Hoseini Khamenei was able to fight off challenges to his authority by strange combinations of shrewd political infighting and unexplained and well-timed disasters.

So now, he told himself to overcome his fears and apprehensions and remember exactly who he was dealing with here, relax. Take command of this situation, he ordered himself. Take charge *now!*

"The Republic has been betrayed, Eminence," Buzhazi began. He knew that word *betrayed* would arouse Khamenei's attention. . . . "My orders were countermanded, and because of this, our main island protectorate in the Persian Gulf, Abu Musa, has been attacked by Gulf Cooperative Council air forces."

Khamenei seemed surprisingly relaxed as he heard the news—well, probably *not* surprising. It wasn't from divine inspiration that he'd first heard about it, Buzhazi knew, but from his contacts in the VEVAK, the Iranian Ministry of Intelligence and Security. Buzhazi had no control of that group—they reported directly to the Council of Guardians and to Khamenei. "What kind of damage was sustained? What casualties?" Khamenei asked.

"Few casualties, thanks to Allah, and only a handful of injuries," Buzhazi said dismissively. "The attack was directed against the Silkworm and Sunburn anti-ship missile emplacements, and the major port facilities. Unfortunately, the attack caused some damage.''

''My information says the damage was considerably more than that,'' Khamenei said.

It had been less than an hour since the attack, Buzhazi reminded himself, and Khamenei already had a briefing from his intelligence people—very efficient work for a pious holy man. This man did not sit contemplating his navel in an ivory tower. He was fully engaged in the operation of the government. ''Regrettably, that is true,'' Buzhazi said. ''But island defenses will be restored by the end of the day, and until then, we have naval and air forces on the scene to maintain security.''

''How fortunate,'' Khamenei said, almost in a whisper, like the hiss of a snake's tongue. ''But your defensive strategies for Abu Musa seem to have been somewhat shortsighted. . . .''

''Eminence, with all greatest respect, that was not the case,'' Buzhazi said. ''The defensive systems I placed on the island were designed to protect the defensive anti-ship missile emplacements from high-and low-altitude air threats as well as massed maritime threats. The island was under surveillance by long-range radars from Bandar Abbas and by short-range radars from Abu Musa Island itself. In addition, we have seven thousand troops on that island to defend against amphibious assaults, all very much aware that our enemies were seeking to destroy those weapons and take those islands from us at any time. All island defenses were fully functional and on full alert.''

''And so why were these defenses so easily destroyed, General . . . ?''

''Because President Nateq-Nouri countermanded my general orders to launch on alert,'' Buzhazi said angrily, ''and instead ordered that, unless the island was unmistakably under direct attack, that all launch orders be issued by the Defense Ministry in Tehran, not by the on-scene commanders.

It was madness! I argued against that policy and appealed to reverse the order . . .''

"The Council of Guardians has not received any such notification or appeal," Khamenei pointed out.

"I was going to present my arguments in person with your representative at the next meeting of the Supreme Defense Council," Buzhazi lied, knowing full well that Nateq-Nouri had never countermanded any of Buzhazi's orders. The policy of "launch on alert"—fire without warning on any vessel or aircraft that crossed Iran's claimed borders or boundaries—had never been an official peacetime policy of the Iranian government except over Iran's most highly classified research centers, bases, or over the capital or the holy cities. The simple fact was that Iran possessed few trained individuals and workable air defense systems for very low-altitude air threats; even if the forces on Abu Musa had had "launch on alert" orders, they probably wouldn't have been able to stop the attackers.

"It appears to be a moot point now, does it not, General?" Khamenei commented.

"My point, Eminence, is that I should be given the tools to do my job if I am to defend the Republic properly from attack by our enemies," Buzhazi retorted. "Abu Musa Island and Greater and Lesser Tumbs belong to Iran, not to Sharjah or the so-called United Arab Emirates or the Gulf Cooperation Council or the United Nations or the World Court. I was given the task of defending the Republic, but my hands were tied by a President, his Cabinet, and a parliament afraid of stirring up resentment and hatred overseas, afraid of losing investors and popularity. What more do we surrender? Do we surrender Kermanshahan and Kurdistan to the murderous Kurds? Do we surrender the Shatt al Arab to the Butcher of Baghdad? Perhaps Turkmenistan would like the holy city of Mashhad?"

"Enough, General, enough," Khamenei interrupted, with a weary tone in his voice. "Why do you not take this matter up with President Nateq-Nouri? The task of commander-in-chief was delegated to him by His Holiness the Imam Khomeini.''

"Eminence, the President's inaction in defense matters is plainly obvious to everyone," Buzhazi said. "He has reduced the budget of the Pasdaran to less than what we need for training and proficiency, and chosen to give it instead to the Basij militias as a form of public welfare and to buy votes for himself. We purchase advanced weapons, but no money is spent for spare parts or for building our own military infrastructure—again, the money goes to public-welfare programs to bribe factory owners and wealthy landowners who support him. Military base construction is at a standstill because he coddles the labor unions. The outcome was inevitable, despite all my warnings and precautions: Abu Musa Island's defenses have been destroyed, and the base is in danger of being retaken by American and Zionist sympathizers.''

Khamenei could obviously recognize Buzhazi's flowery exaggerations, but he paused in thought. The conflict between the military and the civilian government had been brewing for some time, he thought, and this early-morning meeting was perhaps the wake-up call to action he had been anticipating—perhaps dreading. It was time for Iran's clergy to take sides in this dispute: Support the government or support the military?

The Grand Ayatollah had known Ali Akbar Nateq-Nouri, the former speaker of the Majlis-i-Shura, Iran's Islamic Consultative Assembly, and former President Hashemi Rafsanjani's handpicked successor, since before the Revolution, and had watched General Buzhazi's meteoric rise in power, and so knew that the only difference between them was their uniforms. Both men were intelligent, opportunistic, single-minded, power hungry, and ruthless. Both gave lip service to the role of Islam in the government, but neither truly believed that the clergy should have a strong voice in day-to-day affairs—an opinion that happened to be shared by many in Iran. "What is it you would have us do?"

"I have spoken of my plans many times, Your Holiness,"

Buzhazi said. "First and foremost, Iran and its territories must be protected. This is our most important goal, and we must do all we can to ensure it is done." He paused, then said, "We must prohibit all non-Arab warships from entering the Persian Gulf. No aircraft carriers, no guided-missile cruisers, no submarines carrying Tomahawk missiles. These are all offensive vessels, designed to wage war on those who call the Persian Gulf home.

"The *Khomeini* carrier group must be made fully operational and deployed immediately to the Gulf of Oman to screen for foreign warships," Buzhazi went on. "As we have seen, even with proper warning, it still takes far too long for land-based aircraft to respond to an attack on the islands— only the carrier can properly defend the islands against very low-altitude attackers."

"The Chinese aircraft carrier? The rusting piece of flotsam in the harbor at Chah Bahar?" Khamenei said scornfully. "I thought we were using that to house the Chinese advisers, prisoners, Basij volunteers, and jihad members working on the base-construction project."

"The *Khomeini* is operational, and it is ready to help defend our rights," Buzhazi said. "We have a full complement of sailors, fliers, and weapons aboard, and the carrier's escort vessels are also ready to set sail. I had ordered the carrier to Abu Musa Island to assist with island defenses, but as all of our military forces, they were unprepared for this treacherous attack."

The Ayatollah Khamenei paused to consider that request. The *Ayatollah Ruhollah Khomeini* aircraft-carrier project had been a pie-in-the-sky project from the very beginning. The Russian aircraft carrier *Varyag* had been laid up at Nikola-yev, Ukraine, since 1991, completely stripped of all essential combat systems; it had no radar, no communications, no aircraft, no weapons, only its nuclear power plant, a flight deck, and more than three thousand watertight compartments. The People's Republic of China had purchased the 60,000-ton vessel and made it an operational warship, but the world's political consternation at China owning and operating a nuclear-powered aircraft carrier in the fragile South China Sea and Sea of Japan region had been too great—if China had a carrier, Japan wanted five, and the United States wanted to base five more in the region—so those plans were shelved.

At the time, Iran had concluded a $2 billion arms deal with China, and relations between those two countries had been at an all-time high. The carrier had been moved to Iran's new military and oil terminal on the Gulf of Oman called Chah Bahar, where it had once again been laid up in floating storage. No definite plans had emerged for the ship: some said it was to be cut up as scrap, then as a floating hotel, then as a floating prison.

General Buzhazi had other ideas. Over the next eighteen months, the Iranians had begun to install new, relatively modern weapon systems on board the ship, including Russian anti-ship missiles, Russian aircraft, and state-of-the-art sensors and equipment from all over the world—all the while insisting to the world that they were "experimenting" or "assisting" China with its plans to convert the carrier for other uses. Then Iranian MiG-29 and Sukhoi-33 fighter crews had begun practicing carrier landings. Since early 1996, both Chinese and Iranian crews had been training aboard the *Varyag* in carrier deck and flight operations in the Persian Gulf. At the same time, Chinese and Iranian crews had begun firing anti-ship missiles from the carrier, including the huge SS-N-19 Granit supersonic missile, which was designed to sink a carrier-class ship over 200 miles away. In effect, both countries shared the cost of a completely combat-ready aircraft carrier.

"This aircraft carrier, it is ready to fight?" Khamenei asked.

"It is, Eminence," Buzhazi replied. "Twenty fighter aircraft, six helicopters, twelve long-range anti-ship missiles—it is one of the most formidable warships in the world. With our new Russian, Chinese, and Western surplus warships as escorts, the *Khomeini* can ensure that we will not lose our rights to the Persian Gulf."

"It will cause much fear among those who travel the Gulf," he pointed out.

"If it is Allah's will," Buzhazi responded. Normally he didn't care to use the real religious fundamentalist expressions with others, but of course it was necessary and proper to do so with the mullahs. "We fear only Allah, Holiness. Let others fear the Islamic Republic for a change. Your Holiness, we have a right to defend what is ours, and the *Khomeini* is the best weapon with which to do so. It has been in shakedown status far too long—we are ready to put to sea. Give the command, and we shall need worry no longer about protecting our Gulf from attack."

Buzhazi paused for a moment, then added, "Oil prices will of course be affected by this, Eminence." *That* got Khamenei's attention. His political fortunes were tied directly into the price of oil, and for the past several years both had been in a steady decline. "Even if we are not ultimately successful in closing off the Gulf from all foreign warships—if the Majlis and President Nateq-Nouri conspire against your wishes and the loyal people of the Islamic Republic—we will still benefit from the rise in oil prices. Iran can of course continue to ship oil to its Gulf of Oman terminus at Chah Bahar, but oil shipments from Gulf Cooperative Council states will be greatly curtailed."

Khamenei paused once again, but he had decided. The insurance companies would double, perhaps triple the premiums on supertankers transiting the Gulf, and the shortage of oil would shoot prices to heaven. The rewards would be great. But the risks . . . The Faqih nodded. "It shall be ordered," he said. "But we must be in the right always, General. World public opinion may favor Iran because we have been attacked by the oil-hungry West and their Gulf lapdogs, but we must not allow the world to ostracize us once again. We are for peace, Buzhazi, always peace."

"Motashakkeram," Buzhazi said, bowing as he gave thanks. "Your Holiness, I believe so strongly in this, that if you give the command, I shall take full and complete responsibility for the consequences. You may say that I was

the mad dog, that I gave the order, and you may disavow all knowledge of my actions. I know in my heart that it is right, and I stand with Allah because I know he will stand with me. . . ."

"Will you stand with the thousands of our brothers who will be slaughtered by the forces of Satan when the world declares war on Iran for what it has done?"

"Eminence, war appears to be upon us already," Buzhazi pointed out. "I believe we will *avert* further conflict by executing my plan. The world will fear Iran once again. It will be hesitant to start a conflict that might escalate into real death and destruction at our hands. Give the command, Holiness. I stand ready to defend Islam and protect the Republic. I have the strength to do it."

Khamenei hesitated, then turned his back on Buzhazi—so the general could not see the look of concern on his face. But he said, "*Inshallah*, General. So by the will of Allah, let it be done."

"ABC World News Tonight With Peter Jennings"

"Iran's Leader of the Islamic Revolution, Ayatollah Ali Hoseini Khamenei, blasted the Gulf Cooperative Council, the union of six pro-West Persian Gulf nations, today for what he claims was an attack on a, quote, 'defensive security and safety installation,' unquote, on a small island in the Persian Gulf in the early-morning hours, and has called on a 'holy jihad' against the GCC.

"Khamenei claims the attack by what he terms 'terrorists and saboteurs' of the Gulf Cooperative Council's action group called Peninsula Shield killed several dozen workers while they slept, and heavily damaged the island's electricity, fresh water, and living quarters.

"The island, identified as Abu Musa, is one of three small islands that sit very close to the oil transshipment lanes through the Persian Gulf. The islands were claimed by Iran in 1971 but were under joint jurisdiction of both Iran and the United Arab Emirates, one of the member nations of the Gulf Cooperative Council, until 1992, when Iran claimed all of the islands for itself.

"Spokesmen for the Gulf Cooperative Council in Riyadh, Saudi Arabia, declined to comment, except to say that the GCC has often been blamed for actions by anti-Iranian government forces, notably the Mojahadin-i-Khalq, in an effort to stir up resentment and fundamentalist fervor against Iran's Arab neighbors in the Persian Gulf region.

"A U.S. State Department spokesman says he knows no details of the incident, but says that Iran has heavily fortified Abu Musa Island over the past few years with modern offensive anti-ship and antiaircraft weapons, and has resisted all efforts by the United Nations International Court to mediate the dispute. The State Department says no oil tankers or any American vessels or aircraft are in danger and says the Martindale administration is looking into the matter.

"Back in a moment."

ONE

The U.S.-flagged rescue-and-salvage vessel *Valley Mistress* was riding high and fast in the water these days; very few patrol boats had bothered to stop her as she made her way from the Mediterranean through the Suez Canal, down the Red Sea, and across the Gulf of Aden, Arabian Sea, and the Gulf of Oman. Salvage-and-construction vessels were usually hard to search, they rarely had anything fun for customs officials to look at—just a bunch of cranes, tanks, chains, dirt, and nitrogen-and booze-soaked roustabout crews—and U.S.-registered and-flagged vessels rarely carried exciting contraband like drugs, weapons, or humans. In any case, with its U.S. Naval Ready Reserve Fleet designation, the *Valley Mistress* was rarely detained—it carried almost the same right-to-pass exemption as a warship.

The *Mistress* was riding high right now because its 55,000-pound CV-22 Pave Hammer tilt-rotor aircraft, normally secretly stowed on the telescoping helicopter hangar on the aft deck, was off on a mission with several of its commando teams, including Chris Wohl and Hal Briggs; its current cargo was much, much lighter. The *Valley Mistress* was indeed a real salvage vessel, and it did many contract jobs as such all over the world—but it was also a sophisticated spy ship that conducted surveillance and special operations missions for the U.S. government. All sorts of classified missions had been conducted from the *Mistress*'s decks, from shadowing a port, harbor, or vessel to reconnoitering a battlefield, rescue work, and all-out air and land combat. Any job that needed doing, anytime, anyplace, the crew of the *Valley Mistress* could do it.

Retired Air Force colonel Paul White stood on the aft deck of the *Valley Mistress*, arms crossed on his chest, watching the dark shapes working all around him. In addition to leading Madcap Magician, White was the senior officer in charge of the thirty-man "technical" crew of the *Valley Mistress*, which on this leg of their voyage—White's technical crews changed often, depending on the current mission requirements—consisted of engineers, technicians, and sixteen U.S. Marines, none in uniform.

All of the concentrated planning and rehearsing had already taken place, so, like Alfred Hitchcock, who had already meticulously plotted out each one of his shots before setting foot on a new movie set, White's job at this point was simply to observe his team in action, silently monitor their progress via the ship's intercom through his headset, and stay out of their way. Paul White was a thirty-two-year veteran, but had never been in combat except for brief stints as a communications repairman in Vietnam. His specialty was electronics; he was a "gadget guy," designing and building sophisticated systems from spare parts—the parts could be leftover transistors, old radios, or old aircraft. White could take the oldest, most broken-down thing and make it better—and, more important, he could teach others to do it, too.

White's intercom crackled to life: "Lightfoot, Plot."

Without alerting his stance or changing his scan of deck activities, White keyed the talk switch on his headset cord: "Lightfoot, go."

"T-minus-ten radar sweep, no air activity, no surface activity within five miles," the radar operator aboard the *Mistress* reported.

"Copy," White responded. "Report every two minutes, report any surface activity within ten miles, Lightfoot out." White raised his head and watched as the retractable mast carrying the ship's SPS-69 X-band surface search radar began to extend. The range of the SPS-69 was limited to about six miles on a normal mast, but could be extended to almost fifteen miles by hoisting the radar to 100 feet—which was done only at night or in an emergency, because it looked very suspicious to have a search radar up so high on a non-combat vessel. Even more suspicious-looking on a "rescue" craft was the radar that was normally restricted into a housing just forward of the helicopter hangar—an SPS-40E B-band two-dimensional air search radar, which could scan for aircraft from sea level up to a 33,000-foot altitude and out to a 100-mile range. The *Valley Mistress* would probably not enjoy the same relatively unfettered access to most nations' territorial waters if those countries knew the ship had enough electronic search and communications equipment to control a surface or air battle at sea.

Over the din of deck activities, White heard another familiar sound, and he turned toward the starboard rail to see a young man wearing a headset leaning over the rail—*way* over the rail. "Chumming for sharks," as the crew called it, was pretty rare on the stabilized *Valley Mistress* in good weather, but this poor guy had had trouble ever since he'd joined the ship. White smiled and keyed his intercom button: "You okay, Jon?"

The man hurriedly wiped his mouth and face as if surprised someone noticed him, although there were men and women all around him, and he straightened and walked stiffly and unsteadily toward White. Jonathan Colin Masters was thirty-eight years old, but he looked about fifteen. He had short brown hair that looked as if someone—most likely himself—had cut it with hedge clippers; normally a baseball cap worn backward hid his goofy-looking hair, but Masters had lost that hat days ago in one of his frequent visits to the rail. He had disarming green eyes and long, gangly legs and arms—but he also had one of the world's most finely tuned brains on the end of his thin pencil neck.

Masters, a Dartmouth graduate at thirteen, an MIT doctor of science at twenty, was the president of Sky Masters, Inc., an Arkansas-based research company that designed, built, and deployed small specialty aircraft and spacecraft. SMI products took the latest aerospace technologies and miniaturized them: he could turn huge Delta space boosters into truck-mounted launch vehicles, or multi-ton communications satellites into breadbasket-sized devices. He was aboard the *Valley Mistress* to supervise the progress of his latest development.

"Feeling okay, Jon?" White asked as the boyish-looking engineer stepped toward him. The question was serious: repeated seasickness was just as debilitating as any other serious illness or disease, bad enough to cause problems even for a healthy, normally hydrated person; Masters was as skinny as a beanpole and the temperature and humidity in this part of the world were often both in the mid-to high nineties. "Why don't you stay inside where it's air-conditioned?"

"I need windows, Paul," Masters said weakly. "This damned ship of yours has no windows. I need a horizon to get my bearings."

"You must have a few thousand hours' flying time, Jon," White said, adding a lighter tone now that he could see that the young man was feeling okay, "but you've had trouble every single day since we left Italy. Ever get airsick?"

"Never."

"Are you using the scopolamine patches like the doc said?"

"I've worn enough of those damned patches to make me look like I've got a cauliflower growing behind my ears," Masters said, "and that stuff makes me drowsy and it makes food taste like charcoal. I'd rather eat, then barf, thank you very much."

"Maybe if you'd stop eating the burgers and fries like a pig, you wouldn't upchuck so easy." Masters ate junk food and drank soft drinks like a teenager but never gained the weight; it was always the supergeniuses, White thought, who were too busy to worry about unimportant matters such as health and nutrition. All that brain energy he generated must've kept him nice and slim.

"You want to know about the mission preparations or critique my eating habits, Colonel?" Masters asked impatiently. White gave up on the lecturing and motioned for the young scientist to show him the final preparations for the maiden launch of his newest invention.

Assembled on the aft helicopter deck was a sixty-five-foot-long track elevated about twenty degrees, and aimed off the fantail. Sitting on the front end of the track was an aircraft that greatly resembled a B-2A Spirit stealth bomber, its wingspan a large forty-two feet. The High Endurance Autonomous Reconnaissance System (HEARSE), nicknamed Skywalker, was a long-range, high-altitude flying-wing drone, with long, thin swept-back wings and a bulbous center section that was the aircraft's only fuselage. Like the B-2A stealth bomber, its engine section was on top of the fuselage, with a low, thin single air intake on the front and a very thin exhaust section in back; it used a single minijet engine, which was now running at idle power and had been for several minutes as White's technicians did its final checkout. Skywalker wasn't wasting gas sitting out there idling—it could probably run for three days at idle power. Painted in black radar-absorbent material, the craft looked sinister and unearthly, like a giant air-breathing manta ray. Unlike remotely piloted vehicles steered from the ground, Skywalker was a semi-autonomous drone—it would carry out commands issued to it via satellite uplink by plotting its own best track and speed.

Skywalker carried 1,000 pounds of sophisticated communications and reconnaissance gear in its fuselage section. The primary reconnaissance sensor was a side-looking synthetic-aperture radar, which broadcast high-resolution digital radar images via microwave datalinks back to the *Valley Mistress*. The SAR radar, similar to the one in the B-2A stealth bomber but optimized for reconnaissance versus attack and terrain avoidance, was powerful enough to create photographic-like images in total darkness that were clear enough to identify objects as small as a dog, and to electronically measure objects down to a foot in size. It used the same LPI (Low Probability of Intercept) technology as the B-2A as well: very short radar "looks," the radar imagery digitized so that it could be manipulated, enhanced, and viewed off-line, with the radar turned off.

"Everything looks like it's going fine."

"Skywalker's engine has been running fine for exactly ten-point-three minutes, all uplink channels confirm connected and secure—she's ready for a push anytime," Masters said confidently, almost boastfully.

"Good," White said. Some people might get irritated about Master's cockiness, but White enjoyed it. Left free to let his imagination soar, Masters was a true idea machine, a man who could get the job done no matter what the circumstances. "I've got about T minus eight. I'm heading to the recon center—I'm sure you'll want to stay out in the open air until your ship gets on station." Secretly he prayed that Masters wouldn't blow lunch in the confines of the reconnaissance control room—most of the air conditioning in that space was reserved for the electronics, and it was stuffy and smelly enough without the "chain reaction" scent of vomit.

Launch time had arrived. After clearing the area on radar, White ordered Skywalker on patrol. Masters throttled the turbofan engine up to full power; it would need full throttle only for a few minutes, then throttle back to a miserly twenty-liter-per-hour fuel-consumption rate, good for twelve hours of cruising. Then he released the hold-back bar, and the bird hurled itself down the launch rail. It sailed into the darkness at deck level for less than a hundred feet until it had built up climb speed, then, buoyed by its long, thin, supercritical wings, Skywalker climbed rapidly into the darkness. In less than five minutes, it was at 10,000 feet. It made a few orbits over the *Valley Mistress* as Masters and his technicians checked out its systems, then headed north, toward the Iranian coast.

Jon Masters looked pretty together when he stepped into the reconnaissance control room a few minutes later—his wet hair and chest probably meant he had stuck his head in a freshwater shower to refresh himself. "Looks like we got a tight bird, Doc," White told him as he stepped inside. "Skywalker should be on station in about an hour."

Masters found his chair but did not sit in it. He looked around apprehensively. "Can you open a window or door?" he asked in a quiet voice, like a boy shyly asking to use the bathroom. "Man, I need a horizon to align my gyros."

"Sorry, no windows," White said, "and leaving the hatch open spoils our electronic security." White knew that ships, subs, aircraft, or even shore-based electronic surveillance systems could pick up electromagnetic emissions from long distances—passive electronic reconnaissance was one of White's most popular missions—so the *Mistress*'s classified sections were shielded to foil eavesdroppers; that shielding was useless if ports or hatches were left open. He had some crew members turn on ventilation fans. It didn't seem to help—even in the dimly lit little chamber, everyone could see that Jon Masters was turning an especially awful shade of green.

But Masters seemed to settle down quickly as the drone approached its patrol area and some interesting images began coming in. The first one was crisp and clean, with shades of purple and orange providing some contrast and depth. The sensor operators filled the two thirty-inch monitors with a large warship steaming northward; data blocks under the sensor image displayed the target's speed, size, direction of travel, and other characteristics. "Beeaauuu-t-ful!" Jon Masters exclaimed.

Paul White agreed. It was the joint Chinese-Iranian aircraft carrier *Ayatollah Ruhollah Khomeini*, fully loaded and with a full complement of escorts, leaving its port at Chah Bahar and heading into the Gulf of Oman. White had never thought he'd see anything like it in his life—Iran sailing an aircraft carrier in the Persian Gulf region. "I'll get the report out on the satellite," he said, almost breathlessly. "NSA will want to know details."

Although it was not as big as the American supercarriers, it was still a very impressive-looking warship. It had so many anti-ship missile mounts on its decks that it looked like a battleship or guided-missile cruiser welded beside an aircraft carrier. It was a little intimidating to think that the *Khomeini* could bring an awesome array of surface-warfare weapons to bear on a target, and *then* launch attack aircraft to finish the job. The *Khomeini* looked similar to American aircraft carriers from the rear, with its slanted landing section, lighted edges, and four arresting wires; the main difference was in the huge array of armament set up in the aft section—the cruise-missile canisters and defensive missile and gun emplacements on both sides. The "island" superstructure looked like any other, with huge arrays of antennas seemingly piled atop one another on the superstructure and on a separate antenna structure aft; there was one aircraft elevator in front and behind the superstructure. Again, anti-ship cruise-missile emplacements were everywhere. The really unusual feature of the *Khomeini* was the bow section—instead of continuing the large, long flat profile of a "flat-top," the *Khomeini*'s bow rapidly sloped upward at the bow, forming an aircraft "ski jump."

White returned as Skywalker was focused on the carrier's forward flight deck. "NSA's got the word," he said. "No other instructions for us, so we continue to monitor the battle group. We should hear something soon."

"Man, look at the planes that thing is carrying," Masters exclaimed. He started poking the screen, counting aircraft. "They got at least ten fighters lined up on deck."

"They what?" White asked. He counted along with Masters, then said, "That's weird. They got their attack group up on deck."

"What's weird about that?"

"The *Khomeini* is a former Russian carrier, and the Russians usually wouldn't park any of their aircraft up on deck, like the Americans do,'' White explained. ''They'd keep all the fixed-wing aircraft belowdecks and leave only a few fling-wings on the roof for rescue and shuttle service between other ships in the group. That's why they carry only two dozen fixed-wing jets. An American flat-top carries three times that many—but one-third of them can be stowed belowdecks at one time.

''See this? The deck is so small, they line the helicopters up just forward of the forward elevator, and all the fixed-wings on the fantail behind the aft elevator,'' White continued. ''They need all that room because the *Khomeini* doesn't use catapults like other carriers. The Russians originally designed the ski jump for short-takeoff-and-landing jets, like the Yak-38 Forger and the Yak-41 Freestyle, which they canceled, but it works OK—in a manner of speaking—for conventional jets.'' He pointed at the monitor toward the aft section of the Iranian carrier. ''The fighters start way back here, about six hundred feet from the bow. The fighters are secured with a holdback bar, the pilots turn on the afterburners, and they let them go. When they leave the ski jump, they get flung about a hundred feet in the sky—but they *fall* almost seventy feet toward the water as they build up enough speed to start flying. . . .''

''You're *kidding!*'' Masters exclaimed.

''No, I'm not,'' White assured him. ''The jets drop so low that they had to build this little platform here on the bow so that someone with a radio can tell the air boss and skipper whether or not the jet made it, because no one can see the fighter from the 'crow's nest' for about fifteen to twenty seconds after takeoff, and if it crashed the ship would run right over it. The Sukhoi-33s apparently have a special ejection system wired into the radar altimeter that will automatically eject the pilot if there's no weight on the landing gear and the jet sinks below twenty feet. The auto-ejection system is manually activated, and apparently a lot of planes have been lost in training because newbie pilots forget to turn the system off just before landing. They make a successful carrier approach, swoop over the fantail, then *fwoosh*—they're gone, punched out a split second before they catch the wire.'' Masters laughed out loud like a little kid—for the moment, his seasickness was all but forgotten.

"The deck gets very dangerous in operations like this. There's probably only thirty feet of clearance between a wingtip and a rotor tip when a jet's heading for the ski jump,'' White went on. "Plus, nobody can land because aircraft are lined up on the fantail in the landing zone, which means if a jet has an emergency right after takeoff it'll take them a long time to clear the deck to recover it. . . .''

"What's on your mind, boss?" It was Paul White's deputy commander, Air Force Lieutenant Colonel Carl Knowlton.

White shook his head. "Ah, nothin'. It's just weird for all those planes to be on deck at night." He studied the monitor a bit more. "And they've got the ski jump clear. If they were just emptying out the hangar deck to clean it or set up for a party or reception or basketball game or something, like they do on American carriers, you'd think they'd just tow airplanes out of the way across the entire deck.''

"You think they're going flying tonight?"

"Who the hell knows?" White responded. "The Russians never flew carrier ops at night, and the *Khomeini*'s only been operational for about a year, so I'd think night flights would be the last thing on their minds. The Iranians would have to be real stupid to fly planes off a carrier at night, in a narrow channel, not facing into the wind, with a foul deck for emergency landing. Of course, I'd never accuse the Iranian military braintrust of a lot of smarts anyway.'' He paused, lost in thought. "Could be trouble tonight. I'm real glad we got Skywalker up there right now."

They zoomed out Skywalker's sensor to take pictures of the entire carrier, then zoomed in to maximum magnification to take detail pictures of every section of the ship. Occasionally Skywalker's threat warning system would beep, indicating that it was being scanned by a nearby radar, but there was never any indication that anyone had locked on to it, and no aircraft ever flew nearby to chase it away. There was an outside possibility that Skywalker's satellite uplink back to the *Valley Mistress* had been detected and even intercepted, but no one in the *Khomeini* group ever attempted to jam or shut down the signal; White and Masters hoped that Iran didn't yet possess the sophisticated computers needed to unscramble the uplink signals.

"Here's the other stuff I wanted to look at," White said excitedly as the Skywalker drone moved northward again, after orbiting over the *Khomeini* for nearly an hour. The drone had locked its sensor on a ship almost as large as the aircraft carrier, its center superstructure higher and clustered with twice the antenna arrays. "The Chinese destroyer *Zhanjiang*, the pride of the Chinese navy," White said. "Supposedly out here to house the Chinese officers and troops training on the *Khomeini*, but I think it's out here to protect the carrier and to add a little extra firepower to Iran's carrier escort fleet. It's got a full complement of non-nuclear weapons—long-range anti-ship and antiaircraft missiles, cruise missiles, rocket-powered torpedoes, big dual-purpose guns, three sub-hunter helicopters, the works. This one ship has more firepower than the entire Iranian air force, before they started buying up surplus Russian planes."

"So basically the Chinese are escorting an Iranian aircraft carrier battle group," Masters observed. "If anyone takes a shot at them, China gets involved in the fight."

"No one knows what China would do if the group was attacked—or, more likely, what the Chinese would do if the Iranians *attacked* someone," White said. "But Iran and China are pretty closely allied, economically if not ideologically—China's been pumping billions of dollars' worth of military hardware into Iran every year at bargain-basement prices, in exchange for cheap oil. It's a win-win deal for both of them, and I'd think they'd try very hard to maintain their relationship."

"But what for?" Masters asked. "What does Iran need with an aircraft carrier and a guided-missile destroyer?"

"They're the big boys on the block now, Jon," White replied. "You got a carrier, or a nuke, and you're the top dog. Iran maneuvers itself as the leader of the Muslim world by sailing five billion dollars' worth of warships around the Gulf, daring anyone to take a shot at them.''

"Who'd be stupid enough to do that?

"I'm not saying that's their strategy," White said, "but it's a pretty big threat, and they've got a lot of firepower to back it up."

"Like big chips on their shoulders," Masters summarized. "More like bricks. I guess they're out of the terrorist game then, huh?''

"I wouldn't say that at all," White said. "They've mastered the art of terrorism over the years. It didn't earn them any respect, except with other fanatical fringe groups. But now, with a powerful navy and air force, they've got respect—at least, everyone's wary of them now. The U.S. definitely is.''

Skywalker continued its patrol after orbiting *Zhanjiang* for almost an hour—still no sign of detection, even after more than two hours over the Iranian battle group. The operation had been a complete success so far. They decided they'd recall Skywalker after the battle group had headed south around the Musandam Peninsula and entered the Gulf of Oman. They programmed the drone to fly about twenty miles west of the warships instead of directly over them. Using the drone's sideways-looking radars, they kept track of the ships as they sailed southward into the sea lanes.

There was more to see as they scanned the rest of the Iranian battle group: "Holy cow, look at that," Masters exclaimed as they studied the vessel. "Looks like a big sucker. . . .''

Paul White was examining several photographs; he started shaking his head and said, "It's not on the list of known ships in the *Khomeini* battle group. Let's see . . . destroyer from the looks of it . . . huge superstructure, but not as big as a cruiser . . . big missile tubes amidships . . . aha, boys, looks like Iran really did get the Chinese destroyer it was looking for. That looks like a Luda-class destroyer, with two three-round Sea Eagle missile canisters. Skywalker's paid off right away, Doc. I don't think anyone knew another destroyer had joined the *Khomeini* group. This is a pretty significant find.''

Masters still looked green around the gills, but he grinned like a schoolboy. ''Of course it is, Colonel,'' he said, beaming with his usual bravado. ''I'm here to serve up the surprises for you.'' White had the communications section relay a message to the National Security Agency of the new Chinese destroyer's presence. ''Only the best from Sky Masters.''

''Uh-oh,'' Knowlton said, ''Mr. Modest is cranking it up again . . .''

''No brag, just fact,'' Masters said jubilantly. ''The Air Force or CIA should buy a hundred HEARSE drones. You can't get better intel than this—quick, reliable, accurate, and . . .''

Just then, one of the Sky Masters technicians radioed, ''Skywalker is reporting an overtemp in the primary hydraulic pack. Could be a bleed air-duct failure—might've got hit by a bird. Shutting down primary hydraulics . . .''

Masters looked as if someone had just slapped him in the face, and White and Knowlton couldn't help smiling over his sudden discomfort, even if it meant discontinuing their surveillance. ''Recall it!'' Masters shouted. ''Issue the recall command!''

''Recall order transmitted and acknowledged,'' the technician responded immediately. ''Skywalker changing heading . . . Skywalker's on course back to home plate. It's reporting capable of normal recovery; it will be ready for recovery in one hour, forty-two minutes.''

Jon Masters shook his head. ''If the Iranians are any good, Skywalker will never make it back,'' he said. ''Bleed air-duct failure near the primary hydraulic pack means a fire; a fire means visibility. With the hydraulic failure, Skywalker will start trailing hydraulic fluid, maybe fuel, maybe smoke and fire, and dragging control surfaces and maybe its arresting system, and bye-bye, stealth.''

''Then don't aim it right back for the ship, Jon,'' White

said. "Make it head to someplace over land, in Oman, or self-destruct it—"

"I am *not* self-destructing Skywalker while it's still flyable!" Masters shouted. "If it heads directly for us, it'll highlight our position, highlight *us*. I'll have to reprogram it manually. This was not supposed to happen . . . it's designed to head back to its launch base on as direct a route as possible."

"Turn it away, Jon," White warned him urgently. "The Iranians will pick up on that thing and trace it back to us."

"Skywalker reporting fire-control radar . . . intermittent lockon, Ku and X-brand radars, probably Crotale antiaircraft missile fire control."

Masters turned to White, all hint of seasickness gone from his face—he was deadly serious now. "We can surely kiss Skywalker good-bye, Colonel," he said. "And it's not taking any navigation commands."

"*What?*"

"It's in emergency-nav mode, Paul," Masters said. "Conserving power, conserving hydraulics—it might even have its controls locked. It won't evade, won't do anything but fly in a straight line."

"I think we'd better prepare for visitors," White said grimly. He clicked on his shipwide intercom: "Bridge, this is Lightfoot. We've been blown. I suggest you put the ship at action stations, institute Buddy Time procedures, head for the Omani coastline at flank speed, and be prepared for a boarding party alongside, a hostile aircraft overflight—or worse."

"Bridge copies." Immediately the alarm bell rang three times, and the captain announced, "All hands, action stations, all hands, action stations, this is not a drill."

ABOARD THE ISLAMIC REPUBLIC OF IRAN AIRCRAFT CARRIER
KHOMEINI

"Bridge, radar-contact aircraft, bearing two-one-zero, range
seven-point-eight kilometers, speed two-four-one, altitude
two-point-one K, course two-zero-zero."

Major Admiral Akbar Tufayli, Commanding Admiral of
the Islamic Revolutionary Guards Seventh Task Force,
turned his chair on the admiral's bridge of the *Khomeini*
toward the battle-staff area of the compartment. Within the
admiral's bridge, one deck down from the main bridge but
still able to view all of the above-deck activities on the ship,
Admiral Tufayli and his staff could monitor all the ship's
radio and intercom transmissions and, if he so chose, interject
his own commands directly into the system, even to aircraft
in flight or to nearby ships, bypassing all other commanders'
orders.

Tufayli had immense power for a relatively young man.
He started as a common street fighter and gangster, staging
wild, bloody executions of known spies and informants of
the Shah before the revolution. He'd joined the elite Pasdaran
in 1981 and risen swiftly through the ranks, commanding
larger and larger special forces and shock forces. Now he
was the fifth-highest-ranking officer of the Pasdaran, and had
been honored over all other field generals when he'd been
awarded command of the Pasdaran forces—nearly three
thousand commandos, infantrymen, pilots, and other highly
trained specialists—aboard Iran's first aircraft carrier.

Tufayli's battle staff was a mirror image of the ship's captain's own, and they were assembled in the admiral's bridge
now, monitoring all essential ship's departments and reporting to Tufayli's chief of staff, Brigadier General Muhammad
Badi. "General," Tufayli's called out, "is that an *aircraft*?
How did it get so close to my battle group without detection?"

"Unknown, sir," Badi responded. "Though it is possible . . . very small aircraft, weighing less than five thousand kilograms, flying less than two hundred fifty kilometers per hour, and greater than fifteen kilometers from the center of the group, would be squelched from the combat radar display as a non-hostile. Once our attack began, something that small might be ignored or omitted."

"Damn your eyes, Badi, that so-called non-hostile is now an unidentified aircraft less than ten kilometers from my battle group!" Tufayli shouted. "I want it destroyed immediately—no, wait! Is it transmitting anything? Can we identify any signals it might be sending . . . ?"

"Stand by, sir," Badi said. A few moments later: "Sir, the object is transmitting non-directional microwave signals in random, frequency-agile burst patterns. We can detect the signals, but only for very short periods of time. We cannot record or decode the signals."

Tufayli felt his anger rising up through his throat. Badi was very fond of jargon—it was one of his few faults. "Non-directional signals, burst patterns . . . are they satellite transmissions, Badi?"

"They do not appear to be jamming, uplink, or radar energy patterns, so the best estimate would be satellite signals," Badi responded.

"Before that contact gets out of optimal Crotale or SA-N-9 missile range, I want those microwave signals identified and analyzed," Tufayli ordered. "Then I want a listing of all vessels between us and the contact's course to the southwest. Maybe the contact is some sort of reconnaissance aircraft, returning to its home. I want that identified and reported to me immediately."

"Yes, sir," Badi acknowledged, and ordered the battle staff to work on this new problem. "Sir, unidentified aircraft is at eight kilometers, still on a constant heading south-southwest at two hundred kilometers per hour." Badi was handed a report, message form. "No luck in identifying or decoding the signals it is transmitting."

"Very well. Destroy it," Tufayli casually ordered.

Fifteen seconds later, just before the first assault helicopter left the *Khomeini*'s deck forward of the island superstructure, the battle staff turned and watched as a bright streak of fire shot upward from the deck of the Chinese destroyer *Zhanjiang*, then gracefully arced toward the southwest and dived straight down. The first Frenchmade Crotale surface-to-air missile launch was followed by two more, but the other two were unnecessary. Three seconds later they could see a bright blob of light in the sky, and a sharp *boom*! rolled across the water.

"Unidentified aircraft destroyed, sir," Badi reported.

"Very good," Tufayli said. He was still amazed at the incredible power at his fingertips. Yes, the *Khomeini* and its air group was an awesome weapon, but the destroyer *Zhanjiang* had as much long-range killing power as an entire Iranian artillery battalion. Tufayli controlled the skies, seas, and soon the land for 100 kilometers from where he sat, and the feeling was almost beyond comprehension. "Have one of the escorts send a launch to search for wreckage."

"Yes, sir."

"Where is the report on the ships along that unidentified aircraft's course?"

"Still cataloging all vessels along that projected course line, sir," Badi responded. "The flight path takes it very close to the Omani and UAE coastlines, and there are several major oil platforms . . ."

"It won't be an Arab base—no Gulf states possess such sophisticated systems," Tufayli said irritably. "Any major Western vessels reported in this area recently?"

Badi searched the initial list quickly, then put his finger on one line: "Yes, sir, just one. An American rescue-and-salvage vessel, the *Valley Mistress*. Identified by Sudanese coast patrol transiting the Red Sea three days ago, en route to Bahrain . . ."

"Identification?"

"Former Edenton-class salvage-and-rescue ship, three thousand tons, one hundred thirty men, long endurance, helicopter pad, and hangar facilities," Badi responded, reading from a copy of a Sudanese coast guard patrol report that had been forwarded to the Iranian battle group commander. "Privately owned but registered under the U.S. Navy Ready Reserve Fleet. Not inspected since leaving Port Said on its Suez Canal transit."

Tufayli was positive the unidentified aircraft, which he suspected was a small reconnaissance aircraft, possibly a balloon or drone, had come from that ship—it had the right size to handle such complex operations. "Send an electronic reconnaissance helicopter out to take some photos and scan the ship for unusual electronic emissions," Tufayli ordered. "In particular, try to get the ship to respond to a satellite communications transponder enquiry. I want a direct overflight— let us see what that so-called salvage ship does when threatened. Launch photo or decoy flares, drop a bomb, fire a marker rocket toward that ship—anything, but try to elicit a reaction."

Badi issued the orders, and a Kamov-25 reconnaissance helicopter, fitted with sensitive electronic warfare sensors and transmitters, was airborne within five minutes and headed southwest toward the American salvage ship.

ABOARD THE S.S. *VALLEY MISTRESS*
THAT SAME TIME

"Lost contact with Skywalker," the reconnaissance technician reported. "I had a brief lock-on by the Ku-band Crotale radar, then gone."

Jon Masters was mad enough to chew on a bulkhead door. "They got Skywalker, dammit!"

"Well, we're out of the recon business—and the Iranians will be gunning for *us* next," Paul White said. On shipwide intercom, he radioed, "Attention all hands, this is Lightfoot. Our reconnaissance aircraft was shot down by hostile action. We can expect a visit from Iranian patrols any minute now. All stations, begin a code-red scrub, repeat, begin code-red scrub procedures immediately. Initiate Buddy Time profile procedures. Helm, steer a direct course for Omani territorial waters, best speed. All section team leaders, meet me on the bridge. Lightfoot out.''

''Hey, wait a minute, Colonel!'' Masters said. The technicians in the reconnaissance section had immediately begun deactivating their equipment—not by using the checklist, but instead by yanking cables and pulling plugs. It didn't matter if yanking a hot plug caused a computer subsystem to lock up or suffer damage, because they were going to fit hundreds of pounds of explosives to all of it, drop it over the side, then set off the explosives. All paper records went into red plastic ''burn bags'' for shredding and burning; software disks went into ''smash bags'' for magnetic erasure and destruction. ''You called for a code red without even consulting me? It's my gear, you know!''

''Jon, buddy, stop thinking with your nuts or your pocketbook for one damned second,'' White said as he helped prepare the equipment for disposal. The control units were mounted in large suitcase like enclosures, all of which had spaces built into the frames for cooling and access—those same access spaces made it easy to slip half-pound bars of C4 plastic explosives into the equipment cases. Fitted with simple timers activated by seawater, the explosives would sink several feet before automatically detonating. The pieces would be very, very difficult to find.

Yes, they were now in international waters, and soon they would be in Omani territorial waters, but White had no doubt in his mind that Iran would try to recover any evidence that the *Valley Mistress* was a spy ship. They would violate a stack of international maritime laws to get what they wanted.

''It'll take one of those Iranian fighters just five minutes to shoot an anti-ship missile into us and disable the ship,'' White went on, helping carry the first of several dozen containers out to the rail. ''Ten minutes after that we could have an Iranian helicopter assault team dropping on deck. Sixty minutes after that, we could have an Iranian frigate pull up alongside. Now if they find any of this gear on board, we'll be hauled away as spies, and we'll never see the United States again—if they let us live.''

Masters wasn't listening. "But at least let me transmit some of the data, save some of the records," Masters protested. "This is supposed to be an operational evaluation—I'm still trying to collect performance data.''

"It's all going to be fish food in about ten minutes," White said. "Jon, we can't have any signs of anything on this ship except stuff that shows we're a legitimate rescue vessel. We've already got stuff that we can't hide, like the air search radar system and the—''

"It'll just take me a minute to do a system dump," Masters said, pushing past a technician and furiously typing on a keypad. "I'll burst it out on the satellite, and we'll be done with it.''

"Jon, forget it.''

"Lightfoot, bridge," the intercom cut in. "WLR reports inbound sea surveillance signal contact, possible heliborne search radar, approximate range forty miles, bearing zero-two-zero and closing, speed one hundred knots.'' The WLR-1 and WLR-11 systems aboard the *Valley Mistress* were passive radar-detection systems—they did not require the use of radar to pick up an enemy presence.

"We've just about run out of time, folks," White shouted in the reconnaissance center—he forgot about Masters, who was still typing away on his terminal. "We've got about ten minutes to get this stuff overboard before they get within visual range. After that, it all has to go out the SDV access hatch." The same chamber in the bottom of the ship that allowed Swimmer Delivery Vehicles to dock with the ship without surfacing could be used to dump some of the classified equipment while the Iranians were topside—that could give White's crew an extra few minutes.

In less than three minutes, the reconnaissance compartment was cleared out—all except Masters. White wasn't going to wait any longer: "Jon, dammit, pack it up, *now!*''

"I'm ready, it's going," Masters said. "Couple more seconds, and I'll be done.''

White was about to yank the plug himself, when he noticed a blinking UAV SYNC light on the computer control panel, with a SYNC ERROR light underneath. "Jon, what in hell is that?"

Jon saw the blinking light at the exact same moment and hit a key—the light went out. "I don't know," Masters replied. "The computer is trying to sync with Skywalker—"

"Except Skywalker was destroyed," White said. But then what was the computer talking to? "Shit, Jon, shut that thing off! That Iranian helicopter might have an electronic warfare suite that can send satellite transponder interrogate codes. Your computer was sending sync codes to the *Iranians*, trying to lock on to it!"

"I didn't know . . . I didn't realize it was still active!" Masters cried, yanking cables and practically overturning the terminal to shut it down. "Skywalker was off the air, shot down . . . I didn't think to shut down the uplink channel!"

"The Iranians must be reading our satellite transponder data signals," White said. "No way those signals can be mistaken for communication or navigation signals. And if they picked up Skywalker's uplink signals and matched them with our transponder signals . . . shit, the Iranians will know we were talking to Skywalker. We just gave ourselves away to the bad guys."

ABOARD THE IRANIAN AIRCRAFT CARRIER *KHOMEINI*

"Message from Patrol Helicopter Three," General Badi reported to Commanding Admiral Tufayli. "The crew reports non-directional microwave signals emanating from the salvage ship. They report the signals are identical to the signals transmitted by the unidentified aircraft."

"Excellent! We have them!" Admiral Tufayli shouted. "And that unidentified aircraft definitely constituted a hostile aircraft overflying my fleet without proper identification or communications. That is an act of war, and I am permitted to defend my men and vessels by any means at my command. General Badi, what anti-ship strike aircraft do we have ready at this time?''

"One fighter is airborne over checkpoint four, carrying two AS-18 radar-guided missiles and two AA-10 air-to-air missiles," the air operations officer reported. "It is scheduled to return to base in eleven minutes. Its replacement will be ready for launch in five minutes."

The patrol point for that fighter was only five kilometers east of the American warship—perfect! "Divert the fighter over checkpoint four, issue vector instructions to that American spy ship," Tufayli ordered. "As soon as the replacement fighter comes up on deck, launch it as a second strike and air cover; if the spy ship is still afloat, have the second fighter divert as well. We must attempt to keep that vessel out of Omani waters until we can reach it with a boarding party. Divert the destroyer *Medina* and Pasdaran Boghammar patrol boats to the spy ship's location to capture and detain any survivors and to search the wreckage for evidence; have Patrol Helicopter Four and the *Medina*'s helicopter keep visual contact on the spy ship until the *Medina* arrives on station. We will teach the Americans a lesson for spying on my ships!''

S.S. VALLEY MISTRESS

Jon Masters had that last terminal and all the rest of the equipment packed up, rigged, and thrown overboard in record time, and he even helped move several of the cargo boxes into the reconnaissance room, as the crew furiously tried to make the room look more like a cargo container and less like a control room. The underwater explosions reverberated through the ship as, one by one, the fifty-three containers associated with the Skywalker unmanned reconnaissance drone were blown into a hundred pieces and scattered across the bottom of the Gulf of Oman.

"Are we in Omani waters yet?" Masters shouted to White as he trotted back outside for another box.

"Get your life jacket on, Jon," White said grimly. He had just returned from the helicopter deck, where he'd been monitoring the crew as they stowed the surface and air search radar arrays. The SPS-40 was already stowed in its container and was even partially disassembled and the pieces thrown overboard—it would look very, very bad to have the Iranians find a sophisticated air surveillance radar on a salvage ship—but the SPS-69, which had been hoisted 100 feet above the deckhouse, was slow in coming down. It would not be so bad for the Iranians to find an SPS-69 on the *Valley Mistress*, but it would look very suspicious indeed for it to be up on a 100-foot mast.

"It's down in my cabin."

"Then get it," White shouted, grabbing Master's arm and pulling him around so that he was facing down the catwalk toward the ladder leading to the crew cabins, "and don't let me see you without it until we get back on dry land."

Masters stared at White in absolute terror. "Hey, Colonel . . ."

"It doesn't matter if we're in Omani waters or international waters or U.S. waters," White said, "because the Iranians are coming to get us. Now, get your damned life jacket, and make sure you've got your passport on you and no papers, disks, faxes, or computer records in your cabin. If you're not sure, toss the computer overboard. *Move*."

Masters had never seen White this grim, and it scared him even more. "Paul, I . . . I'm sorry about the terminal, about the satellite."

"Forget it," White said. "I think the Iranians were coming for us anyway. Now get going. Meet me right back up here on deck." Masters ran all the way back to his cabin.

"Lightfoot, bridge."

White keyed his intercom button: "Go."

"Air target one now approaching at one hundred knots," the radar officer on the bridge reported.

Shit, White swore to himself, that meant trouble. The helicopter was moving into visual range—reporting to other Iranian inbounds, no doubt. "Any other targets?"

"Negative."

"There will be," White warned him. "Keep me posted. Out."

"Paul?" It was Carl Knowlton, supervising the work on the SPS-69 radar.

"What'd you get, Carl?"

"No good on the radar mast—it's jammed."

Dammit, dammit, *dammit* . . . "Well, I was hoping NSA would buy me a better system anyway," White said. "That patrol helicopter is moving in fast. Blow the radar mast. Sound the bell fifteen seconds prior. Break. All hands, this is Lightfoot, use caution, the SPS-69 mast is coming down hard. Take cover when you hear the alarm bell."

Masters met up with White on the helicopter pad, where they could watch the SPS-69 but close enough to the hangar door so they could run inside if the mast and radar antenna fell toward them. The life preserver he wore was a thin-line Class V jacket, which looked more like a thick Windbreaker than a typical vest, but it still looked three sizes too big on Masters. "My cabin's cleaned out," he told White breathlessly. "I tossed everything overboard, even my pager."

"Good. Thanks." A few seconds later the alarm bell rang, followed shortly by two flashes of light and two loud *bangs* as the mast and the portside guy wires were cut by small explosive charges and the SPS-69 radar antenna and forty feet of mast toppled over to starboard into the sea. Two more explosive charges cut the starboard guy wires a second later, and the antenna disappeared from view. "The damned Iranians owe me a new surface search radar," White said under his breath.

"Bridge, Lightfoot."

"Go."

"We're receiving numerous radio calls from the Iranian fleet, ordering us to heave to for an inspection," the bridge officer reported. "We've told them repeatedly that we are an American Naval Reserve Fleet rescue vessel and cannot be detained on the high seas while under way, but they are still ordering us to heave to. I'm quoting chapter and verse out of the law books, but they're ignoring it."

"Keep on reading 'em the law," White said. "Not that they'll obey it, but keep on reading it to them anyway. Broadcast on international distress freqs, too—maybe a maritime lawyer will jump in."

There was a slight pause, then: "Lightfoot, bridge, they are asking if they can lower an inspector on our hangar deck by helicopter."

"Tell them we need to keep our decks clear."

"They're asking why we're running from them and if we know anything about a spy aircraft that tried to attack them just now."

"Tell them . . . shit, bridge, tell them anything, read them the Bible, read them the law, just keep on looking innocent. But we're not stopping."

"Lightfoot, the Iranians advise us that they're lowering an Iranian customs officer to the helicopter deck to speak with the captain. They state that we were in Iranian waters and they have a right to have customs inspect our vessel. They say if we do not submit to an inspection, they will attempt to stop us by force."

"Tell them we weren't in Iranian waters, but we'll be happy to submit to an inspection at our destination port, Muscat. We're responding to an urgent call, and that's where we're headed. Lowering a man onto our deck at night is too hazardous, so we refuse."

"Oh, shit—look," Knowlton said, pointing to the north. Just as the radar mast hit the water, the Iranian patrol helicopter had appeared. No doubt it had seen the radar mast blown off the ship. A side door was open, and a door gunner could be seen aiming a large gun at them. "That gunner's got a forty-millimeter grenade launcher aimed at us," Knowlton said. "Those suckers are serious."

"Wave, everybody, wave," White said. "We're supposed to be a friendly, non-hostile salvage vessel." He got back on shipwide intercom: "All hands, this is Lightfoot, visitors off the stern, Buddy Time procedures in effect now. Break. Plot, you need to relay AWACS data to me now that our radars are down. That Iranian helicopter sneaked in on us and probably saw us blow the radar mast. Keep the reports coming.''

"Copy, Lightfoot, sorry," the radar officer responded. "AWACS reports air target two, bearing two-eight-three, range twenty-five miles, altitude one thousand, six hundred, speed five hundred knots, probable a fighter from the carrier *Khomeini*.''

"Probable *shit*, that's exactly who it is," White shouted. "Helm, Lightfoot, match reciprocal bearings on air target two, keep it off the stern as best you can. Break. Comm, send out a coded flash message via the AWACS plane to Gulf Cooperative Council or U.S. forces and request some fighter support—we'll be under attack in a couple minutes. Break. Stinger team, report to the helo deck on the double, but stay inside the hangar, out of sight—that Iranian helicopter is sitting right off our stern watching us. CM crews, stand by belowdecks with floaters. Break. All hands, this is Lightfoot, hostile fighter aircraft inbound from the east, report to your damage control stations, Stinger and countermeasures crews responding. Break. Plot, count me down on air target two.''

ABOARD THE *KHOMEINI*

"Sir, Patrol Helicopter Three reports the crew on that salvage ship set off a small explosive charge to sever a tall mast on its superstructure," General Badi reported. "The mast was cut free of the ship and abandoned in the water. Some crew members are on the helicopter landing pad, waving at the helicopter. They appear to be friendly, but they are obviously crowding the deck to show their numbers and prevent anyone from boarding her.

"That could have been the satellite antenna they used to

control that spy plane," Badi said. "Obviously they did not want us to see it on their ship."

"I understand that, Badi. Any response to our hails?" Admiral Tufayli asked.

"They insist they are responding to an urgent call and cannot be stopped," Badi replied. "They will not allow anyone to be lowered on deck."

"Order Patrol Three to flash 'heave-to' light signals to their bridge," Tufayli ordered. "If they do not respond, fire a warning shot across their bow. If they do not respond to that, open fire on the ship until they stop."

Badi looked at Tufayli in sheer horror: "Are you sure, Admiral?" he asked in a low voice. "Fire on an American salvage vessel? This ship has a Naval Reserve designation, sir—it's been verified. We'd be attacking an American naval vessel!"

"I want that ship stopped and its crew placed under arrest," Tufayli said. "It is obvious they are fleeing us to Omani waters to prevent their being discovered as spies, and I will not allow that. Now see to it that vessel is stopped *immediately!*"

ABOARD THE *VALLEY MISTRESS*

White, Knowlton, Masters, and the other men on deck watched as the Iranian helicopter maneuvered around to the *Valley Mistress*'s bow and began flashing bright red and white lights at the bridge.

"Heave-to signal," Knowlton said. "As a general rule, in international waters we'd have to stop unless we really were en route to an emergency."

"Well, we ain't stopping."

"That means they'll try to . . ." Just then, they saw a bright flash of light from the open crew door on the helicopter, and a huge geyser of water erupted just a few dozen yards off the bow. A rolling *boom!* caused everyone on the hangar deck to jump.

". . . fire warning shots next," Knowlton said.

"Question is, would those crazy suckers put one of those grenades into us?" White asked. He answered his own question right away, and keyed his mike: "Comm, any reply from anyone for air cover?"

"Affirmative, Lightfoot," came the reply. "U.S. Air Force is vectoring fighters on our position, ETA fifteen minutes."

"Shit, some of those UAE or Omani fighters would be real welcome right now," White said. "It'll be way too late for U.S. fighters from Saudi. We're in deep shit."

Just then they felt a hard impact on the portside of the *Valley Mistress*, and a cloud of fire erupted just below the bridge. White and the others raced over to the left side of the ship and saw that an Iranian grenade launched from the helicopter door gunner had hit the foredeck just forward of the superstructure at the base of the forward crane. "Stinger crews on deck!" White ordered. "Target helicopter, off the port beam!" He shouted to the others on the helicopter pad, "Everyone but the Stinger crews, clear the chopper pad! Stand by damage and rescue stations!"

The Marine Corps Stinger teams were beside White on the helicopter deck in an instant, and in less than thirty seconds a Marine had a Stinger MANPADS (Man-Portable Air Defense System) missile launcher on his shoulder. Another Marine was beside him, guiding his movements; two more Marines were nearby, ready to load another missile canister and back up their teammates if necessary. "I have the target!" the gunner shouted. Just then, a second grenade blasted into the side of the *Valley Mistress*, just above the waterline.

They saw the Iranian helicopter gunner swing his grenade launcher toward the helicopter deck, and then the helicopter wheeled right, nose-on to the Stinger crew, presenting the smallest possible target. "Batteries released!" White shouted. "Nail the bastard!"

The Stinger missile crewman pulled a large lever down

with his right thumb, which activated the battery and charged the ejection gas system. "My launcher is charged!" he shouted.

"Clear to uncage!" the spotter shouted.

While keeping the target centered in his viewfinder, the launcher crewman squeezed a large button on the front of the launcher tube, which uncovered the seeker head of the missile. He immediately got a low growling sound in his headset—he was locked on. "Target lock!" he shouted. "Clear!"

The spotter took one quick look behind them, checking the blast area, then patted the launch crewman on the rear. "Clear to fire!"

"I'm clear to fire!" The crewman raised the Stinger launcher.

"One away!" he shouted, and squeezed the trigger. There was a loud *pop!* and a gush of white gas from the exhaust end of the Stinger tube. No one could see it in the darkness, but the Stinger missile flew for several yards through the air; then, just as it began to descend at the end of its ballistic travel, the rocket motor ignited and the missile plowed into the helicopter, directly into the engine compartment atop the fuselage. The launcher crew did not bother to watch the result of that hit—they hurriedly made ready for a second launch.

For what seemed like a full minute, nothing happened. Just as Masters thought the missile had missed or harmlessly plunged into the sea, he saw a bright flash of light and a puff of fire; then, as if the helicopter pilot had decided to land, the helicopter descended quickly to the ocean, nosing over slightly just before hitting the water. It was out of sight in an instant. "We got him!" Masters shouted. "Man, I never seen anything like that—it happened so quick, but it was like it was in slow motion."

"The Iranian fighters will be next," White shouted as he hurried back on the hangar deck. On intercom, he shouted, "Countermeasures, launch floater! Plot, where are those fighters?"

On the starboard side of the *Valley Mistress* near the stern, the countermeasures crews released a large raftlike unit, nick-named a "floater," that contained specially designed radar reflectors, signal generators, and infrared energy generators designed to mimic the radar and infrared cross-section of the ship. Once clear of the ship, the floater began shooting chaff rockets into the air. After reaching 300 feet, the rockets be-gan ejecting bundles of hair-thin strips of metal that would expand and bloom into a sausage-shaped cloud. Hopefully that would present a more inviting target on radar than the *Valley Mistress*'s stern.

"Range nine miles. Target bearing one-five-zero." The *Valley Mistress* turned northwest as the fighter swung slightly south—the fighter was maneuvering to try to get a larger profile picture of its quarry, and the helmsman of the *Valley Mistress* was trying to turn to keep the fighter behind the ship.

"Seven miles, bearing two-two-zero . . ." No sooner had the ship finished that first right turn than it suddenly heeled sharply to starboard as the helmsman threw the ship into a tight turn to port. The fighter had turned farther around, com-ing in from the southwest, so the helmsman now tried to point the bow of the *Valley Mistress* at the incoming fighter instead of the stern. "Six miles, bearing . . ."

Suddenly the sea behind the ship exploded into a huge geyser of water and foam, followed by a second explosion. The sound rolled across the deck a second later, hitting them like a double thunderclap. "That motherfucker fired at us!" Masters shouted. "They're shooting at us!" The Su-33 fighter had launched two radar-guided anti-ship missiles, which had locked on to the much larger radar target—the decoy floater. The missiles hit the water less than a thousand yards astern.

"Range five miles, target turning north escape vector bear-ing one-eight-zero . . . range three miles . . ."

"Stinger crews, batteries released!" White ordered. "Nail the bastard!"

Unlike with the attack on the helicopter, this time the

Stinger launcher crewman couldn't see the fighter itself through the view finder, so he had replaced the regular optical viewfinder on his Stinger launcher with a two-inch-square LCD screen, which showed an electronic image of the Stinger viewfinder and the Iranian fighter, along with target flight data and missile status. Data received from the AWACS radar plane orbiting over Saudi Arabia was transmitted via wireless datalink to the *Valley Mistress*, then to a receiver carried by the Stinger launcher crew, and presented on the tiny screen so that the launcher crewman could aim his Stinger system in total darkness.

When the electronic image of the fighter was centered in the screen, the launcher crewman first hit a button on the right hand grip, which fired a radio interrogation signal at the fighter. A friendly plane would have responded to the radio signal—this one did not. "IFF negative! Clear me to shoot!"

"Clear to shoot!" White shouted. Again, the Stinger crew fired. The missile disappeared from view into the darkness . . . but far out on the horizon, they saw a bright flash of light and a stream of fire—another hit.

But there was no celebrating their victory. Everyone knew there were at least nineteen more fast-movers and six more fling-wings out there based on the aircraft carrier *Khomeini*, plus hundreds more based in Iran just a few hundred miles away, that could quickly send the *Valley Mistress* to the bottom of the Persian Gulf. Their little counterattack merely bought them a few precious minutes, perhaps a little hesitation or overcaution in the minds of the Iranian attackers, perhaps a mile or two closer to the Omani coast, where the Iranians might not pursue. But the fight was still on. . . .

ABOARD THE *KHOMEINI*

"Contact lost with Patrol Three!" the radar operator shouted on the intercom. He began reading off last position, altitude, and airspeed, which would be relayed to rescue forces. "Lost contact with attack two as well!"

"What in hell happened?" Admiral Tufayli shouted. "Did the pilot crash? Get me a report!"

"Message from scout helicopter, just before contact was lost," General Badi interjected. "The pilot reported that a missile was fired from the deck of the American salvage ship shortly after they fired their warning shots."

"Missiles? That American ship fired missiles?" Tufayli shouted. "I want that damned ship on the bottom of the Gulf of Oman *now!*"

"The American vessel appears to be still under way. It is crossing into Omani territorial waters, now five kilometers offshore and less than twenty kilometers northeast of Ra's Haffah, heading southwest at twenty knots. The pilot of Attack Two said he had contact on the target, but apparently he struck a decoy."

"Decoys . . . antiaircraft missiles . . . this is no damned salvage ship, and it's no spy ship, either—it is an American *war*ship, and they have declared war with Iran and with my battle group!" Tufayli shouted.

"Sir, Strike Unit Nine is ready for launch," General Badi said. Tufayli looked outside his flight deck windows and saw the long double tongues of flame erupting from the holdback spot, as the Sukhoi-33 fighter-bomber activated its afterburners. A second later, the fighter began to roll down the long flight deck, uncomfortably slow at first but rapidly picking up speed. The afterburner flames described a bright yellow arc through the sky as the fighter leapt off the ski jump, sank toward the water, slowly leveled off, then accelerated with a smooth, shallow ascent into the sky. Passing 200 meters' altitude, the afterburner flames disappeared. "What are your instructions, sir?"

"Destroy that ship!" Tufayli screamed. "*Destroy* it!"

"But, sir, the vessel is in Omani waters now," Badi said. "It is within sight of land, and there are many small villages near."

"I do not care how many people will see this—I want that

American warship destroyed!'' Tufayli cried. "Divert another fighter with anti-ship weapons to follow if the second pilot fails as well, then rearm another fighter for anti-ship operations, and do it *now!*'' Badi could do or say nothing else.

Aboard the S.S. *Valley Mistress*

The first two lifeboats were loaded up with technicians from Sky Masters, crowded shoulder to shoulder in three rows of ten men in each boat. They had just been lowered to the water and were beginning to motor toward the UAE shoreline when the intercom blared, "Incoming aircraft bearing zero-three-zero, speed six hundred knots, range thirty-six miles and closing!''

"Go! Fast as you can!'' White shouted to the crew of the second lifeboat as they finally detached from the lowering cables and started the lifeboat's engine. A third lifeboat was being loaded with the rest of the civilian contractors plus the non-essential seamen—only a handful of seamen, the ten officers, and the thirty members of Madcap Magician remained aboard the *Valley Mistress*. "Lower lifeboat!'' White shouted. "Head for shore and don't stop!'' He keyed his intercom mike: "CM, release floater! Stinger crews, stand by!''

When White returned to the helicopter landing pad, the members of the crew assigned to the countermeasures crew were assembled there, waiting for him. He was shocked to see Jon Masters standing with them. "Masters, what in hell are you doing here? I ordered you to go in the third lifeboat.''

"They needed some help with the signal generator on the floater,'' Masters replied. "It's fixed.''

"That was the last floater, right?'' White asked. He got a nod in reply. "Take lifeboat four and head for shore. Jon, bridge, crew, engineering, you go with them.''

"Lifeboat four is the last one," Masters said. "You won't have a boat."

"We're not leaving without the rest of you," Master Sergeant Steven Cromwell, the senior member of the twenty-four-man Marine platoon attached to Madcap Magician, said sternly. "Our job is to protect the ISA technical group. We don't split up and we don't leave anyone behind."

"If you all get captured by the fucking Iranians, we'll all be in deep shit, Sergeant."

"You said it yourself, Colonel," Cromwell said. " 'Deep Shit' is our middle name. We're not leaving. We'll man an extra Stinger crew if you want one."

"What I want is a Stinger crew in lifeboat four to trail the others and provide air cover in case an Iranian helicopter tries to pursue," White said. "Grab four men and as many tubes as you can carry and head toward the others. You'll have a datalink as long as the ship is still operational—if you lose the datalink, you'll just have to guide by hearing. Get going, Steve." He looked at Jon Masters, then at Cromwell, and said, "Take Dr. Masters with you."

"I'll stay here if it's all the same."

"It is not," White said. "Sergeant, your responsibility now is the safety of the disembarked crew and the civilians. You are to deliver all the members of the ship's crew and the civilian contractors, including Dr. Masters here, safely to the U.S. embassy in Dubai or Abu Dhabi, or any friendly agency or military unit, to ensure the safe delivery of these men back to the United States. You are to take any and all steps necessary to ensure their safety and the security of the ISA cell. Is that clear?"

Cromwell appeared as if he were going to make another argument for staying, but he knew White was right. Most of the ISA cell members were going to be on shore, and White had four Marines to help him here. "Yes, sir," Cromwell responded. He turned to the Stinger crew members and said, "Sergeant Reynard, you're in charge of this detachment." The young Stinger crewman acknowledged the order, and Cromwell saluted White and departed with his men.

Masters still hesitated: "Hey, Paul . . ."

"Get moving, Doc. I want you on that lifeboat."

"Why don't you come with us?" Masters asked.

"Can't leave the ship," White replied.

"But if the Iranians get . . . you know, if they attack . . ."

"You're assuming they'll attack, and assuming they'll hit us, and assuming they'll put us out of commission," White said. "I don't make assumptions. We'll get off the ship only when it's necessary—otherwise we stay."

"But you're ISA, you're Madcap Magician," Masters said. "We need you to reassemble your team. Let the ship's crew take care of the ship. If they get captured, they've got an airtight cover."

"Listen, Doc, I've put too much time in this tub to leave it when it's still slimy side down and running," Paul White said. "It may not technically be *my* ship, but I made it what it is right now. I'm not leaving the *Mistress* until it's not safe to stay. Now get moving, Jon." White turned away, and a Marine was pulling at Masters's arm, practically dragging him to the last lifeboat.

"Nice working with you, Colonel," Masters said, but White was talking on his headset and didn't hear him. One minute later they were speeding away from the ship, trying to catch up with the other three lifeboats. The Marines on board had one Stinger missile assembled and ready for launch, with one Stinger missile "coffin," containing two missile tubes, a spare launcher grip assembly, and three battery units, opened up and ready to load.

As they sped away from the ship, Jon Masters remembered the first day he set foot on the *Valley Mistress*, about three months earlier. He had thought it was the ugliest thing afloat. It had a cleft bow for hoisting things up from the bow cranes up on deck; two huge cranes, one twenty-ton aft and one ten-ton forward; plus lots of standpipes and hoses and other weird things jutting out from the deck and superstructure that just made it look cluttered and made it hard to move around without banging knees or elbows on things. Now it seemed like the most welcome sight on earth, and he wished he was back on deck, complaining about the lack of windows, the poor TV reception, the lack of fresh water, the boring menu, and the out-of-date videotape library.

The dim green light of the electronic viewfinder illuminated the Stinger launcher crewman's right eye as he raised the weapon and pointed it to the north. "Datalink active," he reported. "One fighter inbound from the north, range twenty klicks. I've got another slow-mover, possibly another patrol helicopter, orbiting about ten klicks north of the ship."

"Maybe the fighter and the chopper will have a meeting of their minds," one Marine quipped.

"Button it," Cromwell ordered. "If it flies within four klicks of our position and doesn't squawk friendly, kill it. And I want you bozos to set a new record for readying a second missile for launch. Maxwell, keep an eye out for lifeboat number—"

Suddenly a bright orange ball of fire erupted from the starboard side of the *Valley Mistress*, followed by another directly alongside. The sound of the explosion followed a few seconds later, and to Jon Masters it felt like a red-hot fist punching him in the face. "Oh, shit, they're *hit!*"

"Target bearing zero-niner-zero, ten klicks!" the gunner yelled.

"Helm, starboard turn heading north!" Cromwell ordered. "I want that hostile kept on the starboard beam!" The helmsman swung the tiller over and pointed the lifeboat north. Everybody ducked and scrambled out of the way as the Stinger crew reoriented themselves and reacquired the Iranian fighter.

The *Valley Mistress* was partially illuminated from the fires on the portside—it was already listing heavily. "Get off that thing, dammit, it's sinking!" Masters shouted to anybody that might still be on board the stricken ship. The lifeboat swung farther east as the fighter flew closer. Just then, they saw a Stinger missile launched from the helo deck of the ship. The missile and the gunner on the lifeboat were lined up—the Stinger missile appeared to be tracking perfectly—but then they saw several blobs of bright white floating in the sky, followed by a bright but brief explosion. "Flare decoys," Masters said. "The fighter got away."

"No way!" the Stinger gunner on the lifeboat shouted. "Range three miles! Weapon charged . . . negative IFF response! Two miles . . . lost contact! Lost the datalink!"

"Uncage!" Cromwell shouted. It would be almost impossible for the gunner to find the fighter in the dark, but Cromwell wasn't about to let it get away. The missile's seeker head was their last chance. "Find that fighter!"

The gunner squeezed the uncage button, still swinging right to follow what he thought was its flight path. He got a lock-on signal right away. "Locked on! Clear me to fire!"

Cromwell thought for a moment: if the Stinger missed, they'd have highlighted themselves to the fighter. The helicopter might come after them then . . . but the others might be safe, might have time to make it. "Clear to fire!" Cromwell shouted.

"Missile away!" the gunner shouted as he superelevated the launcher and squeezed the trigger. The missile popped out of the launcher, its main rocket motor ignition seemingly close enough to touch. The Stinger missile heeled sharply north, the motor burned out . . . and seconds later, they saw another bright glob of light and a streak of fire drawn across the night sky. "Got the motherfucker!" the gunner shouted. They saw the streak of fire continue north—it was on fire, but apparently still flying.

"A half a kill is better than nothing," Cromwell said as the crew fitted another missile onto the firing grip assembly. In twenty seconds they were ready to fire a second round.

The helmsman turned the lifeboat back on a westerly heading, toward shore but away from the brightly burning ship. It was hard to pick out details, but the shape was different; it was listing heavily to port, almost capsized, Jon Masters guessed. He had never seen a ship sink for real before—even from this distance, it was horrifying. They could hear hisses and pops and tearing, grinding metal sounds roll across the water; then, several minutes later, nothing. The ship was out of sight a few minutes later, lost forever.

"Do not talk to *us* of treachery and sedition, Madam Vice President," Dr. Ali Akbar Velayati, the Iranian Foreign Minister, said over the phone. His English was good, with a touch of a British accent. "First the United States assists the Gulf Cooperation Council with a wanton attack on Iranian soil—then you violate our sovereignty, our peace, and our right to free access to international waters and sovereign airspace by flying spy planes over our vessels. Not only that, madam, but our vessels and aircraft came under attack by your spy vessel! This is an act of war, and *you* have started it!"

"The United States had no spy vessels or aircraft anywhere near your ships, Dr. Velayati," Ellen Christine Whiting said. "The United States will not tolerate air or naval attacks on unarmed civilian vessels in international or allied waters . . ."

But Velayati was already speaking before the Vice President could finish: "It is vital for the peace and safety of the entire region for all to stop these threats and accusations, pledge assistance to help in rescue-and-recovery efforts, and pledge cooperation in restoring peace to the region," Velayati said. "The Islamic Republic is conducting rescue-and-reconstruction work on our damaged property on Abu Musa Island—the death and destruction, I must remind you, which was caused by you and your Zionist stooges!"

"I can assure you, Minister, that the United States government was not involved in the attacks against Abu Musa Island," Whiting said, "and neither were the Israelis. The Gulf Cooperation Council was responding to the threat of anti-ship, antiaircraft, and long-range missiles placed on your illegal military installations. I can assure you, Minister, that the United States will not tolerate any—"

"I have told you, madam, that Iran is not responsible! Not responsible!" Velayati exploded. "Do not provoke my government, madam! America wants war with Iran! We are not begging for war like America! We want peace! But we will act to protect our people and our homes! We want all warships to depart the Persian Gulf at once. All foreign warships must leave."

Whiting's eyes widened in surprise. "Excuse me, Minister?"

"Madam, the Islamic Republic demands that all foreign warships leave the Persian Gulf," Velayati said. "The presence of offensive warships in the Gulf is a threat to Iran's peace and sovereignty, and may be considered a hostile action toward Iran."

"Minister Velayati, the Persian Gulf is not the private lake of the Islamic Republic of Iran," Whiting said. "Any vessel, including war ships, can freely navigate those waters at any time."

"Then you risk war. You want war with Iran . . ."

"We don't want war with anyone, Dr. Velayati," Whiting said, "but you threatened international shipping and the right to freely navigate the Persian Gulf by placing anti-ship missiles on Abu Musa Island."

"Are we not allowed to protect our property?" Velayati asked. "Are we not allowed to defend our rights and our freedom?"

"Of course you are, sir," Whiting replied, "but those weapons Iran placed on Abu Musa Island were offensive in nature, not defensive."

"And so you say, Madam Vice President, that the presence of the U.S.S. *Abraham Lincoln* and its escort guided-missile cruisers and battleships in the Persian Gulf with their bombers and cruise missiles and nuclear warheads are merely defensive in nature and not offensive?" Velayati asked. "I think not. Yet you insist on the right to sail your warships within just a few kilometers of Islamic Republic territory and fly your spy planes over our vessels. You set a dubious double standard in our own front yard, Madam Vice President.

These are *our* waters, our lands. We have a right to defend them from hostile foreign invaders. Your support of the dastardly Gulf Cooperative Council attack on our islands proves your hostile intent.

"Madam Vice President, the Islamic Republic of Iran will look upon the presence of non-Arab warships in the Persian Gulf to be a hostile act, an act of war against Iran," Velayati went on. "We are calling for all non-Arab nations to remove their warships from the Persian Gulf immediately."

"Leaving only Iran's warships in the Gulf, Minister?" Whiting interjected.

"Iran hereby pledges that we will also withdraw our warships from the Gulf, leaving only those forces precisely equal to those of all Gulf Cooperative Council warships," Velayati replied. "We shall remove the aircraft carrier *Ayatollah Rubollah Khomeini* and our submarines to our base at Chah Bahar and keep them outside the Persian Gulf as well, using them only to patrol the sea lanes and approaches to the Strait of Hormuz and Persian Gulf for signs of anyone violating the agreement."

"It is an interesting idea, Minister Velayati," Whiting said. Across from her, the President shrugged; the President's National Security Advisor grimaced. "We must present your idea to the President and the Congress; we should like to see a formal draft of such a treaty. Until then, Minister, the right of any nation to freely navigate international waters should not be infringed."

"The Persian Gulf is vital to Iran's economy as well as the economies of the GCC and the industry of our customers, madam," Velayati went on, continuing his single-minded preaching. "Because it is so vital, we propose that the Persian Gulf be completely demilitarized. Foreign warships, foreign warplanes, foreign troops should all leave. Iran pledges to do all that is possible to see to it that peace reigns in the Gulf. Can you pledge your support for this ideal, Madam Vice President? Will you take this message to the President?"

"Minister Velayati, I will discuss everything with the

President, of course,'' Whiting said, ''but we need to discuss the attack on the civilian Naval Reserve Fleet vessel, the issue of thirteen persons still missing from that attack, our rights to conduct salvage-and-rescue operations in the area, and Iran's intentions should the United States or any other nation choose to send any vessel, including armed vessels, through the Strait of Hormuz and Persian Gulf.''

''Madame Vice President, Iran feels that the presence of any offensive warships in the Persian Gulf will only increase tensions further,'' Velayati said. ''Iran strongly objects especially to the United States or any other nation sending any warships capable of land attack operations into the Gulf. You desire negotiations, yes, but Iran feels that such negotiations with Hornet bombers and Tomahawk cruise missiles aimed at our cities and military bases is not true negotiating—it is bargaining at gunpoint, and we shall not stand for such. If you truly desire peace, madam, if America truly does not want this conflict to escalate further, you will agree to remove your warships from the Gulf immediately. We shall do the same. Iran will not look favorably upon any nation that decides to send a warship capable of land attack into the Persian Gulf.''

''Minister Velayati, your terms are much too broad for diplomatic discussion,'' Vice President Whiting said in complete disbelief. ''You simply cannot unilaterally decide to close the Persian Gulf to any vessels you choose, any more than the United States can close off the Gulf of Mexico or the Gulf of Alaska . . .''

''We will not accept any interference from America!'' Velayati emphasized. ''If America attempts to sail an offensive land-attack warship into the Persian Gulf, Iran will consider it a hostile act. We do not wish war, but we are prepared to defend our rights and our freedoms! America wants another Desert Storm with Iran! No more Desert Storms! No more warships in the Persian Gulf! No more war!'' And the line went dead.

Whiting dropped the phone back in its cradle, then sat back in the couch in the Oval Office, where she had taken the call. "I'm too young and innocent for this, Mr. President," she quipped. That was an exaggeration, of course. As the former Governor of Delaware and a former United Nations Deputy Ambassador, Whiting was well equipped to take on anyone in an argument.

"Hell, Ellen, Velayati was educated at Oxford—he's supposed to *respect* women," President Kevin Martindale said, trying to help his Vice President unclench her jaw. "I thought he was a pussycat." Whiting was not going to relax that easily—her lips were tight, her eyes narrow and hard as she made her way back to her seat around the coffee table in the Oval Office.

"Okay, ladies and gents, what in hell is going wrong around here?" the President asked. Recently elected and only forty-nine years old, divorced, with two grown children, he was in tremendously good health and vitality although the stress of forming a new government was bound to take its toll on his boyish good looks. Today he was dressed in gray slacks, business shoes, and a conservative white shirt under a thick cardigan sweater. His thick salt-and-pepper gray hair was neatly in place except for the famous "photographer's dream," a thick lock of bright silver hair that curled defiantly down across his forehead over his left eye when he got angry. The end of the lock was pointed, like the Grim Reaper's scythe. If a second one appeared over the *right* eye, heads would roll.

With the President and the Vice President was Secretary of State Jeffrey Hartman; Secretary of Defense Arthur Chastain; Philip Freeman, the President's National Security Advisor; and Charles Ricardo, the White House Communications Director. "This is a new one on me," the President went on. "Iran wants to close off the Persian Gulf to all land-attack warships. The request is so far out in left field that it's laughable, but I got a feeling no one's going to be laughing. First off, I want to hear about that incident with the spy ship. Phil, Arthur, Jeffrey, Charles, let's hear it. Ellen, jump in anywhere. Let's go."

"A covert-action vessel belonging to a technical group of

the Intelligence Support Agency, code-named Madcap Magician, was attacked and destroyed by Iranian air bombardment," Philip Freeman began. Freeman was the former Chairman of the Joint Chiefs of Staff in the previous administration; his popularity and leadership had made him a possible presidential candidate after his retirement, but he had accepted the position of National Security Advisor in the new Martindale administration instead. It had turned out to be a good choice; he was very well respected, not only in the White House but in Congress and throughout the nation as well, on a par with Martindale himself.

"Casualties?"

"No definite word yet, sir," Freeman responded. "The ship carried a crew of one hundred thirty-three. One hundred twenty persons were rescued from the United Arab Emirates; they escaped in four lifeboats before and during the attack. The rest are presumed missing or captured by the Iranian navy. The ship was lost, sunk by aerial missile bombardment."

"Was it on a spy mission?"

"Very definitely," Freeman said. "Operating under Executive Order 96-119, covert surveillance of the Strait of Hormuz and the Iranian heavy warship surveillance and intelligence. The vessel was the base for an unmanned stealth drone the National Security Agency began using to photograph the Iranian warships in the Gulf of Oman."

"Shit," the President muttered. "Sounds like we lost a real valuable asset."

"The vessel had been used as a seagoing platform for tilt-rotor aircraft and Swimmer Delivery Vehicles," Freeman said. "In service for about seven years, just before Desert Storm. The unit had also assisted on the GCC attack on Abu Musa Island recently—they inserted special-ops troops with laser designators to help the Arab crews hit their targets. Yes, we'll miss that platform."

"We never should have sent it in the first place," Secretary of State Hartman said. Hartman was the administration's senior member, a former Wall Street investment house CEO and twelve-term Congressman from New York who brought an insider's knowledge both of Congress and the world of international finance to a rather young White House. Hartman had also brought an extensive web of personal contacts with him—decision makers who preferred the old-boy network over diplomatic or political bureaucracy. "The GCC had no business attacking that island, and we had no business assisting them."

"Intelligence reports said that the Iranians were gearing up to launch an attack on the *Abraham Lincoln* carrier group when it entered the Persian Gulf," Freeman responded. "The Iranians stole those islands from the United Arab Emirates and started basing antiship, antiaircraft, and long-range ballistic missiles there."

" 'Intelligence reports' have been saying that same thing for years now," Hartman said. "And Iran didn't 'steal' those islands—they once *owned* them. The ownership is in dispute, that's all, and negotiations with the United Arab Emirates were ongoing."

"Iran's not negotiating any longer," Freeman said. "It looks like the Iranians are going to block the Strait of Hormuz with their aircraft carrier battle group."

"They're going to park their *what?*" Vice President Whiting asked in complete surprise.

"You heard correctly, Ms. Vice President," Freeman said. "The *Khomeini*, Iran's new aircraft carrier, has put to sea. A fourteen-ship battle group, including two of their three Kilo-class submarines."

"Iran has an *aircraft carrier?* Since when?" Whiting exclaimed.

"Since 1995 at least," Freeman responded, and related the details of its transformation from the ex-Russian carrier *Varyag*.

"This is unbelievable!" Whiting said. "And now they're going to park that thing in the middle of the Strait of Hormuz to block anyone else from entering the Persian Gulf?"

"General, better give us a quick rundown on that battle group," the President said.

"Yes, sir," Freeman said. He referred to his notes only briefly; he had received many detailed briefings on the Iranian military's recent developments and knew the information, updated daily, almost by heart: "The *Khomeini* aircraft carrier battle group is the largest and most powerful seagoing battle group in southwest Asia, with the exception of our own—and in normal day-to-day postures, we're certainly outnumbered, if not outgunned. Most of the ships are ex-U.S. or ex-British frigates and destroyers, but new hardware was acquired over the past three years during the Russians' big arms fire sales, and with arms deals with China.

"Leading the group is the *Ayatollah Ruhollah Khomeini*. Although the Iranians call it a 'defensive aviation cruiser,' it's a pure aircraft carrier, designed for high-performance fixed-wing aircraft, not just vertical-takeoff jets or helicopters. It carries an air group of twenty-four fixed-wing and fifteen rotary-wing aircraft, including two squadrons of twelve Sukhoi-33 Flanker-D fighter-bombers; it can carry probably another six to ten planes above-deck, including carrier-modified Sukhoi-25 bombers and MiG-29 fighters. The ship and the planes are top-of-the-line Russian hardware and weapons—the Iranians spent four billion dollars in the past five years outfitting this ship.

"The *Khomeini* carries lots of anti-ship and antiaircraft weapons as well," Freeman continued. "The *Varyag* was originally designed to carry nuclear anti-surface cruise missiles; we don't think the *Khomeini* has any nukes, but it certainly has cruise missiles, probably ex-Russian SS-N-12 Sandbox, good against ships or shore targets. The Sukhoi-33 fighter-bomber carries the Kh-41 Moskit short-range and AS-18 Kazoo long-range ground-and maritime-attack missiles, along with air-to-air missiles. The *Varyag* was primarily designed as an anti-submarine warfare vessel, and so the *Khomeini* still has a pretty good ASW capability."

"It's a violation of the Missile Technology Control Regime agreement to sell sophisticated missile stuff to Iran," Hartman pointed out. "Russia and China both signed that agreement."

"But Iran didn't officially get them from Russia—they got the missiles from Ukraine, Serbia, and the Czech Republic, as well as North Korea. None of these countries signed the MTCR agreement—none of these countries except North Korea even *existed* in 1989, and North Korea thumbs its nose at the rest of the world all the time," Freeman said. "The bottom line is this: Iran can get its hands on any military hardware it wants, and there's little we can do about it. If we sanctioned every country that sold Iran modern military hardware, we'd alienate three-quarters of our trading partners.

"The Iranian carrier group also includes the Chinese destroyer *Zhanjiang*, a very capable guided-missile destroyer," Freeman went on. "This is supposedly being used to house Chinese officers who are also training on the *Khomeini*, but the destroyer was involved in shooting down the spy plane, so it's obviously responding to orders from the Iranian commanders. The Iranians did buy one conventional Russian cruiser, which they call the *Sadaf;* both it and the *Zhanjiang* carry a big payload of surface, air, and anti-submarine weapons, but its primary purpose is carrier air defense. The group has two ex-U.S. Knox-class frigates to help out with antisubmarine defense, left over from our arms deals with the Shah, armed with Soviet-and Chinese-made missiles and electronics plus four ex-British frigates and four ex-Chinese Houku-class fast guided-missile patrol boats for outer-area screening; these boats carry Chinese-made antiship cruise missiles. The group includes a whole bunch of support vessels."

"Thanks to our 'friends' in Pakistan and Bangladesh, the Iranians have lots of U.S.-made ships and equipment," the Vice President said acidly.

"I wouldn't be surprised to see Iran start flying F-16 fighters soon," Secretary of Defense Chastain interjected.

"That's not a joke, sir," Freeman observed. "We believe Pakistan, Bangladesh, Indonesia, Malaysia, as well as China are supplying Iran with advanced Western hardware. It comes down to simple economics: few countries can afford to turn down the money Iran is paying for arms and advanced technology.''

''Are they a threat to the *Lincoln* carrier group?'' the President asked.

''By itself, they can't stand up against a carrier battle group like the *Lincoln*, sir,'' Chastain chimed in. Chastain, a four-term U.S. Senator and nationally recognized military affairs expert, was well suited for his post in the Pentagon; unlike many political appointees, he knew the U.S. military as well as he knew Congress, and he had made himself familiar over the years with modern warfare and strategic thinking. ''However, they would most likely operate well within range of land-based air forces and it could call upon another one hundred small attack craft to harass our group. I feel certain we could destroy most of Iran's air force and navy in a matter of days. Shadowing the *Lincoln* would just highlight how small the *Khomeini* is next to our ships—you can set the *Khomeini* on *Lincoln*'s deck with plenty of room to spare.'' Chastain's smile flickered, then faded as he asked: ''What about that third Kilo sub, General? Is it in dry dock· as last reported?''

''We haven't located the third Iranian Kilo submarine— we thought it was in dry dock at the new sub base at Chah Bahar, but it disappeared,'' Freeman acknowledged. He turned to the President: ''The Kilo-class subs are diesel subs, no anechoic—anti-sound—coating on their hull, but still much quieter than nuclear-powered subs because they run on batteries while submerged. They can't stay under as long, but when they're under they're hard to find and track, especially in the Persian Gulf and Strait of Hormuz.''

''They could cause a hell of a lot of destruction with two subs and an aircraft carrier, no matter how much firepower we bring against them,'' the Vice President added. The Oval Office fell silent once again; even Chastain, an ardent Navy supporter, couldn't argue with that.

''I think it's unlikely we'll get into a carrier war with Iran,'' Hartman added, ''but it's a major concern. An American carrier hasn't been sunk in combat since the battle of

Midway—it would be a tremendous boost to Iranian morale if they did it, even if they eventually lost the war."

"We're going to see that scenario doesn't happen," the President said resolutely. "I don't like the idea of Iran threatening us or barring us from navigating the open seas, but the *Lincoln* group could be a major target. I'm not prepared to send them in harm's way until we're ready to go all out and defend them with everything we've got.

"Arthur, keep the *Lincoln* group in the Arabian Sea for now until we find out more." The Secretary of Defense reluctantly nodded in agreement. To the National Security Advisor, the President asked, "Phil, any speculation on what Iran might do if they start a shooting war?"

"The new Iranian military doctrine is simple: ensure security and demonstrate its leadership of the Muslim world by strict control of the skies and seas over and near its borders," Freeman said. "Well-armed internal security forces like the Pasdaran hunt down insurgents and rebels and control the border; this leaves the regular military forces free to roam all of southwest Asia. The regular military's primary emphasis is on three areas: the Persian Gulf, the Strait of Hormuz, and the Gulf of Oman; by far, the most important of these areas is the Strait of Hormuz—it's the choke point in the sea lanes to and from the Persian Gulf.

"The conventional theory says that if Iran is provoked, they'll cut off the Strait of Hormuz by application of massive shore-based anti-ship missile attacks, backed up by air-to-surface missile attacks using large numbers of supersonic aircraft, including heavy bombers, and by small, fast attack boats carrying anti-ship missiles or guns," Freeman went on. "The missile sites would be defended with heavy concentrations of ground, sea, and airborne air defense forces that they've built up in tremendous numbers over the past few years. Without the application of concentrated suppression attacks, the Strait of Hormuz would become an impenetrable gauntlet. If successful, Iran could cut off nearly half of the region's oil exports."

"*Half the Persian Gulf oil?*"

"Exactly," Freeman acknowledged. "And the threat doesn't stop there. With a few massive air raids, Iran can cut the Gulf pipelines flowing out of Saudi Arabia, Kuwait, Bahrain, Oman, and the UAE—there goes another twenty-five percent of the region's oil. With their new long-range Backfire supersonic bombers, they might be able to cut the trans-Arabian pipelines running west to the Red Sea—there goes another ten to fifteen percent. The rest—flowing from Iran itself—would presumably be cut by us. If successful, Iran could cut the entire world's oil supply by thirty percent, all by itself, in a very, very short, lighting-fast blitzkrieg."

"No oil from the Middle East," Hartman murmured aloud. "One-third of the world's oil supply . . . almost half of America's oil supply. It would be a catastrophe, Mr. President."

"And we couldn't stop it from happening," Chastain said. "I can say, as we stand right now, that it would take far longer than six months to amass a force equivalent to the one mobilized in Desert Shield, and it would be far more dangerous to U.S. forces. Even if the Iranians made the same mistake as Iraq did and let us accumulate our forces in Saudi, it would take us almost a year to build up a seven-hundred-fifty-thousand-man fighting force."

"A *year!*" Vice President Whiting exclaimed. "You're exaggerating!"

"I wish I was only trying to be conservative, Ellen," Chastain said, "but I believe that's an accurate assessment. At the end of the Cold War, we switched from a deployed counteroffensive force to a defensive expeditionary force—except that the money wasn't spent on boring, low-tech things such as more cargo planes, container ships, and railroad cars. In addition, we've got fewer active-duty forces, and we pulled them out of overseas bases back to the U.S. We've got fewer soldiers, they're farther from the Middle East, and we've got fewer transports to take them where they need to go. Bottom line, Mr. President: we plan on a year and hope for a miracle."

Everyone in the Cabinet Room was stunned into silence.

They all remembered the buildup prior to the Gulf War of 1991; although the first American defensive forces had arrived in Saudi Arabia less than a day after the invasion of Kuwait, it had seemed it would take forever to build up to what could be called an offensive force. Even when Desert Shield had turned into Desert Storm, no one had been sure if they had enough men and equipment to do the job. It had been sheer luck—and they all knew it, although few dared admit it—that Saddam Hussein had decided not to press his attack on Saudi Arabia, Israel, and Turkey during the Coalition's long mobilization, and that Coalition forces had had powerful, oil-rich friends with large military facilities.

"What do we have over there right now, Arthur?" Martindale asked.

"We've got a token force over in the Persian Gulf region right now," Chastain replied. He quickly scanned his briefing notes, his shoulders visibly slumping as he read: "One carrier group currently within striking distance of Iran; one F-16 attack wing and one F-15 fighter wing in Saudi, just forty planes and one thousand men; three Patriot anti-missile and antiaircraft companies, split up between Kuwait, Saudi, and Turkey, plus one training company in Bahrain and one training company in Israel; one bomber wing in Diego Garcia. A total of about fifteen thousand troops—a trip-wire force, nothing more.

"Everyone else is stateside, and I *mean* stateside—we have one fourth of the troops deployed in Asia and Europe now that we did in 1990," Chastain continued. "The air units could set up rapidly in Saudi, Israel, or Turkey—if the Iranians haven't destroyed the big Saudi bases, or if Turkey doesn't prohibit combat forces from staging there, like they tried to do in 1991—but we can't count on any ground forces for several months because we don't have the same size forces forward-deployed in Europe or Asia. Most of our infantry and heavy-armor units would deploy from North America—that would take them an extra four to six months to get to the Middle East. Our sea and air supply bridges will need some time, perhaps six full months, to come up to full capacity. And, of course, there's no easy land bridge to Iran—we can't deploy to an allied country and roll across a flat desert at high speed to get to Iran, like we could against Iraq . . .''

"If I may interject here, Mr. President," Jeffrey Hartman said, "but as distasteful as this may sound, it appears as if we have an even trade—we shot up their island, they shot up our spy ship. I don't believe we are on the verge of war here. Iran is flexing its muscles, to be sure, but the entire world knows that the *Khomeini* battle group is a paper tiger.

"Mr. President, General Freeman, I know losing even one man is hard, but I don't believe that this is a prelude to war, nor should we make it so. After all, we *started* this mess by bolstering the Peninsula Shield attack mission. The loss of those ISA agents was tragic, but we took a gamble and we lost. We should just back off and let everyone cool down. We stirred up one big hornet's nest, Philip.''

"Maybe someone should have taken care of the nest before it got so big that it threatened all the neighbors," Freeman retorted. "The only mistake we made was letting the GCC fight *our* battle for them.''

"So *we* should've sent in a bombing raid on Abu Musa Island?" Hartman asked. "*We* should've bombed that Iranian island? We'd be the bullies then, General.''

"Instead, we've lost a major intelligence-collecting vessel," Freeman pointed out, "and Iran will just park their carrier task force in the Strait of Hormuz and rebuild the missile systems on that island. Do we dare sail a carrier into the Gulf, Jeffrey? What will we have to concede to Iran so we get a guarantee that they won't attack the carrier group?''

"They are not going to attack our carriers, Philip," Hartman said, shaking his head. "This whole thing is a non-issue, General. We back off, let them rant and rave, and things will be back to normal. We've sailed a dozen carrier battle groups past those Iranian military bases in the Persian Gulf and the Strait of Hormuz over the past few years, and the Iranians have ignored us.''

Freeman didn't continue the argument, and that surprised

President Martindale, who studied his National Security Advisor for a moment in silence. In the previous administration, Philip Freeman had been the long-suffering Chairman of the Joint Chiefs of Staff, a lone voice urging a definitive, hard-hitting military policy in a White House that had seemed very reluctant to use military force. Before that, he'd been one of the main engineers of the Pentagon's "Bottom-Up Review," or BUR, a comprehensive review of U.S. military doctrine that was supposed to decide the future of the military forces for the next twenty-five years.

Freeman was a true visionary—even Martindale, leader of the political opposition at the time, had recognized it. Freeman knew that America was done fighting grand intercontinental World War III-scale wars. No longer were nuclear weapons and massive armored columns streaking across the European countryside—or even the Arabian deserts—guaranteed to win wars; in fact, Freeman had written, the nukes and the big, slow, resource-draining weapons systems were sapping the life out of the U.S. military. Speed was life. Wherever and whenever America was threatened, America had to respond rapidly, with the application of accurate, deadly—but not necessarily massive—firepower. Hit and git. Shoot and scoot. It wasn't necessary to flatten the entire battlefield to cripple an enemy's ability to make war—every little cut, every little break weakened him. Philip Freeman had showed why America didn't need thirty bases in Germany or ten bases in England or eight bases in Japan or fifteen carrier battle groups. Global reach and global power could allow America, with proper funding and support from Congress, to fight two MRCs—major regional conflicts, Desert Storm-sized wars—and win, even with fewer forces.

But Freeman had seen his hard work and dedication to duty go to waste, as the best military machine in the world crumbled around him due to a lack of funding and, more important, a lack of strong leadership. The White House and Congress had taken the BUR cuts and effectively doubled them, reasoning that if America could win two Desert Storms with 20 percent fewer forces, it could win one Desert Storm and hold another enemy at bay with *40* percent fewer forces. Congress seemed totally out of control: bases that the Joint Chiefs thought were useless but were located in areas popular with lawmakers were given added funding, while vital logistical and construction bases in major cities with a large civilian payroll were closed.

Foreign-policy disasters had frustrated Freeman as did domestic affairs. He had been deeply hurt after the deaths and public disfigurement of eighteen U.S. soldiers in Somalia, especially since the Somali warlord responsible for the humiliation was not only still breathing, but being flown around by United Nations officials. He had been angry and frustrated over the deaths of U.S. and allied peacekeepers in Bosnia; he had been professionally frustrated when Congress wouldn't budget enough money even for the greatly scaled-down BUR military. He'd seen the U.S. military being sucked into a Vietnam-like quagmire in Bosnia, and seen belligerent Iran, North Korea, and China growing in military strength while the United States was constantly scaling back. War fighting was out, and peacekeeping was in—and to a soldier's soldier like Freeman, it was like stepping into a boxing ring wearing handcuffs.

It had been obvious to presidential candidate Kevin Martindale that these perceptions were tearing Philip Freeman apart. In official press conferences, even a casual observer could tell that Freeman appeared hamstrung by inaction; after his retirement, he'd become almost a recluse. When he emerged from his Billings, Montana, ranch to address a graduation or conference—he'd rarely done press interviews after his Pentagon days—many in the nation, including Martindale, eagerly wanted to hear what he had to say.

And it was that way right now. Philip Freeman's abrupt silence meant that he had a plan, and Martindale couldn't wait to hear it—but first there was much to do. ''I don't hear a firm consensus here, folks, so why don't we put this on the back burner for a short while. I want everybody to gather some more data. We have to know for sure what we're dealing with. Anything more for me?'' They tossed around more ideas and issues, then the meeting broke up. "A word with you for a sec, Phil," the President said. When everyone else except Vice President Ellen Whiting had departed, the President motioned them both to a chair at the coffee table, and they sat informally. "Talk to me, Phil," the President ordered. "What's on your mind?"

"The Iranians could do it, sir," Freeman said.

"Do what?"

"Close off the Persian Gulf. They've got the advantage of substantial land-based air assets, a pretty good air defense network to protect against cruise-missile attack, and a million-man standing army battle-hardened and ready to fight—plus they've got a beefed-up navy, including an aircraft carrier battle group that has the potential to mount a pretty good attack on the *Lincoln* carrier group. The intangibles are a pretty sophisticated chemical and biological warfare capability and possibly an advanced nuclear weapons program, far more advanced than Iraq's. Finally, Iran has a better network of regional and world allies, including China, North Korea, possibly Russia, and possibly many Muslim nations such as Syria, Libya, Pakistan, even Turkey—all of whom could make lots of trouble for us elsewhere in the world, possibly opening up a 'second front,' if you will."

"So this could turn into another Desert Storm-type conflict very easily?"

"Yes, but our response would be far more difficult," Freeman said. "And not only for the reasons I've cited before. Imagine no sea access to the Persian Gulf—all military supplies flown in or sent via road or rail from the Red Sea. Saudi bases and oil fields under attack by Iranian bombers. There would be no direct land invasion of Iran—all amphibious or airborne assaults, similar to D-Day operation—and Iran is three times larger and hillier than Iraq, so the war would probably be longer and much more difficult."

"We're looking at an air war, then," the President said. "A total air war."

"Possibly a total bomber war right from the start," Freeman agreed, "until we got control of the skies, got the carrier battle groups close enough to safely start bombing missions, and secured forward bases in Saudi and Turkey. If Saudi Arabia or Turkey are denied us, the closest bomber staging base might be Diego Garcia, several hundred miles away— and the Iranians can even hold Diego Garcia at risk with *their* long-range bombers.''

''Jesus,'' the President muttered, shaking his head. He held up his hands, as if imploring God for an answer. ''Why is this happening?'' he asked. ''Why does Iran want to do this?''

''I'm praying they *don't* want to do this, sir,'' Freeman replied. ''I believe General Buzhazi, the commander of all Iranian military forces and commander of their Revolutionary Guards, is calling the shots now. He was embarrassed by the GCC's attack on Abu Musa and probably frustrated by Nateq-Nouri's moderate anti-military stance, so he's got the ear of the reactionary clerics. But the mullahs don't have the power they did in the eighties. If Nateq-Nouri can retain control of the government, this thing can blow over, just like Jeffrey said. But if Buzhazi takes charge—a coup, martial law—we're in for a tough time.''

''There are a lot of pretty big 'ifs' in there, General,'' Whiting interjected. ''Any rash action on our part to counter the Iranian threat could make a lot of these 'ifs' come true, like a self-fulfilling prophecy. Let's be careful what we're forecasting.''

The President nodded his understanding, then paused to consider Freeman's and Whiting's words. ''So what are your recommendations?''

''Arthur can make specific military recommendations from the Joint Chiefs, sir,'' Freeman said, ''but I see two things we need to do immediately: move readiness of the bomber fleet up a notch or two, and get some more eyes and maybe some hitting power in the area. I recommend the following: stand up Strategic Command and give them some assets to put on alert in case we need to respond immediately.''

''That's precisely what I'm afraid will escalate this thing, General!'' Whiting interjected.

"Wait a minute, Ellen," the President said, "I'll buy that recommendation, as long as it's done quietly and carefully." Strategic Command was responsible for planning and fighting a nuclear conflict. Normally, it had no weapons, only computers and analysts—it took an Executive Order to give it the bombers, subs, and missiles from other military commands. Except for simulations, Strategic Command had never "gained" any weapon systems in its six-year history. That was about to change. . . . "Talk it over with Defense. Not too much, and all done very quietly—a few bombers, a few subs, perhaps a few Peacekeeper missiles. Bring them up slowly, separately, so it doesn't look like a mobilization, preferably tied into scheduled exercises."

"Agreed," Freeman said.

"As for your other recommendation . . . you have something specific in mind," the President surmised. "Spill it."

"It has to do with certain operations in your old administration, sir," Freeman said warily. The President shifted uncomfortably but nodded, allowing Freeman to go on. "Time after time—over Russia, in the Philippines and the South China Sea, over Belarus and Lithuania, Central America, even over the United States—*something* happened. An invasion force was neutralized, a heavily protected base or enemy stronghold was mysteriously smashed. I know our regular military guys didn't do it; our allies say they didn't do it. I have an idea who did, but I tried to talk to some of the key players several weeks ago, and they weren't talking. You have some very loyal friends out there, sir."

"I heard you had been asking questions," Martindale said. He turned away, then stood up and began to pace the Oval Office. He stopped and stared at one of the rounded walls, his hands behind his back. "Bill Stuart . . . Danahall . . . O'Day . . . Wilbur Curtis . . . oh, God, Marshall Brent, my old teacher . . ." He fell silent, then turned toward his advisers. "Hell, I feel guilty because I haven't thought about them more, haven't had time to pick their brains and have them give me their wisdom and imagination. . . ."

"Mr. President, you used these people because they were

the best, because they knew how much your administration wanted peace but wanted to stop aggression. You wanted to control the escalation of the conflict, because any other response could have led to World War Three.''

"World War Three . . . shit, Brad Elliott . . . HAWC . . . Old Dog . . .'' The President turned, a wry smile creeping across his face. He rubbed the back of his neck, then appeared embarrassed to be doing so. "Just thinking about that old warhorse and what he might be up to makes the hairs on the back of my neck stand up. You have any idea how much sleep that bastard cost me, worrying about what might happen if one of his cockamamie ideas blew up in our faces? Christ, I'm sure he took ten years off my backside. You thought of this several weeks ago, before the crisis?''

"A fight with Iran has been looming for many years, since Desert Storm and Iran's military buildup after the war, sir,'' Freeman said. He saw the President nod in silent agreement. "We had to be ready if Iran, or North Korea, or China struck.''

"You two have lost me,'' Ellen Christine Whiting interjected. "I know General Curtis, and General Elliott when he was with Border Security, and I'm familiar with most everyone you've mentioned in the old administration, and Marshall Brent, of course—he was the greatest, the reincarnation of Abraham Lincoln himself—but I've never heard of HAWC or this Old Dog. And what's all this got to do with Iran?''

"Ellen, back in the midst of the Cold War and the turmoil in the Soviet Union and China, we didn't want to do anything to upset the superpowers, our allies, or the American people,'' the President explained. "We had a military research unit called HAWC—hell, I don't even remember what it stood for, probably some string of military-sounding words just so the acronym came out cool and tough—commanded by Brad Elliott, way before his stint with the Border Security Force. He had a small to medium budget, buried so deeply in the Air Force budget that I think everyone mistook it for a warehouse or a military band or something. It was always getting slashed, and that bastard would march up to the Pentagon and scream and holler and jump on desks until we gave him a few bucks more just to shut him up.

"Anyway, Elliott and his staff could take a piece-of-shit plane like a B-52 bomber and make it *dance*," the President went on, so excited with his reminiscing that he found himself talking with his hands, something he rarely did. "Elliott was building stealth bombers years before the B-2A; he was playing with TV-guided bombs and small satellites and brilliant search-and-destroy cruise missiles years before Desert Storm, even before most experts in the Pentagon ever *heard* of them. He was so good . . . the stuff he turned out was so reliable, so effective, that we . . . used them a few times."

"You *what?*" the Vice President asked incredulously. "Used them . . . as in, sent them off to *war?*"

"Sent them off *before* the war," the President said, still smiling. "Remember that Soviet laser site in Siberia, the one that was shooting down satellites and even taking shots at our intelligence aircraft? Remember how it just up and blew itself apart one night?"

"We all assumed it was the Navy SEALs or Delta Force."

"Delta Force didn't even exist back then," Freeman corrected her. "The defenses were so thick around that site, we couldn't get a plane or a sub in close enough to infiltrate a SEAL or Green Beret team. We thought we'd need an ICBM to take it out." He turned to the President. "That was Elliott? Flying one of his experimental planes?"

"A fucking B-52 bomber, a job older than most of the crew members who flew it. They called it the *Old Dog*. Called Brad Elliott that, too," the President said proudly. "Elliott called it a 'flying battleship,' had it loaded up with smart bombs, decoy drones, even air-to-air missiles, if you can believe it."

"I can't believe this," Whiting exclaimed. "Congress knew absolutely nothing about it?"

"No one knew, except for the White House inner circle," the President said. "Heck, even *I* got briefed *after* the fact! But Elliott did it, Ellen. He was so successful, we used him again and again. A Chinese radar site and a big battleship needed taking out in the Philippines? Nobody else around within a thousand miles, no carriers, no subs—but Elliott's toys would take them out. Elliott's toys destroyed an entire Belarussian armored battalion, a hundred tanks and armored vehicles, in one night—hell, *in one pass*—without anyone in Europe knowing about it.''

The Vice President was still shaking her head. "What happened to him?"

"He was fired, forced to retire," Martindale replied. "He started to make mistakes, got a little overconfident. He was a throwback, too. He'd go out looking for fights—he'd want to fly his hybrid spaceships in each and every little conflict that cropped up in the whole friggin' world. Fortunately for us, he would never quit—*un*fortunately for him, he never learned *when* to quit."

"Sounds like my kind of guy," Freeman said with a smile.

"No, Phil, not anymore. If you're thinking about using him in some way for this Iran thing, forget it. He was a loose cannon. We stayed awake nights thinking of how we were going to explain things to Congress, to the American people, to our allies, if Elliott screwed the pooch."

"I wasn't thinking about Elliott," Freeman said. "I was thinking about McLanahan."

"Who?" asked Whiting.

"Patrick McLanahan," said Martindale. "One of Elliott's deputies. Damned talented youngster. But I thought he was gone, too."

"I found him," Freeman said with a mischievous smile. "I found most of the surviving members of Elliott's gang . . . and I prescreened most of them under NSA Article Three."

"Article what?" Ellen Whiting asked. She hurriedly read through a draft Executive Order that Freeman handed to her. "And you're proposing that we create a military force that acts under sole authority of the White House? The Pentagon will never support it. The Cabinet will never buy it. Congress will never fund it. The American people will scream bloody murder.''

''We've already got the force in place, Ellen,'' Freeman said. ''It's called the Air Force Intelligence Agency, based out of San Antonio, Texas. They've been in business for four years now, assisting the Air Force and other agencies in combat, scientific, and human intelligence operations. The agency is a combination of assets from other forces, including Air Combat Command. These were the guys that helped pick out targets in Baghdad for the stealth fighters; they operated in Iraq and even in Haiti, picking targets for the Air Force. They're experienced with working with the National Security Agency, CIA, and foreign intelligence services. So what we do is team them up with the Intelligence Support Agency to find Iran's mobile missiles and mess up their command-and-control system. If we destroy their communications and command-control network, maybe we can head off a war *before* it starts.''

The Vice President remained openly skeptical; the exasperated shake of her head told her opinion of the legal authority to conduct military operations without notifying Congress, not to mention the commonsense logic of doing such operations without getting the entire Cabinet on board. ''Ma'am, I'm not suggesting we start a war—I'm suggesting that we get some high-tech eyes out there to keep an eye on the region and get some precision, survivable firepower in the area in case something does happen,'' Freeman went on. ''We all know that Iran would very well start a war if we do a Desert Shield-type escalation or overtly threaten them with any show of force—that's why I'm suggesting we do this operation as quietly and as stealthily as possible.''

''But we have political and diplomatic realities to face, General.''

The President held up a hand to the Vice President. ''Hold on, Ellen. Let's let the general dig himself out of this. What are you proposing, Philip?'' the President asked.

''I'm proposing an escalation of technologies, if you will, all employed by the Air Force Intelligence Agency, and all centered around keeping an eye on Iran as it conducts this saber-rattling routine,'' Freeman said. "I want the same B-2A HAWC flew over the Philippines in the China conflict, the one that carried the exotic weapons that no one ever heard of. We'll need specialized crews for this plane. They happen to be civilians, but I think they'll come back and fly for us.''

"Why that particular plane, Phil?'' the Vice President asked. "Why a civilian to fly it?''

"The Air Force doesn't have the new weapons yet—no one has them, except the crews that used to work at HAWC in Nevada,'' Freeman replied. "Even the B-2As still use dumb bombs. Only a handful of fliers know how to use the real twenty-first-century Buck Rogers hardware—and I found them.''

"So you're proposing sending this B-2A loaded up with smart bombs and flown by CIA spies over Iran to blow up a command center—without declaring war or notifying Congress?'' Whiting asked incredulously. Both Freeman and Whiting noticed that the President was perfectly content to let her play "devil's advocate'' and come up with as many negatives as possible, so she charged ahead: "I can't think of a faster, easier way to start a world war, bring down international condemnation on this office, and be branded as lunatic terrorists ourselves!''

"If the force is never, *never* applied within the United States, the American people won't care what we did as long as it got results.''

"You sound like Bud McFarlane or Oliver North all of a sudden, General,'' the Vice President said acidly. "Are you forgetting the Iran-contra debacle? We may have a Republican Congress now, but that doesn't mean they or the American people will like or appreciate what you're trying to do.''

Whiting turned to the President and went on: "Let's assume for a moment that there is legal precedent for forming such a group, Mr. President, that this Air Force Intelligence Agency can legally do these missions. The question you need to ask yourself is, will you take the bombardment of criticism we're undoubtedly going to receive? You cannot hope that General Freeman or anyone else is going to deflect or absorb the negative press for us. Could this be considered an abuse of power? Could this be considered an impeachable offense? Will this affect our chances of a second term—or could this even affect our ability to effectively govern through our *first* term in office?''

The President returned to his desk and slouched, as he was fond of doing in private when he had an important matter to consider. He saw lines lighting up on his phone—his staff was holding all calls for now, but he knew the ones lighting up the phone were the most important ones. Time was running out.

Iran was gearing up its war machine. He could feel it. Just like Saddam Hussein in the 1980s, like Milosevic and the Bosnian Serbs in the 1990s—the signs were all there of an impending calamity, of a dangerous and bloody war. All of these dictators had one thing in common: they wanted to use a strong military force to demonstrate to their friends and foes alike that they were powerful leaders. The instant that a conflict or threat developed, such leaders were too quick to send their bloated military forces off to war. Martindale had always faulted others for not seeing the signs and reacting in time—he was determined not to let that happen again.

History would not treat him kindly if some disaster occurred before the bad guys started hostilities. If the B-2A crashed over Iran while doing a secret reconnaissance, or if one of those anti-radar missiles hit a school or hospital and killed innocent civilians, Martindale would be labeled a warmonger. When he had been Vice President, he'd gladly accepted that title—now he wasn't so sure such a name would be good for his political career. But if the presence of the B-2A kept a conflict from escalating, if it was at the right place at the right time, it would be a major military and foreign-policy victory for him. . . .

"Do it, Philip," the President said. "*Quietly*. Form a team, map out a plan, bring them together, then report back to me. I'll brief the Cabinet myself after I've heard your plan. This plan might die at birth, but get things moving. Baby steps, General. Quietly and gently. Full security.''

"Yes, sir,'' Freeman responded.

He saw Whiting close her eyes, and said to her, "I've answered your question, Ellen—yes, I'll take the heat. If it's legal, I'll do it. I need to do *something*—I can't wait for the Middle East to blow up in our faces before we act. I want something in my hip pocket ready to go, to try to stop the hemorrhaging before it's necessary to go to our allies and to Congress to authorize an act of war.'' He hit the button to the outer office, instructing his personal secretary to give him a list of the most important callers. "That'll be all, ladies and gents.''

But he was wrong, the President knew as he had his secretary dial the first number on his growing priority phone list. This was not all—this was only the beginning.

ABOARD AIR FORCE ONE, SOMEWHERE OVER TEXAS
LATER THAT DAY

As was his custom when traveling on Air Force One, the President wandered back to where several members of the White House Press Corps were busy preparing news items, and he spent a few moments with each person over coffee and bran muffins that had been freshly prepared in one of Air Force One's two kitchens. The President had ditched his usual dark blue business jacket and red silk tie and was wearing a blue cotton Air Force One windbreaker, with two buttons open on his white business shirt underneath. "How's it going back here this afternoon, folks?'' the President greeted them. They all came to their feet as he entered, preceded by a Secret Service agent, and he heard an unintelligible chorus of words and lots of smiling, so he assumed they had all said, "Fine, Mr. President,'' or something to that effect. Traveling with the President of the United States aboard Air

Force One had to be the ultimate assignment for a reporter, and he rarely heard a complaint.

"Please, take your seats, thank you. Got enough coffee back here?" Nods and smiles all around. "Got enough work to do? I could use a hand with this National Education Association speech." He got a faint ripple of laughter. "Anybody got anything for me?"

"We noticed Miss Scheherazade didn't join you on this trip, Mr. President," one lady reporter asked. "Everything OK between you two?"

"Well, according to the briefing I got this morning, I hear some of you in the press have been saying that Monica was mad at me because I didn't attend the premicrc of her new film," President Martindale said with a boyish smile. "I feel like a hunk of raw meat in the tabloids sometimes. The truth is that Miss Scheherazade is filming this week in Monaco . . . oops, I wasn't supposed to reveal that. Sorry, Monica." His mischievous grin told the reporters that he enjoyed playing these media-public relations games. "Anything else?"

"I know the country doesn't seem to care too much about anything else but your love life, Mr. President," a veteran news anchor-person chimed in, his cameraman dutifully behind him taking pictures, "but there are reports from Reuters that Iran attacked a vessel and possibly an aircraft last night in the Gulf of Oman, near the Persian Gulf. Any information on that?"

"No," the President replied. "It apparently wasn't an American or allied ship, because I've received no complaints or protests about it. Anything el—?"

"Are you concerned that Iran is apparently operating this aircraft carrier so close to the Persian Gulf, and they apparently have it fully armed with very sophisticated aircraft and missiles?"

"Lots of nations have ships with extremely sophisticated weapons operating in or near the Persian Gulf, the United States included," the President replied. "The United States and its allies can defend themselves if necessary, but there doesn't seem to be a reason to be concerned. In fact, I've received a very interesting proposal from the Iranian Foreign Ministry to which we're giving a lot of thought—a plan to remove all offensive, land-attack warships from the Persian Gulf entirely. I don't have any details about the idea, but it sounds intriguing, doesn't it?''

"It seems a bit incongruous for Iran to sail its carrier through the oil-shipment lanes, and then to propose that everyone do away with such vessels. . . .''

"Well, that might suggest that the carrier is nothing but a symbol of their resolve, of their desire to be a major player in the region,'' the President offered.

"So you feel the Iranian carrier battle group is no threat?''

"Any nuclear-powered vessel with the firepower that ship apparently has is potentially a threat,'' the President said, "but we're prepared to deal with any threat. However, the prospects for peace look very promising. If President Nateq-Nouri has a proposal, I'm anxious to look at it. I like the idea of demilitarizing the Persian Gulf.''

"Even though you didn't go to the premiere, do you plan to see Monica's new movie, Mr. President?''

President Martindale breathed a silent sigh of relief. Good, he thought, they were moving back to the subject of his personal life again. As difficult as it was to have his private life under the media microscope every hour of every day, the topic of Iran's growing threat in the Middle East was even worse. The veteran anchorperson noticed his relief and nodded knowingly—smug bastard. When it was time for their short one-on-ones, the subject of Iran was sure to come up again. "Actually, I did see *Limbo*,'' the President replied with a smile. "I had my own . . . private screening.''

There was a conspirational "Ahhhhh!'' through the press corps. "And what did you think of the nude scene?'' he was asked for the two hundredth time since the movie opened last weekend. "Do you approve of the love of your life doing nude scenes with Brad Pitt?''

The President let loose one of his boyish, innocent-looking grins again, and replied, "I'll bet Mr. Pitt was asking himself the very same thing about me.''

TWO

One of the most beautiful places on earth had to be Louisiana in the springtime, thought Air Force Lieutenant General Terrill "Earth-mover" Samson. Little humidity, perfect temperature, cool, clean air—perfect. Too perfect for him to be cooped up in the office all day.

The big three-star general was having a great day. It had started with his weekly two-mile morning jog with about one hundred senior officers and NCOs, which he hoped would serve as a motivational fitness incentive for all base personnel. That was followed by a breakfast meeting with local businesspersons to suggest ways in which the Air Force could help improve and revitalize the community and cut down on crime; a rather productive morning in the office answering mail and reviewing paperwork; and an informal Q-and-A lunch with the students at the current session of Eighth Air Force's Non-Commissioned Officer Leadership School. Now, Samson, forty-six years young with the heart of a twenty-year-old and with a cleared-off desk and calendar, was going to goof off this afternoon and do something he rarely had time to do these days—go flying.

Actually, this wasn't going to be a purely fun flight—there was little money in anyone's budget these days for taking a $2 million dollar jet just to punch holes in the sky. Samson had called up the Second Bomb Wing, found a young B-52H Stratofortress instructor copilot sitting around with nothing on the schedule, and asked him to give him a proficiency check. Every flying-qualified officer had to log so many hours, so many takeoffs and landings, so many instrument approaches, etc., every quarter, and Samson was woefully behind—this was a good day to get caught up. Scheduling had found them a plane, Samson had found his flight suit and boots in his office closet, and the check ride was on.

Normally rank has its privileges, and check rides for three-star generals are "pencil-whipped" to a great extent—do a couple of landings, maybe shoot a couple of no-brainer ILS approaches, and get signed off in just a few minutes—but the young IP Samson had tapped wasn't going to "pencil-whip" the commander of the Eighth Air Force, and Samson wouldn't stand for it even if the IP tried. As with any check ride, the IP started Samson off with a fifty-question emergency-procedures written test, including space to write down all sixty-seven lines of "bold print" emergency procedures for the T-38 Talon jet trainer, the steps that were required to be committed to memory word for word. No one was allowed to step inside any Air Force aircraft without demonstrating thorough knowledge of all aircraft systems. With three amused young officers looking on, the big three-star general bellied up to the flight planning table at base operations and got to work.

Samson had more *combat* flying time than *total* time for all three of these young bucks put together, and had forgotten more than they would ever know about flying, but now he had to dig deep and pass a damned written "multiple-guess" test. But without hesitating, Samson got down to it—no compromises, no whining, no shortcuts.

That was the way it had always been for him. Having risen through the ranks from airman basic to three-star general over his thirty-year career, Samson's entire life had been a series of challenges and successes.

In 1968, Terrill Samson, just seventeen years old, had been a high school dropout looking to beat the draft and avoid going to Vietnam and dying in the fields like many of his Detroit gangbanging friends. His parole officer had told him to enlist or face a certain draft notice the minute he turned eighteen; he'd enlisted in the Air Force simply because the Navy's recruiting office was in a rival gang's neighborhood. His mother Melba cried as she signed the enlistment papers for her youngest son, and Terrill was made to promise that he would write. He would never even consider disappointing his mother.

Samson had spent most of the early 1970s carrying buckets of hot tar across griddle-hot construction sites, repairing roads and runways all over southeast Asia in the closing years of the Vietnam War. He'd sent all but five dollars of his monthly military paycheck home to his mother, who would write and ask him if he was safe and if he was making anything of himself. He'd become obsessed with finding opportunities to complete school, volunteer for a job, upgrade his skills, or learn a new specialty, just so he could send his mother a new certificate or document chronicling his accomplishments and proving he wasn't wasting his time.

Since Terrill had no money to do much socializing, he'd spent a lot of time in the barracks, which made him susceptible to a lot of "line-of-sight career development." His squadron first sergeant had ordered him to get his high school diploma so he could raise his squadron's education average; Samson had dutifully complied. Another first sergeant had ordered him to reenlist so his own recruitment figures would look good; Samson had complied again. The tall, good-looking, hardworking, successful black soldier had soon become the Air Force's "poster boy" as the ideal enlisted man; he'd been promoted to staff sergeant in record time, then received an offer to attend Officer Candidate School at Kelly Field in San Antonio, Texas. Anywhere was better than southeast Asia, he and his mother figured, so he'd accepted.

By the end of the Vietnam War, Samson had a bachelor's degree, a reserve commission, and an undergraduate pilot training school slot. Four years later, as a young captain and B-52 bomber aircraft commander, he had a regular commission and an instructor training slot; twelve years later, he'd earned his first star as the commander of a B-1B Lancer bomber wing.

Now Terrill "Earthmover" Samson, often mentioned in the same breath as Colin Powell and Philip Freeman, commanded Eighth Air Force, in charge of training and equipping all of the Air Force's heavy and medium bomber units. He was widely regarded as one of the most successful and intelligent officers, of any race or background, ever to wear a uniform.

He proved that fact again by scoring a respectable 90 on the EP test and a 100 on the bold print test, then submitted himself to a complete review of the missed questions by the instructor pilot, undergoing free-fire questioning until his IP was satisfied that Samson really knew the answers. Again, no compromises. Samson ran through a quick review of formation flying procedures with another T-38 crew that would be flying with them that afternoon, and after a formation briefing, a review of the "Notices to Airmen" and the weather, Samson filed a flight plan to the practice area, suited up, and got ready to go.

Snug in the rubber G suit secured around his waist and legs, with his backpack parachute slung over one shoulder, and his helmet and a small canvas bag holding approach plates, charts, and the T-38 checklist on his other, he headed out from base ops toward the flight line, waving off the supervisor of flying, who offered to give him a ride out to the jet—it was too beautiful a day to waste in a smelly old runway car. He chatted with his instructor and the other T-38 crew members on the way out to the ramp, talked about what was happening around the world and around town and around the squadron—it wasn't often that regular crewdogs got to shoot the shit with a three-star general. No pressure of rank here, no official business, no politicking, no "face time'' with the boss—just a bunch of Air Force fliers getting ready to do what they loved doing.

Samson had almost made it to his sleek white jet when another car pulled up alongside. ''General . . .''

''I don't need a ride, thanks,'' Samson said for the sixth time in that short walk.

''Yes, you do, sir,'' the driver said. ''Flash priority-red message waiting for you at the command post.''

Just like that, Terrill Samson's idyllic day was over. Messages coming into the Eighth Air Force command center all had priorities attached to them, ranging from ''routine'' on up. Samson didn't know what was exactly the highest-priority classification, but the highest he had ever seen was a ''flash red''—and that was in 1991, when the world thought the Iraqis had launched chemical weapons at Tel Aviv and the Israelis were getting ready to retaliate with nuclear weapons.

Samson threw his gear into the back of the staff car, shot a salute and a ''Sorry, guys'' to his crew, and hopped into the front seat. Time to get back to the real world. . . .

● ● ●

''Eighth Air Force, General Samson up.''

''Earthmover, Steve Shaw here,'' came the reply. General Steve Shaw, Samson's boss, was the commander of U.S. Air Force's Air Combat Command, the man in charge of training and equipping all of the Air Force's nine hundred bombers, fighters, attack, reconnaissance, and battlefield support aircraft and the 200,000 men and women who operated and maintained them. ''Pack your bags, you're going TDY.''

Samson, sitting at the commander's desk of the Battle Staff Room at the Eighth Air Force command post, replied immediately, ''Yes, sir. I'm ready right now. I've got a T-38 warmed up for me, in fact.''

''We've got a C-20 with some crews and equipment that'll pick you up out there at Barksdale for a briefing at Whiteman.''

''Yes, sir, I'll be ready,'' Samson said excitedly. Whiteman Air Force Base, near Knob Noster, Missouri, was the home of the B-2A Spirit stealth bomber. Although they had been used in very minor roles in other conflicts, the B-2A bombers weren't scheduled to go fully operational until later on in 1997. What in hell was going on? "Anything else you can tell me, sir?"

"The Iranians look like they're going to try to close off the Persian Gulf," Shaw said. "NSA wants a special task force to put together a quick-response team to hit targets in Iran if the balloon goes up—and the President wants bombers."

"Yes, sir," Samson said. "I'm ready to do it. Who's heading this task force?"

"I don't know," was Shaw's cryptic response. "Top secret, NSA stuff. You'll get the initial briefing materials on the plane."

"I understand. I'm ready to go, sir," Samson said.

"Good luck, Earthmover," Shaw said. "Whoever's leading this task force, I know they're getting the best in the business. When it's over, come on out to Langley and let me know how it went."

"You got it, sir," Samson replied. "Thanks for the vote of confidence. Eighth Air Force, out."

There were a million things running through Terrill Samson's mind the second he hung up that phone. He should call his wife, tell her he'd be out of town (shit, he thought, what a freakin' *under*statement!); he should notify his vice commander, notify the wing commanders, notify his staff, notify . . . "Captain Ellis!"

"Sir? replied the senior controller on duty at the command post.

Samson was heading to the door as he spoke: "Tell General Andleman I'm on my way to Whiteman and that he's minding the store. Tell base ops to notify me immediately when the C-20 calls Shreveport Approach inbound for landing. And tell my wife . . ." He paused, thinking about what he was about to do and what it might mean. "Tell her I'll talk to her tonight. I *will* talk to her tonight."

SACRAMENTO, CALIFORNIA
16 APRIL 1997, 2055 HOURS LOCAL

The new waitress quit after only one day—something about how life was too short to work for a "stressed-out bulldog hyped on speed," or some such comment like that—so the owner of the little tavern on the Sacramento River near Old Sacramento had to fill in waiting tables himself.

It had been many years since he had had to take drink orders. Still dressed in a long-sleeve white shirt, colorful "power tie," Dockers slacks, and black Reeboks, he zipped from bar to tables to kitchen and back, memorizing drink and appetizer orders while wiping tables and setting up place settings, all the while remembering that he had to smile, say a pleasant word, and stay as cheerful as he could. The original owner had bought the bar after his retirement from the Sacramento Police Department more than fifteen years earlier, and he had never seemed cheerful or pleasant. Despite this—or possibly because of it—McLanahan's Pub, only seven blocks from police headquarters, had been one of the most popular cop bars in town. Police, sheriff's deputies, even federal agents working downtown in California's capital had regularly shuttled between Gillooly's, the Pine Cove, and McLanahan's after duty hours. They'd always gotten good advice from a seasoned veteran sergeant, a lot of stories, and a little cajoling and friendly criticism—but never cheerfulness.

The new owner of McLanahan's wasn't a cop, and although his younger brother was slated to start the police academy soon and all of the police photos and memorabilia were still on the walls of the place, it wasn't the same popular cop hangout it had been years ago. Because the clientele was more touristy and more sophisticated these days, McLanahan's had changed as well: they served selections of Napa Valley chardonnays and specialty espresso coffee drinks as well as cold beer and bourbon. Tourists who ordered café mochas and veggie appetizers expected cool, suave Tom Cruise–look-alike bartenders and cheerful, trim-and-tan California-cutie servers, not loud, adrenaline-pumped cops lining the bars being served by gruff, overworked owners.

The second-generation owner, Patrick McLanahan, indeed looked as if he might be more at home in a squad car or on motorcycle patrol than in a bar. Patrick was a bit less than average height, but his broad shoulders, thick forearms and neck, and deep chest made him look much shorter. If the blond-haired, blue-eyed man smiled, which was rare these days, one might almost call him disarming, like a big, cuddly teddy bear. But no one remembered the last time their forty-year-old boss had smiled for real, and now it was easy to see a lot of turmoil going on behind those shining blue eyes.

It was Monday night, and the crowd was small and quiet. A few regulars at the bar, a few cops still hanging around (although shift change was a couple of hours ago), a few strangers getting out of the off-and-on drizzle outside. Quite a contrast from table to table. Three guys and a woman, sitting at different tables, reading the paper or watching the news on TV, all drinking coffee; Patrick guessed they were U.S. Marshals or Secret Service, still on duty or on call. A few San Jose Sharks fans were still here, celebrating the hockey team's latest victory at home over the Stanley Cup champions, the Buffalo Sabres, that they had watched on the big-screen TV here at the bar. One big black guy was by himself in a booth in the corner, still wearing his dark overcoat, watching TV as well—he looked a little rumpled and overburdened, maybe a mid-level manager for the state who had just had an argument with his wife, or a local businessman worrying about the state of Sacramento's economy now that all of the area's military bases had been closed down. He paid for his Samuel Adams with a fifty-dollar bill. His only interaction with Patrick was when he asked him to switch the TV over the bar to CNN, and since there was nothing on ESPN, he complied.

In between serving drinks and wiping tables, Patrick made lots of calls to other employees, asking for help, and after an hour and a half he finally got someone to come in from eleven to closing, so he had a bit more time to circulate and do owner things rather than serve tables. He finally escaped to his office and plopped down in a spare chair beside the woman seated at his desk, who was punching numbers into a computer with the speed and ease of someone very familiar with using a keyboard. "Damn, if I *ever* see another plate of potato skins or another glass of white wine, it'll be too soon. My feet are *killing* me."

Patrick's wife, Wendy, turned and smiled at her husband, and Patrick automatically extended his hand to her and they held hands as they talked. Wendy was in her mid-thirties, with short strawberry blond hair and bright green eyes. Bandages still covered the left side of her neck and her right arm, and her breathing was noticeably labored, but her smile could still melt Patrick's heart like nothing else. Wendy and Patrick were still newlyweds, having married late last year, but an entire lifetime's worth of events had interrupted their new life together, and they spoke and treated each other as life-long mates. "Think about that the next time you chop on a server because she's not going fast enough for your taste, hon," Wendy said. She stifled another cough, and Patrick winced inside as he heard the delicate but raspy noise.

"How are you doing, sweetheart?" Patrick asked. It was the end of Wendy's first full week of part-time work doing the books, payroll, and ordering at the tavern. Patrick had seen some of the country's toughest professional soldiers in sixteen years in the U.S. Air Force, and there was no doubt in his mind that Wendy was stronger and more durable than any of them. Yes, she had lost a lot of weight, and she suffered shortness of breath if she walked around too much, and she required a two-hour nap in the afternoon as well as a full eight hours of sleep at night, but she had been out of the hospital after three weeks and working just a few short months after her horrible aircraft incident.

"Don't change the subject, hon," Wendy said with a stern

smile. "That was the second waitress that quit this week. We're hiring only experienced persons, Patrick—they're not butter-bars. You've got to let them make a few touch-and-goes and get some pattern work on their own before you start a full-scale stan-eval ride on them."

Patrick smiled at all the military aviation jargon. It had been quite some time since he had heard them. "Yes, ma'am," he responded, snapping a left-handed salute, then kissed her hand. She looked at him skeptically, as if afraid he wasn't listening to her indirect criticisms. "Hey, I'm just trying to keep things moving, trying to pitch in. It's easier for me to notice how long an order's been sitting ready to be picked up if I'm just standing by the door. I'm only trying to help, you know, keep things moving . . ."

"The only things that keep moving are the servers," Wendy said. "Let them do their thing—they feel uncomfortable having the boss hovering nearby all the time. Did you ever work better with that slave driver Colonel Anderson standing over you telling you to . . . ?" Wendy paused as she saw Patrick's eyes drift away and begin staring at faces and places long lost but certainly never forgotten. "Sorry, sweetheart," Wendy said in a soft voice. "I hope it's not too painful for you when I mention . . ."

"No, it's okay," Patrick said. "I just hadn't thought about him, or any of them, for a while."

"If I may so politely and delicately point out: bullshit," Wendy said, squeezing his hand. "You think about them all the time. I can see you talking on the phone or sweeping the floor, and all of a sudden you'll stare off into space, and I know you're on the deck of the Megafortress or one of those other creations you built, dropping bombs and screaming around at Mach one with your hair on fire."

"Hey, c'mon, that's all past me . . . us," Patrick said. He glanced at his wife reassuringly, then motioned at the computer screen. "Can you give me a list of applicants? I'll call a few tomorrow morning and find us a replacement."

"I'll take care of it," Wendy said. She turned his face

back to face hers. "We can talk about it, you know—the service. *I* can talk about it."

"There's not much to talk about, is there?" Patrick said, a trace of bitterness in his voice. "We're out, involuntarily retired. Everything we built is gone, everyone we know is gone. We're two grad-school-plus-educated professionals living in a one-bedroom apartment over a bar. We live off your disability payments, we eat bar food, drink bar drinks, and watch bar TV because we can't even afford our own TV." He took her hand and squeezed it reassuringly. "Not exactly the kind of life I wanted to make for you, Wendy."

"Maybe you should soak your head, lover, not your feet," Wendy said disapprovingly. "Where did you suddenly get this sad-sack streak from? You took an early retirement as an Air Force lieutenant colonel—you can't draw your fifty percent retirement salary because you're barely forty years old! You've lived more and done more in the past twenty years than most men would in two lifetimes. You own an established restaurant and tavern in the capital city of the state of California, which earns enough to put a brother through college and pay for your mother's condo in Palm Springs—we live over the bar because it doesn't cost us anything and we're saving up for the lakeview condo up on Lake Tahoe you've always wanted. You've got so many prospects available, you can't count them all. Yes, we eat bar food, but we eat pretty darn good bar food, thank you very much—I don't see any ribs sticking out your sides, if I may say so, lover. Why are you suddenly so down on life?"

"I'm not down on life, Wendy," Patrick responded. "I just wanted more by now, that's all."

"You're unhappy because you're not flying, that's what it is, isn't it?" Wendy asked. "Patrick, you can go flying anytime you want. There's a bunch of rental planes waiting for you at Executive or Mather. You can do aerobatics, you can go high and fast and push the Mach, you can fly a helicopter or a war bird or a racer—you're checked out in almost everything with wings. In fact, I wish you'd get out a little more often, look up your pals in the service, maybe even write a book.

"But you paid your dues as a military aviator, Patrick. Your work is done. You're a genuine hero. You've saved this nation a dozen times over. You've risked your life, hell, I've lost count how many times! For my sake as well as yours, put that life behind you and start a new one, with me, here, right now."

"I will, Wendy," Patrick said. He took a deep breath, squeezed her hand, then got to his feet. "I better see if Jenny's showed up yet."

"Hey," she said, pushing him back to his seat. She held his hands tightly until he looked into her eyes again. "You know, Patrick, Charlie O'Sullivan asked if he could look over our books again, and he wants to bring Bruce Tomlinson from First Interstate over." She interrupted herself with another short fit of coughing.

"You okay, sweetie?"

She ignored the question and continued: "He's really serious about buying the place. He knew your dad from the force. He's got the financial backing to turn this place into a real entertainment spot, bring in big-name groups—we can't even afford to get a dancing permit."

"I'm working on all that, too, sweetheart."

"But we can't afford all the upgrades we need to do unless we mortgage the place again, and that's too risky. You said so yourself," Wendy said. She took his hands and squeezed. "I'm your wife and your friend and your lover, Patrick, so I feel qualified to tell you: as a barkeep, you're a great bombardier."

"*Excuse* me?"

"Do you want to be working for a business that you took on just because you love your father and you couldn't stand the idea of your mother selling?" Wendy asked. "You don't want to be a barkeep, babe. I have no doubt you could make it if you wanted to, but your heart's not in it. You . . ." She stopped again, the coughing lasting a bit longer this time. "Besides, hon, the air quality in Sacramento is not getting any better. My company doctor down in La Jolla says a change might do me some good—San Diego, or Arizona, or Tahoe . . .''

"So you think we should sell?"

"We'd have the money to make a fresh start," Wendy said. "We could go anywhere, do anything. Jon Masters said he'd hire you in an instant, doing God knows what. Any defense contractor in America would hire you, hire both of us, on the spot if we wanted to get into that life again. Hal Briggs talked about us getting involved in his brother's police canine-training facility in Georgia. Or we could just buy a boat and shuttle back and forth from Friday Harbor to Cabo San Lucas all year. We wouldn't be obliged to anyone except ourselves and our own dreams. We could . . .''

But she stopped, and she knew he wasn't listening—he had adopted what the Vietnam vets called the "thousand-yard stare," a flashback. His mind had drifted off once again, replaying some bomb run or aerial chase or dangerous mission where men and women had died around him. Mentioning the names of Brad Elliott, Jon Masters, and Hal Briggs had been a big mistake, she decided. His life, his heart, was still with them, wherever *they* were. If there truly was a purgatory, Wendy thought, Patrick McLanahan must be in it—and she was with him.

She knew that he had forcibly separated himself from them, his longtime friends, to return her to California so she could heal after her aircraft accident—and it had been a truly extraordinary event. A Russian spy named Kenneth Francis James had shot down an experimental bomber in which she had been a crew member. Only two of the seven crew members aboard that bomber had survived; the spy had killed six other soldiers, injured several others, and destroyed hundreds of millions of dollars' worth of equipment in his mad dash to escape. The incident had led to the dismissal of all of the senior officers of Nevada-based HAWC, including Patrick McLanahan, and the closure of the facility.

Patrick had accepted an early retirement rather than demotion and reassignment so he could be with his newlywed during her recovery; to pass the time and do something close to home, he had taken over the operation of the longtime family business in Old Sacramento. She loved him for making that sacrifice for her, but she could tell that he longed to be back in the action, even though he was bitter that the government and the Air Force had destroyed so many lives and careers in the witch-hunt that followed the James disaster. The restlessness, his guilt-based desire to stay with his wife and run the family business, and his anger and frustration were all combining to turn Patrick Shane McLanahan into a dark, explosive, and angry young man.

He said absently, "I'll think about it, sweetie," before rising, robotlike, giving her a peck on the cheek, and departing. As Wendy watched him leave, she knew that he hadn't heard a word she'd said. All he could see was a job not yet finished, a life not yet fulfilled. He had come out of sixteen horrible, hard years in the Air Force with barely a scratch, yet he had been wounded far worse than all the others—his spirit may have even been killed. Just a little bit, perhaps, but just as surely and as finally as the deaths of J. C. Powell, Alan Carmichael, and John Ormack, among all the others that had touched Patrick's life over the past ten violent, unpredictable years.

Patrick's attention had wandered because he had heard the eleven o'clock news come on. As usual the lead story was on the goings-on in the Middle East, and he wanted to hear the latest. So far, a lot of saber-rattling by Iran, and virtual silence from Washington.

"What do you think of all that shit, boss?" asked the bartender, a young kid by the name of Hank.

"I think the Iranians are sailing their carrier around to scare the shit out of the rest of the world, and to prove they're the baddest Muslim country on the planet," Patrick replied matter-of-factly.

"Why aren't we doing anything about them? Is it because we're afraid of getting our asses kicked, like twenty-five years ago?"

"Hank, that was Vietnam, and we didn't get our asses

kicked—we withdrew," McLanahan corrected him. "Iran and Iraq are two different countries in the Middle East, not southeast Asia. Both countries border on the Persian Gulf, a major oil-producing region. We went to war with Iraq six years ago, remember?"

"Six years ago . . . man, I was just in high school then, boss!" Hank laughed. "Did we win that war?"

"Hank, we won that war in *one hundred days!*"

"One hundred days! That's . . . that's like over three months!" Hank exclaimed. "Don't the Navy SEALs and guys like Jean-Claude Van Damme kick ass and clean up in just a day or two?"

"The Vietnam War lasted ten *years*, Hank."

"Oh, yeah, we learned about *that* one in school," Hank said, trying to sound as if he had really been paying attention. "That was the war where Johnson and Nixon kept on drafting war protesters and sending them over into the jungles to napalm villagers and get killed by bamboo poisoned with rat shit, until Jane Fonda caught Reagan bugging her offices and got him thrown out of office . . ."

"Jesus, Hank . . ." Patrick spluttered. Man, this kid made him feel *old*, Patrick thought. He didn't even remember the Persian Gulf War, let alone the Vietnam War or Watergate! All he knew was what he saw on "Beavis and Butthead" or "Hard Copy." "Try picking up a copy of something other than *Mad* magazine once in a while, okay?"

"So why don't we just go in and kick some butt, boss, like we did against Iran . . . ?"

"Iraq, Hank."

"Yeah, right . . . whatever. Why don't we just go in and bomb 'em or something?"

Patrick looked angrily at the bartender, then turned, picked up a towel to do the tables, and said as he walked away, "We don't bomb anybody anymore, Hank. We're peace-keepers now."

Hank nodded, hopelessly confused, and said, "Yeahhh . . . right. We're peacekeepers. . . ." Talking international affairs with Hank was like talking to the dishrag in his hands, Patrick decided.

Yep, only peacekeepers now . . . and targets . . .

The waitress hadn't shown up yet, so Patrick decided to make the rounds. The guys who looked like feds only wanted coffee refills. Patrick tried to strike up conversations with them, hoping to find out if his instincts were right, but none of them were in a chatty mood, which suited Patrick just fine. Patrick found a pretty blond woman sitting with the black gent in the corner booth now; she placed her coffee cup where he could reach it with the pot, and Patrick filled it. He tried to catch a good glimpse of her face, but failed. Was she a hooker, trying to scare up some business? Patrick caught a glimpse of sleek legs, but little else.

It appeared that the black gent hadn't touched his beer in half an hour. Even the sweat on the side of the glass was gone. Patrick reached for the glass: "I'll get you a fresh Samuel A," he said.

"Thanks, young man," the gent said. "Guess I'm paying more attention to the news than to the beer."

"Me too," Patrick offered. "Can I get you anything else? We have some great hot appetizers. Would you like to see a menu?" The woman sitting at the guy's table tittered a bit, covering her mouth. The black guy scowled at her; Patrick ignored it, but inside he was fuming, asking himself, Why the hell am I here? What the hell am I doing? This bitch is laughing at me because I'm taking food orders . . . but I'm not happy doing this. Wendy's right, I'm not happy doing this.

"I heard what you told the bartender about Iran," the black guy said, in a bit of a booming, authoritative voice that made Patrick think perhaps he was a little drunk or distraught. "It's pretty unbelievable when you think about the historical memories of America's young people."

"Not everyone," Patrick said. "Hank's main concern right now is paying the rent, not world affairs. He's a pretty smart guy."

"What makes you think the Iranians are just scaring everybody?"

"Iran's got enough domestic problems without worrying about picking fights with any of its neighbors, or with the United States," Patrick said, not really wanting to get into another inane discussion about the Middle East but unconsciously blowing off a little steam from interacting with ol' Hank. "But the GCC attack on Abu Musa Island stirred up the military. Soon they'll mobilize the Pasdaran—"

"The what?" the guy asked. "The who?"

"The Pasdaran, the Islamic Revolutionary Guard Corps, the Iranian elite troops. The Pasdaran are the Iranian storm troopers, the SS of the Middle East. They're the best of the best, the pointy end of the spear. They have about the same size, speed, and equipment as the U.S. Marine Corps— maybe even better." Patrick pointed to the TV set over the right side of the bar just as a map of Iran was being shown for the hundredth time that hour on CNN.

"What will they do?"

"If the military gets the ear of the clerics in charge of the country, the first thing they might do is close off the Strait of Hormuz and the Persian Gulf. They'll use the *Khomeini* carrier group, backed up by their new fleet of land-based bombers."

"You've lost me, son," the gent said. "Iran's going to do all this? Why?"

"They'll do it if anyone, especially the U.S. or Israel, gets in their way," Patrick said. "If Iran closes off the Gulf and maybe then the Red Sea, all the oil-rich countries lose billions a day. The Gulf states won't risk that—they'll deal with Iran rather than risk losing oil revenues."

"So why don't we just get a Steve Canyon aviator hero-type and bomb the crap out of Iran, like we did in Iraq?" the woman chimed in, her voice slightly sarcastic, as if a mere bartender had any answers she would find useful or informative. Aha, Patrick thought, not a hooker—or at least a very highly educated one. These two were together, and probably with the other three guys surrounding the bar. What in hell was going on?

"We could, but we risk starting a huge Middle East war," Patrick said. "We'd need a pretty thick scorecard to keep track of all the alliances, cooperatives, economic unions, and religious factors in this region." Patrick began wiping a nearby table so he'd be better able to slip away and avoid a prolonged conversation with these two. "We couldn't count on our old friends for help, because Iran is a pretty tough adversary, far stronger than Iraq was. This time, both Russia and China are involved—on Iran's side, not ours. And we've got fewer bombers, tanks, ships, and men to fight a war. We're pretty well on the backside of the power curve on this one." Patrick paused, then added, "Besides, Steve Canyon types are just fiction."

"Too bad," the blonde said.

"That sounds like a fighter pilot talking," the black gent observed. "You a flier?"

"I was in the Air Force once," Patrick said. "Didn't do anything special. Put in my years and punched out." His blue eyes turned stormy once again, and he half turned to the man and told him, "I'll bring that beer right away."

"Sure. Thanks," the guy said. As Patrick was walking back to the bar, the guy raised his voice and added, "When you get back, maybe you can explain how a single B-2A equipped like a Megafortress could slow down the Iranian advances without triggering a Middle East war."

Patrick tried hard to make no outward reaction to the word *Megafortress*, but inside his guts turned upside down. The Megafortress had been one of his top-secret projects back when he was in the Air Force—a highly modified B-52 bomber, what they referred to as a "flying battleship," designed for long-range heavy-precision strikes and to escort other, less sophisticated bombers, such as unmodified B-52s, into the target area. Several other Megafortresses had been built and flown—even flown in combat, over Lithuania and Belarus—but they had all been dismantled and placed in storage or destroyed when HAWC was disbanded. This guy knew about it, knew about *him*, about his past. All that information was highly classified. Was he a reporter? A foreign agent? An industrial spy?

Remaining calm, pretending he hadn't heard the guy, Patrick nonchalantly set the man's beer mug on the bar. "Hank, pour him another Adams," Patrick said, then headed immediately into the office.

"Sure, boss. Hey, I'm gonna need . . ." But Patrick was already through the office door, practically at a dead run.

As soon as he closed the door behind him, he said, "Wendy, head out the back, take the cell phone, and call OSI." OSI, the Air Force's Office of Special Investigations, was their point of contact should anyone try to contact them regarding any classified information. Their nearest office was at Beale Air Force Base up in Marysville, about an hour away, but if they had any agents in the area, someone could be by there right away to intercept. Or maybe they'd call the FBI or U.S. Marshal's office in Sacramento for help . . .

"I think it's too late for that, dear," Wendy said. There, standing next to Wendy, was a stranger in a black trench coat and wearing black gloves.

Patrick didn't hesitate. He quickly stepped forward until he reached the desk, then shoved the computer monitor off its stand at the stranger. The guy instinctively grabbed at the monitor flying toward him, which distracted him and brought his face down to the perfect level—so Patrick swung his right fist, putting his entire two hundred pounds behind it, connecting squarely in the middle of the stranger's left temple. He went down with a muffled grunt and lay still, knocked cold.

"God," Wendy gasped as she stared at the unconscious stranger. "Patrick, *wait*."

Without stopping, Patrick stepped on and over the stranger, grabbed Wendy's left arm, and steered her toward the back of the office to the back door. "Head toward the coffee shop down the street—they'll be open, and the cops hang out there," Patrick told Wendy. "Tell them there's five out front, one black male, three white males, one white—"

"What in hell is going on back here!" a voice thundered behind him. Patrick whirled around and saw the black gent and the woman standing at the office door. The black guy was bug-eyed as he looked first at Patrick, then at the unconscious guy on the floor with the computer monitor lying on his chest, then back at Patrick. The woman studied the scene the same way, but her face registered immense glee. "What do you think you're doing, McLanahan?"

"Wendy, *go!*" Patrick tried to pull her toward the door, but she was not moving. "Wendy, what's wrong?"

"Patrick, sweetie, you just knocked a Secret Service agent out cold," Wendy said with a smile.

"A *what?*"

"He's a 'who,' dear," Wendy repeated, grinning broadly. "Special Agent Frank Zanatti, from Washington, D.C. He's already showed me his ID. I tried to tell you, before you knocked my monitor over."

"Secret Service?" Patrick looked at the unconscious guy in total confusion, then pointed an angry finger at the large black guy standing in his office door. "Then who the hell are *you?*"

"I am Philip Freeman, U.S. Army, retired, National Security Advisor to the President of the United States," Philip Freeman bellowed.

"Fr . . . Freeman? *General Freeman?*"

"Don't just stand there gaping, Colonel," Freeman shouted, "help Agent Zanatti up." He half turned to the woman beside him and ordered, "Colonel, give him a hand. I swear, McLanahan, if you've killed him, we'll all be skinned alive."

The woman standing beside Freeman hurried over to the fallen Secret Service agent. As she did, she passed close by Patrick and, to his amazement, whipped off her blond wig and handed it to him. "Hello, Colonel. Last time I saw you, you were blasting that rat bastard Maraklov out of the sky in *Cheetah.* Never thought I'd ever see you asking me if I wanted a hot appetizer. I couldn't help laughing. Sorry."

Patrick blinked in total surprise: "*Preston?* Major Marcia Preston . . . ?"

"Lieutenant Colonel Preston, Patrick," she said as she gave him a friendly hug. Preston had been former National Security Advisor Deborah O'Day's personal aide and body-guard, a U.S. Marine Corps F/A-18 Hornet fighter pilot, and one of the first female combat pilots in the American military. "It's nice to see you, but let's get General Freeman's man up off the floor, shall we?" Patrick's head was swimming in confusion as they helped Zanatti to an armchair and revived him. After he was up and around, Preston stood and walked over to Wendy and extended a hand. "You must be Dr. Wendy Tork . . . er, Dr. Wendy McLanahan. Marcia Preston." They shook hands. "I've only flown once with your husband, but it was a ride I'll never forget."

"This is Wendy Tork?" Freeman asked in surprise. He too walked over and extended a hand in greeting. "It some-how didn't show up in any files that you two were married. Congratulations. I assume it was just before your . . . acci-dent."

"That's right, General."

"It was an unfortunate, tragic incident, a huge and incred-ible loss," Freeman said, "but out of the ashes will come a newer, even stronger force."

He turned to Patrick and said, "I must ask a favor, Patrick. I need to speak to you right away, and since I see you're one of the only ones on duty, it might be better if you closed up early. We have a lot to discuss. The White House will see to it that you're compensated for your lost time."

The dark, cold expression came over Patrick's face. "Somehow, I doubt that," he said, "but since you've prob-ably scared all the other customers out already . . ."

"Unfortunately, yes," Freeman acknowledged with a wry smile.

"I guess we don't have much choice . . . as usual," Patrick said, and he went to close and lock the doors.

●   ●   ●

Freeman's men swept Wendy and Patrick's apartment for listening devices in just a few minutes—thankfully, there were none—and they sat down to talk over coffee and fresh fruit. Freeman winced as he put a slice of fresh kiwi up to his nose, wishing he had a nice thick, gooey doughnut instead, but he seemed to enjoy the kiwi and helped himself to a slice of mango next. "We're nicknaming it Future Flight," the President's National Security Advisor began. "I'm bringing back your team, Patrick, at least as many as we can. Being the senior member, I want you to command the team. I borrowed Colonel Preston here from the Marine Corps again, and she'll be your deputy."

"What exactly are we going to do, General?" Patrick asked.

"Anything and everything," Freeman replied. "The purpose of Future Flight is to support specialized intelligence operations with long-range, stealthy aerial assets—in particular, a certain B-2A Spirit stealth bomber, which you knew as Test Article Number Two, assigned to the High Technology Aerospace Weapons Center, and which you tested and flew for two years, loaded with various payloads, including reconnaissance, communications, intelligence, and combat strike."

"Sounds pretty . . . open-ended," McLanahan observed warily. "A license to kill, so to speak."

"You'll be attached to the Air Force Air Intelligence Agency—you'll report to Major General Brien Griffith. He'll report to me . . ."

"And you report to the President," Patrick interjected. Freeman nodded. "Sounds awfully dangerous to me—lots of chances for abuse."

"You did it all the time when you were a member of HAWC—"

"And look what happened to us," Patrick snapped. "HAWC is closed down, General Elliott was demoted and forced to retire, and everyone else was scattered to the four winds or kicked out. Lots of careers and reputations were ruined, General. If we wanted to appeal those verdicts, we'd have been thrown in prison for life for violating national security—''

"You retired with an honorable discharge and a pension after only sixteen years of active-duty service, Colonel," Freeman pointed out. "You made out pretty well, I'd say."

"Only because Brad Elliott used the last of his political markers to get us some leniency," Patrick said. "Only because I agreed not to talk, not to go to the press, not to sue. I'm not proud of the way I exited, sir. One reason I'm not in the service and doing what I was trained to do is because Brad did everything the White House and the Pentagon wanted of him, and he was branded a loose cannon and taken down. My only other options were a less-than-honorable discharge or a demotion and reassignment to a remote non-flying specialty.

"My point is, sir, what we learned after ten years was a simple lesson: If the government wants a strike or recon mission done, call on the armed services to do it," Patrick said. "If they don't have the equipment or the training, either get them what they need, or don't do the mission."

"Neither are options, Patrick," Freeman said. "We don't have the funds to equip an active-duty unit with the equipment you developed at HAWC, and we don't have the time to train an active-duty flier on how to use the equipment you designed, tested, and flew in combat. Our only other option is to withdraw all the ISA technical groups from their deployed positions, which would hurt our intelligence-gathering capabilities—to the contrary, we want to *assist* these cells and allow them the chance to do even more."

"ISA can take care of themselves, sir," Patrick said. "If they can't, if the situation is too hot for them, yank them out. If the situation's too hot for ISA, it's probably at the wartime stage anyway."

"That's the whole point, Patrick. Future Flight's mission is to prevent any situation from escalating into the wartime stage by the careful, controlled application of strike assets," Freeman said, "and I'm talking about ISA, and I'm talking about the B-2A stealth bomber. Iran has done exactly the same thing: they've drawn a line at the entrance to the Persian Gulf, daring anyone to cross it. The rest of the world is completely paralyzed with fear; Iran knows this, and they're going to take advantage of it.''

"So your solution is to play high-tech terrorist, too, right?''

"In a manner of speaking, yes!'' Freeman replied resolutely, slapping a hand on his knee. "Who the hell says the United States has only two choices—war or peace?—pardon my language, Dr. McLanahan.''

"Wendy,'' she said. "And your language doesn't offend me, sir—but frankly, your ideas do.''

"Then I'll try to explain them,'' Freeman said. "Listen, Patrick, Wendy: my job is to coordinate the United States' national security affairs *before* they get to the guns and bombs phase. In peacetime, that usually means intelligence operations—trying to find out what the bad guys are doing before they do it, so we can pursue diplomatic and legal solutions and avert war. Sometimes NSA uses field operatives, and in very rare instances we'll use military forces to help out in security or direct-engagement situations. But we're expanding that role now to include military and paramilitary options. Our means are less 'hide-and-seek,' more offensive than pure intelligence operations, but the goal is the same: find out what the bad guys are doing before they do something so we can pursue diplomatic solutions and avert a war.''

"You can sugarcoat it all you want, General,'' Wendy said, "but the bottom line is the same—it's terrorism. If Iranians were doing the same to us, we'd call it terrorism, and we'd be correct.''

"And what about that Gulf Cooperation Council attack on Abu Musa Island?'' McLanahan said. "Iran says the attack was conducted by an American stealth bomber and Israeli F-15E attack planes, which I believe is bullshit, but they got one observation right: the attack had to have been made by precision-guided weapons.''

"So what if that's true . . . ?''

"So the British Aerospace Hawks flown by Oman and the United Arab Emirates don't normally drop precision-guided munitions," McLanahan said, "and the Super Puma and Gazelle attack helicopters normally fire only AS-12 missiles, which are short-range optically-guided missiles, not very useful on high-speed night attacks—they need spotters to find targets for them. And those Peninsula Shield crews weren't trained in using Maverick missiles, especially the imaging-infrared version. That tells me that the missiles were laser guided, probably Hellfires or French AS-30L missiles. And since none of the aircraft involved in the attack carries laser designators, the designators had to be on the ground, which meant you had commando teams lasing targets for the Peninsula Shield pilots. Who were they, General Freeman? Marines? SAS? Green Berets? The CIA?"

"What in hell difference does it make, McLanahan?" Freeman retorted, silently very impressed with this civilian's accurate analysis. "The GCC attacked hostile *offensive* weapon systems—"

"You didn't answer my question, General. Who was it?"

"You don't have a need to know," Freeman shot back. "Why am I arguing about this with you, McLanahan? You of all people, you and your mentor Brad Elliott, Misters Damn-the-Torpedoes, Praise God and Pass-the-Ammunition. The GCC destroyed what they believed was a hostile force on disputed territory."

"Instead of negotiating!" McLanahan said. "General, they performed a *terrorist action!* They weren't defending themselves, they attacked a foreign base without warning or without a declaration of war. That's an act of terrorism."

"That 'foreign base' was getting ready to attack GCC ships and American-flagged tankers transiting the Gulf."

"Really, General? When?" McLanahan interjected. "Iran has had those missiles on that island for years and hasn't fired one missile except for live-fire exercises. But the GCC struck first, and I think the U.S. helped them."

"You're guessing."

"It's not a big stretch of the imagination, sir," McLanahan

said. "It's a logical assumption. The GCC might have started this whole conflict because they got exasperated or impatient about the negotiations over Abu Musa and the Tumbs."

"And now the President has ordered the *Abraham Lincoln* carrier group to stay out of the Persian Gulf for the time being," Freeman pointed out, "which is making many of our Middle East allies nervous—which means Iran is already winning the war that always occurs before the shooting starts, the *psychological* war." McLanahan paused at that—he knew Freeman was right.

"I'm sending in ISA and the team you worked with, Patrick, Madcap Magician, to keep an eye on Iran's carrier battle group and other Iranian military assets," Freeman went on. "Every suspected Iranian nuclear, chemical, or biological warfare base or storage dump will have an ISA agent nearby; every Iranian bomber, fighter, rocket, or missile base capable of striking the *Lincoln* battle group or reaching targets in Saudi Arabia, Turkey, Kuwait, or Israel will have an agent watching it. If the Iranians try to make a move, and one of those special bases is involved, I want to know about it, and I'll recommend that the President order that base put out of commission.

"Now, both of you know the chances of a Navy A-6 or a large flight of Tomahawk cruise missiles reaching an isolated Iranian military base are pretty slim—and you know the B-2A is the only platform that can make it. Loaded with the right mix of anti-air defense and Disruptor-type weapons, we can accomplish the mission with a very low probability of collateral damage or risk to the American crews involved."

Freeman paused as he noticed Patrick's surprised expression, then smiled at the former bombardier. "Ah, I see the name 'Disruptor' got your attention. C'mon, Colonel, you didn't think all of Brad Elliott's little experiments could be kept secret forever, did you? Especially not the Disruptor series."

Wendy looked confused, which pleased Freeman—so Patrick McLanahan *could* keep a secret, even from his wife, who had once held as high a security clearance as he. To Wendy, Freeman added, "General Elliott was very involved in research and development of non-lethal weapons, which he called Disruptors. Elliott and HAWC became proficient enough in killing from very long range with very high precision—toward the end, he began to experiment in ways to simply disrupt, damage, or discombobulate something from long range and with high precision. The Disruptors are non-lethal air weapons, designed to confuse, frighten, interrupt, or intimidate the enemy without killing or destroying anything. We used some of these type weapons in the Persian Gulf War, but some of the new gadgets Elliott concocted put those to shame.

"When Dreamland was closed, we turned some of Elliott's work over to the Air Force Air Weapons folks at Eglin, but most we turned over to Sky Masters. They have some prototypes ready for testing." Freeman turned again to Patrick, the same mischievous smile on his face. "All we need is a seasoned B-2A crew member or two to test and train and get ready to fly. Interested, Patrick?"

"I can't fly a B-2A by myself," Patrick said. "You'll need several crews."

"One for now," Freeman said. "We may recruit more later." Patrick hesitated, looked at Wendy, then shook his head. "Sorry, sir, I'm still not interested," he said resolutely.

"If you agree to begin, you'll be fully compensated by the National Security Agency," Freeman said. "You'll receive pay and benefits equivalent to a GS-19, the equivalent to an O-6 in the military, whether or not you fly a mission. You'll be relocated completely without charge, given dependent and survivor privileges, plus extra personal-support services granted to senior NSA members." He paused for a moment, looking at the floor, then said, "I know you've been thinking about selling the tavern. We could assist with that, or assist in helping you keep it."

"How in hell did you find out about . . . ?" But Patrick already knew the answer—it was easy for anyone, not to mention the National Security Agency, to find out those things.

"In fact, one such opportunity has already presented itself," Freeman said. "One cover we were considering using was Sky Masters, Inc. They're a well-known defense contractor, downsized like all contractors but still viable. They're relocating some of their offices and R-and-D facilities to San Diego, and they have a new rocket test facility on unused government land near Tonopah. We even know that the Top Gun bar on the waterfront in San Diego is for sale—if you wanted to stay in the tavern business, that would be your opportunity. I know Dr. Masters has already given you several job offers. It may be time to accept one. You can of course accept his generous pay and benefits package as well as NSA's. The climate change might be of some benefit to you as well, Wendy."

"Is that your *medical* opinion, General?" Patrick snapped. "If I wanted to work for Masters, I'd have accepted his offers. I didn't because I'm not interested in working for a company that does business with the same government that uses its best people, then discards them like so much dirty tissue paper. That goes for your offer, too. The money and the climate don't concern me as much as the way you treat— or should I say, *mis*treat—those who believe in what they do."

"I've told you what your mission is, Patrick," Freeman said. "Your mission is to *protect* your fellow ISA agents. If the job calls for a military response, we'll send in the military, but we're going to send in ISA and other NSA assets *before* the military, just as we did before you went in as a HAWC bombardier, so we can gather as much intelligence information as possible. I'm just looking for a way to protect those men and women who will risk their *lives* to avert war."

"You haven't convinced me that we won't be called on as the President's private little gang of thugs and assassins," Patrick said warily.

"Colonel, I listened to the entire proposal, and I'm for it," Marcia Preston interjected. "I've worked for the NSA in the past, and we're not a private mercenary group for the White House or the CIA. We've got an honorable mission, Patrick. Our mission is to stop war. Iran is butchering our agents in—"

"In where?" Wendy asked. "What's happened?"

"It's classified," Freeman said. "I didn't want to bring it up. . . ."

Preston looked at Freeman for permission to continue; he granted it with a slight nod. "Happened not long ago," Preston said. "The ISA intelligence vessel *Valley Mistress*—you're familiar with it, of course. . . ."

"Paul White's group?" Patrick exploded. "What happened?"

"They were flying a stealth reconnaissance drone over the *Khomeini* battle group, trying to keep an eye on it," Preston replied. "Drone had a malfunction, and the Iranians tracked it back to the ship . . . and sank it. Thirteen crew members missing, including Colonel White . . ." Freeman held up a hand, ordering her to stop.

"My God . . ."

"We do what we do to beat up on the bad guys, Patrick, not against innocent persons," Freeman said. "We do the job to fix the problem at hand—we worry later about the long-term consequences. That's the unfortunate aspect of our work: we don't have time to analyze or determine the effect of our actions. A problem needs fixing, we fix it; a crisis develops that needs attention, we attend to it. We know what we do is necessary and vital for the national security and safety of Americans—we pray that what we do is for the long-term benefit of all."

Patrick paused for a moment, and now even Wendy was looking at him with a thoughtful glance. But still he said, "No. I . . . I'm sorry about Paul and his crew . . . but I can't. Sorry."

"Then we'll be off," General Freeman said, rising to his feet. "Thank you for your time, both of you. I don't need to remind you, I'm sure, that this entire conversation, this entire interaction, is of the highest secrecy . . ."

"General, tell him the rest," Preston said.

"I think not."

"What is this, some kind of game? A 'good-cop-bad-cop' routine?" Patrick said, rising to his feet as well. "I said I'm not interested. That's final."

"Tell him, General."

"No."

"It's about Madcap Magician," Preston said quickly. Freeman whirled at the Marine, but she finished her sentence: "One of the ISA agents attached to Madcap Magician—"

"Colonel, that's enough!"

"He wasn't killed, but he's going back in to look for Colonel White and anyone else who might have been captured."

"Preston, what in hell is it?"

"Colonel Preston, no!"

"One of the Madcap Magician agents is Major Hal Briggs," Preston said.

"Hal Briggs is with ISA? With Madcap Magician?" Patrick exclaimed.

"At the risk of breaking a major rule of survival with ISA—yes," Philip Freeman replied, after giving Marcia Preston one last warning glare. "Individual technical units aren't supposed to know any members of other units—one captured agent can put hundreds of others at risk. But . . . yes, Hal Briggs was recruited for service by my predecessor shortly after the James spy incident. In fact, he's going to be named its operations commander, if the unit survives and is reconstituted."

"Where is he?"

"He's . . . in-country," Freeman admitted. "Major Briggs . . . er, has a valuable contact, an intelligence officer from the United Arab Emirates who assisted him in the raid on Abu Musa Island. Major Briggs is awaiting clearance to go back in to make contact."

"That agent's gotta be a woman," Wendy said with a smile.

"I must warn you again, Colonel and Dr. McLanahan," Freeman said, pointing a finger at both of them, "that all this information is highly classified—I don't need to tell you what would happen to the persons involved if word as to their identities or position was released.'' Freeman nodded at the Secret Service agents in the room, and they headed for the door. He extended a big, rough hand. "It was a pleasure and an honor to meet you, Patrick McLanahan," he said. "The country—maybe the entire world—already owes you a tremendous debt of gratitude. I'm sorry we couldn't put your talents to work again. Dr. McLanahan, it was an honor to meet you as well. Good day to you both."

But Patrick was looking into Wendy's eyes—and she saw it, the sudden hot spark of energy, the old cocksure hellfire-and-damnation blaze in his eyes that had attracted her to him ten years earlier, back at that bar in Bossier City, Louisiana. Briggs had tipped the scale, she knew—Briggs and White and the memories of their old friends and comrades-in-arms. His gaze was also a question—he knew there was no time to converse, no time to talk it over as they always had before, but he was asking her opinion, asking her permission. . . .

She knew—and she responded: Do it, Patrick, her eyes told him. You want it, I want it for you, and men out there need you. Do it, but don't do it *their* way—do it *your* way!

And Patrick understood, because when Freeman tried to release the handshake, Patrick held firm.

Freeman looked at McLanahan with a puzzled expression. "Colonel McLanahan, does this mean . . . ?" Freeman started—but McLanahan's grip suddenly tightened. Freeman couldn't let go. "Yes, very well, Patr—"

"We use Disruptors," McLanahan interrupted, still clutching Freeman's hand tightly. "Non-lethal weapons only, unless there's a declaration of war—then we go in with everything we've got, and I mean *everything*."

"Ah . . ." McLanahan's grip tightened suddenly; it surprised Freeman. "Agreed," Freeman replied. "That was the plan all along, of course."

"We operate overseas only, not over U.S. or allied territory unless there's a declaration of war or an invasion."

"Agreed," Freeman said again, hiding the pain. "Now if

we could, I'd like to have Colonel Preston give you—''

"We support ISA operations *only*—no CIA, no other agencies or operations. No DEA, no ATF, no FBI," McLanahan continued. "Full disclosure, full verification, open access."

"Colonel, there's time to run down all the options . . ."

The grip suddenly doubled in strength—Freeman didn't think it was possible. He was starting to sweat. "Agree to it, General!" McLanahan said loudly. The Secret Service agents warily took a step toward McLanahan. McLanahan's grip was crushing, making Freeman see stars. "Sweat it! Or is all of this some kind of bullshit agency snow job right from the top?"

"What in hell do you think you're doing, dammit?"

The Secret Service agents started to rush over to Freeman's side. "If those sons of bitches touch me or Wendy, the whole deal's off!" McLanahan shouted. Freeman held up his left hand, halting the agents. "Tell me the truth, Freeman, damn you, if you have the *balls!*"

Something was going to break—his hand, or the Secret Service agents' patience. . . . "All right!" Freeman cried out through gritted teeth, "I agree!"

"Agree to what?"

"No other agencies . . . ISA only . . . full disclosure, full access," Freeman said. McLanahan released his grip, and Freeman jerked away, as if he had just been electrocuted. He gingerly rubbed the circulation back into his hand. McLanahan hadn't even broken a sweat. "That was a childish and immature thing to do, McLanahan," Freeman said. "What were you trying to prove—how tough you think you are?"

"I wanted to give you a little reminder, in case you've been in the Pentagon or the White House too long," McLanahan said, "that good men, my friends and I, are going to be counting on you keeping your promises. If you don't, the pain you just felt will be nothing compared to *theirs*."

Freeman knew he should be furious, but somehow he couldn't fault McLanahan, not after all the man had seen and been through. He let the anger drain away with the pain in his right hand, then nodded. "I'll keep my part of the bargain," Freeman said, "not because of your little macho stunt, but because I goddamn *do* care about the men and women under my command. I don't play games, Colonel McLanahan."

McLanahan snatched up the wig and shook it in front of Freeman. "You all play games, General," he said angrily. "We all play games—but not with the lives of fellow crewdogs. I learned a lot from Brad Elliott in almost ten years, sir, and I've got lots of ideas of my own. You play straight with me, and we'll kick some ass and come home alive. If you don't, I'll make you wish you hired Brad Elliott and had never even *heard* of me."

Freeman did not like being spoken to in this way, but he knew McLanahan was a truly dedicated man. Everything he had heard and read about this guy was true. "If you're finished breaking my fingers and my ass, you're on the government clock now, McLanahan. Your plane leaves Travis Air Force Base in seven hours. Good luck." By impulse, he held out a hand to him, then quickly retracted it. He smiled, nodded, and said, "Kiss your lovely wife good-bye, McLanahan. You're in the ISA now."

WHITEMAN AFB, MISSOURI
17 APRIL 1997, 0649 CT

"Who the hell is it, Tom?" Colonel Anthony Jamieson irritably asked the one-star general standing beside him. The two officers were standing in the cool, damp morning air outside the base operations building at Whiteman Air Force Base, Knob Noster, Missouri, waiting as ordered for the jet carrying the VIPs to arrive. "A Congressman? A Senator's aide?"

"The boss says you don't need to know the answer to that, Tony—yet." Brigadier General Thomas Wright, the commander of the 509th Bomb Wing, Whiteman Air Force Base, and Jamieson's boss, obviously disliked giving that kind of response to a senior officer, fellow pilot, and friend—but it was the only one allowable.

Jamieson could see his boss's indecision and decided to keep on pressing: "Do *you* know who he is?" he asked.

"Not exactly," Wright admitted, "and apparently I don't need to know, either. Listen, Tiger, stop asking all these damned questions. You just have to fly him in the simulator. This is just one of Samson's gee-whiz dog-and-pony-show tours. Have fun, water his eyes—you know the drill. I'll wax your ass in golf afterward."

Jamieson muttered a curse under his breath and fell silent, seething underneath. Tony "Tiger" Jamieson, a twenty-five-year veteran of the U.S. Air Force with over four thousand hours' flying time and experience in several major conflicts from Vietnam to Libya to the Persian Gulf, had been tasked to give a "dog-and-pony-show" ride for a visiting VIP. The former fighter-bomber ace, now the operations group commander of the 509th Bomb Wing, the home of the B-2A Spirit stealth bomber, was not accustomed to being ordered to do these "public affairs things," as he liked to call them, and he would have preferred to turn the whole thing over to the bomb squadron commander or one of his senior instructor pilots, the tall, studly-looking Steve Canyon types with the square jaws and blue eyes that look so good on TV and in the newspapers. But the brass—namely, the wing commander and his boss, the commander of all Air Force bomber forces—wanted Jamieson, so his job was to salute smartly, say "Yes, sir," and perform as expected.

The C-20H military special air mission jet landed precisely at its scheduled time, and taxied quickly to the base operations building; even before the engines had spooled down on the military version of the Gulfstream IV, the air-stair door popped open and soldiers and technicians in fatigues hurried out. The VIPs, led by a three-star general accompanied by a two-star general, a colonel, and two civilians, were quickly whisked right from the plane to the waiting cars without stopping for any pleasantries, as if the early-morning sunlight would shrivel them up like vampires if they stayed in the open too long. Two Humvee security vehicles filled with uniformed and plain-clothes security officers flanked the staff cars; Jamieson was displaced to a second staff car because a plainclothes security officer, armed with a submachine gun partially hidden under his safari-style jacket, took the front seat. He also noted many other persons in utility uniforms disembarking from the C-20 Gulfstream jet, all heading for the maintenance group hangar complex in a real hurry, some carrying catalog cases full of tech orders, some carrying tool-boxes and test-gear equipment—and some, judging by the length of their hair and the width of their midsections, ob-viously not military. They all looked as if they were already late for a big meeting.

Security police units closed all the intersections as the little motorcade made its way to the B-2A Weapon Systems Trainer building. All this excitement only served to make Jamieson even grumpier. Doing these "dog-and-pony shows" was bad enough, but a motorcade and extra security for a lousy civilian? A lot of it had to be for show, Jamieson decided. The visitor was probably some congressional budget weenie investigating security procedures for the B-2A stealth bomber fleet, and the brass had beefed up security to make it look good. Their security was already very tight here at Whiteman, but a good show of force never hurt.

After they were seated in a briefing room in the simulator building, with the doors closed and locked and guards sta-tioned inside and out, Jamieson got his first opportunity to check out the VIP. Too bad it was a guy—the female con-gressional staffers that frequently visited Whiteman were all knockouts, and Jamieson, now single after two divorces ("if the Air Force wanted you to have a wife, they'd have issued you one"), had gotten to know many of them. The guy was about ten years younger, four inches shorter, and forty pounds heavier than Jamieson, with broad, knobby shoulders, thick arms, and weight lifter-like thighs and calves—a for-mer college power lifter turned desk jockey who liked to hang out at the weight machines on occasion, Jamieson decided—with thin blond hair and a fairly new mustache, both a bit longer than the regs allowed and definitely a lot longer than the current crew-cut style common in the late-nineties military. His handshake was firm, his eyes were blue and sparkling with energy, and he looked as if he might have wanted to smile when the introductions were made, but something dark and painful inside him vetoed the idea of showing any emotion at all, let alone a happy one. Bags under his eyes and lines in his face showed signs of tension, of aging beyond his years.

Jamieson was also reintroduced to another VIP who was going to monitor the simulator ride: the commander of Eighth Air Force himself, Lieutenant General Terrill "Earthmover" Samson, the man responsible for manning, training, equipping, and deploying all U.S. Air Force heavy bomber units. Samson was America's "bomber guru," the man who was single-handedly responsible for the continued presence of the B-2A stealth bomber and the other heavy bombers still in the Air Force inventory. When everyone else had been telling Congress to get rid of the "heavies," Samson had been trying to convince Congress that America still needed the speed, flexibility, and sheer power of the intercontinental-range combat aircraft. Jamieson had met him once, a few years earlier, when Jamieson had been installed as Operations Group commander of the 509th.

Samson often brought influential congressmen and Defense Department bureaucrats in to see the B-2A stealth bomber in order to drive his arguments home. Because civilians were not permitted to fly in the plane (the third seat in a B-2A, located at the flight engineer's station behind the right seat, was no longer fitted with an ejection seat), a few special VIPs sat in on B-2A simulator sessions flown by other crew members. Jamieson assumed that this guy was going to get a real special treat and sit in the right seat while he flew the simulator. No problem: Jamieson could fly the beast without help just fine, from the left seat.

"Good morning, gentlemen, welcome to Whiteman Air

Force Base," General Wright began. "I'm Brigadier General Tom Wright, commander of the 509th Bomb Wing, the home of four thousand dedicated men and women who take care of the world's most sophisticated warplane, the B-2A Spirit stealth bomber. As you may know, the 509th has the distinction of being the only American military unit to employ nuclear weapons in anger—as the 509th Bomb Group, we dropped the first two nuclear bombs on Hiroshima and Nagasaki in World War Two. Our unit crest is the only military crest authorized to depict a mushroom cloud on it. We take great pride in our past as well as responsibility and leadership in our future.

"Today, we employ a weapon system that is far more sophisticated and far more important to our national defense than the thermonuclear device—the B-2A Spirit stealth bomber. We will be introducing you to the world's deadliest war machine by giving you a short unclassified background briefing on the aircraft, a thirty-minute classified familiarization ride in the B-2A Weapon Systems Trainer, a tour of our facilities, a meeting with some of the outstanding officers and airmen of our major units, and of course a look at the aircraft itself. Without further ado, I'd like to introduce you to the 509th Operations Group commander and our most experienced B-2A aircraft commander and instructor, Colonel Tony 'Tiger' Jamieson, who will conduct today's simulator familiarization session. Colonel Jamieson?"

Jamieson had already set up all the standard briefing stuff, and he flipped on the digital slide projector and got to his feet: "Thank you, sir. I'm Tony Jamieson, Operations Group commander here at Whiteman. I'm responsible for overall operational and administrative charge of five squadrons in the wing, about two thousand men and women, dealing directly with combat flying activities, training, and deployment: the 393rd Bomb Squadron 'Tigers,' the first operational B-2A squadron; the 715th Bomb Squadron 'Eagles,' which is due to receive its first B-2A aircraft later this year; the 509th Air Refueling Squadron 'Griffiths,' which fly the KC-135R Stratotanker aerial refueling tankers; and the

4007th Combat Crew Training Squadron 'Senseis,' which fly the T-1A Jayhawk and T-38 Talon jet trainers and operate the B-2A part-and full-task weapons-system simulators. The Senseis conduct all B-2A initial, recurrent, and instructor ground and flight training. Also under my chain of command is the 509th Operational Support Squadron, which include the life support, weapons loaders, flight line security, weather, intelligence, and mission-planning officers.

"My job is simple: provide General Wright with the maximum number of mission-ready tactical aircrews ready to go to war at a moment's notice," Jamieson went on. "We do this by maintaining a rigorous training schedule to keep all crews fully proficient, including using the simulators and Jayhawk jet trainers for normal proficiency training, thereby maximizing the number of bombers and tankers available to go to war. We feel the combination of the part-task and full-motion simulators and the specially configured Jayhawks can keep our crews proficient without too much training time in the bomber itself, which allows us to deploy the B-2A as much as possible without sacrificing capability or training—in fact, we can deploy all of our B-2A bombers overseas and still train aircrews to full mission capable status here at home.

"The name of the game here at Whiteman is 'quick strike'—the ability to successfully strike any assigned target anywhere in the world with any weapon in our arsenal within twenty-four hours of a warning order," Jamieson continued. "In simple terms, in case of war or if ordered to deploy to an overseas base, my group and I move as a team as quickly as possible, brief and launch the combat-ready bombers and tankers, load our prepositioned mobility packages into the first available transport planes, and begin attack operations and/or deploy to our forward operating location, depending on our orders."

"I hate to burst Colonel Jamieson's obvious pride bubble," General Samson interjected with a smile, turning toward the stranger, "but I must add that the 509th is not yet fully mission ready. We're at least a year ahead of our planned initial operational capability schedule of January one in the year 2000, and we could fly combat missions with the ten planes we have here right now, but the 509th won't be officially combat capable for another year or two.''

Jamieson took a deep breath as he clicked the button and brought up the next slide. Man, this was a total waste of his time, he thought. The VIP looked disinterested and distracted, as if thinking about a hundred things happening thousands of miles away. Probably already has his report written, Jamieson concluded. ''This morning, after showing you around the base a bit,'' he went on, ''we will present an overview of the 509th Bomb Wing organization, a briefing on current and near-future technology, then present standard flight mission planning profile in the—''

''Colonel, we can stop this right here,'' General Samson said, holding up a hand. ''Tony, I apologize. I've had to lead you on a bit. My orders were to conceal the real purpose of this visit as much as possible using my own discretion, so I made this visit look like a VIP tour. It isn't.'' He motioned to the civilian seated beside him and said to Jamieson, ''Tony, I want you to give this gentleman a full B-2A emergency procedures simulator check ride.''

Jamieson nearly dropped his jaw in surprise. Was this some kind of *joke?* ''Of *course,* sir,'' Jamieson responded sarcastically. ''Give a check ride in the B-2A stealth bomber to a civilian. Not an orientation ride, but a check ride. Yes, *sir.*'' He turned to the stranger with an amused grin and asked, ''So. How did you do on your open-book and closed-book exams, sir?''

''I think I did pretty good, Colonel,'' the VIP replied, in a deep, monotone voice, opening his briefcase.

Jamieson scowled at the guy's smart-ass comeback, then laughed as if dismissing the thought of this guy passing a B-2A bomber crew-member exam. But all traces of humor disappeared when the VIP picked out a folder with a red TOP SECRET cover sheet on it, and extracted a single sheet of paper—a 509BMW Form 88, ''B-2A Record of Aircrew Training and Performance.'' Jamieson examined the form with a dumbfounded expression, then muttered, "What is this shit?"

"It's all genuine, Colonel," the VIP said, as if reading Jamieson's mind. He had indeed finished his open-book and closed-book exams, with near-perfect marks, along with a 100 on a "bold print" emergency procedures test, a complete publications inspection—this guy apparently had a complete and up-to-date set of B-2A tech orders, including the classified 1TO-B2A-25-1 weapons-delivery manual—an oral exam, and a complete Class I flight physical and psychological stress exam. He was even certified under the Personnel Reliability Program, the program used to certify any person who had responsibility for nuclear weapons or components. A few of the sign-off blocks had been blacked out so he couldn't read who the evaluator was, but all of the other blocks were signed off by Eighth Air Force Standardization/Evaluation instructors, with General Steve Shaw himself, the four-star commander of Air Combat Command, in charge of all Air Force combat air forces, as the final approving authority.

"Yeah, right. And I'm the Prince of fucking Wales," Jamieson snapped. He swung around to Samson and tossed the form on the table. "What's going on, General? Who is this guy? Why is Eighth Air Force Stan/Eval signing him off?"

"Tony, I'll answer all the questions you have . . . later . . . maybe," Samson said. "But all your questions will be moot if this gentleman can't fly. I need you to give him an EP check ride."

"Excuse me, sir. I don't know what's going on here, and I don't think I *care* to know, but if you're asking me to 'pencil-whip' this guy, General, ask someone else," Jamieson said firmly. "We got standards to follow."

"I'm not asking you to sign him off if he doesn't know the procedures, Tony," Samson said. "If he's not qualified, I want to know about it."

"He's not qualified then, sir," Jamieson said resolutely, refusing to be bullied by the hulking three-star general before him. "All B-2 crew members must be U.S. Air Force pilots with at least one thousand hours' jet flight time, they must be selected by the 509th wing commander and the commander of Air Combat Command, and they must be graduates of B-2A Combat Crew Training here at Whiteman. I help screen and select every B-2 bomber candidate, and I personally know and fly with every graduate from the 4007th CCTS. I don't remember seeing *him*.''

''Tony, I want you to evaluate this gentleman as if he were fresh out of CCTS and ready to undergo unit mission-ready qualification,'' Samson said evenly. ''General Wright has already certified him as ready to begin unit certification—it's your job to evaluate his readiness to certify him mission-capable.''

Jamieson glared at Wright, who remained impassive. Tom Wright obviously knew much more about this little con game than he had let on, and he had not shared his knowledge with his old friend and longtime wingman. Either Wright was turning into a true mindless staff weenie, or this was *really* heavy shit going on with this stranger. ''But the fact remains, sir,'' Jamieson went on, ''that I *know* he hasn't been through CCTS. If I continue, I'll be knowingly violating the law. Are you asking me to do that?''

''The fact is, Colonel,'' Samson said, ''that he *has* been through initial B-2 flight training—I can't tell you which one, that's all.''

''But there's only one initial B-2A flight training school, sir.''

''No, there *isn't,* Colonel,'' Samson emphasized, ''and that's all I can say about the matter. Now get out your scenario book and the rest of your evaluator shit and give this man an EP check ride, and do it *quietly.*'' The argument ended right there, with Samson shooting an angry glare into Jamieson's brain. The newcomer was quiet, keeping his mouth shut and his eyes averted through this discussion.

They took a break for a half hour while Jamieson brought in the materials for an emergency-procedures simulator examination—one simulator was already set up for the evaluation, he learned—and when he was ready, he began briefing the mission profile. It was a simple profile: preflight, taxi, takeoff, an aerial refueling, a high-altitude bomb run, a low-altitude bomb run, and return to base—although these check rides never ended up looking anything like the briefed profile. The simulator instructors—there was only one man on the simulator console today, a civilian Jamieson had never seen before—could insert hundreds of different malfunctions and emergencies into the scenario at any time.

The EP check ride concentrated mostly on "bold print" and warning items, which were actions that each crew member had to commit to memory perfectly and execute flawlessly. EP check rides were the most demanding. A bust in any "bold print" or "warning" action or more than one or two busts in a less-serious "caution" action meant instant flight decertification. Few new guys ever passed an EP check ride the first time, and even experienced crewdogs who didn't keep up with their studies had trouble on "no-notice" checks.

When Jamieson finished briefing, the stranger got to his feet and began to give the mission commander's portion of the flight briefing. "Hold it," Jamieson interrupted, totally caught off guard, "you don't have a part to brief in this scenario. You fly the profile and—"

"I'm your MC on this flight, sir," the newcomer responded, in a deep, rather reserved but no-nonsense tone of voice. The MC, or mission commander, on a B-2A stealth bomber acted as copilot, offensive-systems officer, and defensive-systems officer, although either pilot could complete the mission alone in an emergency. "The MC always briefs his actions on takeoff and the route of flight—"

"When I need you to give me something, mister, I'll tell you—"

"Let him brief, Tony," General Wright said. "We want to hear this."

"Thank you, sir," the stranger said immediately. "I'll be briefing the mission commander's portion of the emergency-procedures simulator flight check. I'll be evaluated on three main areas: knowledge of all procedures and tech order directives; performance as mission commander during normal and emergency situations; and performance as the flying crew member during emergency situations. Since Colonel Jamieson didn't give one, let's start off with a time hack. . . ."

Without seeming to notice or care about Jamieson's protests, the guy launched into a standard crew briefing, outlining his responsibilities, the mission timing, the route of flight, the attack route, the assigned targets, alternate landing bases, and his actions during all critical phases of flight. He completed the preflight briefing competently and succinctly—he clearly knew his stuff.

Jamieson was amazed. The guy was obviously a former bomber crew member, with a lot of experience in many different combat aircraft, and he knew very technical and detailed information on the B-2A stealth bomber and current attack procedures. He had no detectable accent—not New England, not southern, not Texas, not midwest. Who was he? Why hadn't Jamieson ever heard of him?

Samson thought of the U.S. Air Force's tiny fleet of B-2A stealth bombers as his own personal responsibility, almost his personal property, so no one was going to go up in one unless Tiger checked him out first. Besides, it was always a good thing to do a favor for a three-star general, especially a guy like the Earthmover. Terrill Samson spent almost as much time testifying on Capitol Hill on behalf of an expanded heavy bomber fleet as he did at his headquarters at Barksdale Air Force Base in Bossier City, Louisiana, and one word from him in the right ears in Washington and at the Pentagon was worth perhaps another order of sophisticated "brilliant" weapons, another upgrade on a B-52 or B-1B bomber, maybe even another B-2A bomber wing—not to mention the addition of one, maybe two, stars on Jamieson's shoulders in the not-too-distant future. . . .

Nobody, not even the big fearsome-looking three-star general, told "Tiger" Jamieson whom to fly with, but he was intrigued by the secrecy and urgency surrounding the stranger and this mission, so, like an idiot, he agreed to cooperate.

• • •

"Ground position freeze." The high-resolution video display out the cockpit windows froze, as did all of the cockpit instruments and readouts. "Record current switch positions and flight parameters and get me a mission printout." Instantly the visual display shifted—they were now over a large expanse of desert, with the runway lights of a large airport complex barely visible in the distance. "Thank you. Everyone take five, then reconfigure the simulator for the next session. You too, MC. Step outside and take five."

The civilian sat back in his seat in the cockpit of the B-2A Weapon Systems Trainer, or WST, *The Spirit of Hell* (all of the B-2A bombers were nicknamed after a U.S. state except the WST, which was nicknamed after the place most crewdogs associated with their time spent in it), and consciously let his muscles relax. "We've still got an engine-out approach and landing to do, Colonel," he said, staring at the scenery depicted on the high-resolution video screens as if he were really looking off into the distance. "I'm ready to go as soon as we reconfigure."

"I don't need to see an approach," Jamieson said. He turned to the younger man beside him and scowled. "You know just enough to be dangerous, in my opinion. You know a little about a lot of stuff in the beast, but not nearly enough to fly it in combat. The evaluation is over."

"We're here to complete an emergency-procedures evaluation, Colonel," the civilian said. "The curriculum calls for an engine-out."

"I don't need to see an approach," Jamieson insisted, wiping sweat from his eyebrows and scowling at the stranger beside him, "and I designed the entire B-2A initial, recurrent, upgrade, and instructor training curricula—I don't need you to tell me what it says." The B-2A WST, or Weapon Systems Trainer, was the world's most realistic simulator, and it often left its users exhausted and stressed after even a simple combat scenario. The stranger looked completely relaxed, Jamieson noted, with not a drop of sweat anywhere on his body. Either he was sedated or he had ice water for blood. "I got no doubts you can fly an approach, run a checklist, maybe even land the thing with one engine out, even though you're not a B-2A pilot—or any kind of pilot," Jamieson said. "You just don't have what it takes to fly the Beak, period." The civilian was taking Jamieson's words pretty well—very little reaction, just sitting still and looking at nothing in particular.

The guy had just gone through an emergency-procedures scenario that would've killed most crewdogs, no matter how experienced they were. The sim operator had thrown in an emergency action message and a scramble launch—Jamieson hadn't done that since his B-1B Lancer bomber days five years ago. They'd then had a complete failure of one of the B-2A's primary hydraulic systems, and after a short but intense argument, they'd decided to proceed with the mission. The sim operator had thrown in what appeared to be a series of minor glitches, most of which were handled automatically by the B-2A's sophisticated flight-control computers. In the end, on the bomb run, all those little malfunctions had turned out to be a staggering huge malfunction, one that threatened to scrub the mission or even force the crew to eject.

They hadn't ejected—the stranger had handled all of the malfunctions. Jamieson had to admit (to himself only, of course) that he had no idea why the B-2A hadn't just flipped over on its back and plowed into the ground, or hadn't been cut to ribbons by the multiple layers of air defense weaponry that had been inserted into the scenario. Normally in an EP sim, when the action in the cockpit was getting too rough and the crew coordination was breaking down, the sim operators would begin to reduce the outside distractions—they would flatten the terrain, improve the weather, or reduce the number of threats—so the crew had at least a chance to catch up and get some productive training out of the simulator session, even if they flunked the exam. It wasn't realistic— the number of threats usually *increased* as the mission went on, not decreased—but it kept the session from being a total washout.

Not only had the stranger *not* flunked the exam, but the

sim operator hadn't reduced the number of threats. They'd somehow made it to the target area, laying a string of bunker-busting 2,000-pound bombs on a command-post complex on the high-altitude pass, and a cluster-bomb attack on an air base and radar-site complex on the low-altitude run—and gotten all of their weapons off on time and on target. Jamieson didn't know if they would be armed weapons—the MC was running so many damned checklists, juggling so many malfunction screens, and pulling and resetting so many circuit breakers that even Jamieson couldn't keep up—but they had made their attacks and then actually departed the target area with at least two engines and all crew members still alive. That was more than most crews could claim if they had been loaded up as they had been. Returning to base was not a requirement in an emergency-procedures sim session.

"Listen, son, for a civilian, you're a damned good student, and I think you'd make a great crewdog," Jamieson went on, "but a B-2A flight-crew candidate has to attend twelve months of Air Force pilot school, spend five to seven years in combat strike aircraft, pass a screening program that accepts only one in two hundred applicants, attend a tough six-month B-2A combat-crew training course here at Whiteman, a six-month in-house qualification course, then spend at least two years as a B-2A pilot before upgrading to the right seat as mission commander. You've showed me a few things this morning that tell me you can handle a program like that."

Stop trying to stroke the guy, Jamieson shouted at himself. This guy had done none of these things necessary to fly the Spirit. He wasn't qualified, period. Sure he knew systems, and he knew the basics of flying, but that didn't give him the right to play MC with a billion-dollar warplane.

"Any specific critique items, Colonel?" the guy asked quietly.

"A few—not that it makes any difference," Jamieson replied. "Go-no-go decision making was your biggest screw-up. A responsible, thinking crew never, *never* takes a primary hydraulic problem away from home plate. The plane's too valuable; we have only ten of the damn things flying. If it's a major bold-print malfunction item, bring it home and fight another day. We would've given you the engine-out approach right away if you had called the command post and brought the Beak back for landing like you were supposed to do. Then we would've sent you through the bomb run with only the electrical fault, and you would've possibly avoided the fighter attack because you would not have had the hydraulic failure or the split ruddervator. If you knew your tac doctrine, you'd know all that.'' Jamieson didn't remind the guy that they had somehow *survived* the fighter attack. A stealth bomber that wasn't stealthy was a sitting duck for any air-superiority fighter—the MC had (again that word) *somehow* maneuvered the bomber so that it had survived the requisite two missile and two gun passes. Yes, they had been shot up, but they were still alive and still flying! The guy earned a big fat ''attaboy'' for his work. Unfortunately, Jamieson wasn't the guy who was going to give it to him.

''Maybe the persons your mission is supporting need you over the target when you said you'd be there,'' the civilian said. ''Maybe they're counting on you. Maybe lives depend on—''

''It's not worth risking over a billion dollars' worth of hardware, weapons, gas, and manpower,'' Jamieson interrupted testily. ''We're heavy into flight safety here, son. There are always backups to every strike mission. No one plane is that valuable.''

''That's not always the case, sir. They put four engines, four independent hydraulic systems, four independent flight-control systems, and four independent electrical systems on the B-2A for a reason: to continue the mission should one, two, or even three of them fail.''

''This is my critique of your performance, mister, not a debate.'' Jamieson interjected. ''I'm explaining why you wouldn't pass a check ride—we can talk about tactics and doctrine in Snobsters over a couple beers.'' Snobsters was Whiteman's old officers' club, now the all-ranks, all-services casual bar. ''You studied hard, son, and you got a good full-speed-ahead attitude. It's obvious you played on heavy bombers before, many, many years ago, but frankly, son, you don't know shit about modern-day bombers. The days of swapping spares and using bubble gum and baling wire to keep a bomber in the air, no matter what, are dead and gone—and good riddance. Today, the crew's responsibility in the new Air Force is to monitor and manage systems. If things start going tits-up, you bring the beast home and go to your backup plan. You're good, son. You're a good systems operator . . ."

"So what's the problem, Colonel?" the civilian asked, removing his headset and letting his longish blond hair hang loose in sweaty strands—aha, the guy's not a friggin' machine. He *does* sweat! "If you say I can fly the B-2A . . ."

"Sir, give me a few months and I can teach a *monkey* to fly the Beak," Jamieson said, unstrapping from his seat and heading for the rear entry hatch to the simulator cab, "but I wouldn't want to go to war with the son of a bitch. A monkey can drop bombs, work the MDUs, maybe even fly an approach if you give him enough bananas—but he won't back you up and he won't make good decisions. I need an MC that will not just run a checklist, but make sound decisions based on tactical doctrine and years of experience in a flying unit. You don't have it. Sorry." He turned and headed for the exit, then turned back to the stranger and added, "I'm sure you're a good aviator and a good student, and with time and training I'm sure you can get the job done. But not now."

As Jamieson was leaving, he heard the civilian say, "Thank you for the lesson, Colonel." It was a low, sad voice—but there was a certain cocksure ring to it, a hint of defiance, perhaps?

Jamieson did not reply. The guy was better than he had let on, Jamieson had to admit. Yeah, decision making was important, but that's why God had invented aircraft commanders and crew coordination. Jamieson would prefer to have a knowledgeable systems man in the right seat any day over a second-guesser or a self-anointed tactics expert. Jamieson reluctantly admitted that he regretted the Air Force's decision to put a second pilot in the right seat of the B-2A stealth bomber rather than a pilot-trained navigator or engineer; or, even better, leaving the third seat in and bringing a navigator-engineer-bombardier along. He had criticized the guy for knowing a little about a lot; in fact, the man knew quite a bit about almost everything, and that made him a valuable asset on a bomber crew, no matter what kind of wings he wore—or even if he wore no wings at all.

The door to the cockpit cab opened, and the crew chief for *The Spirit of Hell* met up with Jamieson. "We're done for the day, chief," Jamieson said, as he stepped from the cab to the steel platform surrounding the full-motion simulator. "You're cleared to reset the box after the printout's ready."

"Uh, sir . . . ?"

"Where's the printout?" Jamieson asked—then he stopped short when he saw the armed guards in the doorway to the simulator room. "What's going on, chief?" he snapped. "What in hell are those security guys doing in here?"

"I asked them," Lieutenant General Terrill Samson said. The big three-star general was in the simulator instructor's control room, carrying the mission-data printout and a large catalog case with a large combination lock on it. Jesus, Jamieson thought, the guy is *huge!* How did he ever fit into the cockpit of a military jet trainer? "Thank you, chief. If you'll excuse us, I need to talk with Colonel Jamieson. Let me know when the maintenance troops arrive, please." Soon they were alone in the control room. Jamieson noticed that everyone in the entire simulator bay had departed, except for the guards, who were armed with Uzi submachine guns.

Jamieson was tall, but the commander of Eighth Air Force towered over him. It was a little intimidating even for a guy like Jamieson, who was not easily scared by other men. Tony Jamieson had over four thousand hours' flying time in a dozen different Air Force combat aircraft, including more than sixty combat sorties over Iraq, and anyone who could beat those numbers got Jamieson's instant respect and attention. Terrill Samson was such a man. "Hello, General," Jamieson said to Samson. "What's with the guards?"

"We're going to be doing a few modifications to this simulator," Samson said, "testing out a few new items. It'll be down for only a day or two; you'll have to use the second box by itself for the time being. How did it go with our boy?"

"Fair to poor," Jamieson replied. "He's knowledgeable and all—book stuff, numbers, some good systems knowledge, not a bad stick—but he doesn't know tac doctrine and procedures."

"Could he be a B-2A Combat Crew Training Unit student?" Samson asked. CCTU was the 509th Bomb Wing's B-2A six-month initial training program. "If so, what stage would he be in?"

"His pilot skills are average, but based on his systems knowledge, I'd say he was a second-or third-stage student, upper level . . ."

"So you're saying he's as good as an average pilot who's been through about half the CCTU program, Tiger?"

"There are lots of candidates out there with better piloting skills," Jamieson said quickly, still not wanting to admit that the guy was pretty good for fear of appearing to compromise on his deliberately set lofty standards for B-2A crew members. "He seems to have lost a lot of heavy iron piloting skills."

"He never *was* a pilot, Tiger," Samson said with a smile. "He's an ex–bomber-*navigator*, B-52s mostly."

Jamieson was surprised—no, shocked was the word. The bomber part didn't surprise him, but Jamieson would've bet that the guy had been flying nothing but a desk for years. "Where'd he learn to fly, then?"

"HAWC," Samson replied, "and that's classified. *Highly* classified."

"HAWC?" Jamieson sputtered. "You're shitting me . . . er, sorry, sir, I mean . . . man, this guy used to fly for HAWC? When? What did he fly?"

Samson closed his eyes, as if the very mention of the word *HAWC* caused him great physical or mental stress. "Tony, do me a big damned favor and keep your questions to yourself," Samson said impatiently.

Jamieson did exactly as he was told—he knew as well as Samson what the Department of Defense did to those who breathed a word about its most super-secret research facility. Only the best engineers and fliers got to work at HAWC— even hotshot veteran sticks like Tony Jamieson didn't dare apply to work there for fear they'd be rejected or that working under such a constant level of strict security would destroy their private lives.

The aircraft and weapons HAWC worked on were classified at the highest levels of national security, and any inquiries or even a casual mention of the place or the organization required a report to the Air Force Office of Special Investigations. Jamieson knew that Samson had to report him to AFOSI just for having this conversation—and that such a report would change Jamieson's life forever, because of the level of official scrutiny he'd be under from now on. With all of the recent security breaches rumored to have occurred at HAWC, everyone even remotely involved in the facility would be closely monitored; their public and private lives would no longer be their own, but would be documented and examined by the Department of Defense until death closed the file.

"Excuse me, sir, but there's a whole lot you're not telling me," Jamieson probed. "You say this guy is ex-military, a civilian, but he's got access to B-2A tech orders, weapons manuals, and he's riding the sim with the radar on? No person without a special-access clearance has ever seen the radar in operation before—he not only watched it work, but *knew how to work it in a combat situation!*"

"No more questions, Tiger," Samson said. "I need to know one thing: would you fly with him, right now, in combat?"

"Not in a million friggin' years!" Jamieson retorted. "Why should I, sir? I've got thirty of the world's best pilots in my wing, already fully trained and qualified to fly the Beak. Why should I fly with someone who's not checked out?''

''I'm not asking you to choose between a mission-ready crew member and him,'' Samson urged. ''I'm asking you, would you fly with him if—''

''If he was the last man on earth?'' Jamieson interjected. He had no idea where this was leading, but it wasn't good. ''He could back me up on most tasks, but . . . no, sir, I wouldn't fly with him. It'd be a waste of a good airframe.''

''On today's sim ride, Tiger, what would have been the chance that he would've hit his assigned target?'' Samson asked.

Jamieson shrugged. ''You saw the results, sir: he hit his assigned targets, so I guess the answer is one hundred percent,'' Jamieson admitted. ''But I'd give him only a seventy-five percent chance of reaching his target in the first place, and that's bad, because he could have brought his bomber home and gotten it fixed and taken a one hundred percent plane into combat. What's his chance of bringing the plane and his crew home with all the malfunctions he let accumulate? Maybe twenty percent, tops. He exercised poor judgment.''

''What if the mission absolutely had to go off on a certain date and time?''

''Use the backup planes,'' Jamieson replied. ''You need one bomber to take out the target: launch three. Send one home after the last inbound refueling, then send another home just before ingressing Indian country. Fly the best one to the target and bomb the crap out of it.''

Samson nodded; it was the correct response. If he had forgotten it, he was grateful to Jamieson for pointing it out— and angry that his superiors had forced him to forget the basics of employing strategic air power. But the wheels were already in motion here; Samson was committed to following his own directives until they could be followed no more. ''What if you had only one bomber available?'' Samson asked. ''What then?''

"Sir, I wouldn't get forced into that predicament in the first place," Jamieson said resolutely. "Don't let the bean counters talk you into limiting your options in order to save money or reduce risk—as if they knew anything about reducing the risk to anyone but themselves. If you aren't left with any options, recommend scrubbing the mission or find another way." Just then the civilian came into the simulator control room, carrying his charts and checklists. "You'll have to wait outside, sir." But the guy didn't move—and Jamieson noticed that his entire demeanor, his entire bearing, had changed. He didn't seem like the quiet, contrite civilian bureaucrat anymore.

"General?" the guy asked. "What about it?"

Jamieson felt his face flush with anger. "I said wait outside, mister . . ."

The stranger was still ignoring the Ops Group commander: "I need to know right now, General."

"Did you hear what I said, buddy?"

"Tiger . . ." Samson interjected. Jamieson looked at the three-star general with a shocked expression—the stranger was practically *ordering* Samson around here! "I . . . we have something to ask of you."

"What's going on, sir?" Jamieson asked. He turned to the civilian. "What's your story, mister?"

"This gentleman is . . . joining the 509th for a while, Tiger," Samson began. "We're going to take a B-2A bomber, load it with state-of-the-art precision standoff weapons, and fly bombing missions overseas—except they won't be Air Force operations. We need a B-2A aircraft commander, preferably the best in the business—General Wright says it's you, and I agree."

"What the hell is this, General?" Jamieson retorted. "Who in hell does he work for?"

"You're not authorized to reveal anything," the stranger said to Samson.

"I told you I wasn't going to allow any of my people to commit to this project without full disclosure," Samson said to the stranger. "Jamieson's been cleared. We tell him, or the deal's off."

The civilian looked at Samson, then at Jamieson's angry, confused features, then nodded to Samson. "All right, sir," retired Air Force Lieutenant Colonel Patrick S. McLanahan said resolutely. "In the vault."

The 509th Operational Support Squadron building was a huge three-story, 20,000-square-foot electronic vault, guarded night and day by humans and by a dazzling array of electronic eyes and sensors. The reason: the OSS received real-time intelligence information from all over the world and processed it continuously, building and refining a series of preplanned strike packages for the B-2A stealth bomber and other long-range bombers. When the Russians moved an SS-21 missile from one launch site to another, or when Iran deployed a new fighter, or a new terrorist base camp in Sudan opened, or a new surface-to-air missile site in China was activated, the computers in the OSS adjusted mission charts, flight plans, strike routings, target lists, and threat predictions on dozens of computerized mission packages. If the stealth bomber crews were tasked to perform a strike mission, the 509th OSS would simply dump the latest flight plans and intelligence data into two videocassette-sized cartridges and print out the latest sixteen-color charts straight from the computer databases. The crews would load the cartridges into readers in the planes, and the mission would begin. Satellite uplinks to the B-2A bomber would allow crews to receive the latest intelligence data and update their mission computers continuously in-flight, right up to seconds before bomb release.

There were several briefing rooms within the OSS building, where aircrews received pre-mission briefings and received the latest intelligence information. General Wright led Samson, Jamieson, and the stranger to one of the larger briefing rooms and posted a guard inside and out.

His face impassive, his voice even and firm, the stranger got to his feet, faced Jamieson, and began: "What I'm about to tell you is classified top secret, Colonel."

"I figured that much," Jamieson interjected, not quite ready to be intimidated by this guy. "Just tell me who you are and what you want."

"My name is Patrick McLanahan, lieutenant colonel, United States Air Force, retired," the civilian said. "I . . ."

"McLanahan! I recognize that name," Jamieson said. "You were involved in the raid on Chinese forces in the Philippines a few years ago, like I was. The President gave you some award or commendation, but no one knew who the hell you were, where you came from, or what you did."

McLanahan nodded. "That's right, Colonel." Three years earlier, naval forces of the People's Republic of China had attempted an invasion of the Philippines following the U.S. military withdrawal. Jamieson himself had led a force of three B-2A bombers on secret raids against Chinese air defense positions in what had been the first use of the B-2A bomber in combat . . .

. . . at least, the first *known* combat mission for the B-2A. Obviously there had been others . . .

"There was a fourth bomber, Tony," Samson explained, as if he were reading Jamieson's mind, "and it didn't launch from Whiteman. It was in-theater before the Whiteman birds deployed to Guam, doing special reconnaissance and defense-suppression stuff. It—"

"Defense suppression? Reconnaissance? We didn't have any defense-suppression weapons on . . ." He finally stopped and made all the connections. "This guy . . . this guy went in ahead of the Air Battle Force bombers with defense-suppression weapons? I thought we took out the coastal radars and long-range shipborne radars with cruise missiles."

"HAWC was tasked to employ several of its test-bed aircraft over the Philippines and to use some of its other development weapons and space technology to support air operations," McLanahan explained. "The President wasn't sure if he wanted to commit massive U.S. forces against the Chinese, so he sent HAWC units in secretly to soften up the Chinese air defenses, make them more vulnerable to U.S. air attacks. The idea was if they found themselves more open to attack, it might draw them back to the negotiating table faster.''

''Obviously it worked—the Chinese navy backed off in a matter of days,'' Samson said proudly. ''It was a great victory for strategic air power.''

''Well, HAWC can't seem to get out of its own way lately, from what I hear,'' Jamieson said with a sneer. ''I heard rumors of a plane crash, another stolen plane, right?''

''I'm not going to go into details about what happened at HAWC, Colonel,'' McLanahan said, trying not to show the flush of anger and frustration—and the flood of awful memories—that rose up within him.

''But HAWC was closed down, right?'' Jamieson asked.

''Tiger, drop it,'' Samson warned.

''That's all right, General,'' McLanahan interjected. ''Yes, Colonel, HAWC was disbanded. Weapon-test operations went to Eglin Air Force Base; flight-test ops went to Edwards. Most of our more exotic airframes and weapons were either destroyed or placed in secure storage. Some were dispersed to active-duty units after cleaning out the classified stuff. In fact, the 509th was slated to get one of our experimental airframes, Air Vehicle 011. The test crews and technicians were reassigned; the senior staff members were given early retirements, including me.''

''You don't look too retired to me,'' Jamieson said. There was a knock on the door at that moment, and two more Air Force officers were shown inside by uniformed and plainclothes security officers.

''Colonel Jamieson, I didn't come here to be evaluated *by* you: I came here to evaluate *you*,'' McLanahan said. He motioned to the newcomers and said, ''Colonel Jamieson, this is Major General Brien Griffith, commander of Air Force Air Intelligence Agency; Colonel George Dominguez, the chief B-2A maintenance officer assigned to this task force; and Marine Corps Lieutenant Colonel Marcia Preston, my deputy and liaison officer with the office of the White House National Security Advisor. Colonel Dominguez, Colonel Preston, and I are the chief officers of a task force of the Air

Intelligence Agency, code-named Future Flight. We're going to take charge of Air Vehicle 011.'' Jamieson's jaw dropped open in surprise as McLanahan continued, "We are going to use the B-2A to fly covert reconnaissance and defense-suppression missions in support of National Security Agency operations."

"You're CIA?" Jamieson retorted. "You're a goddamned CIA agent?"

"I'm a crewdog, not a CIA agent," McLanahan said.

"You're a contractor, a *former* crewdog working for the CIA," Jamieson corrected him. "You got canned because of some fiasco at HAWC, so now you sell your services to the guys with more money than brains—"

"You don't know shit about me or my mission, Colonel!"

"I don't fucking *care* to know!"

"All right, both of you, shut up," General Samson interjected. "Colonel, you listen to what this man has to say. I'll give you an opportunity to talk. Now you listen."

"Yes, sir," Jamieson relented. "Sorry, but I'm a little confused and a little angry that I'm being 'volunteered' for some illegal ops. So what does this Future Flight want with me?"

"General Griffith is taking command of Air Vehicle 011 and assigning it to Future Flight," McLanahan explained. "My job is to assist Colonel Dominguez in equipping it, then to recruit, train, and fly reconnaissance and defense-suppression missions in the Middle East. I've chosen you to be my aircraft commander."

"*What?*"

"I've been tasked with forming a group that can support secret high-risk deep-strike and reconnaissance operations worldwide. The B-2A stealth bomber is the best strike platform out there; the President and the National Security Council agree. I've been tasked to recruit B-2A flight and support crews from the active-duty ranks, among others, to support group operations."

"You mean, you're forming a secret squadron to fly B-2A bombing missions?" Jamieson asked incredulously.

"That's the most asinine thing I've ever heard. Pardon me, General, but I don't believe what I'm hearing here."

"You go ahead, Tiger," Samson said, fixing McLanahan with a satisfied smile. "You got something to say, say it."

"So what about it, McLanahan?" Jamieson asked, arms crossed on his chest.

McLanahan didn't need to be an expert on body language to know that Jamieson wasn't going to buy any explanations—those crossed arms were like a wall erected against any suggestions. "I don't have to explain anything to you, Colonel. My instructions were to recruit you to fly missions for me and my team and see to the refit of my plane."

"*Your* plane?"

"Air Vehicle 011," McLanahan said. "Colonel Dominguez's techs are modifying it as we speak."

"Modifying it? Are you crazy? That's our best plane!" Jamieson cried. "That bird is tweaked tighter than any other bird Northrop's ever cranked out! It's got the lowest radar cross-section, the best engines, the best hydraulics, the best . . ."

"It should have the best of everything—I spent two years on that bird back in Dreamland, redesigning and improving almost every aspect of that plane's performance," McLanahan said. "Air Vehicle 011 used to be Test Vehicle 002 . . ."

"The one that was supposedly tested to destruction?"

"Yes, sir," McLanahan said. "HAWC rescued it, rebuilt it—we probably spent a quarter of a billion dollars on making it airworthy and upgrading it. I spent plenty of long nights with the engineers to squeeze every knot of performance out of that plane, before the Philippines conflict. That's the plane I flew into combat—twice. It's the only bird in the fleet already modified to carry reconnaissance pods, anti-radar missiles, cruise missiles . . ."

"It can't be the same one," Jamieson pointed out. "AV-011 doesn't have a MILSTD data bus yet for the release systems—it's only hardwired for dumb bombs. It can't carry any 'smart' weapons without a—"

"We didn't use MILSTD buses on test articles at HAWC," McLanahan said. MILSTD, or Military Standard, was the generic term for the standard electrical and electronic circuits and systems developed by the U.S. military for civilian contractors—every weapons design used MILSTD, so the plane could "talk" with the weapons or other systems. "They were too slow, too old, and too easy to jam or disrupt. We borrowed a few commercial-grade data buses from a company in Arkansas—sixty-four-bit logic, clock speed well into triple digits, fiber optics ready, secure and hardened. It's all plumbed for our own data bus—the Sky Masters people I brought with me are going to reinstall the system in about three hours. Ever have any problems with the radar?"

"No," Jamieson replied, "but we haven't had much trouble with any of our radars."

"If your troops opened up the SAR on AV-011, you wouldn't have known what to do with it," McLanahan said proudly. "We modified some of its subsystems for reconnaissance as well as for targeting and terrain avoidance, far beyond Block 30 standards. Range is doubled, resolution tripled, and it has air, sea, and electromagnetic spectrum search as well as ground mapping, terrain following, and targeting—the radar can act as a signal processor for programming anti-radar missiles and for jamming. We were doing terrain-following years before Block 30 was announced."

Now Jamieson was intrigued. He'd always suspected that organizations like HAWC did cool stuff like this, and he had always wanted to be a part of it—but was this the way to do the job? "I still don't buy it, McLanahan," Jamieson said. "You'll be conducting military missions in support of . . . who? The National Security Council? The CIA? The Boy Scouts of America?"

"Listen, Colonel, I was given a task to perform—to get you and Test Vehicle Double-Ought-Two ready to fly, for *me*," McLanahan said impatiently. "We were assured full cooperation by General Samson and General Wright. In exchange, I agreed to tell you a little bit about what's going on. I was not authorized to answer any questions, and I'm sure I've told you far more than I'm supposed to tell. Now you'll agree to cooperate in this project and prepare to—''

"Hey, mister, I don't fly for nobody unless I know the *whole* story," Jamieson said. "I'm not participating in any secret backroom espionage Ollie North–Air America stunt that's gonna get me in front of some congressional committee or a court-martial. You tell me what's going on, and then I'll *think* about helping you.''

McLanahan noticed General Samson's satisfied smile, as if he were saying, "I told you he wouldn't take kindly to threats, boy." "General Samson said that approach wouldn't fly," McLanahan said, "which is why I decided not to take the tough-guy approach with you.''

"You're smarter than you look, McLanahan . . .''

"So I'll just say this, Jamieson." McLanahan stepped closer to Tiger Jamieson and regarded him with an amused stare. "You will agree to accompany me on this mission and cooperate, or . . . I'll get someone *else*.''

"You'll *what?*" Jamieson was as surprised as if he'd just kissed him on the lips. "You can't do that . . .'' Jamieson instantly decided it was a bluff. "Yeah, right, don't make me puke, McLanahan," Jamieson said acidly. He noticed the shit-eating grin on McLanahan's face, then turned to Samson—the big three-star was not smiling. "You're crazy, McLanahan," Jamieson sputtered nervously. "Who else are you going to get?''

"Doesn't matter. I'll find someone.''

"Hey, buster, I trained each and every B-2A crewdog on the entire *planet*," Jamieson said, jabbing a thumb into his own chest to drive the point home, then jabbing a finger at McLanahan, "except maybe you, and I'm not *totally* convinced you're fully qualified. I've forgotten more about the Beak than everyone else put together *knows*. You can't get no one better because there *ain't* nobody better.''

"I'll get Ed Carlisle," McLanahan said calmly. "He's the 715th Bomb Squadron commander, young, lots of hours, bright guy, and the 715th hasn't stood up yet.''

"Carlisle? 'Boondock' Carlisle, the only guy ever to get

lost while flying a B-2A bomber?'' Jamieson exclaimed.
''The guy's got fifty million dollars' worth of navigation gear
sitting in front of him, and he still managed to fly out of the
RED FLAG range during an exercise—he was nearly in Los
Angeles before he figured out where he was. The guy's a
former Navy pilot, for God's sake!''

''He's also written the book on B-2A combat tactics,''
McLanahan repeated, standing up and packing up his briefcase. ''He's a forward thinker, an innovator, a planner—
you're just a throttle jockey. The bottom line, Jamieson, is
this: you're either in with me, or you're out. We're going to
take aerial strike warfare into the next century, *today*, and if
you're not with me, you'll be left behind. So what's it going
to be?''

''Don't fuck with me, McLanahan,'' Jamieson said angrily. He realized that McLanahan was serious—he was *not*
going to select him if he didn't cooperate! ''You're obviously not thinking about the success or failure of your project—you're only out to throw your weight around. This is
some kind of damned power trip for you . . .''

''I don't play games, Colonel,'' McLanahan warned.
''I've been given a job to do, and I'm doing it. I'm wasting
my time talking to you.''

''I think you're both two prima donnas who're only out
to see who can pee the farthest, and I'm sick of it. Button
it, both of you,'' General Samson said angrily, aiming a huge
finger at both McLanahan and Jamieson. ''McLanahan, I
agreed to backstop this project because of one thing: you got
the best players working for you, dedicated guys who won't
let America down no matter how bad the bureaucrats, poli-
ticians, and spooks want to screw things up. Now Carlisle is
damned good, but he's more valuable to me as a staff officer
and squadron commander—''

''Wait a minute, General,'' Jamieson interjected, ''where
does that leave *me*?''

''I said *button it*, Jamieson!'' Samson shouted. ''Tiger,
you're a damned fine officer and a great pilot—but you are
not the last word in strategic aerial strike warfare. This is not

a beauty contest, Jamieson, this is serious business, and I want it done right or not at all.

"Now, McLanahan has proven to me that he can fly the Beak without breaking it, so I'm authorizing the refit of Air Vehicle 011 and the transfer to McLanahan and his Intelligence Support Agency group. In my mind, there's only one B-2A crew member who I trust to do this mission, and it's Tony Jamieson. There's no alternative, no option—it's you two, or nobody. And the choice is still voluntary—Colonel Jamieson can accept or reject the offer, with no *official* consequences." He turned to Jamieson. "Talk to me, Tiger. Now's your chance to talk—do it."

"This is total *bullshit*, sir," Jamieson said angrily. "Since when do we turn tricks for a bunch of spies? If they want a target taken out, why don't they just crank out a warning order and an air tasking order? We'll blow up anything they want. We don't need McLanahan. I've got the best aviators in the world waiting right now to go to war, especially with Iran. Just say the word, and we're locked and loaded."

"Colonel, they've got a ship that carries precision-guided weapons, anti-radar missiles, and reconnaissance gear that even *I've* never heard of," Samson said. "How long would it take you to train a crew to use the equipment?"

"I don't know, sir," Jamieson replied testily. "Maybe a week, maybe a month—maybe it's so automated that it doesn't require any special training, just turn it on and watch it work. Make McLanahan our tech rep or our civilian instructor—but don't make him part of the flight crew."

"Colonel, you know the answer as well as I do, and that ain't it," Samson said, turning toward Jamieson and impaling him with the most evil, deadliest stare he had ever seen. "Face it—this wing is not operational. Your crews and your planes are at least a year, probably two, from going into combat. McLanahan and this Future Flight is the best we've got, and I want you part of it."

Jamieson still didn't like it, still resented the break from his long-established and trusted chain of command. But it was the opportunity of a lifetime. "Who would I report to?"

"Me," McLanahan replied. "The plane, the weapons, the personnel—I own them all, as of right now."

"But you're a civilian," Jamieson protested, though with less vehemence than before. "I don't report to a damned civilian."

"My boss is General Griffith; he reports directly to Philip Freeman, in regards to this mission," McLanahan added. "And Freeman reports to the President."

Jamieson still had not finally agreed, but McLanahan knew he had his man. He turned away and nodded at General Samson. "Thank you for your help, sir. I'll report to you and General Wright on the progress of the work on AV-011 at our noon briefing. Colonel Jamieson, you've got sixty minutes to clear your desk; then we meet back here at eleven hundred hours for an overview on the mods to tail number AV-011. Bring your tech orders and checklists; we'll be updating them with lots of new stuff." To Samson, he asked, "Anything more for me, sir?"

"Just one more thing, Patrick," Samson said. "I've been fighting for exactly this kind of role for our strategic bomber force for years. I never expected a group like the Intelligence Support Agency to be the one sponsoring my program, but it's being done, and that's the important thing. But I've built a career out of seeing that this kind of mission succeeds, and I'll still be fighting even though it's out of my hands once you sign for the plane. This will *not* turn into another Iran-contra debacle, or—and I don't mean this personally—another Brad Elliott operation."

"I do take that personally, General," McLanahan said, his fiery blue eyes narrowing in clear, immediate anger. "Brad Elliott is a good friend of mine."

"Then I apologize," Samson said quickly but, in McLanahan's estimation, not sincerely. "But I reemphasize my point: We go all out, we play to win, but we do this by the book. Agreed?"

The fair-haired, blue-eyed young man was silent for a moment. Samson was just thinking that this was someone he could work with, a fellow crewdog who would work on the "inside," give a fresh perspective to the White House brain trust . . .

. . . until McLanahan's features suddenly turned dark, and his blue eyes narrowed into dark cobalt pits, and he stepped closer to the big three-star general and said in a low voice, "You're right, General: we'll do this by the book—*my* book. This is not an Air Force operation, and this is not *your* operation, it's *my* operation, is that clear?" Samson was too stunned by the guy's sudden change in demeanor to respond.

"General Samson, this team was picked for one reason only: to protect the lives of the agents on the ground that are following the orders of their leaders in the White House," McLanahan went on. "If we fail, men and women die— some of them my friends. If they die, they are not just forgotten—it will be as if they *never existed*. I was given this opportunity to form a team to help them survive, and that's exactly what I'll do."

Jamieson was watching General Samson as the big three-star tightened his jaw muscles, but instead of exploding, he nodded, jabbed a finger in McLanahan's direction, and said calmly, "Fine, *Mr*. McLanahan. You do your thing. When you need Eighth Air Force's help to bail your ass out, just call." He nodded at Jamieson, turned, and walked away.

McLanahan's eyes followed Samson as he departed; then he turned to Jamieson and asked, "Anything to add before we get started, Colonel?"

"Yes: I think you're an asshole, *Mr*. McLanahan," Jamieson replied matter-of-factly.

"Thank you, Colonel," McLanahan said. "It's nice to be working with you, too."

IN THE GULF OF OMAN, ISLAMIC REPUBLIC OF IRAN
19 APRIL 1997, 0612 HOURS LOCAL

It was General Buzhazi's first look at the aircraft carrier *Ayatollah Ruhollah Khomeini* since the thing had been towed into port two years earlier, and frankly, it didn't look that much better—the crews had cleaned it up greatly, but now it seemed more cluttered, more disorganized. Two years earlier it had been in mothballs in a Russian shipyard in Nikolayev, Ukraine, abandoned and heavily cannibalized for scrap steel, wiring, even lightbulbs and screws—it had even been set on fire by shipyard protesters. After being brought to Bandar Abbas, it had been towed down to Chah Bahar and used briefly as a floating prison for work crews, where it had been even further abused by the inmates during that construction "jihad." Then, it had been the biggest, ugliest ship Buzhazi had ever seen in his life—and Iran was paying the People's Republic of China $500,000 per *month* to use it!

Now it had over three dozen combat aircraft on board and three thousand men working on it. Iran was still paying only a half a million dollars a month to use it, but now China was paying Iran millions per month for training, billeting, and installing new, modern equipment.

"Welcome aboard the pride of the Islamic Republic's attack fleet, sir," Pasdaran Major Admiral Akbar Tufayli said effusively, as Buzhazi stepped off the Mil-8 helicopter that had flown Buzhazi from Bandar Abbas out to the carrier. Akbar Tufayli was one of Buzhazi's young, energetic "lions" in the Pasdaran-i-Engelab. When the Pasdaran had been an independent, elite military force during the War of Liberation with Iraq in the 1980s, Buzhazi expected that Tufayli had had grand ideas about his future as a major commander, given his political and family connections, but when the Pasdaran had been integrated into the regular Iranian army, all of Tufayli's chances for greatness had been reduced. Because of this, Tufayli sought out the highest-visibility positions, the ones no one else wanted to touch; then he would lie, cheat, steal, whine, beg, and murder his way to success. He thought of himself as bold and fearless, when in fact he was stupid, rash, and always looking for a scapegoat.

Well, he'd certainly picked the biggest, most highly visible position now: commander of the Middle East's first aircraft carrier. With a new, fat emergency budget following the GCC attack on Abu Musa Island, and lots of favorable attention from the mullahs, Tufayli was in a pretty good position to move up the Pasdaran chain of command. Being the first sometimes got men the glory, but most often it was a no-win situation. Tufayli's future, as they say, was his to destroy.

"Thank you, Admiral," Buzhazi said. "I wanted to see for myself if all is in readiness—including the 'special' shipment . . ."

"It is indeed, sir—I have my best men on it," Tufayli said. "I will show you right away." Dodging running men and jet aircraft engine blast, Tufayli led the way across the steel non-slip deck, over countless hoses, ropes, cables, chain, to the huge island superstructure and the hatch that would take them below. Buzhazi noted with some amusement that the huge white flag with the hammer and sickle of the Soviet navy was still barely visible on the flat side of the superstructure just above the hatch—Allah help us, he thought, if we don't even have enough paint to cover *that* properly, what kind of shape can this tub be in when it comes time to take it into combat?

The aircraft hangar deck was so choked with planes, men, aircraft-moving equipment, tools, spare engines and fabricated steel parts, and thousands of unrecognizable odds and ends that the flag contingent could hardly pass through. Here, Chinese maintenance officers worked side by side with Iranian officers, but only Iranians worked on the planes themselves—the Chinese maintenance workers crowded around and watched. All but two of the *Khomeini*'s twenty-four fighters and all but two of the ship's sixteen helicopters were parked down here, all in various stages of repair—none of them looked as though they could fly right now if needed.

Security was tightened considerably as they moved forward to the double-walled steel bulkhead that separated the hangar from the missile bay forward. The next compartment forward was just as high and wide as the hangar deck, and almost as long, but unlike the hangar deck, there was plenty of room to move around, and it was blissfully quiet, almost somber, as befitting the kind of weapons fitted here. "Here we are, sir," Tufayli announced proudly. "This compartment is the reason that, even without its Sukhoi-33 fighters, the *Khomeini* would still be one of the most devastating warships on the planet."

There before them, in two rows of six, stood the steel launch canisters of the *Khomeini*'s P-700 Granit medium-range attack missiles. Each canister was six feet in diameter and thirty-six feet long, stretching far above, all the way to the flight deck. Cranes and hoisting devices were strung everywhere on deck to move the 11,000-pound missiles in the compartment. "We have no reloads now, sir," Tufayli said. "but when we have enough missiles to allow for reloads, they will be stored in a shielded magazine in the area by the bulkheads fore and aft. All the carrier's missiles, including the P-700s, are transferred through the hatch on the portside—we have the proper equipment to allow under-way missile transfers, although most transfers will probably be at dockside. Missiles are transferred from the magazine via the cranes to be loaded in the launch canisters."

Tufayli motioned to the weapons officer. A warning light began to flash, and one of the launch canisters began to lower itself down to the deck, like a giant sequoia slowly falling to the forest floor. Once on the deck, the top part of the canister swiveled open toward the side of the ship, revealing the missile inside.

It looked like a long, thin, winged needle, with a narrow cylindrical body, short, narrow, steeply angled wings, and small aft wings. A small air intake could be seen on top of the missile. On the aft end, two long cylindrical detachable booster motors were mounted nearly flush with the engine exhaust tailpipe. The missile was a spongy light gray color except for the nose cap, which was hard red plastic, and a section near the front that was outlined in yellow and black.

"The P-700 Granit anti-ship missile, the largest and most powerful anti-ship weapon in the world," Tufayli said proudly. "It can fly over twice the speed of sound to ranges in excess of six hundred kilometers. It is guided by its own inertial navigation computer until within fifty kilometers of its target, when it activates its own onboard radar, locks onto the largest radar target in its line of sight, and guides itself precisely on target. The missile blasts out of the launch canister on those two rocket motors to about Mach one, when the turbojet engine takes over. It flies a powered ballistic path up to thirty thousand meters' altitude until very close to the target, when it executes a high-speed dive—almost impossible to shoot down with any known antiaircraft weapons. This rubbery coating burns off during its flight to protect the guidance and warhead sections.''

"And the warhead?" Buzhazi asked.

Tufayli turned to the weapons officer, who assured him that all nonessential personnel were out of the compartment, then he nodded to Buzhazi. "Yes, sir," he said, "this is what you wanted to see—the NK-55 thermonuclear warhead''— and Tufayli slapped his hand on the yellow-and-black bordered section. The sudden *slap!* sound made them all jump. "Selectable yield from five-hundred-kilogram high explosive to three-hundred-kiloton nuclear. Barometric and radar altimeter fusing, detonating two to three thousand meters above the target, with impact backup.''

"Do you think it is *wise* to slap that warhead like that, Admiral?" Buzhazi asked acidly.

"Perfectly safe, sir," Tufayli the idiot replied, not understanding Buzhazi's meaning at all—Buzhazi meant to ask if he thought it was wise for Tufayli's *career* and continued good *health* to be scaring the chief of staff like that.

"Yes . . . and the other canisters . . . ?"

"Still all one-thousand-kilo high-explosive contact warheads on all the rest," Tufayli replied. "We look forward to getting more warheads such as this one for our other missiles.''

"That appears unlikely," General Buzhazi said, "unless we can convince the President that the Islamic Republic needs more nuclear warheads to counter our enemies in the Persian Gulf region and elsewhere.''

"President Nateq-Nouri would be happier, I think, if Iran had *no* warships or missiles at all," Tufayli said. "This proposal to ban all warships from the Persian Gulf and Gulf of Oman? Ridiculous. You should advise the President that it would be in all of our best interests to continue an aggressive weapons buildup and develop a better indigenous weapons manufacturing—"

"Yes, yes, Admiral, you are correct, of course," Buzhazi interrupted, shutting off this egotistical, strutting popinjay. Any other officer would be immediately dismissed for trying to tell Buzhazi how to do his job—but he needed Tufayli to outfit this battle group and get it out into the Gulf of Oman, where it would have maximum psychological effect against the GCC and the West . . .

or could be best used to spearhead a drive to close off the Persian Gulf, and ultimately propel himself to the presidency.

"How soon can you be on station in the Gulf of Oman, Admiral?" Buzhazi asked, as he headed for the hatch to go back up on deck.

"We have a few minor repairs to conclude, nothing too serious," Tufayli said. "We should be fully operational, with a full complement of aircraft and weapons, in two days."

Judging by the looks of things in the aircraft hangar, Buzhazi thought, this idiot Tufayli wouldn't be ready to fight for two *years*, but he didn't say that. Instead: "Very well, Admiral. Good work. In two days, I will see you on station in the Gulf of Oman, ready to counter any seagoing force which may threaten the sovereignty of the Islamic Republic. Good luck, and good hunting."

"Thank you, *sir!*" Tufayli said in his best academy parade voice. "You will be pleased and gratified by the trust you have placed in me."

Just don't get sunk by your own stupidity, Tufayli, Buzhazi thought. Do what I will tell you to do, *whatever* I tell you to do, and you will do just fine. When it comes time to launch that missile, don't think about it—just do it.

"A mysterious attack on an island in the Persian Gulf that some claim was perpetrated by the United States against Iran; a bold so-called defensive move by Iran's new aircraft carrier battle group into the Gulf of Oman, punctuated by a recent deadly attack against an unarmed rescue vessel; a military arms buildup by Iran, Turkey, and Pakistan unprecedented in two decades," Tim Russert, the host of NBC News' "Meet the Press," began. "In the aftermath of the collapse of the Soviet Union and the glut of high-tech weapons of mass destruction on the world's arms market, the Middle East is becoming an even more dangerous powder keg. Is it ready to explode?

"Joining us to help put all this in perspective is today's very special guest, the Vice President of the United States, Ellen Christine Whiting. Madam Vice President, welcome to 'Meet the Press.' "

"Thank you, Tim." The image of Russert, the "saber-toothed teddy bear," flashed in her mind, almost making her laugh, and instead prompting her famous "ten-million vote" smile.

"Finding the first one hundred days challenging enough, Madam Vice President?" Russert asked.

It was the patented Russert disarming tactic, she thought: hit the guest with his boyish, chubby-faced smile, then the light, easy banter, the brainless question she could answer while half-asleep. He liked to make his guest feel at ease, as if this were going to be an easy Sunday-morning chat, then *whammo* . . . "It's a challenge I've been savoring ever since I was a young campaign volunteer in Frederick, Maryland, Tim," Whiting replied. "But let's get right down to the issues your viewers want to hear about."

"Indeed, let's," Russert said with a smile, but his voice

turned decidedly harder after being upstaged like that. "Let's first talk about what seems to be on everyone's mind, Madam Vice President, and that's the attack on those disputed Iranian islands, allegedly by the Gulf Cooperative Council, the launching of Iran's huge nuclear aircraft carrier battle group, the attack on that rescue vessel with the loss of about a half dozen lives and a dozen still unaccounted for, and the administration's apparent wait-and-see, do-nothing attitude. What's the latest on this, Madam Vice President?"

"Tim, at the risk of sounding like a broken record—and I know most of your audience still remembers what a record is—we're looking into exactly what happened out there in the Persian Gulf," Whiting replied. "The Gulf Cooperative Council is preparing a full report on their attack on Abu Musa Island, but claims it was a defensive, preemptive strike on Iranian offensive missile emplacements that threatened ships in the Persian Gulf oil lanes. Given Iran's huge military buildup on that island since their illegal annexation of those islands in 1992, their explanation seems somewhat justified."

"And Iran's claims that U.S. and Israeli commandos were involved in the raid?"

"Nonsense," the Vice President replied. "This appears to be a GCC operation, and the White House was not notified of the action before or during the attack.

"As far as the salvage ship *Valley Mistress* attack, the U.S. company, Jersey Tech Salvage, out of Elizabeth City, is currently under investigation by the Justice Department for its recent activities," the Vice President continued. "Apparently the ship that was attacked by Iranian aircraft was involved in some . . . illegal operations, taking advantage of its U.S. Naval Reserve Fleet designation. These operations have something to do with shipping weapons, possibly to Iraq, possibly to anti-Iranian government rebels."

"So the reports that this was a spy ship are completely false?"

"The ship may have done some government or defense work in the past," the Vice President acknowledged, "but it was not operating under a government contract when it was

attacked and hadn't received a government contract since the
Gulf War. The President has asked the Justice Department
to thoroughly investigate Jersey Tech Salvage and all other
contract and Naval Reserve Fleet companies to see that
abuses are quickly stopped.''

"But what about the Americans reportedly being held by
the Iranian government?"

"We are not positive whether or not anyone *is* being held,
or if they are American citizens or legal employees of Jersey
Tech Salvage," Whiting replied. "Iran is not cooperating
with anyone, yet they continue to throw unsubstantiated rumors and wild accusations around every time a reporter
cruises near. Now Jersey Tech is not cooperating with State
Department officials because they're under investigation by
the FBI. It's very frustrating.''

"But surely the United States has spies, intelligence personnel, in the area? Can you tell us anything they've
learned?"

"Tim, you know I can't talk about any ongoing intelligence operations," Whiting said seriously, letting her smile
turn stern and disapproving, as if gently scolding him. Her
hope was that the viewers would scold him in their minds
and side with her, not him. "That's strictly off limits. As a
veteran journalist, I'm *very* surprised *you* asked me about
that.''

"I wasn't asking you for specific information or specific
sources, just general information . . ."

"Tim, you know about this—we've talked about it before," the Vice President said, not recalling if they had or
not, but trying to sound as if she were pumping her for information he knew was supposed to be off the record. "We
can't go into specifics, as you very well know. Let me say
this"—a brief pause as the camera moved closer, building a
little anticipation that she was about to reveal a very inside
piece of information—"yes, we have analysts working
'round the clock, studying events all over the world.

"But I have to tell you, Tim, that one source of information we use has been the press, not just in the U.S., but

all over the world, and frankly the media has the intelligence community going around in circles. The intelligence folks follow up every news item, every piece of so-called evidence, reinterview so-called experts, and check every lead, even if it's only to completely discount it. It may be enlightened speculation to the press, but every bit of speculation adds to the confusion.''

''But what about Iran's aggressive military buildup, and their apparent drive to become the warlords of the Islamic world?''

''I don't think the American people want us *speculating* on something as important and as far-reaching as this, Tim,'' Vice President Whiting said. ''The press can afford to speculate all it wants, and when we hear a news item from a supposedly respected and authoritative source, yes, we check it out. In this particular case, the media has been all over the place, so that hasn't been a good source lately. The fact is that Iran is not on the warpath—far from it. In fact, they've proposed a bold new peace initiative that would eliminate the threat of that aircraft carrier from the Persian Gulf. No one seems to believe Iran is serious about that initiative except the President.''

''So the White House is going to do nothing else about Iran, Madam Vice President?'' Russert asked.

''Tim,'' the Vice President responded in an exasperated tone, exaggerated slightly for the viewers at home, ''it sounds like you're suggesting that we send American troops twelve thousand miles from home back to the Persian Gulf to threaten Iran simply because they are choosing to deploy weapon systems such as the *Khomeini* carrier group. It seems as if you're suggesting we do *something* just *because*. I don't agree with that view, Tim.

''I think the American people out there want us to be ready to act if America, her allies, or her vital interests overseas are threatened. Otherwise, I think America wants our military forces to stay home with their families. We will proceed with extreme caution, and trust that diplomacy and common sense will win out.''

THREE

"Let's go into COMBAT mode," McLanahan announced.
"Give me consent."

Tony "Tiger" Jamieson flipped a red-guarded switch near
his left elbow, checked all the rest of his switch configura-
tions, then nestled his butt deeper into his seat and tightened
up his lap belt and shoulder straps. "Consent switch up.
Clear to engage."

McLanahan pressed a small switch light on the eyebrow
panel marked COMBAT, and just that quickly, the checklist
was complete for arming the weapon systems, configuring
the threat warning and defensive systems, and preparing the
computers, aircraft systems, and avionics for combat. Both
men checked the MDUs (Mission Display Units) as the computer reported all of the subsystems' status, and then prepared themselves to penetrate enemy territory. It took only
thirty seconds to confirm that the computer had switched all
systems into COMBAT mode. "We're in COMBAT," Mc-
Lanahan announced.

"Confirmed," Jamieson responded—and that was the

most he had had to do in the past three hours.

There was one thing that Tony Jamieson hated more than anything else, and that was sitting idle. As a B-2A Spirit stealth bomber mission commander, he did anything but— the MC was by far the busiest crewman aboard. Although they still called the B-2A left-seaters the AC—the "aircraft commander,"—he was no longer responsible for the success of a mission, as were other aircraft ACs. The AC's job was to fly the plane and monitor the systems—in the B-2A stealth bomber, it meant to follow the "blue line," the computer-generated course line on his lower-center MDU, and to respond to computer-generated WARNINGS, CAUTIONS, and ALERTS, or WCAs. Any good AC kept up with the mission progress and was ready to complete the mission from the left seat if something catastrophic happened to the mission commander; although the B-2A was ultrareliable and redundant and the AC rarely intervened, he had to be prepared to drop weapons, navigate, communicate, and operate all of the defensive systems from the left seat if necessary.

The damned problem was, Jamieson wasn't prepared to do that in Air Vehicle 011. This fucking plane had been so heavily modified by the plane's current MC, Patrick McLanahan, the now-defunct HAWC, and his Intelligence Support Agency engineering pukes that he didn't recognize a thing on the right side of the plane. From his studies over the past several days, he knew that he could do a number of things from the left seat, but in the heat of battle he seriously doubted if he could fly the plane and run a checklist at the same time. All he'd really done so far on this mission was a preflight, takeoff, two air refuelings—one east of Hawaii, the other north of Diego Garcia in the Indian Ocean—airspeed adjustment to make sure they were on time, and a flip through MDU pages, checking stuff. That, and look out the window as they chased the sunset.

Long flights in the B-2A bomber were comfortable and relatively stress-free, but in this plane it was even more brainless than in the Block 10 and Block 20 planes at Whiteman. Navigation was managed by an automatic navigation system run by dual redundant inertial reference units fed by a Northrop astro-tracker—first developed for the SR-71 Blackbird spy plane—that could track and lock on to stars even in daytime for accurate heading data, and a Global Positioning System satellite navigation system for position and velocity data—the B-2A's navigation accuracy could be measured in a few feet, even without using the radar.

The fuel-management system was automatic and completely hands-free. Jamieson trusted the automatic navigation and flight-control systems enough to take short catnaps throughout the flight when things were quiet (he would never, *ever* admit he trusted McLanahan well enough to watch over things). The seats were big and comfortable—unlike most ACES II ejection seats, which were narrow and hard—and the cockpit was very quiet. You could take the "brain bucket" off, put electronic noise-canceling headsets on, and listen to the single-sideband HF radio channels from all over the world while monitoring the plane and the computers. Station and oxygen checks every thirty minutes, mission status reports by satellite every hour, and sit back and wait for the action to start. The GLAS, or Gust Load Alleviation System—the pointed "beaver tail" on the back of the B-2A's short fuselage—smoothed out the occasional turbulence bumps with ease.

Jamieson didn't know if McLanahan ever napped. Whenever a message came in on the satellite receiver, he was right there to receive it; whenever the computer alerted them to a significant navigation turn point or mission checkpoint, McLanahan was always right there to respond. Jamieson used the chemical toilet mounted behind the mission commander's seat quite often—Jamieson had never subscribed to the "low-residue" diet recommended for long overwater flights and had brought along two big box lunches filled with fried chicken, bologna sandwiches, raw vegetable sticks, and fruit juice, plus sticky buns that could be warmed up in the bomber's microwave oven in the tiny galley beside the entry hatch, and plenty of coffee. On the other hand, McLanahan had brought only Thermos bottles of cold protein drinks, plus coffee and lots of water; even so, he'd cleared off for relief only twice. Had to be the "B-52 bowels," Jamieson decided—since the big B-52s carried only a cramped, uncomfortable, smelly "honey bucket" instead of a real chemical toilet on board, some crew members got accustomed to flying very long missions without using it.

Their flight path took them over the Pacific and Indian oceans, on a less direct course far from the normal transoceanic flight routines in order to avoid visual detection by a passing airliner. Since this was a secret mission, they didn't need to give position reports or talk to anyone when crossing international boundaries. McLanahan activated the radar for a few seconds every time they passed close to land, but mostly kept it in standby to prevent stray electronic emissions from giving away their position. They had no anti-collision lights or transponder beacon codes activated—they were counting on the "big sky" theory to keep them away from other aircraft.

They'd overflown the Hawaiian Islands four hours after takeoff and received their first refueling about 120 miles west of Honolulu. They passed within radar range of Guam, overflew the Philippines, and shot a two-second radar image each of Vietnam, Malaysia, and Thailand—all without one challenge from any nation's air defense systems. They were nothing but ghosts.

Approaching the Maldives in the northern Indian Ocean southwest of Sri Lanka, out of radar range of India's potent Soviet-built air defense network, they refueled from a U.S. Air Force KC-10 Extender tanker. Now, with full tanks and in long-range cruise mode, the real magic of this incredible warplane was obvious: they could just as easily fly all the way back to Hawaii now if they wanted. The computer listed all the alternate and emergency airfields available to them with their full tanks—they ranged as far north as Anchorage, Alaska, as far south as Auckland, New Zealand, or Cape Town, South Africa, even as far west as London! If they included civil airfields on the list, runways big enough for a standard Boeing 727, they had their choice of about three hundred airports within max fuel endurance range.

That kind of power really impressed Tony Jamieson, and it was what drove him to the big bomber game and the B-2A Spirit stealth bomber in particular. The power he commanded was unlike anything ever believed possible. With only two aerial refuelings, he could fly halfway around the world—but more impressive, he could fly over their fleets, their capitals, their cities, their military bases, and he could unleash devastating weapons on all of them, and those on the ground would *not know he was ever there*, even after the missiles hit! He knew the U.S.S. *Abraham Lincoln* aircraft carrier battle group was just a few minutes farther east in the Arabian Sea—they had flown within *sixty miles* of the group—but the greatest seaborne battle group in the world had had no idea they were nearby.

Eleven hours after takeoff, they'd finally come within radar range of the Arabian Peninsula. McLanahan knew there was an American E-3C Airborne Warning and Control System radar plane flying in southeast Saudi Arabia, to observe all air and sea activity near the Iranian aircraft carrier fleet; Saudi Arabia also operated a sophisticated peninsula-wide air defense command-and-control system called Peace Shield Skywatch, which linked seventeen regional radar sites to a central control facility in Riyadh. But the bomber had overflown Saudi Arabia, then southern Iraq, and then down along the Persian Gulf into southern Iran without one squeak of a radar locked onto them or one challenge on any radio frequency, even though there were lots of Saudi, Iranian, and American fighter patrols up that night. Less than sixty miles away was the Strait of Hormuz and the Iranian military city of Bandar Abbas, one of the most heavily defended places on earth. Just 100 miles south of the strait in the Gulf of Oman was the huge *Khomeini* aircraft carrier battle group, challenging all those who tried to enter the Persian Gulf.

"I don't friggin' believe this," Jamieson exclaimed. "We're flying over no-man's land here. One missile jock gets lucky, and he bags himself a B-2A stealth bomber." McLanahan made no reply—probably the first indication that night that he was nervous. The threat indicator on Mc-Lanahan's supercockpit display was showing massive amounts of threats all around them: numerous SA-10 surface-to-air missile sites near the larger cities in western Iran; a cluster of mobile SA-8 missile units and ZSU-23/4 antiaircraft artillery sites in Iraq, all radiating and searching the skies; and a handful of high-performance MiG-29s over Iran, not too far away. They were bracketed by long-range search radars, but not one of them showed any indication of locking a continuous-wave or height-finder signal on them.

Tensions in the region were always high, but since the invasion of Abu Musa Island and the deployment of the *Khomeini* carrier group, it seemed everyone had every man and every piece of military hardware they owned out in the field, ready for battle. "What in hell are we doing up here, McLanahan? This is nuts . . ."

"There's an ISA rescue mission being executed now over Bandar Abbas," McLanahan said—he knew that Jamieson *knew* why they were doing this mission, but he had to get his AC's mind off the threats surrounding them and back on the mission right now. "That salvage vessel that got hit by the Iranians the other day? It was an ISA ship. They took several captives, and the ISA's going to get them back."

"I heard it was a civilian vessel," Jamieson said.

"It was civilian, but it was being used by the Intelligence Support Agency to run surveillance on the *Khomeini* carrier group."

"So *that's* why the Iranians are pissed," Jamieson commented. "Can we blame them?"

"We can and we do," McLanahan said. "They were conducting surveillance only, no closer than thirty miles to any ship, operating over international waters and airspace."

"So when the ragheads said that the crew of the ship shot down two of their fighters . . . *that was true?*"

"In self-defense, and only after the ship was attacked by fighters from the *Khomeini*." McLanahan said. He looked at Jamieson. "Any more questions, Colonel?"

"Touchy, touchy," Jamieson said. "Just wanted to listen

to you explain our mission—I wanted to see how much of a brainless little government robot you've become.''

''Glad to see you're keeping yourself amused,'' McLanahan said. He continued: ''Our intelligence says the crew members that were captured aboard the ship were taken to Suru Prison near Bandar Abbas. The infiltration group is going right into the prison itself. We're going to provide air cover for them.''

''We fly all this way, I expect to blast something apart,'' Jamieson said, with mock grumpiness. ''A carrier would make a mighty big boom, for instance—''

''Stand by, target area's coming up,'' McLanahan interrupted. With little else to do, Jamieson leaned over to watch McLanahan operate his cosmic equipment. It was nothing like any of Whiteman's Block 10 or Block 20 planes—in fact, it was nothing like the future Block 30 planes, not yet in production, or any other concept Jamieson had ever seen for the B-2A.

Dominating the right side of the B-2A's cockpit was a huge rectangular monitor, larger than three normal-sized multifunction displays put together. McLanahan called this his ''supercockpit'' display, and the term fit. Air Vehicle 011 obviously had had this equipment in it earlier, when it had been known as Test Vehicle 002 at Dreamland, because it had taken less than a day for engineers to reinstall this huge screen. Instead of fixed-function buttons around the edges, the display had function buttons on the screen itself that could be selected using the trackball, by touching the big screen, or by using spoken commands. McLanahan was obviously very adept at it—he used all three methods simultaneously, which allowed him to operate his controls with incredible speed.

For most of the flight, the supercockpit display was configured to resemble a normal B-2A right-side cockpit: graphic depictions of three B-2A MDUs, showing aircraft and computer status ''home'' page; the Horizontal Situation Indicator with compass, artificial horizon, and autopilot steering indicators; and navigation displays with present position, heading, ground speed, and time and distance to go to the next way point. Occasionally, McLanahan would call up a graphic typewriter keyboard and use it to compose satellite messages to the National Security Agency—heck, Jamieson mused wryly, McLanahan even used a weird layout, called a Dvorak keyboard, that he operated with speed and precision but would be three times as hard for anyone else to use.

Closer to the target area now, just minutes away from the action, McLanahan still had the three standard MDU displays on the screen, except they were about one-fourth their normal size and relegated to the upper portion of the screen where he and Jamieson could still monitor them. The rest of the screen showed a digital chart of Hormozgan Province of southern Iran, including the Strait of Hormuz and the city of Bandar Abbas. The province was fairly rural and hilly, with only one medium-sized city, one small city, and perhaps two dozen towns and significant villages in the entire 18,000-square-mile area.

The city of Bandar Abbas and its many military bases and military-industrial centers were protected by modern long-range SA-10 Grumble, medium-range Hawk, and short-range antiaircraft missile sites, along with numerous medium- and short-range antiaircraft artillery sites. In addition, the airfield at Bandar Abbas had the largest tactical air force in Iran outside of Tehran, with modern MiG-29, ex–U.S. Air Force F-4 Phantoms, and ex–U.S. Navy Tomcat F-14 fighter interceptors airborne on patrol. Jamieson and McLanahan were flying well inside the normal lethal range of the SA-10 Grumble surface-to-air missile, hoping that their plane's stealth characteristics would keep them safe. Those thick, multilayered defenses would be deadly to any aircraft trying to fly into Bandar Abbas, and only the B-2A Spirit stealth bomber had the capability to approach the area and knock out those missile sites.

Gunnery Sergeant Chris Wohl was making a final preflight inspection of his men's personal equipment, checking for proper survival clothing; although the CV-22 Pave Hammer tilt-rotor aircraft was safe and reliable even in harsh combat conditions, Wohl always made sure that its occupants dressed as if they'd have to walk or swim back to base.

As was typical with Intelligence Support Agency operations, the men wore a mishmash of clothing items, mostly generic military-style clothing intermingled with civilian clothes, with all patches and labels removed and local clothing makers' labels sewn on. Some shaved, although it had to be done without soap or shaving cream to avoid telltale aromas that might attract dogs or guards; most did not shave and had short Middle East–style beards. Hair was usually cut very short and washed with unscented soap, or shaved completely bald. Headgear usually consisted of full-face ski masks or balaclavas worn over an extra watch cap to better protect the ears from frostbite. Most of the unit wore thick woolly mittens over thin wool or cotton glove inserts, with cutouts in the mitten palms to allow them to extend a trigger finger. The men were lightly armed—a few had AK-74 assault rifles, but most others carried small submachine guns like the .45 caliber Uzi or the 9-millimeter MP5. They carried a variety of favorite side arms and two days' worth of patrol supplies—the rest they would gather from the land as they traveled.

All of the men in the unit were experienced professionals, so this was just a quick safety inspection, not an instructional one, but Wohl began a short briefing and a special mission topic during his quick inspections. "Listen up," Wohl said, as he continued his inspections, "just to bring you all up to speed: Our target area tonight is the naval prison medical facility at Suru, a few klicks south of Bandar Abbas. Our route of flight will take us northwest around Abu Musa, feet-dry at Bostaneh Point, twenty klicks west of Bandar-e Lengeh, then terrain-following across the Laristan range, along the Kol River, and touchdown just outside Bandar Abbas.

"This is our second infil into this area, and as you all know, we got creamed over the Tumb Islands the other night, so stay heads-up tonight. We're checking three different exfiltration points tonight outside Bandar Abbas. If our guys are out there, I want them brought back on board the Pave Hammer without a scratch. You all know the code words and code signs. Anyone who doesn't return a recognition signal is a hostile. We're not going in to slaughter civilians, but you will protect your own sorry butts and those of your fellow grunts to the maximum extent.

"Assignments: Monroe will be the wheel; Bennet is port guard; Reid's on starboard guard; I'll be the ramp guard. Guards, remember, don't go out too far or your gunners watching your back will lose sight of you, and he's likely to blow your ass away. Guards, use your recognition signals; flash them whenever you see the aircraft, since a gunner probably has you in his sights and his finger's tightening on the trigger. Schiff is tail gunner, Morgan is port gunner; Andrews, you're starboard gunner. Gunners, radio out for signals before you open fire, and wait to get a return signal—but if you don't get one, shoot first, then call out your hostile's position. You don't get extra credit for shooting off a whole can of ammo—make your shots count. Our call sign tonight is 'Japan.'

"You got the standard escape-and-evasion plan memorized, I hope, but the basic plan is head west and stay away from everyone and everything. You should all know where our backup and emergency pickup points are; I'm going to ask all of you to point them out for me on your map on the way out, and if you miss even one, you'll be on KP for a week.

"I remind you that we're going into the area with the

Iranian military on high alert, which means a very good likelihood we could see action and might even be knocked down,'' Wohl continued, scanning each of his men's eyes to try to gauge their readiness for this mission. ''If we're shot down, remember to evacuate out the back of the aircraft, not the sides. Grab a buddy or a crewman or extra gear, but don't waste time evacuating the aircraft if things are going to shit. Get as far away from the crash site as possible after the crash. Most guys who get captured after a force-down are captured near their aircraft within ten minutes, so the farther you can get away from your force-down point in the first ten minutes, the better.

''Move only at night, avoid all contact with civilization as much as you can, and move during daytime only long enough to get oriented, then get back into deep hiding,'' Wohl went on. ''Make your way to a pickup point, but stay away from roads, railroads, rivers, or streams—that's where the bad guys will be looking for you. Trying to blend in with the locals is a Hollywood stunt, not a valid escape-and-evasion technique. Don't make contact with anyone unless you're hurt, but I goddamn guarantee that you better be hurting *real* bad, because if you ask someone for help you'll likely be captured and tortured and then the pain will be unlike anything you've *ever* experienced.

''When you get to a pickup point, don't just march right into it—take a few hours and check it out first. If you're able, backtrack and check your rear—we don't want the ragheads setting up any ambushes for your rescuers. And remember to preserve the pickup points for other unlucky saps who might need it in the future. Don't just bolt out of a spiderhole when you see the angel coming down for you— if the bad guys aren't on your tail, police your area and recamouflage everything before the pickup to make it tougher for the ragheads to find the hiding spots. Okay. What are your questions for me?'' No responses.

''Good. I got one more thing to say,'' Wohl went on. ''We got three guys hurt on the last sortie, including the FNG, Major Briggs. They're all right, but they'll be out of action for a few weeks. I wanted to remind all you swinging dicks that sometimes no matter how much you shake your snake, that last drop can still roll down your pants. The latest prelaunch intel had the antiaircraft stuff moved off the Tumb Islands onto Abu Musa; we didn't know they had put more stuff on Lesser Tumbs until it was too late. Shame on us. Shit happens. Forget about the last mission and concentrate on this one. Don't let it get you down. We're here to find Colonel White and our shipmates and bring 'em back alive.

"We got some help tonight—apparently some other ISA cell is going to stir up some shit for us tonight," Wohl said. "Maybe it'll keep the ragheads off balance, maybe it won't. Forget about them and concentrate on your work tonight. Our job is to go in, check the escape-and-evasion areas, rescue anyone that might be out there waiting for us, and come back alive. Let's get loaded up."

Wohl had picked the men personally for this patrol, so he really was not looking into each individual's face as he went down the line just before boarding the chopper—he could usually recognize each man by his build or choice of weapons or voice or attitude. He came to the last and most senior man in his squad, the "wheel," who would coordinate the flight crew's activities with the ground team. Monroe had his balaclava on, shielding his face against the freezer-like chill of the hangar. "Ready to do it tonight, Monroe?" he asked him. No response, just a thumbs-up and a rather nervous shuffling of the feet. Wohl looked and saw the man's right finger extended out of his mitten, covering the trigger guard of his suppressed IAI Uzi .45 submachine gun—this bad boy, he thought, was ready to go . . .

. . . but unfortunately, he wasn't *going* to go! "You are one stupid son of a bitch, Briggs," Gunnery Sergeant Chris Wohl said in a low voice. "You are just too stupid for words. Did you really think I wasn't going to notice you on my aircraft?"

Hal Briggs pulled off his balaclava. "How'd you know it was me, Gunny? You didn't even look at my face or my eyes."

"You're the only one who always sticks his trigger finger outside your mitten and covers the trigger guard when he gets nervous," Wohl said. "I noticed it the first mission we flew. Now, what the hell are you doing out here? I thought the flight doc ordered another week of bed rest."

"I'm sick of bed rest," Briggs said. "I'm fine. I'm ready to go."

"The doc didn't sign you off yet."

"Fuck the flight surgeon, Gunny," Briggs said. "I'm ready to go on this patrol—hell, I've *got* to go on this patrol or I'll go nuts."

"You were ordered to stay in bed, sir," Wohl said. "The doc ordered it, and I ordered it. Sick or not, sir, I'm going to kick your ass if you don't start obeying orders."

"You can do an operational evaluation on me," Briggs suggested. "Plenty of room in the Pave Hammer. Besides, Monroe can't fly tonight—he's got a cold or a sinus infection or something."

"Bullshit," Wohl said. "Stop treating me like your senile old aunt baby-sitting you when you want to sneak out to the drive-in, Briggs. You wanna override doctor's orders and go on a patrol, just come out and say it."

"I'm saying it already, Wohl," Briggs said. "I want to go."

"Disapproved," Wohl said quickly. "You look OK to me, but I did talk to the doc today—he said he found blood on a towel in your room. You been hiding shit from the flight doc, Hal?"

"Dr. Sabin checks the towels in my damned room?" Briggs exclaimed angrily. "I want him to stay the hell out of my room."

"Did you or didn't you?"

Briggs didn't reply. Instead, he asked, "How do *you* feel, Gunny?"

"I feel fine."

"You sure?"

"Stick your tongue up my ass and take my temperature if

you really care,'' the Marine said irritably. ''Otherwise, get out of my face.''

''Why didn't you get hit, Wohl? We were standing side by side, less than an arm's length away from each other. Three guys went down when that antiaircraft artillery site opened up on us—two guys on one side of you, then me on the other side of you. You're sitting in the middle and don't get a scratch. Why the hell not?''

''Because a Marine sucks in a triple-A and spits out fire, Briggs,'' Wohl said with a perfectly serious expression. ''We eat barbed wire and piss napalm.''

''Yeah, yeah, hoo-rah and all that jarhead shit.''

''It ain't jarhead shit, Briggs,'' Wohl said earnestly. ''I don't know why I didn't get hit, Briggs. Maybe I'll get it on this trip—would that make you happy, Briggs?''

''C'mon, Gunny, I didn't mean it that way. I'm just bored and ready to get my ass in the air again, and I can't believe I got hit by the golden BB. I'm too young and too good-looking to get nailed by a triple-A site older than my uncle. . . .''

''I'll tell you what I believe, Briggs: I truly believe I won't get hit because I'm a U.S. Marine. I truly believe I'm too tough and too strong and too dumb to get hit by a little Iranian Zeus-23/4.''

''Give me a break, Chris . . .''

''I'm serious as a stock market crash, Hal,'' Wohl said. ''You see, you're smart, a *real* college boy, not a correspondence-course college boy like me. You knew it was a ZSU-23/4, knew about how deadly it is to low-flying aircraft that stray within lethal range . . . hell, you probably know its rate of fire, its reliability, its crew complement, its maintenance procedures.''

''Yeah, I do. So?''

''So I'm not being critical, Briggs, but maybe you got tagged because you *believed* you'd get tagged. You thought it was perfectly logical and understandable and proper that if we come across a Zeus-23 that's not supposed to be there, you'd get hit by a ricochet. I, on the other hand, believe that only lily-livered pussy-whipped, pudd-pounding, tired-ass, numb-nut legs—or any *officer*—are weak enough to be put down by something as low-tech as a Zeus-23.''

''What about Barnes and Halmar?''

''They got it because they were sitting next to *you*.''

''Gimme a break, Gunny.''

''The point is, Briggs, I did not *allow* myself to die. I'd allow myself to die rescuing our shipmates, die with one or two fellow buddies on my shoulders, but not die by a lousy piece-of-shit Iranian ack-ack gun. And if it doesn't kill me, it makes me stronger.'' Wohl paused, shrugged, then added with a faint smile, ''Or it could've been the nonstop praying I'd been doing, and the extra thin-line Kevlar jacket I was wearing that night.

''Now, stop screwing around and go get Monroe out here so we can get this show on the road. You want to help, go monitor the situation display in the command center. Just don't let the flight doc see you.''

Monroe wasn't too far away—he'd told Briggs that it would never work, so he'd been standing by, ready to go—and soon he was aboard the CV-22 Pave Hammer tilt-rotor and the rescue mission was under way. Again, Briggs was left behind.

Dammit, he thought, it wasn't fair! Just because he didn't snarl and growl like a bitch in heat like all these other borrowed Marines, he had to sit on his ass and get his room searched by the flight surgeon without his knowledge!

After returning his prized Uzi and its spare magazines to the armory, Briggs checked in with the command center. Nothing would be happening for at least twenty-five minutes until the CV-22 went feet-dry. Last mission, they hadn't made it that far—an antiaircraft artillery site on Tumb as Sughrd, or Lesser Tumb Island, had opened fire on them as they passed nearby, and they'd been hit by a half-second burst. The CV-22 had sustained minor damage; three crewmen had been wounded by flying shrapnel, including Briggs.

This time, with a little luck, Madcap Magician was going all the way into the claws of the beast: Bandar Abbas, the largest military complex in Iran and one of the largest in the Middle East. Intelligence had suggested that the survivors of the *Valley Mistress* might have been taken to Suru prison. They were going to check out the prison's security and try to find any weaknesses, in case they decided they had to break in; then they would check the safe areas.

Like all areas of every country in which they operated, Madcap Magician had a series of safe areas and escape-and-evasion plans formulated that every crewman was required to memorize before each mission. During the infiltration, every crew member was kept apprised of the team's present position, their heading, and speed, so in case the aircraft was forced down, every man knew where he was and which way to proceed to the nearest safe area. At specific times for each area, a survivor would make his way as carefully as he could to a contact point, where—with a little luck—a rescuer would be there to find him.

But every day that went by lessened the chance of a successful rescue. The Iranian army, the Revolutionary Guards, reserves, and Basij militias were everywhere, near every city, town, highway, road, railroad, bridge, and river, looking for infiltrators. A guy on the run couldn't hold up for very long even if his health was perfect—if he was injured, as a result of an escape or fight, he'd be in bad shape.

He'd lost Colonel Paul White and ten of his best men, and he hadn't even gotten a chance to lead them yet. . . .

1 LAFAYETTE SQUARE, WASHINGTON, D.C.
THAT SAME TIME

The gentleman being escorted by the tuxedo-dressed bellman through the cherry-paneled corridors of the luxurious Hay-Adams Hotel in Washington already had his jolly, glad-handed face on when he entered the small, secluded dining room. His contact and another man, probably an assistant or aide, were already waiting for him. The double doors were closed behind him; the warm room enveloped him like a calfskin glove. Nothing like this in Tehran these days, he thought. "Ah, my friend Robert, it is good to be here with . . ." But his politically practiced visage changed abruptly when the man in the room turned to him.

"Mr. Sahin, please come in," Philip Freeman, the President's National Security Advisor, said. It was obvious that his presence was a complete shock to Sahin. He extended a hand in greeting, but Philip Freeman did not accept it. Then Sahin looked for a chair and did not find one. It was obvious this was not going to be a civil sociable meeting.

Businessman and professor Tahir Sahin was one of a rare and unusual breed, vital to governments all over the world— a well-spoken, well-traveled, educated man welcomed and employed by all sides of a dispute. A son of a wealthy landowner in eastern Turkey, Sahin's Muslim family had escorted and guarded the Ayatollah Khomeini during his exile to Iraq via Turkey in 1963. A young Tahir Sahin had then accompanied Khomeini to the holy Shi'ite city of Najaf in Iraq and spent several years with him, acting as interpreter and bodyguard.

Sahin had seen firsthand the transformation of Khomeini and his vision of a worldwide Islamic revolution, and in time Sahin had become infused with much of the same burning passion as Khomeini. When Khomeini had been deported from Iraq and moved to France in 1978, Sahin had returned to his native land and become instrumental in spreading the word about Khomeini's impending revolution to Turkey and everywhere else he traveled in his business. When Khomeini had made his triumphant return to Iran and established his Islamic republic, Sahin had been an honored guest many times. With his Turkish passport and Iranian identity papers, signed by Khomeini himself, Sahin could travel anywhere in the world with complete safety and security.

It was after the closing of all diplomatic relations between the United States and Iran following the U.S. embassy siege in 1979 that Tahir Sahin's real worth had stood out. Sahin had been part of the secret "arms for hostages" deals with

the United States to the benefit of the Iranians, but had also
helped secure the release of British, French, Italian, and
American hostages held captive by pro-Iranian radicals in
Lebanon. Although not credentialed with the U.S. State Department or recognized professionally by any country, Sahin
had been acting as an unofficial messenger between the two
governments, keeping the lines of communication open between two countries who did not have embassies in each
other's country.

The downside to having a pro-Iranian, pro-Islamic fundamentalist man like Sahin roaming freely around Washington was that he was reportedly a deputy director of an
organization called the Niru-ye Entezami-e Johuriye, or Institute of Strategic Security Studies. The ISSS was known as
an Iranian defense "think tank," which advised rich Middle
East countries on emerging defense technology and strategies; but it was also widely believed to be an international
intelligence front operation, designed to feed information
through diplomatic channels back to Iran. If Sahin hadn't
been funneling messages back and forth between Washington
and Tehran, he'd have been kicked out of the United States
years ago as a suspected spy.

It was painful for Freeman to be meeting a likely Iranian
spy like this, but there was no better way to impress upon
Iran the seriousness of the situation that was before them
now.

Tahir Sahin put his glad-happy face back on and nodded
enthusiastically at his hosts. "It is indeed an unexpected
honor to be here with you, General."

"I have a simple message for President Nateq-Nouri and
General Buzhazi," Freeman interrupted. "The President of
the United States views the attack on the civilian salvage
vessel *Valley Mistress* by the *Khomeini* carrier battle group
and the capture of its crew as an act of aggression against
the United States. The President is demanding their return
immediately."

"Please, General Freeman, please," Sahin interrupted,
holding up his hands as if in surrender, "but I am nothing

but a small businessman. I am not an ambassador or an emissary of any country . . ."

"And this is not a diplomatic visit," Freeman interjected. "I'm asking you to deliver a message, Mr. Sahin—if you can do it, you'll be providing a great service for both the United States and the Islamic Republic of Iran. If you can't deliver the message, then we've all wasted our time here."

Sahin nodded thoughtfully. "I will of course endeavor to do as you wish, General Freeman," Sahin said. "I hope I have the good fortune to have the opportunity to speak with Minister Velayati or Minister Foruzandeh."

"See to it that this message is delivered immediately, Mr. Sahin," Freeman said. "We are going to play a little game with the Islamic Republic of Iran."

"A game, General?"

"Yes, Mr. Sahin. Every day that an American is held captive by Iran, or his whereabouts are not known, the United States will attack a military target inside Iran. You will not know where, or when, or how, only that it will happen. The United States will not publicize this; no public comments will be made. The targets will be vital military installations and command-and-control targets. The goal of the strikes will be gradually to weaken Iran's air defense, command, mobility, and long-range strike capability so that if war does break out, Iran will have difficulty defending its borders from attack or will find its forces substantially weakened or unable to mobilize."

Tahir Sahin laughed a hesitant, nervous laugh. "This . . . this is very odd, General Freeman," he said. "This . . . this is tantamount to terrorism!"

"Call it what you will," Freeman said. "If the captives are not released, Iran will suffer the consequences."

"Does this concern the proposal by the Islamic Republic to exclude all foreign warships from the Persian Gulf?" Sahin asked. "Is this an attempt to induce Iran to capitulate?"

"This has nothing to do with the Persian Gulf," Freeman said. "In fact, the President is seriously considering that proposal, and he may agree to it with some modifications. This only concerns the thirteen men missing from the salvage vessel *Valley Mistress*. The President wants those men immediately released unharmed and unmolested in any way—no questioning, no interrogation, no coercion.''

Sahin shook his head, his eyes blankly scanning the room in complete surprise. ''This is a very unexpectedly belligerent and arrogant stance the President is taking, General Freeman,'' he said. ''Is the President truly in control, or is it possible that the military has taken over the White House?''

''The President is in control, I assure you,'' Freeman replied. ''If *I* were in control, I'd have destroyed all of Iran's military bases one by one, sent Iran's carrier to the bottom of the Gulf of Oman, and had U.S. troops occupy Hormozgan Province by now.''

''Do you believe such a belligerent, intractable attitude will help improve relations with Iran or assist in negotiations, General?''

''Perhaps you don't understand, Mr. Sahin: the United States is not negotiating anything at this time,'' Freeman said, turning to leave. ''The attacks will commence and will continue until our demands are met. The President may open negotiations for the removal of land-attack warships from the Persian Gulf, but as for the topic of the survivors of the *Valley Mistress*, we will not negotiate. The attacks will commence and will continue until our demands are met. Good day, Mr. Sahin.''

''This is . . . this is highly irregular!'' Sahin blurted out as Freeman reached the door. ''I must take with me some proof of this discussion, some sign that you and I spoke—''

''The only proof you need is the news that a military target inside Iran has been destroyed,'' Freeman said. He checked his Ulysses-Nardin multi-zone watch and added, ''In fact, the first attack should be happening at any moment. It will be in retaliation for the illegal and unwarranted attack on the *Valley Mistress*. Good day to you, Mr. Sahin.''

ABOARD THE B-2A SPIRIT STEALTH BOMBER AV-011,
OVER IRAN
THAT SAME TIME

McLanahan finished typing in commands on the supercockpit display. "SAR configured," he announced. "No terrain returns, no large cultural returns, moving-target mode enabled." He turned to Jamieson: "Ready, AC?"

"I was born ready, MC," Jamieson said gruffly. "Take the shot."

"Here we go," McLanahan said easily, "radar enabled . . . radar transmitting . . ." then, just two seconds later, he announced, "radar's in standby."

"Two seconds is plenty long for the ragheads to track us, MC," Jamieson pointed out angrily. "A standard SAR shot is one second *max*, dammit."

That point was most important while they were so close, because in order to transmit the synthetic aperture radar, COMBAT mode was temporarily suspended. Part of going into COMBAT mode was the activation of the B-2A stealth bomber's AN/VUQ-13 BEADS system, the Bomber Electronic Attenuation Defensive System, or the "cloaking device." BEADS electrified the outer surface of the B-2A bomber and the cockpit windshield with positive ions, in effect turning the aircraft into a giant electron magnet.

With the "cloaking device" activated, very little electromagnetic energy could penetrate the positron field—electrons were "sucked" into the field and dissipated behind the aircraft; similarly, electromagnetic energy radiated *from* the bomber was also absorbed. Along with the radar-absorbing materials in the bomber's non-metallic composite surface and the low reflective makeup of the composite structure, BEADS reduced the bomber's radar cross-section by 60 to 70 percent, depending on the range and power of the radar. The remaining 40 percent of the reflected radar energy was diverted in different directions by the unique shape of the bomber itself. The end result: less than 1 percent of the radar energy of even the most powerful radars in the world returned to its sender after hitting the B-2A Spirit stealth bomber.

The drawback to BEADS was that if electronic emissions couldn't go in, they also couldn't go out. In COMBAT mode, the crew couldn't transmit on the radios, couldn't receive radio or satellite messages or navigation signals, couldn't use the MAWS defensive missile tracking system, and could not use the synthetic aperture radar. The "cloaking device" automatically deactivated itself when the crew took an SAR shot or bypassed the safety interlocks to use the radios or get a navigation fix while in COMBAT mode. Even though a typical SAR shot was very short, in that short time frame the B-2A bomber's radar cross-section grew several times larger than normal—very dangerous when so close to enemy air defenses.

To Jamieson, activating the SAR and shutting off BEADS was like dipping his dick into a tank filled with piranhas—the less time in there, the better. He might not get attacked the moment he stuck it in, but the longer it stayed in there, the better his chances of getting it bitten off; and sure as hell, the piranhas would be ready and waiting for the *next* time he dipped it in.

"This isn't a standard SAR shot, AC," McLanahan said. "Besides, the SAR computer decides how long the exposure will be, based on the mode programmed, the environmental conditions, the signal strength—I don't control it . . . stand by, second shot coming up . . . ready . . . now . . . radar in standby, SAR routine ended, radar disenabled."

"A second shot? What in hell is that for? Jesus, McLanahan, that thing's going to kill us!"

"Threat scope's clear, AC."

"Lucky for us," groused Jamieson. "What in hell was the second shot for?"

"Watch." Jamieson watched the big supercockpit screen—and was amazed at what he saw. Overlaid on the chart of

Hormozgan Province was a radar picture filled with tiny blips. "Here's all the small cultural returns we picked up," McLanahan explained. "Since an SA-10 or Hawk on its transporter-erector-launcher might be stationary or moving, we've got to check both, so all are displayed. I simply instruct the computer to search for returns that match the size of a Grumble or Hawk TEL, either in road-march configuration or in launch position . . . now." In a matter of seconds, all but a handful of the dots disappeared. There were about two dozen blips remaining.

"We've got a few, but not as many as before. From here, we can just pick one, and we check it out. The SAR will not pick up decoys unless they're close to the same mass as a real missile, so inflatable decoys or decoys made out of wood won't show. But before we search, I'll be looking for a few other items. According to our intel guys, a presurveyed launch point will have a fence surrounding it. I'll tell the computer to pick out any returns that look like that."

"This radar will pick up something as small as a *fence*?"

"With ease," McLanahan said. Sure enough, several such objects were selected. McLanahan rolled a cursor over one blip that was sitting a few hundred yards off a small secondary highway, then entered in some voice commands. The blip began to grow in size until it filled the supercockpit screen—and to Jamieson's amazement, he could easily identify the return. "Holy shit, it looks like a cattle car!"

"I'd say that's what it is, too," McLanahan agreed. It was easy to do—the image was as sharp and clear as a black-and-white photo in daytime. He entered a command and the image disappeared and switched to the next blip. After automatically enlarging again, they finally found their quarry. "We got one."

Jamieson was astounded. There it was, a nearly photographic radar picture of an SA-10 Grumble surface-to-air missile on its transporter-erector-launcher, similar in size and appearance to a Patriot missile system. They could clearly see every detail—its fins, the shape of its nose cone, even that the driver's side door of the tractor truck pulling the

TEL had been left open. "This is unbelievable!" he exclaimed. "We goddamn found a mobile SA-10 missile deployed in the field!"

McLanahan was typing commands into his supercockpit terminal. "And now NSA and the Intelligence Support Agency know where it is, too," he said. "We're flight-planned to be in the orbit for the next fifteen minutes—let's see if we can find some more."

For the next fifteen minutes, McLanahan systematically checked the blips on the supercockpit display, changing the search parameters after every search—blips on the road, blips on the rail lines, blips inside fences, blips out in the open, blips moving, blips not moving—then went back, rechecked the original size parameters, expanded them out slightly to get more returns, then searched again. In fifteen minutes, they had charted six new air defense missile sites near Bandar Abbas—including several decoys set up close to the real missile sites. The Iranians had set up a piece of steel sewer pipe on a flatbed tractor-trailer, very close to the size and appearance of the real SA-10 Grumble.

"Threat scope's clear," McLanahan said. "Search radars only. Ready to stir up some dirt?"

"Go for it," Jamieson said.

"Stand by for bomb doors," McLanahan said. "Doors coming open . . . now . . ." Jamieson and McLanahan felt a rumble in the B-2A bomber's normally rock-solid fuselage as the four massive "barn door" bomb doors opened. Just as the doors opened, a "10" symbol with a diamond symbol around it appeared, and they heard a low, slow *"Deedle . . . deedle . . . deedle . . ."* sound in their headphones. "SA-10 searching . . ."

"C'mon dammit," Jamieson muttered, "launch, son of a bitch, *launch!*" The B-2A bomber was now at its most vulnerable position: with its bomb-bay doors open, its radar cross-section was just as large as any major aircraft. And as it launched missiles, the missile's track through the sky would point directly back at the retreating B-2A, showing the way for enemy gunners to take a shot and bag a billion-dollar bomber.

"Launcher rotation completed, stand by for missile launch . . . missile one away . . . two away . . ." Jamieson expected to feel a lurch or a bump or something as the 4,000-pound missiles left the plane, but there was nothing, except for the graphic depictions of shapes leaving the little bomb-bay drawing on his MDU.

The diamond around the "10" symbol on the threat scope began to blink, and they heard a higher-pitched, faster *deed-ledeedledeedle* warning sound. "Height-finder active!" McLanahan shouted. He put his fingers on the supercockpit screen on the buttons marked MAWS and ECM. "Launchers rotating . . . stand by . . . three away . . . four . . . five . . . six missiles away . . . bomb doors moving . . . bomb doors closed. . . ."

Just then, both the diamond and the "10" symbol began blinking, and a computer-synthesized voice announced, "MISSILE LAUNCH . . . MISSILE LAUNCH . . . McLanahan immediately hit the MAWS and ECM buttons. The Missile Approach and Warning System was an active missile defense system on the B-2A bomber designed to actually protect the bomber, not just jam a missile's tracking systems. As soon as the SA-10 missile launch was detected, a small radar dome extended from a compartment near the B-2A bomber's tail, the radar slaved itself to the azimuth of the SA-10 missile site, and the radar began scanning the sky for the missile itself.

The MAWS's ALQ-199 HAVE GLANCE radar tracked it, displayed its position to the crew on the pilot's main screen, and a computer suggested which way to turn to evade it by making corrections to the terrain-following autopilot. The computer also ejected bundles of chaff—thin slivers of metal that would create huge radar-reflective clouds in the sky and hopefully decoy the Hawk radar—and also sequenced the ECM (electronic countermeasures) track breakers' jamming signals to allow computer-controlled jammer-free "corridors" that would "point the way" for the

Grumble's radar to lock on to the cloud of chaff.

As the SA-10 missile rose through the sky toward the B-2A bomber, the next and most high-tech aspect of the MAWS system activated—MAWS shot high-powered laser beams at the approaching missile, blinding its seeker head and overheating the missile's guidance electronics. In less than three seconds, the Grumble was deaf and blind, flew harmlessly behind the B-2A, and then self-destructed as it began its death plunge toward the Persian Gulf.

"Good connectivity on all missiles," McLanahan reported. "Good signal . . . I've got flight-control surface deployment on all missiles, good guidance. They're on their way."

In thirty seconds, the first attack was over—and Jamieson realized he hadn't done a thing, hadn't even touched the throttles, and his right hand was resting only lightly on the control stick. They'd needed no evasive maneuvers, no threading their way around terrain trying to hug the ground to hide from enemy radar, no coordinated defensive maneuvers.

It was so sterile, so robotic—almost inhuman. Shadows of steel, death from nowhere, from everywhere . . .

But it didn't stay quiet for long. Seconds later, the search-radar signal had changed, and Jamieson saw a bright yellow arc on the threat scope, aimed very close to the B-2A, slowly becoming narrower and narrower until it was a line. Fortunately, the line also began to offset behind the center of the scope, meaning that it was not locked onto the B-2A. "Height finder active again," McLanahan said. "Looks like they're locked on to one of the JSOWs. JSOWs have responded . . . looks like missile number two is tracking."

The missiles McLanahan and Jamieson released were called AGM-154 Joint Standoff Weapons, or JSOWs. They were small, lifting-body cruise missiles that could be fitted with a variety of warheads, payloads, avionics, sensors, guidance packages, or propulsion units, so they could mix a number of these missiles on the bomber and perform many different missions. These JSOWs had special Disruptor payloads on board called "screamers" that would transmit high-frequency, high-powered jamming signals across the entire frequency spectrum and completely overload any antenna system within range. The JSOW missiles would orbit over the air defense missile and radar sites, broadcasting high-intensity "screamer" signals, blanking out radar scopes and overloading radio networks for as long as sixty-minutes—plenty of time for the Intelligence Support Agency teams to enter the area.

The B-2A crew again heard a slow, low pitched *Deedle . . . deedle . . . deedle . . .* warning tone in their headsets, and saw the "10" symbol with a diamond around it: "SA-10 acquisition radar at Bandar Abbas . . . cruise missiles one and three locked on . . ." As each antiaircraft missile system came up, the JSOW missile's seeker head would lock on, plot the emitter's location, and reprogram its internal auto-pilot to fly to that point and destroy the radar. Another warning tone, this time with an "H" symbol: "Hawk system acquisition radar . . . missile four tracking . . . looks like the Iranians already got another Hawk set up on Abu Musa Island. They didn't waste any time."

"Forget the commentary, McLanahan," Jamieson said. "Just make sure none of those sites locks on to *us.*"

"Our track breakers are in standby, search radars only sweeping us," McLanahan reported. He typed on his keyboard, and the bomber turned slightly south. "I'm heading a bit more to the right to stay away from that Hawk on Abu Musa," McLanahan said. "If they sneaked an SA-10 on that island, too, I want to stay far away from it. The screamers should activate in a few seconds."

The effect was frightening and surprising at the same time—as if on cue, every Iranian air defense site within fifty miles opened fire. Eight SA-10, four Hawk, at least a dozen Rapier, and a handful of ZSU-23/4 and ZSU-57/2 sites appeared to be firing guns or launching missiles.

"Jesus H. Christ, I don't believe it!" Jamieson muttered. Out the cockpit windows, McLanahan and Jamieson could see the sky below ablaze with missiles flying aimlessly through the sky, and boiling red and yellow from the clouds of antiaircraft artillery shells sweeping the skies. The "screamers" had activated all of the Iranian air defense site's attack response systems, and the sites had reacted as if a massive air invasion were under way. In seconds, every missile on its launcher was in the sky, and every shell had been fired . . . and they had hit nothing but empty air. Several warships docked at Bandar Abbas had also opened fire, and they even detected an anti-ship missile launch from one of the docked ships—where that missile was headed, McLanahan had no idea. Jamieson could not believe the concentration of antiaircraft systems active right now: they were flying less than forty miles south of that massive concentration of weaponry.

The scene looked much the same ahead as they continued eastward toward the *Khomeini* battle group in the Gulf of Oman—the carrier was lit up like a Christmas tree with threat radars, and the destroyer *Zhanjiang*, several miles farther southeast, was radiating as well. The threat scope clearly outlined the defensive box around the carrier: smaller vessels with short-range antiaircraft systems were surrounding the carrier, and the long-range systems of the larger escorts overlapped those of the carrier itself, forming several layers of antiaircraft protection for Iran's prized possession.

"We've got four 'screamer' JSOW missiles programmed for the *Khomeini* group, with two in reserve," McLanahan summarized. "I'm getting ready for the SAR exposure."

Jamieson was still in shock at the reaction from the Disruptor flyover. "I can't believe it—they all opened up, all at once . . . it'll take them two days to rearm those air defense sites!"

"Maybe not two days," McLanahan said, "but they'll have to reload all those sites, maybe replace some overheated gun barrels and burned-out launchers. But just about the time they're ready to fire again, the 'screamers' will reactivate, and maybe they'll launch against them again and waste some more missiles and ammunition. Eventually the JSOWs will get hit or run out of fuel and crash somewhere, but we hope not before our guys get in, poke around, and get out again. And if we're lucky, the 'screamers' caused enough overload damage to take out a few older Hawk or Zeus-23 sites. It just increases their chances of penetrating those air defenses. Now, let's see if we can do it to their carrier and that Chinese destroyer.''

Jamieson had at first distrusted McLanahan's Disruptor weapons—he'd wanted to see a pretty big blast if they'd had to fly all this way!—but even he had to admit that this next attack, if it worked, was going to nail the Iranians really good.

''I've got the final launch point fix in,'' McLanahan continued. ''Stand by for missile launch . . . ready . . . doors coming open . . . missile one away . . .'' One by one, McLanahan counted down the weapon releases until four missiles had left the two internal rotary launchers. With two missiles still in the bomb bays in reserve, the B-2A bomber banked hard right and headed back toward the safety of UAE airspace, away from the Iranian fleet and their deadly antiaircraft weapons.

Following McLanahan's programmed flight plan, the four missiles arced north of the Iranian battle group, then turned south-southeast toward the Gulf of Oman, roughly following each other in trail 500 yards apart. The ''screamer'' missiles began their orbits just six miles east and west of the carrier group. The four missiles did appear on the Iranian's radars, but they were so small and flew so slowly that they were electronically squelched from the displays as non-hostiles.

**THE ISLAMIC REPUBLIC REVOLUTIONARY GUARD AIRCRAFT CARRIER *AYATOLLAH RUHOLLAH KHOMEINI*
THAT SAME TIME**

''Sir, Bandar Abbas air defense sector reports unidentified aircraft inbound, bearing two-five-zero, eastbound at five hundred knots!'' the combat information center intercom suddenly blared. ''Bearing now two-three-zero, last reported range from us eighty-five kilometers and closing . . ."

"*What!*" Pasdaran Major Admiral Akbar Tufayli shouted. That jarring pain was suddenly back in his jaw, tripled in intensity. The newcomers were over the Trucial Coast—from the direction of the United Arab Emirates! Was this another GCC attack? "What speed, what altitude?"

"Multiple contacts . . . three, perhaps four formations, speed five hundred, altitude ten K meters and descending."

Major Admiral Akbar Tufayli, commander of the *Khomeini* battle group and nominal commander of the carrier air group, swung on his absolutely flabbergasted chief of staff, Brigadier General Mohammed Badi. "The threat has been eliminated, you say? Those radar contacts are on an *attack profile*, Badi! Those are UAE attack planes, and they are attacking Bandar Abbas and this battle group!"

"It is . . . it is unbelievable, sir!" Badi stammered. "The UAE pilots or their British mercenaries do not have the skill to perform night attacks against maritime targets!" Like many Middle East countries, the United Arab Emirates hired pilots from all over the world to fly their attack planes—but no skilled attack pilot would ever consent to fly a *suicide mission* such as this! "They have no guided weapons, only gravity bombs and the cannon! Surely they know they will be chopped into pieces long before they get within range to drop their bombs?"

"That is, if we successfully stop them!" Tufayli cried. "Engage at longest possible range! Then launch the alert fighters! I want each and every GCC fighter destroyed and the wreckage strewn across the coastal plain for all those reporters to photograph! I want to demonstrate the power of this battle group to the entire damned *world*, right now, *tonight!*"

"Hostile aircraft turning!" The *Khomeini*'s radar operator screamed over the intercom. General Tufayli made a mental note to tell his section chief to brief his men to remain calmer on the intercom—the operator's voice had gone up at least one octave in the past few minutes as the unidentified attack planes closed in. "Range sixty kilometers, decreasing slowly, altitude now below two thousand meters. Heavy jamming detected.''

''They appear to be heading for Bandar Abbas,'' Badi observed, ''but they could turn in our direction at any moment. No report on what type of weapon they are using.''

''We must assume they have standoff weapons—unless they try a low-altitude suicide bombing run,'' Tufayli said. He stared out the observation windows at the *Khomeini*'s flight deck. ''How much longer on the interceptor launch?''

''Just a few minutes, sir.''

''Damn you, Badi, I want air cover up as soon as possible to chase down those attackers! I want those fighters airborne *now!*''

''Yes, sir,'' Badi acknowledged. Badi could do nothing but pick up a phone and tell the air operations commander to speed up the launch.

Tufayli watched as crews raced for the rescue helicopters on deck forward of the island superstructure. The rescue helicopters always launched before the fighters, and took up stations beside and behind the carrier, ready to provide search-and-rescue services in case a fighter had to ditch after takeoff. ''If any of those attackers penetrate within fifty kilometers of my battle group, I will execute every last air defense on this ship!''

The first rescue helicopter was just lifting off the deck and taking position on the portside, ready to rescue any crewmen who might have to eject shortly after takeoff. It had taken more than five minutes to scramble a crew and get a helicopter airborne—that was totally unacceptable, thought Tufayli. He was going to whip this crew into shape first thing in the morning with nonstop drills. . . .

The general turned from the helicopter deck forward to the short holdback point near the center of the carrier in front of the island superstructure, where a Sukhoi-33 fighter, loaded with two R-73 long-range air-to-air missiles and two R-51 short-range heat-seeking missiles, was readying itself for takeoff. This fighter had a small missile load and a partial fuel load so it could use the shorter 100-meter takeoff run, while another, heavily armed fighter could use the 200-meter run along the portside of the ship.

Admiral Tufayli was impatient, but he knew that night carrier operations were the most dangerous and the crews were working at their best speed. "Range to those fighters?" he asked.

"Range to nearest air target, forty-seven kilometers. They appear to be attacking the air defense sites at Bandar Abbas."

The GCC fighters had hesitated, Tufayli thought, they'd had second thoughts about attacking the carrier. Two had already paid for the hesitation and had been destroyed by missiles from Bandar Abbas. Soon the rest would be destroyed by *Khomeini*'s fighters. Soon the world would know of the power of this Iranian carrier. . . .

Suddenly a warning horn sounded throughout the ship—the collision-warning klaxon! At the same time, several missile and close-in weapon cannons began firing. "What is it?" Tufayli shouted. "What is going on? *Report!*"

"Unidentified aircraft, range . . . range, indeterminate!" a combat officer responded. "They seem to be right on top of us! Multiple contacts all around us! They are *everywhere!* Heavy jamming reported . . . sensors are overloaded!" Tufayli and Badi scanned the skies as missiles ripple-fired into the sky and defensive guns roared, but no aircraft could be seen—wait, *there!* "I see a hit!" Tufayli shouted. "Off the starboard bow . . . we hit one!"

"No!" Badi shouted over the roar of the erupting defensive systems. "That was *our* helicopter! We have accidentally shot down our rescue helicopter! Cease fire, damn it! Cease fire!"

It took several seconds for all of the *Khomeini*'s weapons to stop. "Get another helicopter airborne immediately," Tufayli shouted, "and then get those fighters up! And find those enemy aircraft!" In just a few moments, another Mil-8 helicopter had its rotors turning, and had lifted off from the helo mooring pad aft of the carrier's superstructure, and a few moments later, two Sukhoi-33 fighters launched from the *Khomeini*'s ski-jump flight deck.

But then it happened again—suddenly every radio and every radar screen was completely jammed, drowned out by noise, and the threat receivers and radars reported enemy threats all around the carrier group. The battle group's air defense commander had no choice—he ordered his loaded and ready weapon systems to open fire at the identifiable targets. In just a few moments, the *Khomeini*, the *Zhanjiang*, and most of the rest of the larger warships in the battle group had expended most of their ordnance.

"We have lost radio contact with our fighter patrol," General Badi reported. "His radios have malfunctioned. And the carrier commander feels it is too dangerous to continue flight operations."

"And Bandar Abbas is under attack as well," Tufayli said. "Order both fighters to continue their patrol for as long as possible, then recover at Chah Bahar."

"Yes, sir," Badi said. Then, stepping closer to his superior officer, he said in a low voice, "Sir, these strange jamming signals and the false targets they have generated have severely reduced our air defense capability. If we came under missile or bomber attack now, we would be highly vulnerable—we are down to less than fifty percent weapon load, and it will take almost an hour to service and reload some of our mounts!"

"So? Get on it, General."

"I am suggesting, sir," Badi said, "that perhaps it would be wise to evacuate the *Khomeini*. The battle group is virtually defenseless right now—no long-range detection, limited short-range detection, dwindling weapons stock, and limited or no fighter coverage. Even shore-based defenses cannot assist us. If this is a prelude to an attack, you have time to escape, perhaps with the prisoners."

"I will not!" Tufayli retorted. "It will seem as if I am running in the face of an attack!"

"Sir, Chah Bahar can be notified that you are transferring prisoners to the naval security facility there, to begin their interrogation," Badi suggested, emphasizing the word *trans-ferring* so that Tufayli would be sure to catch his meaning. "You could see to their transfer *personally*."

Tufayli considered the idea once again, then nodded. "See to it, General," the admiral said. "Get the prisoners ready to transfer—I will see to their interrogation personally." He clasped Badi on the arm in silent thanks, as his chief of staff hurried to carry out "his" instructions.

Surrounded by armed guards and staff members, Admiral Tufayli was spared the ignominy of looking into the faces of the sailors and Pasdaran troopers he passed as he made his way to the fantail to take the helicopter to Chah Bahar. Already waiting near the fantail was a group of men in ragged, oil-soaked clothing, handcuffed, with black cloth bags over their heads.

Tufayli stepped close to the man at the head of the group of prisoners and said over the roar of warning horns, shouting men, and helicopter rotors: "I see you are being treated well, Colonel White."

"Why, it's Admiral Akbar Tufayli," Paul White said, his moisture-starved voice a hoarse croak. His face was still caked with grease, oil, and salt from the hours he spent in the ocean trying to escape after the *Valley Mistress* had been sunk. "What's that I smell, Admiral? Smells like a war going on . . ."

A guard hit White in the solar plexus with a rifle butt; a few of the Marines surrounding him tried to break free of their guards to defend White but, weak with hunger and thirst, they were pulled back easily.

Just then, a klaxon sounded throughout the ship, and again the ship's defensive systems opened fire, seemingly in all directions. This time, the weapons fire lasted just a few short moments, then abruptly ended, though the klaxon was still sounding. Several officers ran up to Tufayli and gave him several reports and messages. "What was that, Admiral?" White said. "You've run out of SA-N-9 missiles? Is that possible? You must've shot down one, maybe two dozen attackers to use up your long-range missiles like that."

"You shall join your spy ship at the bottom of the Gulf of Oman if you do not remain silent, Colonel White," Tufayli warned. "The interrogation staff at Chah Bahar will find your knowledge of Farsi very interesting."

"We taking a trip somewhere, Admiral?" White asked. "Maybe that wasn't war I smelled a second ago . . . maybe I smelled something else? Is it coming from *you*? What could it be, Admiral?"

In response, Tufayli whipped off White's hood and said, "I warned you to remain silent, Colonel White. You must learn a harsh lesson." Tufayli took a rifle from one of his guards, pulled one of the Marine guards away from the group, lifted the rifle to his head, and pulled the trigger. The Marine's head burst apart like a ripe melon.

Everyone around them jumped at the rifle report; the sound of the headless corpse hitting the steel non-slip deck seemed even louder. White's eyes bulged in horror, and he looked as if he were going to sink to the deck himself on wobbly legs. "Any more deaths caused by attacks by your fellow American terrorists will be on your head, Colonel White," Tufayli said. "You and your men will stand trial for all of this."

"And I'll see you in hell for what you've just done," White said weakly. "You *bastard!*"

"Ah, not as glib as you were just a moment ago, I see," Tufayli said. "Good. This will teach you to hold your tongue." He raised his voice and said to all of them, "The United States has declared war on the Islamic Republic of Iran, so you are all prisoners of war. And since you are combatants not in uniform and are presumed to be spies, you shall not enjoy the privileges of prisoners of war as outlined in the Geneva Conventions. This means you are subject to a military tribunal without recourse. The penalty for espionage in the Islamic Republic is death by hanging. Of course, you may confess your crimes and admit your real identities, in which case your sentence can be commuted to life in prison—perhaps even a trade can be arranged for other prisoners."

"Fuck you, Akbar," White said. "You're the one who's going to die, and I hope I'm the one who does it."

"Since you men are obviously not willing to speak openly in front of your commander here, we shall wait until we arrive in the military prison at my base at Chah Bahar," Tufayli went on, smiling as the hood was again placed over White's head. "The prisoner-exchange option and the chance to return to your homes is of course not available to you if you are dead, so I encourage you to accept my one and only offer. You will have a few moments to consider it, but when we arrive at Chah Bahar, I will have your answer. Confess your guilt or die."

MINA SULTAN NAVAL BASE, SHARJAH, UNITED ARAB EMIRATES
THAT SAME TIME

"Officer quarters" at Mina Sultan, the only military base in the emirate of Sharjah in the United Arab Emirates, were simple one-window, one-room concrete block buildings with flat metal roofs, purposely built with far less quality than Arab buildings to avoid the appearance that the UAE was showing any preferences toward non-Arabs in their country. Each building had its own coal-fired stove, a Fiberglass combination sink and shower with an electric thirty-liter water heater, a Porta-Potty bolted onto the back door opening, a bed, a desk with a single overhead light and a phone connected only to the duty officer at the command center, and a chest of drawers. Sometimes Briggs wished for one of the enlisted and non-commissioned officers' rooms, which were nice, modern, air-conditioned dormitory-style brick buildings. Briggs unlocked the door, reminding himself to start placing little telltales on the door to check when the damned flight surgeon, Dr. Nick Sabin, went through his room, or maybe he'd just slap a hasp and padlock on the door and . . .

Briggs flipped on the light and, to his amazement, found

none other than Nick Sabin himself hog-tied on the bed, his ankles and wrists bound behind him, his mouth bound with duct tape. He was still alive and unhurt, thank God, and madder than hell.

The big Colt .45 pistol was out and in Briggs's hand in a flash, and he took immediate aim on the dark cloth in front of the only other enclosure in the building, the Porta-Potty. Sabin was flopping around on the bed muttering something, but Briggs had tuned him out. He shut off the light, crouched behind the bed, and shouted, "Come out of there *now!*" in English and in the best Arabic he could muster. "I said, come out!"

"I am right here, Leopard," came a soft, silken voice. Briggs whirled. The dresser had been pushed out several inches from the wall—dammit, he'd been so focused on the john that he hadn't noticed—and she had been hiding behind it. He saw her hands were empty, saw . . . that it was Riza Behrouzi, the GCC commando! What in hell was going on here?

"Get out from behind there!" Briggs shouted. "Hands on your head! Flat on the floor!" Behrouzi complied as he ordered. "If you move, I promise I'll fucking blow your head off!" Briggs leapt over to the Porta-Potty, ripped off the dark curtain, and aimed the pistol inside, even down inside the shithole—empty. He checked under the bed, under the desk, all around the stove—nothing. He locked the front door, checked that the plywood covering on the one window was secured, holstered his .45, then searched her right down to the skin, as roughly as he would search any other prisoner or suspect. He found no weapons.

"What in hell are you doing here?" Briggs asked, remembering not to use either her code name or her real name in Sabin's presence. He turned the woman over—and immediately his ears felt hot and his throat felt dry. God, she was so beautiful. This was like a damned *dream!*

"I came to see you," Behrouzi replied, as Briggs let her up. She shook her head at Dr. Sabin, still trussed up on the bed. "I found this one rummaging through your room. I was going to report him to the security police when you arrived.''

''Oh, really!'' Briggs couldn't wait to hear Sabin's explanation. He carefully peeled away the duct tape around his mouth—good thing he kept his hair short.

''She *jumped* me!'' Sabin shouted indignantly the instant the tape was removed. ''She nearly broke my neck!''

''I have a feeling she could have done that easily if she wanted, Doc,'' Briggs said with a wry smile. Sabin obviously didn't see the humor in it, though. ''Were you in my room when she attacked you?''

Sabin looked a bit embarrassed but nodded. ''I came to check up on you,'' he explained. ''I knew your team was going out on another mission, and I didn't find you at the command center, and I'm not allowed in the ops hangar, so I thought I'd check here . . .''

''I don't like anyone coming into my room when I'm not here, Doc,'' Briggs said, his voice not as stern or displeased as he'd first meant it to be. Briggs just took his time undoing the tape binding the doctor's wrists and ankles as they spoke.

''Fine—then I'll confine you to the clinic,'' Sabin said irritably. ''I only let you out of my immediate care because you were making life miserable for me and my staff, but it was under the premise that I keep you under close observation. And since you don't think it's necessary to send over stool or urine samples as I asked you to do, yes, I search your laundry and your commode. Since this is how I'm treated for trying to accommodate your wishes, I'll be the asshole and confine you to the clinic until I'm good and ready to release you. How's *that* sound?''

Hal started undoing the duct tape much quicker now—the flight doc was *really* pissed. In a moment Sabin was untied and back on his feet. ''Sorry, Doc,'' he said. ''I'm a little jumpy when the team's going out on a mission.''

Sabin looked at his outfit and nodded in disgust. ''You were trying to go out with them, against my orders, weren't you?'' he observed. Briggs's silence confirmed his suspicions. ''Not only will I put you back in the clinic, but I'll put a twenty-four-hour guard on you.''

"That's not necessary. I'm fine, really," Briggs said. "If I have any problems I'll be sure and let you know. And you obviously put a real big bug in the gunny's ear, because he booted me off. But you don't need to confine me. I'll do as you say."

"Good. You'd better." Sabin turned to Behrouzi and asked Briggs, "Now, can you please explain who this is, and what she's doing here? *You* obviously know who she is."

Briggs hesitated—he didn't know how to address Riza in front of any outsider. But Behrouzi extended her hand, gave Sabin a mind-blowing smile that melted both men's hearts, then showed him an ID card. "I am Riza Behrouzi, assistant to the deputy general, Directorate of Military Intelligence of the United Arab Emirates." She handed her ID card over to the doctor, who gave it a careful examination before handing it back. "I was ordered to interview Major Briggs immediately, since he and his forces came under attack by an unknown ZSU-23/4 system on Tumb as Sughrd on their last mission."

"Here? Now? That seems a little strange."

"Truthfully, Doctor, the Directorate had heard that Major Briggs was dead," Behrouzi said with a half-amused, half-embarrassed expression. "Little of what the Americans do here at Mina Sultan Naval Base is well known in the UAE. We are also looking for Gunnery Sergeant Wohl, who apparently is also alive and well. Do you know where I can find him? I need to interview him immediately."

Sabin looked at Behrouzi suspiciously, then at Briggs. After years of serving with special operations forces, he knew that the less he said and the more suspicious he was, the better. "You should be talking to the base commander or the operations commander, Major Behrouzi," the doctor said. "I'm not exactly sure how you got on base without an escort, but Major Briggs seems to know you and is willing to vouch for you. I can't help you any further. Major Briggs, are you well enough to escort Major Behrouzi to base headquarters, or should I call security?"

"I'll handle it, Doc," Briggs assured him. Sabin smiled

and nodded—it was obvious that Briggs not only had the situation under control, but was as anxious as a love-struck teenager to be alone with this woman. The flight surgeon rubbed his aching arms and wrists once more, received another mind-blowing smile from Riza as an apology, then departed.

When Sabin departed, Behrouzi turned to Briggs and began, "Leopard . . . Hal, I am sorry I surprised you like this . . ."

Briggs didn't let her finish. He pulled her into his arms and gave her a deep, longing kiss, and she returned it with every bit as much passion, holding him even closer. Both of their eyes were smoky, almost tearful, when they parted. "My God, Riza," Briggs said breathlessly, "I've missed you so much."

"I have missed you as well," Behrouzi said. "I heard of your last mission just tonight. Were you hurt? The doctor said you—"

"I'm fine," Briggs interjected. "Just a scratch."

"A scratch? Let me look." She zeroed in on his left shoulder as if she knew exactly where to look, and she unbuttoned his rough cotton shirt and peeled back his underwear. Heavy dressings covered the wound on both sides of his shoulder. "Entry and exit wounds, Hal? It is much more than a scratch," Behrouzi said breathily. "I am so glad you are safe." They kissed again, drinking even more deeply from each other than before. "You wanted to go on a mission? Tonight? Are you mad?"

"The team is flying into Iran, inspecting every safe area between here and Bandar Abbas."

"Looking for Colonel Paul White and the survivors of the attack on your ship, I know," Behrouzi said. "I have information for you—information on the whereabouts of your commander."

"Paul? He's safe?"

"For now," Behrouzi said ominously. "He and twelve crew members were taken aboard the Iranian aircraft carrier *Khomeini* after his ship was . . ." Briggs tried to hide his thoughts, but his suddenly averted eyes were a dead give-away for a trained observer like Behrouzi. "The carrier . . . the Americans will attack the aircraft carrier?"

"I can't tell you, Riza," Briggs said. "We were told there'd be plenty of distractions while we made our infiltration into Bandar Abbas . . ."

"I shall see about the carrier," Behrouzi said. She took out a cellular telephone, got the Dubai Directorate of Military Intelligence duty desk, and spoke to the senior controller at the command center. A few minutes later, she had her information: "Peace Shield Sky watch reports that there appears to have been an aircraft accident near the *Khomeini*—a helicopter or fighter crashed at sea, and there have been reports of antiaircraft fire. After the accident, one helicopter was reported departing for Chah Bahar—none toward Bandar Abbas."

"That means they're taking their prisoners to Chah Bahar!" Briggs said.

"Leopard, that helicopter could be a simple medical evacuation, or it could be just the carrier commander and his staff," Behrouzi said. "And my intelligence information may be faulty and they could not be on the carrier after all, or they could be held on the carrier, or there could have been more than one helicopter . . ."

"Or this could be the best chance we've got to rescue our teammates," Briggs said. "If we can get a strike team together, I'm going to give it a try. I've got to notify the team and tell them to back us up—there's no time to waste!" Briggs was on the phone in an instant, notifying his command center that Wohl and the CV-22 team should return as soon as possible. "Riza, you're wonderful," Briggs said. "You may have saved the lives of all the survivors . . . but I have to go."

"I shall go with you, of course."

"Riza, this mission won't be sanctioned by anyone . . ."

"You think you shall go alone?" Behrouzi asked him with a smile. "Will you sprout jet-powered wings and fly five hundred kilometers to Chah Bahar?"

"I'll find a plane or a ship to take me," Briggs said. "The team will be back in less than an hour. Another hour for refueling and a briefing, ninety minutes en route . . ."

"*If* your mission is approved by your superiors," Behrouzi added. "And by then, it will be daylight."

"I told you, I'm not talking about a sanctioned mission—I'm talking about rescuing my men," Briggs said. "They're *my* men—at least they're supposed to be, if they'd ever let me prove it to them. I could take a cargo plane, parachute in, reconnoiter the base, and report back here."

"Are you sure you are thinking properly?" Behrouzi asked cautiously. "Are you doing this because it is your duty and you feel you can succeed—or are you doing this to gain the favor of the men who now must serve under you?"

Briggs fell silent and scowled at Behrouzi—but, dammit, she was right. "I'm not thinking straight," he said aloud, not really talking to Behrouzi but to himself. "This is not how Chris Wohl would do it. He'd play it by the book, gather intelligence, collect the data, assemble a plan, brief it with his superiors, get approval, assemble his troops and equipment, then brief his troops. He'd be methodical, calculating, and always damned effective. But . . ."

Briggs stopped and looked at Behrouzi's concerned expression. "But, Hal," she said softly, "you are not Chris Wohl. You are Hal Briggs. You are the Leopard."

It was then that the light finally went on in Briggs's brain. "Riza . . . you're right," Briggs said. "I'm *not* Chris Wohl. I wasn't trained by the Marine Corps. I was trained by my uncle, the sheriff of Camden County, Georgia; by General Brad Elliott, by John Ormack, by Patrick McLanahan, by a team of engineers and crewdogs. They always said, 'Just get the job done. Don't plan everything to death. Train and study hard, then use that training to decide on a course of action—then do it.' And that's exactly what I'm going to do." He turned to Behrouzi excitedly. "I need a plane, Riza."

"I have my liaison aircraft available right here at Mina Sultan," Behrouzi said excitedly. "Any other aircraft, I must take time to requisition . . ."

"What is it?"

"A surplus aircraft from your Marine Corps," Behrouzi said, "an OV-10D. I believe you called it a Bronco-D."

"Your personal aircraft is an observation-and-close-air-support aircraft . . . ?"

"In my country, we have little use for a plane that fulfills only one role," Behrouzi said with a smile. "This belongs to Sheikh Rashid's eldest son, who is the Minister of Defense of the United Arab Emirates. When General Rashid is away, the Directorate is permitted to use it to transport myself and others to meetings and exercises all over the region. I am well trained in how to use it for ground attack as well."

"So it still has its weaponry, its cargo bay?"

"Of course," Behrouzi said matter-of-factly. "It is a D-NOS aircraft, configured for night reconnaissance as well as for ground attack and observation, with an AAS-36 FLIR turret, a Gatling gun in a helmet-aimed turret, laser designator, satellite navigation, missile warning system, chaff, and flare dispensers. His Eminence the Sheikh spares little expense for his toys."

"Major Behrouzi, it sounds like just the magic carpet I need right now," Briggs said happily. "Care to offer a guy a ride tonight?"

"Only if I can ride with you, Leopard," Behrouzi said. "If what I think you have in mind is what you will do, I wish to . . . how do you say, 'be where the action is,' no?"

In reply, Briggs gave her a kiss. "You're on, Major Riza Behrouzi. Lead the way."

Just twenty minutes later, Behrouzi and four men—Hal Briggs and three United Arab Emirates troopers, members of the Emir of Dubai's Royal Guard Brigade commandos—were crammed in the tiny aft cargo bay of the OV-10D-NOS (Night Observation System) Bronco attack plane, speeding down the runway of Mina Sultan Naval Base, on their way to Chah Bahar Naval Base in Iran.

They didn't have a flight plan, clearance, permission, or a real concrete plan of action, but they did have a warplane. The OV-10D-NOS twin turboprop attack-and-observation plane had a full attack payload configuration: fully fueled centerline and wing fuel tanks, 1,500 rounds of 20-millimeter ammunition for the six-barrel steerable Gatling gun, two pods of four AGM-114 Hellfire laser-guided missiles on the fuselage sponsons, and one AGM-122A Sidearm anti-radar missile mounted on the outboard side of each of the wing fuel-tank pylons. This Bronco also had chaff and flare ejectors installed in the tail booms to assist in decoying enemy antiaircraft radars and heat-seeking missiles. It seemed as if it took every available foot of Dubai's 9,000-foot runway to get the heavily laden Bronco into the warm, humid air.

Shortly after leveling off at cruise altitude, Briggs was on the plane's radio on the UHF emergency frequency: "Genesis, Genesis, this is Redman, if you copy, come up on Storybook, repeat, Genesis, this is Redman, come up on Storybook." Briggs then flipped over to a special UHF frequency that they had used back when Briggs had been the commander of security operations at the High Technology Aerospace Weapons Center. One of the ranges they'd used for weapons tests had been called "Storybook," and each range had had its own discrete frequency. Redman was Briggs's security detail's call sign.

"Who are you calling, Leopard?" Behrouzi asked.

"A friend that I think is flying tonight," Briggs said. He keyed the mike: "Genesis, this is Redman on Storybook. How copy?"

"Loud and clear, Redman," came the reply. "Fancy meeting you here. Seen any red-tail hawks lately?"

"Only in Amarillo," Briggs replied. "Nice to hear from you again, Old Dog."

ABOARD THE B-2A SPIRIT STEALTH BOMBER, AV-011

"This is an open frequency, remember," Patrick McLanahan said from the flight deck.

"What in hell do you think you're doing, McLanahan?"

Jamieson asked. "Are you nuts? You'll blow us for sure!"

"This is the team, the guy we're supposed to be supporting," McLanahan said. "He knows security better than either of us, and if he took the chance to call, it must be serious."

"Shit, this is going to get us killed—we're still too damn close to the bad guys here," Jamieson groused. But now he was intrigued as well: "So what's with this 'red-tail hawk' and 'Amarillo' business?"

"A private code," McLanahan said. "A job we did not long ago." He keyed the mike: "What's happening?"

"Got any screamers left?"

Jamieson looked as if he had seen a ghost as he stared in complete surprise at McLanahan. "He knows . . . how in *hell* does he know about our JSOWs?"

"He was there when we first tested and built the things at Dreamland, AC," McLanahan explained with a smile. "I don't know if he was briefed on our mission, but he sure as hell seems to have figured it out." On the radio, McLanahan replied, "Affirmative, Redman. Where do you need them?"

"Follow the lights," came the response.

"What in hell does *that* mean?" Jamieson asked.

"It means he's going in somewhere, probably into Iran," McLanahan said. "Give me a one-eighty—I'll see if I can pick him up on radar."

"A *one-eighty!* You mean, fly *back* to where we just creamed an Iranian aircraft carrier?" Jamieson retorted. "Are you insane?"

"C'mon, Colonel, where's your spirit of adventure?" McLanahan asked. "We've got the gas, and we're outside Iran's radar coverage."

"Hey, my butt thinks my legs have been cut off," Jamieson said. "We've still got twelve more hours' flying time to go." But he quickly relented, took control of the Spirit, and turned westbound toward the Strait of Hormuz again.

"What's your altitude, Redman?"

"Shoshone," came the reply.

"You two are just too fuckin' cute," Jamieson said. "Another code word from your days in Dreamland?"

"Exactly," McLanahan said. "Shoshone Peak, in restricted area 4202A, sixty-five hundred feet above sea level. SAR coming on." McLanahan configured the B-2A's radar, then shot a one-second sweep of the sky. The choice was fairly easy—there was only one aircraft near that altitude. "Level off at Brawley for confirmation."

"Roger," came the reply. A few moments later, McLanahan took another SAR shot and zeroed in on the same return—sure enough, it had leveled off at 9,500 feet above sea level—the same height as Brawley Peak in southwestern Nevada near Hawthorne.

"Radar contact, Redman," McLanahan said. "Continue on course. We can keep an eye on you for a while, and if we see red lights, we'll try to turn them green for you."

ABOARD THE OV-10D-NOS BRONCO ATTACK PLANE

"Thanks, Genesis. See you when I see you. Out."

"Can they help us, Leopard?" Behrouzi asked.

"I think so," Briggs said with a smile big enough to be seen in the dim light of the Bronco's cargo bay. "Whatever happened over Bandar Abbas and over the *Khomeini* carrier group tonight, I got a feeling these guys are gonna make it happen over Chah Bahar."

BALUCHISTAN VA SISTAN PROVINCIAL NAVAL BASE, CHAH BAHAR, IRAN
23 APRIL 1997, 0408 HOURS LOCAL TIME

A flash of intense light like a billion-watt lightbulb instantly destroyed his night vision; followed by an earth-shattering explosion, louder than any sound he had ever heard in his life; then an incredible shudder that felt like ten earthquakes rolled into one. The normally unshakable deck heeled over to starboard as if a giant child's hand had tossed them against the toy box, then the deck rolled hard to port, and the port rail was awash. Men were screaming, their faces yellowed by the fires, their voices as loud, maybe even louder—if that was possible—than the sounds of explosions and tearing metal.

For the second time since being transferred to the prison facility, Carl Knowlton was replaying the death of the S.S. *Valley Mistress* in his tortured mind's eye. It had been the most horrifying experience of his life. He had seen the aftermath of the Iraqi Scud missile hit on the barracks at Khobar during the Gulf War, where 117 American soldiers had been killed or wounded; he remembered the thousands of square miles of burning oil fields of Kuwait, when he thought that he was seeing a bit of hell right here on earth. But the air attack against the *Valley Mistress* had been the worst by far. The ship had felt so small, so helpless, as the sea rushed in to claim it. As the sea had poured into the crippled ship, the old bitch had literally screamed—its oil-fired engines first grinding to a painful halt, then tearing themselves apart, then exploding from the stress and rapid cooling. The scream had been like a loud siren, like a wild animal caught in a trap. . . .

This time, though, Knowlton had not been awakened by his nightmare, but by the sounds of real sirens—air raid sirens. He rolled painfully to his feet, his pants creaking from caked-on sweat, oil, and salt. The oil-fire burns on his arms, shoulders, and neck were wrapped in someone's T-shirt, the pus and sweat making the cloth stick painfully to the burns.

"You all right, sir?" a young Marine lance corporal, J. D. McKay, asked. "You cried out."

"Sorry, Corporal," Knowlton said. "Real bad dream."

"The guards might come back if they heard you—we gotta be careful," McKay said. McKay had a right to lecture a superior officer: the Iranian Pasdaran soldiers had obviously recognized who McKay was right after his capture, because they had separated him and beaten him senseless, bludgeoning his face, breaking in teeth, ripping out hair, and breaking fingers. He definitely did not want to attract any more attention to himself.

"Right. Sorry." Embarrassed, Knowlton stepped over to the one window in the room he and the Marine soldier occupied. The window was too high; Knowlton couldn't see anything, and he was too weak to pull himself up onto the sill.

"Hop up, sir," McKay said. Knowlton turned. McKay was crawling on his hands and knees toward the sound of the siren coming through the window.

"No, McKay, I can't . . ."

"Get up, sir, and see what's goin' on," McKay said, and the young Marine offered his back—probably the only part of his body not broken—as a footstool. Knowlton clapped the young soldier on the back, then painfully climbed up to peer out the window, pulling himself up onto the wall by the bars on the window to avoid putting his full weight on the kid's back.

The window was open but covered with metal louvers, so he could see only a few slivers of open sky outside. Still, it was enough: "I see searchlights," Knowlton reported. "Jesus, hard to believe anyone on this planet uses antiaircraft searchlights anymore . . . I see a SAM lifting off north, looks like a Hawk, missile flying southwest . . . there goes a second Hawk . . . no secondaries, no flashes . . . third Hawk lifting off . . . still nothing." He climbed down off the Marine's back. "Somebody's out there, dammit. I think . . . I *hope* it's one of ours. . . ." He pulled off his T-shirt, painfully ripping off the scabs and loose flesh from his burns. He tore a long strip of white cloth from the bottom of the T-shirt, then removed his trousers, tore a long strip off each pant leg, and began knotting the three pieces of cloth together.

"What are you doing, sir?"

"Trying to create a flag for whoever's out there," Knowlton said. "If they see it, they'll know where to look for us." He ripped a piece of reinforced trim from the T-shirt's collar, tore it into thin strips, and tied that to the louvers so it could not be seen from the cell; then he stuffed the trousers and T-shirt pieces out the window through the louvers. It was hard to tell from inside the cell that anything was hanging outside. Knowlton stepped off the Marine's back. "Thanks, McK—"

Just then the cell door burst open, and two guards entered. They jabbered excitedly in Farsi, and pulled Knowlton across the room and up against a wall. They then kicked McKay in the rib cage, sending him writhing in pain into the corner. They yelled at both of them for a few moments. Knowlton held up his burned hands to defend himself as best he could, but they saw his burns and decided they had seen enough and departed. They did not even think to look up at the window.

"Jesus Christ, those motherfuckers," Knowlton cursed as he rushed over to the young Marine. He looked bad, but no worse than he had with Knowlton standing on his back looking out the window. He lifted the Marine up and propped him up in the corner so he could breathe easier. "You okay, McKay?"

"The name's J. D., sir," the Marine said, with a weak smile. "I'm not feelin' very military right now."

"I hear ya," Knowlton said. "Me neither. You breathing okay, J. D.?"

J. D. clasped his broken ribs with his bent, twisted fingers. "For now," he said. "I just hope the beatin' was worth it. . . ."

ABOARD THE OV-10D-NOS BRONCO ATTACK PLANE

"Down to twenty bundles of chaff, Major," the weapons officer reported in Arabic on interphone. "Twenty-five kilometers until we reach the shore."

Riza Behrouzi swore to herself, then replied in Arabic, "I won't argue with the results, Lieutenant Junayd—we're still alive. Just make sure it stays that way."

"Yes, Major," Junayd replied. "Eighteen kilometers to go." As bad as it was up in the cockpit, the young gunnery

officer thought, it would be even worse for the five poor
souls back there.

The Bronco's threat warning receiver was beeping well
before they crossed into Iran's territorial waters; the first
long-range radar at Chah Bahar picked up the Bronco 100
miles into the Gulf of Oman, and they started their descent
to get under radar coverage then. At fifty miles, even though
they were flying less than 600 feet above the dark waters of
the Gulf of Oman, the radar had picked them up once again;
at forty kilometers, the first L-band Hawk acquisition radar
was detected, and a few miles later they detected the Hawk's
X-band target illuminators. That's when they decided to go
down to fifty feet, using the AN/AAS-36 Forward-Looking
Infrared (FLIR) camera and the radar altimeter, which measured the altitude between the belly of the plane and the
surface directly below, to keep from crashing.

When the first Hawk launched at twenty-five miles, it was
like a nightmare come alive. The cockpit crew could actually
see the missile lift off, its bright rocket-motor plume clearly
visible on the horizon. They could see the bright yellow arc
as it described a powered, semi-ballistic flight path through
the sky. The pilot punched out chaff, racked the Bronco into
a tight right turn using max back pressure on the control stick
to get the tightest turn—but the Hawk followed. A second
Hawk went up, followed by a third. The Iranian missile
crews knew that the attacker might evade the first missile,
but doing so greatly reduced the attacker's speed, which
made it likely that a second or third missile could claim a
kill. The pilot set the radar altimeter warning bug to thirty
feet; Briggs, Behrouzi, and the three UAE commandos in the
cargo bay heard almost constant warning tones as the pilot
edged lower and lower, trying to evade the missiles. When
the pilot banked hard, the radar altimeter completely broke
lock, the warning horn sounded constantly, and the commandos all feared that it would be the last sound they'd hear
before crashing into the sea.

"All chaff expended," the gunner reported. They would
be going in completely unprotected now.

Every hard bank threw the cargo bay occupants harder and harder against their harnesses, but each jarring move made Behrouzi smile. "They are working well," she said to Briggs, motioning toward the cockpit. The noise level was very high in the Bronco's cargo bay because they had removed the small rear door before takeoff—it would make it easier to do what they needed to do once they got over the Iranian naval base. "I think they do better than I."

Hal Briggs was smiling, too, but his smile was just a facade—inside, his guts were twisting with worry, doubt, and downright fear. Had he made the right decision? He hadn't expected to involve the lives of six other soldiers on this mission—and he certainly didn't expect to involve Riza Behrouzi. In his fantasy, he envisioned doing a HALO (High Altitude, Low-Opening) parachute jump, solo of course, his trusty Uzi his only companion; he'd land on the rooftop of wherever the prisoners were being kept, blast his way inside, rescue the hostages, steal a cargo plane, dodge enemy fighters on the way out, bring them all back alive, be the hero, and fall blissfully into Riza's waiting arms.

Well, this was reality: he was leading six strangers right into the well-prepared and well-armed clutches of the Islamic Republic of Iran's army. They were still five minutes from reaching landfall, and already they were heavily under attack. Worse, he still didn't know where the hostages were—or even *if* they were here in the first place!—and he had no idea how he was going to get them out. Stupid. Dumb. Asinine. If he survived this, Wohl was rightly going to kick his ass into the next century—or shoot him, if his rash actions caused the deaths of any of his men.

"How are we doing, Lieutenant?" Behrouzi called up front to the weapons officer. "Was that three Hawk missiles you evaded?"

"Yes, Major," the weapons officer replied.

"Very good," Behrouzi said in Arabic, her smile just as strong and as mind-blowing as always—it was more than enough to distract even Hal Briggs. "Expect a second volley in a few seconds and be sure to destroy it with the Sidearms.

If it does not come up, prepare for a Rapier or ZSU-23 radar. I don't wish to swim to our target tonight.''

"I'll do my best, Major—ah, damn you . . . my God . . . *there! Shoot!*'' the weapons officer shouted. The commandos in the cargo bay could hear the threat warning receiver beep, and the Bronco entered another impossibly tight break to evade another missile launch. But moments later they heard a loud *fwooosh!* from the right wing as the first Sidearm anti-radar missile left its rail, and a few moments later, the threat tone abruptly ended.

"Very good, Captain,'' Behrouzi called up to the pilot, smiling even more broadly, wishing that she could be watching the pilot's actions as he fought to outmaneuver these Iranian missiles. "Keep up the good work. Let me know when you have the prison complex in sight.'' The weapons officer's response was choked off by another hard break, this time to the left, followed by another Sidearm launch. "What was that, Lieutenant? Another Hawk?''

The weapons officer was completely flabbergasted—here he was, fighting for his life, just milliseconds from getting a missile in the face or crashing into the sea, and a senior government intelligence officer, an assistant to the commanding general and the son of the Emir of Dubai, was making conversation! "That . . . *Allah preserve us, climb!* . . . That was a Rapier J-band Blindfire radar, Major.''

"Ah, very good, the Iranians made a mistake,'' Behrouzi said gleefully. "They activated their short-range air defense systems too soon. Did you get it, Lieutenant?''

"I . . . I don't think so, Major.''

"That was the last Sidearm missile—we're on our own now,'' Behrouzi said in Arabic. "That Rapier is your first priority, Lieutenant—be sure you kill that unit right away. Range to shore?''

"Twenty kilometers.''

Behrouzi was silent—and Briggs knew why: they were still several minutes away from being able to attack any of the air defense sites with their Hellfire missiles. The longer-range Hawk missile batteries could still track and shoot at them, no matter how low they flew.

Briggs clicked on the radio: "Genesis, this is Redman. The lights are bright in Broadway now. How copy?" No response. "Genesis, this is Redman, anytime now, buddy." Still no reply. He removed the headset and tossed it aside. "Looks like our angel has flown back to heaven."

"It was perhaps too much to hope for," Behrouzi said. On interphone, she asked, "Range to shore, Lieutenant?"

"Eighteen kil—" He was interrupted by the threat warning receiver's blaring alarm again—it was another Hawk missile site. Behrouzi looked into Briggs's eyes, and he could sense her fear—the Hawk was locked on, and there was nowhere to run now. "Hawk acquisition . . . Hawk target illuminator . . ." They then heard the fast, high-pitched *deedledeedledeedle!* as the threat warning system detected the Hawk missile launch. The speed at which the Hawk system had gone from acquisition to illuminator to missile launch told them that the Hawk had a solid lock-on. The pilot started his evasive maneuvers, but everyone could sense that the maneuvers were sharper, more desperate . . . there was a second launch warning tone, then a third. . . ."

"Missiles in the air! Missiles tracking!" the gunnery officer shouted. "More missiles . . . I see more missiles in the air!" One after another, it seemed as if the sky was filling with missiles, and now a few antiaircraft artillery sites opened up far in the distance, like a shower of fireworks. "There are missiles everywhere!" the gunner shouted hysterically. "They are everywhere! They—"

The interphone went dead, and the Bronco's wild evasive maneuvers were cut short. A terrific explosion shook the Bronco as if a giant hand had slapped it, and there was a tremendous screech, like a man crying in terror . . . but they were still flying. Behrouzi tore her headphones off and shouted, "There is a loud squeal in the radios. I cannot hear anything!"

For the first time in what seemed like years, Briggs smiled. "That's my angel," he said. "Good going, Mack."

It took several minutes for the squealing to subside in the radios and interphone. When she was able to be heard over the persistent side tones, Behrouzi asked the gunner, "What has happened, Lieutenant?"

"Every missile site in Iran opened fire on us all at once," Junayd replied excitedly, "but all the missiles seemed to fly in every direction but ours. Then some artillery sites opened fire—but they were sweeping the skies erratically. I am still picking up missile tracking, illuminators, and uplink signals, but I see no missiles or gun sites attacking. It was as if they fired all their weapons at once at some large mass of targets overhead. . . ."

"That is good, Lieutenant," Behrouzi said. "Our American commander brought an angel with us on the flight—I hope it stays. Range to shore?"

"Nine kilometers, Major."

"Good. Well within Hellfire missile range. Do you have that Rapier site yet?"

"Major, please, I'm doing the best . . . wait . . . target identified!" the weapons officer cried out suddenly. "I see it!"

"Be sure it's not a decoy, Lieutenant."

"I see the Sidearm impact point—the Sidearm hit a wall right in front of the unit and missed by just few meters. Locked on!"

"Well, kill it, then, pilot, don't just narrate," Behrouzi screamed up to the pilot—the pilot of a Bronco controlled the attack missiles, while the weapons officer controlled the Gatling gun. Just then, the commandos heard a loud, sustained *fwoooshhh!* as the first Hellfire missile left its launch tube, followed by a second launch a few seconds later.

In this engagement, since the range of a Hellfire and a Rapier were almost the same, the first one to fire would probably be the winner—and Behrouzi's crew won. "Target destroyed!" Junayd shouted. "Target destroyed!"

"Very good," Behrouzi said. "Be on the lookout for antiaircraft artillery sites, but it's rare to find antiaircraft artillery units active on a naval installation.

"Now I want a careful surveillance of the facility, looking for any evidence of where those captives might be held," Behrouzi went on. "You have the diagram of the security headquarters, correct, Lieutenant?"

"Yes, Major," the weapons officer replied. "Our navigation coordinates are programmed for the detention facility, which is right next to the base hospital. We'll look there first."

"The longer you take, the less fuel you'll have for your return flight, Lieutenant," Behrouzi reminded the cockpit crew in an almost humorous tone.

"I understand . . . I have the hospital . . . I see the detention facility. It appears to be dark inside, Major—no sign of occupation. I see only a few lights on in the ground-floor security headquarters. The building appears deserted, no perimeter lights on in the detention facility, no vehicles outside. The hospital looks as if it is fully staffed."

Behrouzi turned to Briggs and said in English, "You must decide, Leopard," she said. "The crew says the detention facility appears deserted—no lights, no sign of activity. The hospital appears to be fully staffed. Shall we try?"

"The detention facility," Briggs said immediately.

"We may have only one chance at this."

"I was in the security business for ten years," Briggs said resolutely. "Prisoners always go to the secure facility. If they're hurt and you're going to treat them, you bring the doctors *into* the facility, not take prisoners *out* to an unsecure area. And I never allowed anyone to park outside my secure areas—too easy to hot-wire a car and blow through a gate, or set booby traps, or take cover during a raid. We go in the detention area, inside the perimeter fence. Directly on the rooftop if possible."

"Very well, Leopard," Behrouzi said, her smile showing that she was pleased with his resolve. She pulled out her chart of the Chah Bahar Naval Base and, in Arabic and English, briefed their intended target, then ordered her three commandos to get ready.

The Bronco pilot made a high-speed approach from the

seaward side of the base at very low altitude. The weapons officer designated targets for the Hellfire missiles, identifying occupied buildings that looked as though they were headquarters buildings or communications centers, and at the same time took shots with the Gatling gun at every power transformer, large vehicle, fuel-storage tank, or anything else that he thought might disrupt things down on the base and cover their activities.

The last run was at the security headquarters, which was the lower floor of the security and detention building. They shot Hellfires at the spots where they knew important rooms were located—the communications stations, the armories, the power transformers—and shot out yard lights and any lighted doorways with the 20-millimeter Gatling gun.

"I see a long strip of cloth tied to the outside of a window on the second floor," Junayd yelled back to the cargo bay.

"Does it form a letter?" Briggs shouted back. "A letter in the Roman alphabet?"

"Yes," Junayd replied, using maximum power on his FLIR targeting scope. "It forms the letter *M*."

"That's one of our guys," Briggs said, smiling broadly for the first time. "Madcap Magician. They're down there. Let's get ready!"

The weapons officer Junayd saved two Hellfires to blow big holes in the side of the security headquarters. About 600 yards from the building itself, the pilot started a hard climb, so he was directly over the detention facility at the crest of the climb at 600 feet. At that point, the five commandos in the Bronco's cargo section made their static-line parachute jumps.

Briggs was going out first. He braced himself against the open door at the rear of the cargo bay, hands and toes outside. As the Bronco started its steep climb, Briggs found himself looking directly down into the security headquarters complex, a square three-story building surrounded by twelve-foot-high barbed-wire fences. Then, just before the Bronco reached the top of its climb, Briggs simply let himself fall through the opening.

He heard the roar of the twin turboprops at maximum continuous power only for a brief instant, and then he heard the wail of air-raid and emergency sirens from the base. The static line yanked his 'chute out of its pack immediately. He heard the loud *crrack . . . whuumpp!* of four other 'chutes opening above him—*very* close above him. He looked up and saw Riza dumping air out of her 'chute right away, trying to catch up with him. The three UAE commandos were doing the same, all attempting to land at the same time as their leaders.

By the time their 'chutes opened, they were less than a hundred feet above ground—they barely had time to get their bearings before they had to steer their parachutes over the detention facility rooftop. Two of the Arab commandos missed the building completely, and Briggs's and Behrouzi's 'chutes actually ran into each other as they maneuvered for their target. Briggs obviously had had a lot less recent practice in parachute infiltrations; he was drifting over to the edge of the rooftop so fast that he had to dump all the air completely out of his 'chute from fifteen feet to make it to the roof. Behrouzi and her third Arab commando hit directly in the center.

"Are you all right, Leopard?" Behrouzi asked as she helped Briggs to his feet. He had taken a bad fall, landing heavily on his left leg, but he was on his feet and moving quickly.

"We lost two," Briggs said to Behrouzi in reply, as he quickly clipped Simrad GN1 night-vision goggles to their helmets. Something was torn or sprained in his left knee, but he tried to ignore the pain.

"No, I directed them to land on the ground and secure the building," Behrouzi said. Her GN1 night-vision goggles and those of the commando with her were already on. "Keep alert—please do not kill them."

"I'm hopin' they don't kill *me*," Briggs said. "Let's move!" It was too easy to breach the roof access door and make their way inside.

The toughest resistance was on the second floor of the

three-story building—all the Iranian guards on the first floor had retreated up to the second as the UAE commandos started their surprise assault; the majority of the Pasdaran guards were already stationed on the second floor. Briggs didn't care—if it moved, it died. He was not going to try to be neat or merciful.

The hallway was lit by emergency lights—those were shot out immediately. Briggs and Behrouzi then threw infrared Cyalume light sticks into the hallways, which would brightly light up the area only for persons wearing night-vision equipment. When Briggs confirmed that Behrouzi's first two commandos would stay on ground level and would not stray into the line of fire, the killing began.

Briggs led the way, Behrouzi following with a Dragon twelve-gauge, twelve-round semi-automatic shotgun filled with breaching rounds, and the third commando following as rear security, carrying a suppressed MP5 submachine gun. Trotting through the four corridors, his Uzi with its sixteen-inch suppressor fitted and loaded with thirty-round magazines of subsonic .45-caliber cartridges, Briggs gunned down anyone in front of him that was alive. He rarely needed more than two rounds to take down a guard—one shot to the chest, one to the head.

As he finished the second corridor, he heard shots coming from the next corridor to the left. He sprinted around the corner and saw a guard unlocking cell doors and firing a pistol into a cell, then moving on to the next cell. Briggs dropped the guard with a three-burst round from thirty feet. "Magicians!" Briggs shouted. "Strike a pose!" He then checked the fourth corridor—all guards subdued. Behrouzi sent her Arab commando to guard the main stairway, and she and Briggs began checking each cell.

The cells appeared to be small dormitory-type rooms, remodeled to be prisoner and punishment-reprimand facilities. Usually it took only one shotgun blast on the top outwardly swinging hinge to crack and pull the door open. When Briggs, now with a Cyalume light stick around his neck, glanced into the occupied cell, he saw two men lying on the floor, facing away from the door, arms outstretched with only the middle fingers extended, and with one leg bent and crossed over the other leg, pointing at the other man in the cell next to them. That was Paul White's unspoken code-sign for a friendly.

"On your feet, guys," Briggs said. "I'm here to get you out."

The first cell he breached had Knowlton and McKay inside. "Jesus—it's Major Briggs!" Knowlton said as he helped McKay up. "I've got him, Hal. He's hurt bad."

"Thanks for the flag outside," Briggs said, handing Knowlton a pistol from a dead Iranian guard. He was off, checking more cells. "Follow me and stay close."

The search was not pretty, and after a very short time Briggs wasn't feeling too heroic. There were prisoners in the cells other than Madcap Magician members. Briggs did not kill them, just searched them to make sure they had no weapons, but even though Behrouzi warned them in Arabic and Farsi not to leave the cell or try to run until they had departed, all of them bolted for the door as soon as Briggs and Behrouzi had left the cell, and they were gunned down by the UAE commandos guarding the exits. They could take no chances with the lives of their own.

But the final tally heartened them all: nine Madcap Magician members well and rescued. Two more members had been killed by the Pasdaran guards; one more was critically wounded. The main captive missing was Paul White himself. "Carl, do you have any idea where the colonel is?" Briggs asked.

"No," Knowlton replied. "He was separated from us right away."

"Any idea if there are any others in this building?"

"I don't know, Hal, sorry," Knowlton said dejectedly. "I was unconscious most of the time, exhausted. I don't know how many men made it after the attack on the *Mistress*, how many we lost . . ." Briggs quickly polled the other Marines, but they couldn't be sure how many others had been captured or killed in the attack, either. Their best guess was that they had everybody. "I wasn't able to make contact with the others or try to find anything out, Hal, I'm sorry. . . ."

"Forget it, Carl," Briggs said. "We'll search the entire building."

But there was no time for that—one of Behrouzi's UAE commandos ran upstairs to report that several heavy infantry vehicles were on the way. "Shit, it didn't take long for them to organize a response."

"Our best chance is on the road," Behrouzi said. "We should try to steal a vehicle, try to make it out into the open countryside. The Pakistan border is only a hundred kilometers east." Briggs knew she was right—if they stayed in that building, they'd quickly be surrounded and chewed to pieces.

But as they ran outside, they immediately drew heavy-caliber weapon fire from the infantry vehicles. The commandos' weapons were useless against the Iranian infantry—they'd brought weapons only for close-range work, not to shoot it out with infantry forces. "Back inside!" Briggs shouted. "We got no choice!"

Just then, the first infantry vehicle began to sparkle, then jump, then it burst into flames—and seconds later, they heard the OV-10D-NOS Bronco fly overhead. The UAE Bronco crew had not high-tailed it for home after dropping their paratroopers—they were burning most of their return fuel on covering their commando's withdrawal. "Now's our chance!" Briggs shouted. "Run for the hospital! We'll try to—!"

The night air suddenly erupted into an ear-shattering blast of gunfire. One of the heavy armored vehicles following the infantry forces was not a troop carrier—it was a ZSU-23/4 air defense vehicle. Its four 23-millimeter cannons fired at a rate of 3,000 rounds per minute, blanketing the sky with deadly radar-guided shells. The Bronco was shredded by the murderous gunfire, cut into pieces and burning long before it hit the ground. The commandos and the rescued hostages had no choice but to retreat back into the security headquarters building. Two UAE commandos and two Madcap Magician Marines stayed on the ground floor, ready to take out the first wave of attackers; the rest headed up onto the roof.

"One lousy rescue this is turning into," Briggs said. All of the Madcap Magician Marines were now armed, and together they made a formidable force—but everyone knew their options were quickly running out.

"You came for us—that's the important thing, Major," Corporal McKay told Briggs.

"He's right, Hal—if you would have waited, we'd be dead," Knowlton said. "No one was talking, so we weren't good sources of information; we knew the U.S. government wasn't going to acknowledge us or try to make a deal for us. They were going to discard us right away."

"We may still be discarded."

"But at least we're fighting," McKay said. The Marine had broken fingers, swollen eyes, and could hardly breathe—but he was still ready to fight. "Thanks for giving us that chance, Major—I mean, 'Commander.' "

The building was quickly surrounded by the armored vehicles and heavily armed soldiers, and the assault began immediately. Heavy 100-millimeter breaching cannons blew large, man-sized holes in the walls on the ground floor, followed by dozens of volleys of smoke and gas grenades, then by Iranian Pasdaran troopers in a hastily organized full frontal assault. The American and UAE soldiers dropped several Pasdaran soldiers as they came toward the stairwells, but were quickly forced to retreat as their number grew. The commandos were much more successful at picking off the Pasdaran troopers up on the second floor, but soon the second floor, too, was filled with gas. One American Marine was shot in the chest and was carried up to the third floor by the others. Soon they had to retreat from that position as well, but with each retreat they were taking out plenty of Pasdaran troopers.

Up on the roof, the sound of approaching helicopters meant that their time was quickly running out. At the same time as the helicopters approached, the ground units, carrying the dead Marine, made their way onto the roof. "Too many to count," was the simple report from a surviving Marine.

A few moments later, three Iranian Navy SH-3 Sea King helicopters could be seen through the darkness. All of them were trailing rappelling lines, ready to drop soldiers onto the roof. All of the commandos took cover as best they could around the raised rim of the roof.

Suddenly a breaching charge blew open the roof-access door, and smoke and tear gas poured through. Briggs fired, and two Pasdaran bodies piled up on the stairway sill. They were quickly dragged away by other troopers, and no others emerged. The doorway was open—a few grenades tossed through would make short work of everyone on the roof. Briggs cleared everyone from the portion of the roof facing the doorway and assigned commandos to cover it. "Anybody got any ideas?" Briggs shouted.

"I am afraid we need to consider a surrender, Leopard," Behrouzi said. "We are outnumbered and outgunned."

"I don't think the Iranians are interested in taking prisoners, Riza."

As if to prove the point, just then one of Behrouzi's UAE commandos jumped to his feet, dropped his MP5 submachine gun, stretched his arms out, and began shouting something in Arabic at a nearby SH-3 helicopter. "Get down, you fool, no!" she shouted in Arabic. But it was far too late. A heavy-caliber machine gun on the SH-3 opened fire, and the UAE commando was immediately cut down.

"They aren't going to let us surrender," Briggs said grimly, "So we're going to have to fight our way off this roof. We've got the darkness to cover us. We'll try to pick up as many gas masks as we can along the way and take out as many of them as we can. Everyone just keep moving, keep—"

Suddenly one of the SH-3 Sea King helicopters exploded in a huge fireball, less than 200 feet from the rooftop. Then down below, one, then two of the armored vehicles surrounding the security headquarters building burst into flames, followed by several rocking explosions in the security building itself. Briggs and Behrouzi cut down three, four, five Pasdaran troopers trying to rush up onto the roof—but they weren't attacking, they were *fleeing* some devastation behind them. Seconds later, another Sea King helicopter exploded, followed by the ZSU-23/4 air defense unit. The ammunition cooking off inside the ZSU-23/4 completely shredded the vehicle from the inside out.

"What is it, Leopard?"

"I think . . . I *hope*, it's the cavalry," Briggs said.

Sure enough, it was. Out of the darkness, a large aircraft appeared. It swooped in toward the security headquarters building with incredible speed for an aircraft its size, its huge twin propellers acting as helicopter rotors. A Gatling gun mounted on its nose spat fire in several directions at ground targets as the huge aircraft moved with delicate precision toward the rooftop. With the nose and an FLIR turret peeking over the edge of the roof, the CV-22 Pave Hammer tilt-rotor aircraft settled just a yard above the rooftop, rear end in. The cargo ramp was open, and commandos were running out and taking security positions around the rooftop.

Marine Corps Gunnery Sergeant Chris Wohl ran over to Briggs and Behrouzi as several Madcap Magician commandos helped the others to the CV-22 tilt-rotor. "Let's go, Major," Wohl said. "We're outta here."

Briggs felt like hugging the tall Marine. "How in hell did you find us?"

"Later," Wohl said. "Right now, let's get the hell outta here. We're bingo fuel, and we've got a tanker waiting for us off the coast."

In less than a minute, everyone was evacuated off the rooftop, and the CV-22 was wave-hopping its way out over the Gulf of Oman. The CV-22's threat warning receiver beeped a few times, but they observed no missile launches or fighter pursuit. In ten minutes they were out of Iranian territorial waters, and a few minutes later they were refueling behind a U.S. Air Force HC-130N special operations tanker that had been dispatched from Bahrain to support the Madcap Magician rescue mission.

"Practically the entire UAE government was watching you guys heading off toward Chah Bahar," Wohl explained once they were safely refueled and on the way back to Dubai. "Peace Shield Sky-watch reported the OV-10D Bronco belonging to General Rashid heading for Iran—they thought the Emir's son was defecting or something. When I heard about it on the air defense net, I had an HC-130N scramble from Manama Air Base in Bahrain, we took a token onload over the UAE, and immediately headed toward Chah Bahar. Somehow, I knew it was you: first the message about the carrier and the lone chopper heading toward Chah Bahar, then the recall message . . ."

"I almost got everyone killed, Gunny," Briggs said. "I lost two Americans, I got four UAE commandos killed, I lost their Bronco . . ."

"Yes, you did," Wohl said sternly. "You executed an impossible mission without proper planning, intelligence, and preparation, including the basics like how in hell you were going to get your asses out of the target area and safely back home. You put yourself and your troops in mortal danger. It was stupid, Briggs, really stupid. You exercised poor, immature, and completely rash judgment as a commander. . . ."

Wohl stopped, then nodded resignedly and added, "But you pulled it off, goddamn your Air Force birdbrain black ass. You saved ten guys, ten of *your* guys, and you didn't leave anyone behind. You improvised, adapted, and overcame. You used incredible bravery and guts, and showed real leadership. I wouldn't have done it that way, but I'm not the commander of Madcap Magician's strike force—*you* are."

OVER THE GULF OF OMAN
THAT SAME TIME

"Shamu One-One, this is Nightmare on AR primary, how copy, over." Silently, McLanahan prayed. Be there, you guys, dammit, be there. . . .

"Nightmare, this is Shamu One-One, read you five by," the KC-10 Extender aerial refueling tanker copilot responded. "We're just about min fuel at Watchdog. What's your position? Over."

"Nightmare is two hundred west of the ARIP, headed your way," McLanahan responded, breathing a sigh of relief. They were one hour late to their scheduled refueling, near the U.S.S. *Abraham Lincoln* carrier group in the Arabian Sea, and now the B-2A was critically short on fuel—but so was their tanker, a converted Douglas DC-10 used by the U.S. Air Force for long-range aerial refueling and cargo hauling. If the KC-10 Extender couldn't stay to hook up, they would have to abort to Diego Garcia in the Indian Ocean—and surely this meant their cover would be blown. One didn't have to be a math major to draw a parallel between all the attacks on Iran and the sudden appearance of a B-2A bomber on Diego Garcia.

"We're headed your way, Nightmare," the copilot of the KC-10 said. "We're working on an alternate divert site for ourselves to get you your full offload. If you can take a partial offload, it would sure help us out. Over."

McLanahan pulled up a large chart of the Pacific and Indian Ocean regions and ran several range calculations through the navigation computer. "We can take a three-quarter off-load and abort to Guam if we can't get a tanker to meet us," McLanahan reported. He paused, showing Jamieson the calculations: "We can also take a three-quarters off-load, fly across India, southeast Asia, and China, and get our normal refueling west of Hawaii. Tempting, isn't it?"

"We're not authorized to overfly any non-international air-space," Jamieson said, "no matter how much gas it'll save. But yes, it is tempting. Take the partial off-load, we'll plan on aborting to Guam."

"Agreed," McLanahan said. He relayed the information to the tanker crew, who were very excited to hear that they wouldn't have to try to get landing permission in Oman or fly anywhere near Iran right now—any aircraft, especially U.S. military aircraft, flying anywhere near the Persian Gulf would definitely be putting the lives of its crew at risk right now. Like a huge, angry swarm of bees, the entire Iranian air force was up, fully alerted, and looking for revenge. With a partial off-load to the B-2A, the tanker could safely make its way back to its staging base at Diego Garcia, a small island in the Indian Ocean leased by the United States from Britain for use as a military air and naval base, about 1,500 miles south.

They agreed on a "point parallel" rendezvous, in which both aircraft would fly toward each other 1,000 feet apart in altitude. About thirty miles apart, the tanker turned in front of the bomber so it would roll out about four to five miles ahead of the bomber, within visual range, and then Jamieson would fly the B-2A up into the precontact position. The rendezvous was automatic—the tanker's navigation computers performed the entire operation, backed up by occasional updates by the B-2A's synthetic aperture radar transmitting in air-to-air mode—and a few short minutes later, the KC-10's flying boom was nestled into the B-2A bomber's in-flight refueling receptacle. The fuel transfer began. The B-2A needed gas badly, so the KC-10 crew turned up the transfer pumps and got the transfer rate up to 3,000 pounds of fuel per minute—enough gas to fill up *sixty* automobiles every minute.

The fuel transfer was about half completed when suddenly the tanker's director lights—the rows of colored lights on the tanker's belly that told the pilot where to fly to stay in the proper refueling envelope—flashed on and off rapidly, and the refueling boom popped out of the bomber's receptacle. McLanahan was watching the tanker and checking to make sure the fuel was being distributed to the proper tanks when he saw the flashing lights and immediately shouted, "Break away, break away!" Jamieson chopped the throttles and started a 3,000-foot-per-minute descent, making both crew members light in the seats from the sudden negative gravity. "Boom's clear! Tanker climbing!" McLanahan reported.

"What happened? What is it?" Jamieson asked, scanning his instruments. "Was it a pressure disconnect? Boom malfunction?"

"The tanker's lights are out," McLanahan said. "I lost sight of him . . ."

"Get him on the SAR," Jamieson said. "We need this refueling."

Just then on the radios, they heard a thick Middle Eastern-accented voice say in English, "Unidentified aircraft, unidentified aircraft, this is Interceptor Seven-Four, air force of the Islamic Republic of Iran, on emergency GUARD frequency. You have been observed flying into Iranian airspace in violation of international law. You are ordered to follow me to a landing at Chah Bahar air base. Turn left heading three-five-zero degrees immediately or you will be fired upon without further warning!"

"*What?*" Jamieson shouted. "What kind of bullshit is this? We're not in Iranian airspace!"

McLanahan made no reply—but he did reach up and hit the COMBAT switch light. The light began to blink because Jamieson's consent switch was not in the proper position. "Give me consent for COMBAT mode, AC."

"What are you doing?"

"*Do it*, Colonel!" McLanahan shouted. "Keep on descending—take it down to two thousand feet, *fast!*" Jamieson was about to argue again, but he flipped his consent switch to CONSENT, AND THE COMBAT light turned steady.

As Jamieson nosed the bomber over and pointed the B-2A's beaked nose seaward, McLanahan displayed the threat scope on his supercockpit display. There was the KC-10 tanker, transmitting rendezvous beacon codes. "Shut down your transmitters, Shamu," McLanahan prayed aloud. Another symbol, a flashing inverted-V "bat-wing" symbol with a yellow triangle emanating from its nose and overlapping the KC-10 symbol, also appeared on the scope.

"What is it?" Jamieson asked.

"An Iranian MiG-29," McLanahan replied. "He's got the tanker locked on his attack radar."

"An Iranian MiG! What's he doing way out here? We're a hundred miles outside Iranian airspace!"

"The Iranians are sweeping the skies for whoever invaded

Chah Bahar, Bandar Abbas, and their carrier battle group,'' McLanahan surmised. ''They're looking for *us*.''

''And they found our tanker instead!'' Jamieson cried. ''Shit, they're trying to get him to land back at Chah Bahar!''

''To replace the hostages Briggs got out of prison,'' McLanahan said. ''Jesus!''

''We gotta do something!'' Jamieson shouted. ''Get on that machine of yours. Call the Navy, call Washington, but get some help!''

McLanahan immediately burst out a message via satellite to the National Security Agency, warning them of the intercept and requesting that the U.S.S. *Abraham Lincoln* launch fighters to try to pursue and to ask American fighter patrols over the Arabian Peninsula to intercept the group over the Gulf of Oman on their way back. ''Messages sent,'' McLanahan said as they leveled off at 2,000 feet above the ocean.

''American tanker plane, this is Interceptor Seven-Four on emergency GUARD frequency. Change heading immediately or I will be forced to fire upon you. You have been observed trespassing in Iranian airspace and attacking Iranian military and civilian property. Turn left to heading three-five-zero now. This is your last warning!''

''Iranian interceptor, this is Shamu One-One,'' the pilot of the KC-10 tanker radioed back. ''We are an unarmed aerial refueling tanker aircraft. We are carrying no cargo or weapons. We were not in Iranian airspace. We are on a round-robin ICAO flight plan, destination Diego Garcia. Please maintain your distance. Do not approach this aircraft. Do you read me?''

McLanahan switched off COMBAT mode so he could talk on the UHF radios; as soon as the electronic masking field around the bomber de-energized, he keyed the mike: ''Iranian interceptor, this is Ghostrider Zero-Five, from the U.S.S. *Abraham Lincoln*, United States Navy.'' McLanahan didn't know the call sign of the fighter squadrons aboard the *Lincoln*, nor did he know anything about Navy fighter tactics—he just hoped this would sound good. ''We have you on radar one hundred twenty miles south of Chah Bahar at angels three-zero. We are rendezvousing with that American tanker aircraft you are pursuing. Back off immediately or we will attack from long range. Ghostrider flight, combat spread, arm 'em up.''

''I hope the hell you know what you're doing, McLanahan,'' Jamieson said. He quickly placed the B-2A back in COMBAT mode as the MiG-29's attack radar swept the skies around them. For a brief moment the fighter radar locked onto the B-2A—the MiG-29 had an excellent and very powerful ''look-down, shoot-down'' radar, and it was only five miles away—but as soon as COMBAT mode was reengaged, the MiG's radar broke lock. The MiG scanned the skies again, using long-range scans, then locked back onto the KC-10 tanker.

McLanahan deactivated COMBAT mode once again, then keyed the UHF radio mike: ''Iranian interceptor, we are detecting you locking on to our tanker with your attack radar at our twelve o'clock, eighty miles. I warn you, shut off your radar and return to your base, or we will attack from long range. Ghostrider flight, lock 'em up, now.''

That time, the MiG-29's radar slaved precisely at the B-2A bomber and locked on, the Iranian fighter's radar triangle switching from green to yellow and back to green as it attempted to maintain a lock on the stealth bomber. While not engaging COMBAT mode, the B-2A still had a very small radar cross-section, but not small enough to evade a MiG-29 at close range. McLanahan considered telling the KC-10 pilot to do evasive maneuvers now while the MiG wasn't locked on to him, but it wouldn't do any good; the MiG-29 could reacquire the big KC-10 with ease. McLanahan called up the B-2A's electronic countermeasures control panels, ready to activate all its defensive systems . . .

. . . and it was just in time, for as soon as the radar triangle surrounding the B-2A bomber on the threat scope changed to a solid yellow, it changed to red. They heard a rapid *deedledeedledeedle!* warning tone, followed by a computer-synthesized ''MISSILE LAUNCH . . . MISSILE LAUNCH . . . !''

McLanahan immediately activated COMBAT mode and all of the countermeasures equipment. The HAVE GLANCE system promptly locked on to the incoming missile and fired its laser beam. "Two missiles in the air!" McLanahan shouted. "Break left!" Jamieson threw the B-2A bomber into a hard left turn and jammed the throttles to full military power.

With COMBAT mode engaged and the B-2A bomber's "cloaking device" reenergized, absorbing every watt of radar energy striking the bomber's electrified skin, the only solid radar-reflective object in the MiG-29's radar sweep was the cloud of chaff the B-2A ejected, and that's what the two radar-guided missiles struck. The radar triangle changed back to green, then disappeared.

Jamieson descended down to 100 feet above the Gulf of Oman, daring the Iranian MiG to fly down to that dark expanse of open ocean to pursue. "He might be trying a heater shot," McLanahan said, warning Jamieson to get ready to counter a heat-seeking missile shot. But the MAWS radar showed the fighter still up at 30,000 feet, not yet pursuing.

"C'mon, this guy's got to be running out of fuel," Jamieson said. "We're nearly three hundred miles away from his base."

"With three external tanks for an air patrol mission, he's good to go for almost a thousand miles," McLanahan said. He deactivated COMBAT mode once again, keeping the MAWS tracking the fighter. "Iranian interceptor, this is Ghostrider flight of two, you just committed an act of war," McLanahan radioed. "Turn back immediately or we will . . ."

But the ruse didn't work. The B-2A's threat scope showed the MiG-29 briefly transmit with its N-019 pulse-Doppler radar, lock on to the KC-10 tanker once again, then flick off. The MAWS radar tracked the MiG-29 until it closed within five miles of the KC-10 . . . "Jesus, *no!*"

"Mayday, Mayday, Mayday, Shamu-One-One on GUARD," the pilot of the KC-10 Extender shouted on the international emergency frequency. "Position, two hundred miles south of Chah Bahar airfield. We have been attacked by an Iranian fighter, repeat, we are under attack! We have been struck by missiles fired at us by . . .'' And the radio went dead.

''Good-bye, Yankee cowards,'' the Iranian pilot radioed, and the MiG-29 turned and headed back toward Iran.

As Jamieson set up an orbit over the area, McLanahan sent another message to the National Security Agency and the Air Intelligence Agency, detailing the events. Using intermittent bursts of the SAR, they orbited the Gulf of Oman over the KC-10's wreckage for another hour until no more radar-significant debris could be detected. Silently, afraid to speak, frozen and riddled by guilt and anguish, the B-2A crew started to climb and set a course for Diego Garcia to arrange another refueling for the long trip home.

THE PENTAGON BRIEFING ROOM
23 APRIL 1997, 0904 HOURS ET

''I just wanted to express my concern over recent events in the Middle East,'' Secretary of Defense Arthur Chastain began. ''Apparently, late last night Iran time, Iran fired several volleys of missiles from air defense sites in the Strait of Hormuz and from their aircraft carrier in the Gulf of Oman.

''The President immediately spoke to President Nateq-Nouri of Iran, who explained that there has been an air defense integration problem with the aircraft carrier battle group, and that a false alert over Bandar Abbas in the Strait of Hormuz caused a similar false alert over the aircraft carrier, causing the missile launches. At last report, no vessels or aircraft were in danger of being struck by these missiles.

''The President conveyed his deep sense of concern over this apparent demonstration of power, and he said that such demonstrations might affect the proposed summit of Middle East nations and negotiations over Iran's proposal to exclude land-attack warships from the Persian Gulf region. The President, as you know, has endorsed President Nateq-Nouri's proposal and has even suggested expanding the ban to land-attack aircraft. The President is awaiting a formal draft treaty before presenting it to the congressional leadership.

"To summarize: Iran apparently fired several dozen air defense missiles, anti-ship missiles, and antiaircraft artillery guns into the sky last night, Iran time. No aircraft or ships were struck, and no countries were in danger. Neither the United States nor any of the countries bordering the Gulf has put its forces on alert in response to this demonstration of power. The Defense Department speculates that this was either a malfunction, a response to a false attack alarm, or some kind of demonstration of air defense power that, frankly, wasted a lot of missiles and bullets for nothing. The President has said that he is still committed to peace in the Persian Gulf region and will not let such blatant demonstrations sway him from that objective. Thank you. What are your questions?"

". . . No, we are in direct and constant communication with President Nateq-Nouri and Foreign Minister Velayati of Iran, and they assure us that Iran is not gearing up or mobilizing for war in the Persian Gulf or Gulf of Oman, or anywhere else for that matter," Chastain replied. "He did admit that there are very pro-military persons in the Iranian government that see the Persian Gulf demilitarization treaty as a sign of weakness and as undercutting Iran's sovereignty and national defense. Privately, some analysts have speculated—and this is *only* speculation—that these hawkish military leaders staged this air defense demonstration not only to threaten the Gulf Cooperative Council states and others sailing the Persian Gulf, but members of their own government as well. Yes?"

". . . Yes, we've heard that other Iranian military bases reacted as well, and that Iranian fighter planes were flying around on full alert, but they are farther away from international waters and from routine monitoring by Gulf Cooperative Council forces, so we don't know much about those reports. . . ."

". . . Yes, Iran's chief of staff General Buzhazi is claiming that the United States is flying stealth bombers over his country and is threatening to attack. The idea is ridiculous. The United States has a grand total of ten B-2A bombers in the inventory, and all ten of them are still at Whiteman Air Force Base in Missouri, and they've never left. In addition, the bomb wing there is not scheduled to be operational until October first.

"Let me make this point very clear, ladies and gentlemen: Iran is not threatening war with anybody, so why should we fly any aircraft over their country? In fact, President Nateq-Nouri has gone a long way toward promoting peace for the Middle East, and the President of the United States will do nothing to hinder that. What the right-wing fanatical military leaders or the fundamentalist clerical leaders of Iran will do, and whether or not President Nateq-Nouri can control them or gain their support, is a question I just can't answer."

FOUR

"You arrogant, incompetent *fool!*" Islamic Republic of Iran
President Ali Akbar Nateq-Nouri shouted angrily. He and his
Cabinet ministers were meeting with military chief of staff
and Pasdaran commander Buzhazi in Nateq-Nouri's office—
the meeting had been bombastic, angry, and threatening to
go out of control right from the start. "How dare you march
into my office, deliver a report like *this* to me, and have the
unmitigated gall to tell me that *I* am preventing you from
doing your job! I should court-martial you for dereliction of
duty—no, I should have you sent to prison for the rest of
your life for insubordination *as well* as dereliction of duty!
But this will wait for a better time—the Supreme Defense
Council is waiting."

The Iranian Supreme Defense Council was the approving
authority for all military matters in Iran. Along with its president, the Defense Minister, it consisted of the Prime Minister, Hasan Ebrihim Habibi; Buzhazi's friend, protégé, and
confidant and commander of Iran's air forces, Brigadier General Mansour Sattari; ground forces commander General Ab-
dollah Najafi; commander of the navy Rear Admiral Ali

Shamkhani; chairman of the Majlis's Armed Services Committee, Qolam Adeli; and Hamid Mirzadeh, director of the Islamic Republic News Agency and the chief of war propaganda.

"What in the name of God . . . ?" Nateq-Nouri exclaimed under his breath, as he entered the cabinet room. Buzhazi noticed with delight that Nateq-Nouri had just realized that both Imams representing the Leadership Council were present for this meeting. The religious leaders of the Council, together with the Faqih, His Eminence the Ayatollah Khamenei, exercised ultimate political power in the government and ultimate spiritual power in most of the Twelver Shi'ite Muslim world. It was unusual to have anyone representing the mullahs here at a Supreme Defense Council meeting—everyone was here but His Holiness, the Leader of the Islamic Revolution, Ayatollah Ali Hoseini Khamenei himself.

"Is this a trial or an execution, Mr. President?" Buzhazi asked sotto voce to Nateq-Nouri.

"I advise you to shut your insolent mouth, General," the President said as they took their seats at the cabinet table.

Buzhazi saw with interest that a political crony of the Defense Minister, an old *lingham*-sucker named General Hosein Esmail Akhundi, was sitting behind Defense Minister Foruzandeh. So apparently they had already picked his replacement, Buzhazi thought with interest. Akhundi had no military education, no experience—nothing but money and political contacts, and had been awarded a commission and instant promotion to general with seniority by presidential decree. He represented Nateq-Nouri's slant away from the powerful, hard-line expeditionary military that Buzhazi was trying to build, and a clear movement toward a toothless dragon used merely to bully other Muslim nations.

Just before he took his seat, Buzhazi turned to his aide and said, "Bring him here and wait for my command." The aide hurried off to do as he was ordered—this demonstration had been arranged in advance.

Nateq-Nouri nodded to the two Imams present. "We are honored to have the representatives of the Leadership Council in our presence today. We are here to receive the report from General Buzhazi on the attacks against the Islamic Republic that occurred earlier this morning. As you all know, there were three separate incidents: an unknown air attack against Bandar Abbas; the mishaps aboard the aircraft carrier *Khomeini* that caused considerable damage to that vessel; and the assault on the security complex at Chah Bahar Naval Base.''

The Iranian President turned to Buzhazi. ''General, we shall surely get to the matter of the *Khomeini* soon, and your theories about what happened to that ship and the Chinese destroyer. But I wish to query you on the attack at Chah Bahar first, since this was obviously an assault made by GCC and American forces. Your report states that our radar planes and ground radar stations detected the intruder almost *two hundred kilometers* from Chah Bahar, and yet *not one* fighter launched? How is that possible, General?''

''The intruder aircraft was flying less than three hundred twenty knots, it was a single aircraft, and it was flying on an established airway,'' General Buzhazi explained. ''Night intercepts are dangerous, and several fighters from Chah Bahar were on patrol searching for the attackers overflying Bandar Abbas, so no additional fighters were launched against this lone, non-threatening target. When the intruder did not answer any of our challenges, it was engaged by ground-based air defenses at maximum range.''

''And it evaded all of them?''

''The aircraft was equipped with very sophisticated defensive equipment, including chaff dispensers and threat warning receivers,'' Buzhazi noted. ''The aircraft was shot down over the base . . .''

''After shooting up more of our armored vehicles, even *after* dropping five paratroopers right on our security facility!''

''. . . and we have examined the wreckage of the aircraft,'' Buzhazi struggled on. ''It was the personal aircraft of Sheikh Muhammad ibn Rashid al-Maktum himself, the son of the Emir of Dubai—a sentence of death should be placed on this infidel immediately. The aircraft was fully armed and was also equipped for low-altitude flight and precision navigation.

"But the main factor was the state of the air defenses around Chah Bahar. As I said in my report, sir, the Hawks placed there were some of our poorest-maintained units. I have ordered SA-10 units and more Rapier air defense units, but my requests have been constantly overridden . . ."

"There was no use in putting a costly SA-10 air defense site at a naval base that is still uncompleted after five years in construction and an oil pipeline terminal that is still uncompleted after ten years," Minister of Defense Muhammad Foruzandeh interjected. "Chah Bahar is nothing but random piles of concrete buildings, mostly vacant or in partial stages of completion, surrounding an obsolete air base and a shallow-water port facility that cannot accommodate anything larger than a tugboat, let alone a major warship or a supertanker. Your budget has been increased every year for the past three years to complete that base, and yet the projected completion date is moved back every year. Where is all that money going, General? To your private offshore bank accounts, your homes in Indonesia and South America, your private jets?"

"How dare you insinuate that I have embezzled government funds!" Buzhazi retorted. "I demand an apology!"

"Enough, *enough!*" Nateq-Nouri shouted. "The general will have his opportunity to answer all of these charges very soon, I guarantee it." He got to his feet and paced behind his desk. "So then a single aircraft shoots up the base, destroys the power plant and all base communications, then drops five"—he shook his head as if scarcely believing what he was saying—". . . five paratroopers into a security compound with *thirty-two armed Pasdaran guards* on duty, kills or wounds each and every one of them, rescues all the American prisoners, then holds off an entire infantry *company* of Pasdaran shock troops until they are extracted by another *single* American aircraft? I cannot believe this, Buzhazi. The

Islamic Republic will be the world's laughingstock by the end of the day."

"Mr. President, we were unprepared for the arrival of those prisoners from the *Khomeini*," Buzhazi said. "The security facility had a normal complement of troops for the number of inmates already present, which were all low-risk disciplinary cases. The base commander already had orders to double the guards at the facility when he learned of the transfer of the prisoners."

"That seems to be the reason for *all* that has happened in the past few hours, General—you were unprepared," Nateq-Nouri said. "You were unprepared for the assaults on Bandar Abbas or on the *Khomeini* carrier group, unprepared for the attack and assaults on Chah Bahar . . . So, you have a theory as to how all those attacks made it through your vaunted defenses, General?"

"The same as the mysterious unidentified aircraft that 'attacked' Bandar Abbas, sir—they were cruise missiles, decoys, launched by American stealth bombers," Buzhazi said. He could see Nateq-Nouri, Foruzandeh, and most of the others roll their eyes in exasperation. "Yes, stealth bombers, gentlemen. The same as was reported by the MiG-29 pilot over the Gulf of Oman with the American KC-10 aerial refueling tanker. The Americans are conducting illegal, warlike reconnaissance flights over our country with stealth bombers, launching sophisticated decoy missiles over our forces that fool our air defenses into thinking we are under massive attack so we quickly expend all our weapons."

"I see, I see," Defense Minister Foruzandeh said scornfully, clearly unimpressed by Buzhazi's explanation. "We are all going to blame this on shadows of steel, on bombers loaded with intelligent cruise missiles that fly with complete impunity over our radars and missile fields. General, you have said yourself that the American stealth program is a sham, a program foisted on the American people to benefit the aircraft manufacturers and to bankrupt the former Soviet Union by forcing them to spend billions on weapons to defeat them."

"The American stealth bombers and their new generation cruise missiles are *real*, Minister," Buzhazi said. "That is what I have been trying to prepare our country to defend itself against!"

"This testimony will make fascinating reading at your court-martial, General."

"Do not threaten me, sir!" Buzhazi shouted. "If you wish to relieve me of my office—if you have the *stomach* to try to remove me—you may do it at any time." Nateq-Nouri looked as if he were ready to kill his military chief of staff with his bare hands. "But you may not threaten me with punishment for trying to do my duty!"

"It has been how you have tried to 'do your duty' that has bankrupted our country and forced us to the brink of war with the Americans," Nateq-Nouri said angrily. "It will continue no more. Dr. Velayati."

Ali Akbar Velayati, the Foreign Minister, held up a communiqué, nestled in a blue diplomatic folder. "A message from the American Secretary of State," Velayati said to Buzhazi and the rest of the Defense Council, "received late last night. The United States accepts in principle the Islamic Republic's proposal to ban all landattack warships from the Persian Gulf, including aircraft carriers, and to allow the Islamic Republic to maintain an equal number of warships in the Persian Gulf as Gulf Cooperation Council warships."

"How dare they issue a statement like that, after wantonly attacking our air defense forces as they did last night?" Buzhazi retorted.

"Silence, General Buzhazi," President Nateq-Nouri ordered. "Continue, Dr. Velayati."

"The United States wishes to schedule a summit of all interested nations for this September, where a treaty will be signed," the Foreign Minister went on. "Secretary of State Hartman further recommends that this proposal be extended to the boundaries of the Gulf of Oman and the Gulf of Aden west of the sixtieth meridian . . ."

"What?" Buzhazi retorted. "The sixtieth meridian? That

is . . . that is just west of Chah Bahar. . . . Sir, do you realize that is almost the *entire coastline of Iran!*''

''And that *is* the entire coastline of all of the Gulf Cooperation Council states,'' Nateq-Nouri said. ''We shall have an equal number of warships as all of our adversaries in the oil-transit areas, but we will be free to sail expeditionary warships from Chah Bahar Naval Base if we so choose—but they will not be allowed to enter the Gulf of Oman, the Gulf of Aden, the Strait, or the Persian Gulf if they exceed the number of warships of GCC states.''

''This is utterly insane!'' Buzhazi shouted. ''You cannot do this!''

''Pending successful treaty negotiations between now and September, ratification by the Majlis, approval by the Council of Guardians, and the blessing of the Faqih,'' Nateq-Nouri said, ''we will sign such an agreement. We shall then seek a new treaty to limit similarly the number of attack planes over the Persian Gulf region.'' Buzhazi was completely speechless—he was watching his newly redesigned military going right down the drain.

''As proof of our good intentions and our desire for peace and prosperity,'' Nateq-Nouri went on, ''I am ordering that the aircraft carrier *Khomeini* and the destroyer *Zhanjiang* be returned immediately to the People's Republic of China. Their presence only exacerbates the tensions in the region. In return, the United States has promised not to send another aircraft carrier or marine aircraft assault ship into the Persian Gulf or Gulf of Oman. We are most heartened by these developments and feel this is the beginning of a new era of peace.''

''Peace! What peace?'' Buzhazi exploded. ''Did you not hear what I have said, Mr. President? I believe the United States overflew our country, violated our sovereign airspace, and attacked our cities and our aircraft carrier with stealth aircraft and cruise missiles. In return, we are agreeing to disarm ourselves? Sir, the Americans attacked our aircraft carrier because they knew what kind of threat it was to their security and the security of their Gulf Cooperative Council and Zionist lackeys. We cannot surrender to their blackmail and threats!''

"It is already done, General—I have so ordered it,'' Nateq-Nouri said. "That monstrosity has always been an embarrassment to the Islamic Republic, General. The money we spent in so-called training can better be spent on our cities, on the needed infrastructure in the remote provinces, and on our people. We can spread the Islamic revolution easier with well-educated, successful citizens than we can by force. It is so ordered.''

One of the Imams, the Ayatollah Bijan Kalantari, raised his hand, and a crier behind the Imams ordered silence. "General Hesarak al-Kan Buzhazi,'' the old man said in a deep, surprisingly strong voice, "the loss of prestige in the eyes of the true believers around the world has offended the Faqih, and he has demanded an explanation. You may speak in the presence of Allah, his servants of the Leadership Council, and all those true believers present here, and may you be struck down by the hand of the righteous if you do not tell the truth.''

This was it, Buzhazi thought as he got to his feet. His days were numbered, his replacement was present, and the firing squad was undoubtedly waiting outside for him—his fate would be decided by the words he was to say right now. . . .

"Our aircraft carrier, the city of Bandar Abbas, and the Chah Bahar Naval Base were attacked by the air and naval forces of the United States,'' Buzhazi said in a firm, loud voice, pointing a finger directly at a stunned President Nateq-Nouri, "as part of a conspiracy between our traitorous pro-West, pro-Zionist President, Ali Akbar Hashemi Nateq-Nouri, the American Central Intelligence Agency, the Gulf Cooperative Council states, and the United States government. Before Allah and all of you, I swear this is true—and I have proof.''

The cabinet chamber exploded in bedlam. Nateq-Nouri was on his feet in indignation, sputtering unintelligible words, shooting a shocked expression all across the room . . .

. . . because, to Buzhazi's surprise, the allegation had hit home. The president looked as if he were ready either to kill Buzhazi or run out of the room like a madman—and the image was not lost on the rest of the Supreme Defense Council. Everywhere Nateq-Nouri looked, he saw another confused and suspicious face—staring back at *him*.

"Admit it!" Buzhazi shouted at Nateq-Nouri. "Admit the truth! Admit that you conspired with the United States to dismantle the Islamic Republic's navy!"

"You will be silent!" Nateq-Nouri shouted at Buzhazi. "I will not dignify such outlandish claims with a denial! You are a liar and an inept despot seeking only glory and power for yourself—"

"Admit the truth!" Buzhazi interjected. "Admit that you have been keeping regular contact with members of the U.S. State Department and the American President's National Security Advisor, informing him of our nation's military secrets and operations and in return receiving favors and tribute from the Turkish and American governments!"

"That is another lie, Buzhazi!" Nateq-Nouri shouted. But his denial was not as strong as the first, and came after a brief hesitation, and that silenced the chamber almost as quickly and as surely as if Nateq-Nouri had admitted his guilt. Nateq-Nouri quickly added, "Well-known associates of members of the Ministry of Foreign Affairs have had brief contacts with American bureaucrats, yes—but that is because we have no embassy in Washington, and a more direct form of communication was deemed necessary. That is all."

"So you deny that your so-called associates—spies in your employ—spoke directly with General Philip Freeman, the American President's National Security Advisor and overseer of American Central Intelligence?" Buzhazi asked.

"General Buzhazi, you are creating some kind of wild conspiracy fantasy. These were routine back-channel informational nongovernment contacts by Iranian loyalists, and you know it. I will not tolerate this," Nateq-Nouri said angrily. "I am the President and commander in chief, and I order you to be silent or I will place you under arrest. I do not report to you, only the Faqih and the people . . ."

"Very inspirational, very touching, Mr. President," Buzhazi went on, "but you refuse to answer my question or refute my charges. Are you or are you not in contact with the American Central Intelligence authorities? Are you or are you not working in concert with the corrupt and immoral United States and the Arab traitors to Islam in the Gulf Cooperative Council, to preserve your own power and position at the expense of the Islamic Republic of Iran's military forces? Did you or did you not know that the *Khomeini* battle group would come under attack, but did nothing to stop it and even ordered me to withhold my defensive forces and even to dismiss me, so that the attack against us could succeed?"

"Silence, General, or I will have you placed under arrest!" Nateq-Nouri shouted. "I will not tolerate this any longer!"

The Ayatollah Kalantari held up his hand, and the crier shouted the order, "Silence all, the Imam shall be heard!" The cabinet room immediately fell silent.

"Excuse me, Mr. President," Kalantari said, in a low, barely audible voice. "The charge of conspiring with the Americans and the Gulf Cooperative Council, two of our chief adversaries, is a serious one. General Buzhazi risks much by leveling such a charge against you. If he is proved false, he is disgraced before the Supreme Defense Council and is subject to immediate imprisonment. Although the general is still your subordinate and faces disciplinary action if he wears the uniform but does not obey your command to be silent, we wish that this matter be resolved. We wish to hear your response to these charges."

"My response is that General Buzhazi is a liar, and is levying these charges merely to cover up his desperate attempt to precipitate a war with the Gulf Cooperative Council and the United States, his failed military operations, and to try to avoid demotion or dismissal," Nateq-Nouri said. "I strongly deny all his charges, and as commander in chief I hereby relieve him of command of the Pasdaran and the armed forces of the Islamic Republic."

The Imam turned to General Buzhazi and said evenly,

"General, you may speak. President Nateq-Nouri has denied your charges. Under pain of dismissal and disgrace, you must prove your allegations. What is your response?"

"Here is my response, Your Holiness," Buzhazi shouted, raising a hand. The doors to the Cabinet chamber swung open, and two armed guards escorted a prisoner inside. The man wore a green-and-yellow prison jumpsuit and was chained at the wrist, ankle, and neck, plus handcuffed in front of his body for added effect. Both eyes were swollen and discolored, and his fingers were heavily bandaged. The barefoot prisoner walked with a great deal of pain.

"This man was pulled out of the Strait of Hormuz on the night of the enemy reconnaissance on the *Khomeini* carrier group," Buzhazi shouted, pointing a finger at the man in chains. "He was aboard the vessel that shot down two of our carrier-based fighters that evening. We have reason to believe that this man's vessel was the launch and control vessel for a small but sophisticated stealth reconnaissance aircraft that was photographing the *Khomeini* carrier group and was in fact passing along information to the American CIA, forces of the Gulf Cooperative Council, and Israel. Our fighters sank his vessel, but not before several of his fellow crewmen abandoned the ship and escaped safely to the United Arab Emirates."

Buzhazi looked at his prisoner and smiled eerily. "We recovered several bodies as well, some of whom appear to be American military personnel, possibly American Marines." The prisoner closed his eyes, as if in great pain; the assembled men noticed this and nodded, as if he had just admitted the fact. "Their clothing had been carefully stripped of all identifying tags. My staff says this is a typical procedure for a spy vessel."

The Ayatollah Kalantari motioned for the guards to bring the prisoner forward, toward the Cabinet table; room was made for him at the table, and he stood before the Imams, battered and weak but head erect, staring at the clerics and the others assembled around the table. "Your name, sir?" Kalantari ordered. "You have permission to speak."

His order was translated by his crier, and the response translated for the Council: "My name is Paul White," the prisoner replied. "I'm the executive officer and purser of the S.S *Valley Mistress*. Look, Your Honor, I haven't been able to call my family and tell them I'm all right, and I haven't been allowed to call the U.S. consulate. Your jets sank my ship, several members of my crew are dead, and I demand to know—"

"Silence, Mr. White," Kalantari said through his translator. "You will be allowed to contact your family only after your identity and purpose for your voyage have been confirmed."

"But, Your Honor, I was nowhere near your aircraft carrier," White interjected. "My ship was at least fifty miles away—"

"Silence, or you will be returned to your prison cell," Kalantari said. "Answer my questions. What kind of ship is this *Valley Mistress?*"

"It's a rescue-and-salvage vessel," White responded. "We can raise small ships, recover items from deep water, tow large vessels, conduct major power-plant and hull repairs afloat or—"

"What were you doing in the area shadowing our aircraft-carrier group?"

"I run a salvage operation, Your Honor," White said. He cracked a thin smile and shrugged, giving the council members a sheepish expression. "Frankly, Your Honor, your ships were in pretty poor shape, and you were pushing them hard. My ship can . . . er, *could*, take any one of your ships in tow, including your carrier, and we can fix any power plant with the exception of course of your nuclear stuff. We're pretty good at minor repairs, too—motors, engines, appliances, electronics. Plus, we carry a goodly amount of supplies—oil, gasoline, diesel, frozen food, electronics, videotapes—and many vessels invite us to trade with them. But I never came near you guys, Your Honor. Usually if someone needs help, we'll come running, but we never approach unless waved in because we're afraid of making you nervous, and you got all the guns. I swear, we never—''

"If I may, Your Holiness?" Buzhazi asked. Kalantari raised a hand, permitting him to continue the questioning. "Do you also carry Stinger antiaircraft missiles as part of your 'rescue' inventory, Mr. White?" Buzhazi asked through the interpreter.

"Stingers? I don't know anything about any Stingers, Sir...."

"Our patrol helicopter observed two Stinger missile launches coming from your ship, Mr. White . . . or should I say, *Colonel* Paul White," General Buzhazi interjected. Reading from a folder handed to him by an assistant, he continued in a loud voice: "Colonel Paul White, supposedly retired United States Air Force. Your last military assignment was the 675th Weapons Evaluation Group, Hurlburt Field, Florida, as an engineer working on weapons and equipment for secret special operations units—this Hurlburt Field is very close to the American special operations headquarters in Florida and the United States Air Force's special operations wing at Eglin Air Force Base. Six months after your official retirement in 1990, you are manifested as the purser aboard the salvage vessel *Valley Mistress* as you transit the Red Sea, and later as you transit the Strait of Hormuz, destination Bahrain, just before the start of hostilities against Iraq . . ."

"Hey, General, everyone knew a war was starting in the Persian Gulf—I wasn't alone," White said. "Lots of opportunities for a good salvage company, as long as no one confuses you for a warship and puts a bomb down your stacks."

"How does a retired Air Force officer secure a position on a salvage vessel sailing through the Middle East?"

White shrugged again and replied, "I needed the work, and they needed an electronics guy. Lots of jobs were opening up before the war—even in Iran. Everyone knew the shit . . . er, pardon me, sir, everyone knew there was going to be trouble."

"It seems your *Valley Mistress* was right on the spot in many such conflicts," Buzhazi went on. The rest of the

Council, except Nateq-Nouri, were fixed at absolute attention. "Your ship was in the Philippines before the start of hostilities with the Chinese; in the Yellow Sea just before the accidental conflict between North and South Korea involving the hypersonic Aurora spy plane; in the Baltic Sea just before the start of hostilities between the United States and Russia over Lithuania; in the Adriatic during the recent Marine invasion of Bosnia; and even in the Bosporus just before hostilities between Ukraine and Russia."

Buzhazi gave the folder back to his aide. "In each one of these incidents, Colonel White, the United States had sent secret paramilitary and special forces troops into the area to conduct espionage, demolition, search-and-destroy, sabotage, assassination, and kidnapping missions. In several such instances, helicopter-borne forces appeared out of nowhere, and it was determined in some situations that the aircraft could have come from nowhere else but your ship. Your ship, it has quite a large helicopter platform, does it not?"

"It *did*—before your fighter jocks sank it, killed my men, and put me out of business!" White retorted. "Listen, General, Your Honor, sure, I was at all those places, but I run a salvage-and-rescue company—we're *supposed* to go where the fur is flying, if you know what I mean. Sure, I used my buddies in the Air Force to find out where something was going to go down. We always sit near where something might happen because we make our money by recovering items of value. Yes, we have a large helicopter pad and a small hangar facility, but that's because a helicopter gives us added speed and reach—we are a *rescue* company also, as well as salvage. Lots of private companies and contractors have used our facilities, but I've never had any spies on board! That's crazy, General."

"Then perhaps you can tell us," Buzhazi said, accepting a large black-and-white photograph from his aide, "why a salvage ship would be using an SPS-69 air search radar?"

"A what? Excuse me, General, but I don't know what that—"

"An SPS-69 radar, capable of searching for aircraft out to

ranges in excess of one hundred fifty kilometers,'' Buzhazi explained. ''A rather sophisticated piece of equipment for a salvage vessel. Our naval forces found such a device just a few hundred meters from your ship. Here is a photograph of the antenna after it was recovered from the bottom of the Strait of Hormuz.''

''Oh, you mean *that* old piece of . . . er, that old thing?'' White responded innocently, trying to smile through the pain in his legs and back. ''We recovered that off the coast of Florida near the U.S. Navy's junk area. We use it for publicity photos for the company—it makes our ship look real high-tech. I honestly have no idea what that thing did. If you say it's an air search antenna, General, I believe you, but we certainly don't go around tracking aircraft. Why would we?''

''We have also found significant amounts of debris on the bottom, mostly electronic devices—they appear to have been destroyed by small explosive charges planted inside them, as if someone did not want them identified,'' Buzhazi went on. ''We are retrieving them as quickly as possible, and we will make identification shortly. The commander of the *Khomeini* carrier group also reported encoded satellite transmissions from your ship, which he believed were used to send signals to a stealth reconnaissance aircraft that overflew the battle group.''

''I swear, Your Honor, I don't know what he's talking about!'' White pleaded. ''We use satellites for navigation and communications, sure, but we don't use it to steer stealth reconnaissance planes—I don't even know what that is.''

''You are a spy, Colonel White,'' Buzhazi shouted, ''employed by the American Central Intelligence Agency and working in concert with Ali Akbar Nateq-Nouri to undermine our country's defensive military forces and make us vulnerable to the despotic, imperialistic West.''

''A spy! CIA! *Me*, working with *your* President? That's insane!'' White retorted in shock and surprise—it was the best acting job he had ever done, because he was fighting for his life. He turned to Nateq-Nouri and said, ''Tell them, Mr. President. Tell them I'm not working for you.'' He affixed Nateq-Nouri with a determined, warning stare and, carefully emphasizing his words, said, *"Tell them* I don't know a damned thing about the CIA or spying or anything but fixing radios and running a salvage ship."

"General Buzhazi is lying, Mr. White," Nateq-Nouri said in Farsi, understanding White's English well enough without having to wait for the translation. "He is trying to cover up his failures by accusing me and anyone else he can of conspiracy. You may indeed be a spy, and I would suspect as much, but we are not working together, and I never would."

Buzhazi turned to the Ayatollah Kalantari. "Your Holiness, I ask that the prisoner be held in maximum security until more evidence of his espionage activities can be collected. I anticipate this will take at least four to six more weeks. No one in the United States has complained yet about Colonel White's absence, lending even more credibility to his role as a spy."

"Your request is granted," the Ayatollah Kalantari replied. "We find more than sufficient evidence to hold this man to stand trial for espionage and for attacking and destroying Iranian government property on the high seas. Take the prisoner away."

Guards grabbed White and pulled him toward the door. "Hey, General, Your Honor, can't I call my family? Can't you treat my injuries? Why are you treating me like an animal? I don't know anything about Stinger missiles or radars or spies or anything! I'm innocent, I swear to God and on my mother's eyes, I'm innocent!"

"Do not use the name of God to cover your lies!" the Ayatollah Kalantari shouted. "Blasphemer! Tool of the devil! Take his filthy carcass away!"

White ignored Kalantari and Buzhazi, looked directly at President Nateq-Nouri and said in passable Farsi, as if no one else were in the room, "Mr. President, think of the future. Your chief of staff is betraying you. You *need* help. Help me, and I will help you."

"You see! You see!" Buzhazi exclaimed. "The prisoner knows our language, and he attempts to communicate with his co-conspirator! That proves Nateq-Nouri's guilt!''

"I demand to notify the American authorities of my capture!" White shouted in Farsi. "I demand justice! What kind of government is this?" But they all ignored him as he was dragged out of the council chamber.

When all was quiet again, Kalantari addressed Buzhazi: "This is remarkable testimony, General, and will be given full weight in regard to the United States' treacherous activities." He cleared his throat. "However, although highly inflammatory and serious, nothing we have heard proves President Nateq-Nouri's complicity in any conspiracy against the military. If you have any evidence, now is the time to present it or accept the consequences. Do you have any such evidence?"

"I do, Your Holiness," Buzhazi replied. Time for the final toss of the dice. His aide passed him a folder. "A transcript of a phone conversation between the senior assistant minister of defense, Minister Foruzandeh's chief deputy, and a Turkish civilian named Dr. Tahir Sahin. Sahin had apparently just met with the American President's National Security Advisor and the American Secretary of State and warned Foruzandeh of an imminent attack on the *Khomeini* battle group by unnamed American military forces. The attack began minutes after this phone conversation; Minister Foruzandeh met with President Nateq-Nouri and Foreign Minister Dr. Velayati about a half hour later. Yet no one in the Minister of Defense's office, the Foreign Ministry, or the President's office bothered to contact me or warn anyone of the impending attack, even though Minister Velayati's office did make several calls to the United States and to the unbeliever Muhammad ibn Rashid of the United Arab Emirates."

"Again, General Buzhazi is dramatizing routine diplomatic contacts," President Nateq-Nouri interjected. "Yes, I directed Dr. Velayati to contact the UAE foreign office, but only to advise them that military aircraft would be departing Bandar Abbas on emergency air patrols over our own airspace—it is a routine courtesy call, nothing more, designed to prevent any danger of appearing as if we are attacking them.''

''A 'routine courtesy call,' put through directly to the tool of Satan, the Emir of Dubai himself? It sounds like more than a simple 'courtesy call,' Mr. President. Yet you did not think it necessary to notify me or your field commanders of information of an impending attack on the aircraft carrier battle group or on Chah Bahar Naval Base—an attack that was conducted by an attack aircraft *owned* by the Emir of Dubai *himself*, flown by UAE commandos in the employ of the Emir of Dubai? It sounds as if you cleared this attack plane to attack yourself, Mr. President! The conspiracy is clear, Your Holiness!''

''The attack was already in progress by the time we were in contact with Dr. Sahin, a loyal and trustworthy servant of Allah and of this government—there was nothing we could do except prepare for the possibility of hostilities breaking out all across the region, if this was part of a larger attack against us.'' Nateq-Nouri turned angrily at Buzhazi. ''None of this would have happened, Buzhazi, if you had not sunk that American vessel in the first place!''

''I was trying to protect our military forces from another sneak attack by the Gulf Cooperative Council states and their overlord, the United States,'' Buzhazi shot back. ''Because of your order, I was prevented from employing my ground forces adequately to stop any further attacks, and the result is what you have seen.'' He turned to Kalantari. ''Your Holiness, we have suffered great damage, and it is because of this man. I demand that he resign his office and turn control of the government over to the Leadership Council until the crisis has subsided and new parliamentary elections can be held. If he will not step down voluntarily, I ask that the Leadership Council strip him of his office and conduct an investigation of his criminal activities. To allow him to continue his evil activities for even one more day may harm the Islamic Republic for decades yet to come! I demand—''

''Silence, General,'' the Ayatollah Kalantari interjected. The President and the general glared at each other, Buzhazi

with a satisfied grin, Nateq-Nouri with a confused and over-
whelmed expression. "General Buzhazi, you have not yet
proven your case before us, but the charges are serious and
the evidence against the President, although circumstantial,
is compelling." He turned to Nateq-Nouri and said in a low
voice, "Speak Mr. President. What will you do?"

Nateq-Nouri was thunderstruck. Buzhazi was going to win
either way, and there seemed nothing he could do to prevent
it. It was time to save his own skin, so there would be a skin
to save later on when Buzhazi's plans failed and Iran's military forces were crushed. "Your Holiness, the Leadership
Council and the Council of Guardians has the power at any
time to assume administrative leadership of the Islamic Republic," Nateq-Nouri said. "I serve at the pleasure of Allah,
His Holiness the Faqih, and the chosen of the Leadership
Council. I swear to you that I am no traitor, and that I have
not conspired with anyone against the Islamic Republic. But
if you wish me to step down, I will agree." The Cabinet
officers surrounding Nateq-Nouri couldn't believe their ears.
It was obvious that General Buzhazi, disgraced in the eyes
of everyone in government, had been shooting in the dark
with his accusations and wild stories—but no one had expected Nateq-Nouri to bend to his threats and accusations!
Was there really something to all of Buzhazi's charges?

"I promise that if you have need of my services in the
future, when General Buzhazi's lies are uncovered and all is
in turmoil, you may call upon me, and I will serve the Republic once again," Nateq-Nouri went on. "I ask that I be
provided with a security detail of my own choosing, because
I fear I am not safe from the Pasdaran troops and Capital
Guards commanded by General Buzhazi."

"Your request is granted," the Ayatollah Kalantari said.
"Until a tribunal is convened to hear the general's charges
against you, you shall enjoy all the rank and privileges of
the President of the Republic, and you may form whatever
personal guard you desire."

The Ayatollah Kalantari turned to the members of the Supreme Defense Council and said in a loud voice, "It is

hereby ordered that His Holiness the Faqih, the Leader of the Islamic Revolution, Ayatollah Ali Hoseini Khamenei, assumes leadership of the government of the Islamic Republic of Iran this day and assumes the role of commander in chief of the armed forces of the Republic. President Nateq-Nouri, his family, and his associates are not to be harmed in any way by any man, upon pain of punishment of the Leadership Council.''

Well, Nateq-Nouri thought, it was not a total victory for Buzhazi. Under Khamenei, the government would lean further to the right, but it would not move any faster and would probably crawl to all but a complete stop. Buzhazi still didn't have his total . . .

''It is also hereby ordered,'' the Ayatollah Kalantari continued, ''that because of the nature of the military emergency that exists with the wanton attack upon the military forces of the Republic, that a state of national emergency exists in Iran, and that it is necessary to establish martial law within the Republic. It is hereby ordered that General Hesarak al-Kan Buzhazi shall retain his full rank and privileges and should now have full authority over all government offices and services to do so as he shall see fit to protect the government of the Islamic Republic of Iran and the lives of all the true believers. It is the will of Allah and the command of His Holiness the Faqih, so let it be done. General Buzhazi, the Council is at your command.''

''No!'' Nateq-Nouri shouted, jumping to his feet. ''This cannot be! Iran is not under a state of emergency—it is an emergency created by Buzhazi for his own aims!'' But the Imams representing the Leadership Council were heading for the door, eyes averted, refusing to speak. It was Khamenei, Nateq-Nouri decided. The Faqih had decided that now was a good time to flex some Iranian military muscle. The only way to bypass the constitution and advance those plans was to put Buzhazi in charge, and that meant martial law.

Buzhazi got to his feet, amused eyes on Nateq-Nouri. ''Guards, escort Their Holinesses out of the chamber,'' Buzhazi shouted. At that moment, several dozen armed Pasdaran soldiers rushed into the Cabinet chamber, heavily armed, with assault rifles at port arms. A dozen Pasdaran guards surrounded the two high priests as they departed the chamber. As soon as they departed, the chamber erupted into complete bedlam. "Silence!" Buzhazi shouted. "Come to order immediately, or I will see to it that you are all removed!"

Several Pasdaran guards rushed over toward Nateq-Nouri, and were immediately blocked by a small contingent of Nateq-Nouri's personal bodyguards, seven ex-Syrian special forces soldiers. Although outnumbered three to one, it was obvious they would protect their charge to the last man. "Hold!" Buzhazi ordered. "His Holiness the Ayatollah Kalantari has ordered that the former President not be harmed or detained in any way. The former President shall be *escorted* safely out of the chamber and immediately to his residence, where he shall be placed under *protective* guard. Colonel, see to it immediately."

Nateq-Nouri was surrounded by his own personal guard, then by Pasdaran troops, and then by his advisors and Supreme Defense Council ministers sympathetic to him, but he raised his voice enough to be heard above the throng around him: "General Buzhazi, your days on earth are numbered, and I shall be there to see your last day, just before the firing squad's bullets riddle your worthless body."

"Brave words from a traitor," Buzhazi shouted back. "All but Nateq-Nouri must stay. I have a few more matters to discuss."

"I swear to Allah, I shall see to it that you are hanged by your own words," Nateq-Nouri said, as he let himself be led out of the chamber.

As the room cleared and grew ever quieter, several shocked and incredulous eyes turned toward General Buzhazi. "You must be mad, Buzhazi, utterly mad," Muhammad Foruzandeh, the Iranian Defense Minister, finally said acidly. "You know all that the President has said is true—he is not a traitor, and the back-channel communications he has had are perfectly legal and aboveboard—you have used them many times yourself in the past.''

The Prime Minister, Hasan Ebrihim Habibi, spluttered, ''You dare attempt a military coup against the legitimate government?''

''Silence, all of you,'' Buzhazi said. ''This is no coup, gentlemen—this is an order from the Leadership Council that the Islamic Republic is in grave danger and is in need of help right away. Nateq-Nouri is weak and has chosen the way of cooperation and free exchange with the very agents of imperialism and oppression that seek to destroy us. I on the other hand refuse to sit by and watch my country suffer.

''Effective immediately, by the power invested in me as military leader of the Islamic Republic, I hereby suspend and disband the Majlis-i-Shura, the Supreme Court, and the High Judicial Council, until further notice.''

''What?'' several of the civilians shouted. In one sweep, Buzhazi had just dismantled Iran's civil representative government—the 270-member Islamic Consultative Assembly, the Supreme Court, and the entire federal judiciary branch of the government. This left only the three major religious organs—the Leadership Council, led by Leader of the Islamic Revolution, Khamenei; the Council of Experts, led by the Ayatollah Meshkini; and the Council of Guardians, led by the Ayatollah Yazdi—along with the military, to rule the Iranian government. All of these mullahs were very pro-military and extremely fundamentalist, dedicated to exporting the Islamic revolution—led by them and the Shi'ite Muslim sect, of course—all over the world. Now, under martial law, they had the military backing them up. ''Buzhazi, you do not have such authority!''

''Under martial law, crimes against the government will be punishable by military courts, and reviewed by the Council of Guardians and the Council of Experts,'' Buzhazi said. ''The Cabinet and the Supreme Defense Council are also hereby disbanded; the Cabinet ministers retain their positions and authority, but now report to me through my General Staff officers. The newspapers *Kayhan, Ettela'at, Tehran Times*, and all other public or political organs will immediately suspend publication; only *Jum-hurie-Islami* will be allowed to continue operations, under command of the Office of Public Affairs of the General Staff. All broadcasting, except for Radio Naft-e-Melli, will immediately suspend all operations; INTELSAT earth station operations and radio relay station operations, except for military-only base operations, will be suspended immediately until military control can be concluded. . . ."

"There will be panic in the streets of Tehran, General," Prime Minister Habibi said angrily. "You cannot simply shut off all media sources and expect to control a population of seventy million."

"I shall deploy the entire Niru-ye Entezami-e Johuriye Eslami-ye Iran, reinforced and led by the Pasdaran, to maintain order in the cities," Buzhazi said sternly. "The Security Forces of the Islamic Republic have a duty to maintain order and uphold the law. I will mobilize the Basij and federalize them under active-duty control of the Pasdaran to reinforce the internal security forces and border guards.

"But most important, I will issue orders to my staff to carefully instruct all members of the Cabinet on how to conduct your day-to-day operations in the face of this emergency. Martial law does not mean the end of the Republic, only that extraordinary measures must be taken to ensure our safety and security. I expect all government offices and ministers to properly convey that message. Further instructions will be issued by my chief of staff. You are all dismissed. Summon my battle staff and get them in here immediately."

Buzhazi was intently studying a chart of the Middle East, with Iran centered on it, when the senior members of the Islamic Republic's joint chiefs of staff hurried into the Cabinet room. "I want full territorial security established immediately," Buzhazi ordered. "The Strait of Hormuz is hereby off limits to all foreign warships. I want every vessel in our inventory in the strait shadowing every vessel that passes through."

"We will need the reserves, sir," army commander, Brigadier General Mohammed Sohrabi, said.

"Then order a full reserve mobilization," Buzhazi said. "Use the Basij to fill in as necessary, but I want the sea lanes full of Iranian patrol vessels immediately—not six or twelve months from now—shadowing every tanker and every cargo ship that moves through the strait. And I want full air patrols as well—around-the-clock, low-altitude, sustained combat air patrols. I want our forces to be visible to anyone within two hundred kilometers of our shores. Test the GCC and American air forces. How do the Americans put it? Play 'Red Rover' with them, probe their weaknesses."

"I may have found one, sir," air forces commander Brigadier General Mansour Sattari interjected. "We *saw* the American's stealth bomber last night."

"You *what?*" Buzhazi dismissed his other staff members, and sat down with Sattari, his handpicked man, hopefully soon to be his chief of staff when he became President. "How was this done?"

"Sir, stealth works because of two things: the stealth aircraft absorbs some radar energy and redirects the rest into thin lobes that point in directions other than back at the transmitter—the net result is that the transmitting radar antenna gets very little of its signal returned, so it fails to correlate the data and form a radar return," Sattari explained. "The energy absorbed by the skin of the plane and other systems—the so-called cloaking device these aircraft are rumored to employ—is relatively small, perhaps ten to twenty percent. The rest of the energy is still out there, but it is simply not returned to the radar system that it should."

"Get on with it, Mansour."

"Sir, the problem is not that we cannot receive the signals, or that the signals are not strong enough—the problem is that the antenna that must receive the signal is in the *wrong place*. If it were possible to move the receiving antenna and synchronize it with the transmitting antenna, or use several different antennas so synchronized, the redirected radar energy would be detected and the plane would appear on radar.

"For very brief moments, this occurred last night. Purely by chance, we had two radar facilities in perfect synchronization, an A-10 Mainstay radar plane over the strait and a radar facility at Bandar Abbas; both stations were electronically linked with each other, sharing radar data. When the radar aircraft transmitted, the ground station received, and the stealth bomber appeared on Bandar Abbas's radar screen. It was lost a second later, not enough time to track it or even reacquire it, but it *did appear*."

"So if we synchronize two radars deliberately," Buzhazi said, "or even more than two, we could spot the aircraft long enough to track it."

"Yes, very possible," Sattari said. "I have my best engineers on the problem right now. I assumed that you wanted to protect the *Khomeini* carrier group as best as possible, so I am setting up the system using the *Khomeini*'s long-range radar as the master, with Chah Bahar's long-range radar and with an A-10 Mainstay radar plane's radar as the slaves. We must precisely match their frequencies and timing so that when the master transmits, the slaves receive, and vice versa. The slaves then report their findings back to the master by datalink, which assembles the data and puts it together into an image. The best part, sir," Sattari went on, smiling a satisfied, evil smile, "is that the stealth aircraft *may not even know it is being tracked!*"

"How is that possible, Mansour?"

"Because we will be vectoring fighters in on the aircraft using long-range search radars only," Sattari explained. "The stealth aircraft believes it is invulnerable to these radars. The radar of the fighters that will have the honor of shooting down the stealth bomber will not be locked on to the aircraft until very close in, and they may be able to lock a heat-seeking missile on long before the stealth bomber's crew suspects that we see them!"

"Excellent, Mansour, *excellent*," Buzhazi said excitedly. "You will receive a promotion to deputy chief of staff if this works. Implement the system immediately. Then see to it that we have massive fighter formations in the air. If the Americans launch four fighters, I want *eight* to counter them.''

"Sir, it may be unwise to begin such a mobilization so suddenly. It will inflame the entire world against us!" Sattari protested.

"The world, and especially the Americans and the Gulf Cooperative Council, will soon learn how dangerous it is to provoke us!" Buzhazi said. "I want the Strait of Hormuz sealed tight, and I want the *Khomeini* battle group to spearhead it, supported by fighters and bombers from Chah Bahar. The Persian Gulf will be ours now!"

ANDERSEN AIR FORCE BASE, YIGO, GUAM
24 APRIL, 1997, 1838 HOURS LOCAL

The dream was so real, he could feel it, hear it as clearly as if he were there with the doomed plane—the screams of the KC-10 cockpit crew as their tanker began spiraling in its death dive into the Gulf of Oman; the horrible crushing impact as the plane hit the water at terminal velocity; the feel of the cold sea, as hard and unyielding as rock, as it crushed their bodies, then dissolved them into the brine. They were shouting, *screaming* his name, cursing it, cursing him, cursing his parents, cursing his stupidity. . . .

Dammit, *he* had killed them, Patrick McLanahan thought. He *never* should have requested that tanker to come anywhere near Iran after the attacks on Bandar Abbas, the *Khomeini* carrier group, and Chah Bahar. He *knew* the Iranian air force would be on high alert, *knew* they'd be patrolling the skies looking for revenge. . . . He could feel the ocean swallow them up, feel the salt water carry them out, away from help, away from home. . . .

It was salt water, yes, but not from the Gulf of Oman— they were tears. Patrick found himself crying in his sleep, mourning the loss of the KC-10 Extender crew. But as he awoke, he found they were not only his own tears, but from . . .

"Wendy!" Patrick exclaimed. "My God, it's *you*." He embraced his wife warmly, and they held each other tightly for several long moments. The bandages were off her neck now, and a bit of hypoallergenic makeup covered the wounds. Her hair was longer, tied in a complex-looking weave on the back of her head.

"I came in and I saw you crying in your sleep," Wendy said to her husband. "It hurt me so much to see you like that. I didn't want to wake you, but I didn't want you to be in such pain."

"Wendy, what are you doing here?"

"When you radioed NSA to tell them you got a tanker and that you were going to land on Guam, Jon Masters loaded up his DC-10 launch aircraft, chartered about a half dozen other cargo planes himself, and we hurried out here," Wendy said. "He's got every NIRT-Sat and PACER SKY satellite, every ALARM booster, every Disruptor-class weapon in his inventory out here, and he's after blood for what the Iranians did to the *Valley Mistress* and its crew."

"You're with Sky Masters now?"

"I signed up shortly after you left with General Freeman," Wendy said. "I'm his new vice president in charge of development. Jon got us a condo in San Diego, a car, a plane to take us to his plant in Tonopah, the works."

"The tavern . . . ?"

"I leased it out to that development group," Wendy replied. "I'm sorry I didn't ask you first, Patrick, but we both know you weren't happy there. This way you still keep ownership of the place, we have a little positive cash flow coming in, and you're free to save the world instead of busing tables. You can have it back next year, or you can sell it to the group at any time. I hope you don't mind, but . . ."

Patrick took her hand, squeezed it reassuringly, then kissed her fingers. "You did the right thing, Wendy," Patrick said. "You're right: I wasn't happy there. But I didn't have the courage to say so." His eyes drifted away for a moment, staring at some scene replaying in his mind's eye.

But Wendy took his face in her hands and said sternly, "*Stop* that right now, Mr. McLanahan. I know what you're doing: you're imagining those KC-10 crew members dying after being shot down."

"You heard about that?"

"Not officially . . . but yes, Jon Masters monitors everything," Wendy said. "We heard what you did with his Disruptors over Bandar Abbas, over the *Khomeini* carrier group. But we found out that you weren't tasked to go in and launch 'screamers' against Chah Bahar. Hal Briggs put that rescue mission together himself, then called you, *in the blind*, asking for your help. Patrick, that strike was a complete success! I heard Briggs found many of the survivors, got them out. Why are you so unhappy?"

"Wendy, that KC-10 crew, they'd still be alive if I hadn't told them to come get us all the way into the Gulf of Oman," Patrick said. "I wanted to get a refueling so I could continue back to Whiteman instead of having to abort to Diego, so I practically *ordered* those guys to come in and get me. They died because of my stupidity."

"Those guys died doing something they loved to do," Wendy said. "If you hadn't asked them to come get you, they would've come in anyway. They accepted the risks because they wanted to fight, wanted to make a difference, wanted to be part of this operation as much as you did. It's a shitty job and a shitty way to die—you said so yourself. You know about it as much or better than anyone. But I know you, Patrick: the second you step onto that ramp, you'll want to be back up there. Wait until you see the stuff Masters brought with him—you won't be able to wait to shoot a few of those things off."

Sure enough, his eyes began to glisten with anticipation as she mentioned Jon Masters and his new missiles. He started to sit up in bed, but Wendy placed a hand against his chest and pushed him back down.

"If you get up, if you go out there, you do it with no regrets," Wendy said. "You can't have it both ways. The things you will say and do once you go out there will set other lives, other futures in motion, do you understand, Patrick? It will cut some of those futures off, and it will affect them all—some good, some bad. If you say yes to the next mission, you put other lives in jeopardy again. Can you live with that?"

"I want revenge, Wendy," Patrick said, sitting up in bed, his eyes blazing into hers. "I want to make the Iranians pay for what they did to the *Valley Mistress*, what they did to that KC-10 crew. Is that okay with you?"

"What you'll get is more killing, Patrick," Wendy said. "It won't stop until someone calls for peace instead of war. You're a war maker, not a peacemaker, Patrick. Is that okay with *you*?"

"You're damned right it's okay with me!"

"Then stop giving me that thousand-yard stare," Wendy said angrily. "Stop crying in your sleep mourning other warriors who only want what *you* yourself want! If you're going to go out there and kill, do it well and get it over with and come home and be a husband and father. Don't feel guilty because you're doing something you believe in. Do it and let's go home—*together*."

In reply he drew her to him and hugged her as if he would never let go.

DUBAI, UNITED ARAB EMIRATES
THAT SAME DAY

The pallbearers were all in uniform, and they carried the wooden coffin with military precision down the street about a mile to the military cemetery. The coffin was open, the body of the UAE commando in full dress uniform, draped with the flag of both the UAE and of the emirate of Dubai, and piled high with flowers atop the flags. Along the way, mourners stopped and bowed their heads. Some touched their fingers to their lips and held them up to the passing coffin;

a few even touched the coffin itself, or the shoulder of one of the bearers.

The procession was led by Riza Behrouzi, acting as representative of the Emir himself, but custom dictated that she walk behind the air forces commander, the highest-ranking military man in the procession, and be with the commando's wife and family. The commando's wife walked straight, her head uplifted, her chin strong, as did her three children; again, per custom, the commando's mother cried openly and loudly, announcing the heroic death of her son to every stranger she encountered on her way to the grave site.

Behrouzi didn't notice at first, but soon she realized that the air forces commander was whispering excitedly to one of his aides. Riza looked up and, to her astonishment, saw two rows of U.S. Marines on the side of the road leading into the cemetery—and there, standing in the center of the road in front of the cemetery gates, was Hal Briggs himself, dressed in his Air Force class-A uniform, wearing his Rangers beret. He and his Marines wore side arms in ceremonial white web belts—it was highly illegal for foreigners to carry weapons in the emirate of Dubai, even U.S. soldiers—and the Marines also carried ceremonial swords at carry-arms. Riza immediately realized that the eight Marines present were the ones that had been rescued from the Iranian prison in Chah Bahar!

The procession stopped several yards from Briggs, unsure whether or not to continue, not knowing if these armed Americans might be a threat. The air forces commander looked as if he were going to explode with indignation and anger for interrupting their procession in this manner, but before he could do or say anything, Briggs commanded, "De*tail*, render arms"—the Marines lowered their swords, spinning the hilts so they gleamed in the sunlight—"hu!" and the Marines raised their sword hilts to their chins, the blades angled above them toward the casket. Briggs saluted the coffin, held it for a long moment, lowered it, then ordered, "De*tail*, ready"—they lowered their swords again, spinning them as they extended them again—"hu!" and they placed them again pointing up in front of their shoulders at carry-arms position. On a final command from Briggs, the detail sheathed their swords and returned to attention.

The air forces commander from Dubai could stand this interruption no longer, and he stormed over to Briggs, stood just a few inches in front of his face, and began to scream epithets at him in Arabic and English. Briggs just stood there at attention, eyes caged, face completely impassive. "I order you, whoever you are, to stand aside and let us pass!" the air forces commander spat in English, "and then I will see to it that you are removed from this country in *disgrace*!"

"Yes, *sir*," Briggs said. He saluted and moved to step aside . . .

. . . but Riza Behrouzi caught his arm. "You and your men will accompany us to the grave site, Major Briggs," she said. "It is so ordered."

"Briggs? *This* is Major Harold Briggs, the one who led the expedition into Iran, the one who got our men *killed*?" the colonel said in Arabic. "This incompetent ass dares bring his men to this holy place?"

"It is a great honor to have them here, Colonel," Behrouzi said. She motioned to the Marines on the side of the road. "These are the men that were rescued by our soldier's heroism. They have come to pay their respects to their comrade."

"They have done so, then," the colonel said. "Now get them out of my sight immediately!"

"Sir, I have one last request . . . ," Briggs said.

"You will remain silent!"

"I will hear it, Colonel," Behrouzi said. "It is an order." The dead commando's mother had a look of sheer horror on her face at the sight of a woman, even such a high-ranking woman as Behrouzi, raising her voice to a military officer. "What is your request, Major?"

"Thank you, ma'am," Briggs said. By way of reply, he raised his voice and said, "*Detail*, take positions of honor, *hu*." And at that, the Marines stepped forward to the casket directly beside each pallbearer, close enough to touch the casket but not so close as to block their way.

"What is this . . . no, *no*, I forbid it!" the air forces commander retorted.

But at that same moment, one of the UAE pallbearers looked into the eyes of the Marine next to him, nodded, and allowed the Marine to take his position. The Marine put the casket of the dead commando on his shoulders; the UAE pallbearer touched his fingers to his lips, touched the Dubai flag, and stepped away, taking a position beside the American at attention.

"This is strictly forbidden! This is not permitted! This is an insult!" But one by one, the Marines were allowed to take the UAE pallbearers' places, until the casket was completely borne by armed U.S. Marines.

"It appears as if your men have decided that their dead should be carried to his final resting place on the shoulders of American Marines," Behrouzi said in Arabic. "It is not your position or mine to argue." The dead commando's mother was still wailing away, more from fear, protest, and confusion now than sorrow, but a stern glance from Behrouzi and a defeated look from the colonel silenced her outrage. "Major Briggs, take your place at the head of the procession as commander of the detail of honor."

Briggs saluted again, then stepped over in front of Behrouzi and the dead man's family, in a position to the left and one pace behind the air forces commander. Before he did so, he turned to the dead commando's family, bowed his head, and rendered a salute. "On behalf of my men and their families, madam, thank you for your sacrifice. God bless you and your country," Briggs said in a low voice, then once again saluted and bowed his head. His words, understood or not, were accepted by the widow, and his salute was returned proudly by the dead man's eldest son.

The procession continued, to the astonishment of the onlookers, into the cemetery, where no non-Muslim had ever before set foot, and the ceremony continued in peace.

• • •

"That was a very beautiful thing you did today, Leopard," Behrouzi said that evening. She had invited him to dinner at her quarters at Mina Jebel Ali Air Base in Dubai. "Thank you. It was a thing no Dubai soldier will soon forget."

"I tried to get permission to attend the funeral, but no one would return my calls," Briggs said. "I finally decided just to do it, just show up. I'm sorry if it embarrassed the colonel."

"He is one of those hard-liners who believe in nothing but religious and ethnic purity," Behrouzi said. "They are not just in places like Iran or Saudi Arabia. He may squawk to the Emir all he wants—the soldiers support what you did, and the Emir loves all his troops." She gave him a satisfied smile, and added, "Again, you see, when you know something is right and you take the initiative, you can succeed."

"I don't feel as if we're succeeding at all, Riza," Briggs said. "The Iranians still have Colonel White, and now they've declared martial law and are trying to seal off the Persian Gulf. Most of America hardly knows what's going on out here. They know oil prices are skyrocketing and Iran has been shooting off a few missiles at shadows, but no one in my country realizes how close we are to a global crisis. Hell, half of America couldn't find Dubai, the United Arab Emirates, the Gulf of Oman, or the Strait of Hormuz on a map, even though half their oil passes through those places every day!"

"You are beginning to sound like a tired, bitter old soldier, like the ones that sit out in the marketplace every day smoking their hookah pipes, fingering their worry beads, making up stories about fantasy exploits in battle, and complaining about everything and everybody, especially know-nothing civilians," Behrouzi said with a heart-churning laugh. "We chose this life, Hal Briggs. Being a soldier means being a servant to the state, a servant of the people. Our training and experiences give us knowledge of the world that is foreign to our own people, and it can be frustrating. Do not give in to your frustrations. You have learned to fight well—you must learn how to live—and love—well, too."

Briggs smiled and nodded at Riza. He looked at the untouched beer on the table. Where Riza had found any alcoholic beverage, much less his favorite beer, here in the heart of Muslim Arabia, he had no idea. "I've got to be going . . ."

"The briefing is not until twenty hundred," Behrouzi said. "We have time."

"I should see to my troops."

"You have trained them, counseled them, and fed them today—let them enjoy a little rest, too," Behrouzi said. "We start all over again tomorrow night. Tonight belongs to the living, to *us*—at least for the next forty-five minutes." She rose, took his hands, and helped him to his feet. "For the next forty-five minutes, I am yours to do as you wish, Leopard," Behrouzi said. She untied a pale yellow silk scarf from around her neck, letting it fall beside her breasts, and she followed his gaze as his eyes explored her body. "I am *your* prisoner."

Behrouzi turned her back to Hal Briggs, then removed her blouse, keeping the silk scarf across her neck. She then felt Briggs's strong hands on her shoulders, massaging her shoulders, then her arms, then her breasts from behind. He slipped her brassiere off her shoulders, lightly touching her naked breasts, barely touching the skin. The almost imperceptible touch of a finger against her erect nipples was so exquisite that it made her gasp. Still from behind, he removed her boots, then her slacks and underwear, and he gently touched her skin, softly exploring every inch of her body.

The room was cold, but his fingers felt as if they were on fire. He did not squeeze her, just continued touching her here and there. It was like some sort of exotic torture technique—she longed, then ached, then begged to be grasped. But he didn't stop. His fingers gently touched her buttocks, then her neck, then imperceptibly her nipples. She reached behind her, grasping for him and finding him erect and quite hard. "Stop this torture, Leopard," she breathed. She reached up and looped her hands behind his neck, stretching her lean body up and pressing her buttocks into his groin. "Take me, Leopard, *now*, please."

Briggs ran his fingers up along her sides, gently around her breasts, then down her arms to her hands. Goose pimples leapt across her brown skin, and she gasped in excitement. Kissing her neck, he clasped her hands in his, brought them down her back near his groin again . . . then, the scarf was pulled away from her shoulders and, before she knew it, her hands were secured behind her back with the scarf. "Yes," she breathed. "I am yours now, Leopard . . ."

"Turn," he ordered.

She slowly turned to face him, her face aching from her longing, her lips parted from her labored breathing. Riza Behrouzi was thin, but her arm and shoulder muscles were thick and heavily defined; her breasts were small, round, firm globes over a smoothly muscled chest; her stomach was flat; her buttocks were round and thin; and her legs were strong and powerfully muscled. She had an athlete's body, but it obviously had not been shaped in a gym or spa with weights or fancy machines—it had been chiseled out in the harsh highlands and deserts of the Middle East, exercised by carrying guns and cameras, and hardened by numerous confrontations with soldiers and interrogators and informants of many nationalities. Like his, her body was a weapon—but, at least not for the next few precious minutes, it was not going to be used to kill or to spy.

Slowly and deliberately, he began to remove his clothes before her. It was almost like a striptease, revealing one tantalizing feature of his hard, chiseled body after another in slow, agonizing bits. Her chest was rising and falling heavily, as if she had just run up six flights of stairs, well before he finally unfastened his belt, eased his trousers off, and revealed himself to her. Her eyes told him that she was at once both intimidated by him and eager to sample him.

"That was delicious, Leopard," Behrouzi said breathlessly. "It is my turn to please you now."

They made love quickly, wildly, explosively. Both knew what was out there waiting for them; both knew how much time they didn't have, what was expected of them, what other governments and officials demanded of them. For now, right now, all they demanded of the rest of the world was each other, if only for a few brief, passionate minutes. His scars, and hers, were visible to each of them, but it didn't matter.

Like a nighttime commando raid, it was over quickly; but, like combat, they were both filled with an intoxicating mixture of tingling excitement, adrenaline, and weariness when it was done. They stayed tightly intertwined until their internal timers told them their time together was running out. He helped her to her feet, then embraced her once again as if this would be the last time. After she dressed, they were both on the phone again immediately, talking to their respective command centers, ordering all the charts, intelligence data, support personnel, and soldiers they might need.

Neither of them would ever forget the moment they had shared together . . . but now it was time to join the fight once again.

IN THE ARABIAN SEA, EAST OF THE GULF OF OMAN, 300 MILES SOUTHEAST OF CHAH BAHAR NAVAL BASE, IRAN 26 APRIL 1997, 0251 HOURS LOCAL TIME

"Aardvark-121 flight, Wallbanger, vector heading two-eight-five, take angels thirty, your bogey is bearing three-one-zero, three-zero-zero bull's-eye."

"121 flight copies," Lieutenant Scott "Crow" Crowley, lead pilot of the two-ship F-14B Tomcat flight, responded. Perfect timing, he thought—he had just about taken on a full tank of gas, and his wing-man, Lieutenant (j.g.) Eric "Shine" Matte had just tanked a few minutes earlier. "Lizard-520, disconnect." Crowley hit the AR/NWS/DISC button on his control stick and watched as the large cloth-covered basket-shaped refueling drogue popped off his refueling probe on the right side of his cockpit. The KA-6D tanker of VA-95 Green Lizards quickly reeled in the drogue and cleared the flight of two F-14B Tomcat fighters from FG-114 Aardvarks, from the U.S.S. *Abraham Lincoln*, to the bottom of the refueling block. Once level 2,000 feet below the tanker, the F-14s executed a tight left turn and headed northwest on their new vector.

"21 flight, check," Crowley radioed as soon as he finished his post-air refueling checklist. He knew that Matte would be finishing his checklist as well, and then hurrying to catch up and stay in formation, which for them was loose fingertip formation.

"Two," was Matte's quick reply. That meant everything was OK—fuel feeding OK, full tanks or as nearly full as possible, instruments OK, systems OK, oxygen OK, GIB (Guy in Back, the radar intercept officer) OK. Crowley looked at his fuel and deducted about half an hour's worth of his wingman and a bit more "for the wife and kids" and guessed he had about two hours' worth of "play time" out here before they had to head back to the *Lincoln*, which was about 300 miles behind them right now.

Each F-14B Tomcat was similarly equipped for this medium-range Force CAP night patrol: two 1,000-liter external fuel tanks on the pylons under the engine air inlets; two radar-guided AIM-120A AMRAAMs (Advanced Medium-Range Air-to-Air Missiles) and two AIM-9M Sidewinder short-range heat-seeking missiles on the wing glove pylons; and four huge AIM-54C Phoenix long-range radar-guided missiles on the fuselage stations. With the *Lincoln* battle group so far out in the Arabian Sea, the primary threat to be countered by the F-14 air patrols was from Iranian long-range fighter-bombers and long-range patrol aircraft, so these Tomcats carried two extra Phoenix missiles per fighter—the Phoenix missile had a range of over ninety miles, well within radar detection range but far enough out of the range of most of the Russian-made air-launched anti-ship cruise missiles that Iran had in its inventory.

A few minutes after receiving their vector from the E-2C Hawk-eye radar plane, from VAW-117 Wallbangers, orbiting 200 miles northwest of the *Lincoln* carrier group, Crowley's radar intercept officer had the bogey on radar: "Radar contact, one-seven-five miles, off the nose."

"Aardvark flight, that's your bogey," the Hawkeye radar officer said, verifying the RIO's report. The Tomcats now took over primary responsibility for the intercept.

It was a cat-and-mouse game that had been played every night for the past few nights. These were "ferret" flights, probes of the *Lincoln*'s air defense capability, by a wide variety of Iranian aircraft, from top-of-the-line MiG-29 Fulcrum, MiG-25 Foxbat, and MiG-31 Foxhound supersonic fighters to giant lumbering P-3 Orion and EC-130 surveillance aircraft. The smaller Iranian combat aircraft—already at the limit of their fuel reserves, because the *Lincoln* was still very far offshore—would simply drive in as close as they dared toward the carrier group and watch to see what sort of response the Americans would make. With one E-2 Hawkeye orbiting over the carrier and one Hawkeye stationed between the carrier and the Iranian mainland, the carrier group had "eyes" out at least 200 miles around the ship, and a narrow corridor of radar coverage on a straight line from the carrier to Chah Bahar Naval Base, over 400 miles away.

Most times, the Iranian "ferret" planes would zoom in— probably recording all of the electronic signals generated by the *Lincoln*, its escorts, and its patrol aircraft—then, once it was "paired" with a Tomcat, it would turn around and head for home. The Iranians knew all about the F-14 Tomcat and the AIM-54 Phoenix missile—because they still employed both of them. In the mid-1970s, when the Shah had been in power, the United States had transferred 100 of the advanced fighters to Iran; the exact numbers were unknown, but Iran probably still had a dozen operational Tomcats and about 100 Phoenix missiles in good condition. The Iranians knew to give the Phoenix missile a lot of respect, so at the first squeak of the Tomcat's AWG-9 radar, they usually turned tail.

But not this time. . . . "Wallbanger picked this guy out at almost three hundred miles—that's the limit of his radar," Crowley observed, thinking aloud. "He's gotta be a big guy. You got numbers on him, Sunrise?"

"Range one-five-zero miles, still closing fast," Crowley's RIO, Lieutenant Adam "Sunrise" Lavoyed, reported. "Altitude angels forty, speed . . . shit, speed *seven hundred*."

"He's not an Orion then," Crowley said. Iran flew American-made P-3 Orion subchasers—another leftover from the Shah's regime—which were capable of carrying Harpoon or Exocet antiship missiles, but Orions were big, lumbering turboprop-powered planes, max cruise speed about 380 knots—this one was going almost twice as fast.

"What's our bull's-eye?"

"Coming up on three hundred bull's-eye," Lavoyed responded, giving range back to the carrier.

"What are we up to tonight, asshole?" Crowley muttered on interphone to the unknown aircraft. "Who are you? What are you?"

Just then, Lavoyed shouted, "I'm picking up a second bogey . . . shit, Crow, second bogey climbing through angels forty . . . angels fifty, speed twelve hundred . . . I'm picking up a third bogey, right behind the second, passing through angels forty, speed eleven hundred knots . . . bandit one turning northwest and accelerating!"

"Kitchens," Crowley shouted, jamming his throttles to max afterburner and raising the nose to pursue. On interplane frequency, he yelled, "Home plate, Kitchen, Kitchen, I am tracking two fast-movers passing angels fifty, speed Mach two. . . ."

"Go weapons hot, go weapons hot," came the reply. The call "Kitchen" was an all-inclusive call warning of the launch of a large anti-ship missile. For years the standard Soviet bomber-launched anti-ship missile, the AS-4 Kitchen, was a 14,000-pound liquid-fueled cruise missile that could fly at over three times the speed of sound for more than 200 miles—and the Tu-22M Backfire bomber could carry as many as three of these huge weapons. The AS-4 was armed with a 2,200-pound conventional high-explosive warhead, big enough to sink a small warship with one missile . . .

. . . or, in Cold War days, a 350-kiloton nuclear warhead, big enough to destroy an entire carrier battle group.

"Shine, you got the second Kitchen, I got the first," Crowley shouted on interplane frequency.

"Two!" came the strained reply—Matte's heart was in his throat right now, just like Crowley's—you could hear it in his voice.

In the blink of an eye, Crowley was in range, and he fired his first Phoenix missile—the first time in his career he had launched the big P. He squinted against the glare as the Phoenix raced off its rail and arced to the right and skyward, the huge blast of the Phoenix rattling his Tomcat's wings and shaking the canopy. Crowley had to pull his Tomcat in a hard right turn to keep the AWG-9 radar locked onto the Kitchen missiles long enough to guide the Phoenix until its own radar could lock on. When he was sure he was locked on, he fired a second Phoenix, now on a tail chase. Crowley considered firing his third and possibly even his fourth Phoenix, but by then the Kitchen missiles were out of range—they were flying well over Mach two, twice the speed of sound and faster than the Phoenix missile itself!

Crowley watched the rest of the incredible chase in complete fascination. He saw a bright flash, then another, far off in the distance. "Clean misses," Crowley's RIO reported. "Bandit two heading straight for home plate at Mach two-point-four, angels sixty and still climbing." Crowley could see that Lavoyed still had the AWG-9 radar locked on to the first Kitchen missile, but they were well outside Phoenix range. It was up to any other fighters airborne and the *Lincoln*'s air defense screen to stop the first Kitchen now.

Matte was more successful: "Splash one Kitchen!" he shouted happily. "Got it!"

"I missed," Crowley admitted on interplane frequency. "C'mon, *Lincoln*, nail that bastard!"

Far off in the distance, Crowley could see a few flashes of light, and he could even see a faint streak of light shoot up in the sky—it was the *Lincoln*'s escorts, the outer air defense screen ships, launching missiles. A split second later, they saw a huge lightbulb *POP*! of brilliant white light very high in the dark sky. "Splash one Kitchen," the combat officer aboard the E-2C Hawkeye reported. "*Lake Erie* got it." The U.S.S. *Lake Erie* was one of *Lincoln*'s AEGIS guided-missile escort cruisers. "Aardvark-121, bandit one is retreating, fly heading one-one-zero, maintain angels thirty, this'll be vectors back to your tanker. Aardvark-122, squawk normal . . . 122, radar contact at angels three-five, 121, your wingman is at your two o'clock, thirty miles, above you."

"121, roger," Crowley acknowledged. As he waited for Lavoyed to lock on to the Tomcat in front of him, he held out his right hand in front of his eyes—his hand was shaking. "Jesus, Shine," he said on interphone, "the Iranians launched two missiles at the *Lincoln*. That was a close call!"

"Those were Backfire bombers launching those things, too," Lavoyed added. "Intelligence has been speculating that the Iranians bought Backfire bombers from the Russians for years—I guess it's true,'cause they just used one to launch Kitchen missiles at our carrier."

It took twenty minutes for the two F-14 Tomcats to join up and maneuver themselves behind a new KA-6D tanker. The radios were crazy with chatter. The *Lincoln* was launching three extra flights of F-14s, making six flights of two total; they were also in the process of launching a third E-2C Hawkeye radar plane to cover the airspace farther north of the group. The group was transitioning from a peacetime ForCAP, or Force Combat Air Patrol—which generally extended 100 to 200 miles from the carrier—to a BarCAP, or Barrier Combat Air Patrol, which would double that distance. Soon, almost anything that launched from Iran would be intercepted, and any aircraft that was large enough to carry an AS-4 Kitchen missile would surely be destroyed long before it got within range. Undoubtedly the battle-group commander was rearranging the seaborne escorts as well, spreading his forces out a bit more to get air defense missiles out farther from the carrier, while keeping one or two guided-missile cruisers or destroyers in close to provide last-ditch protection for the carrier and its five thousand crew members.

Crowley had just maneuvered his F-14 behind the KA-6D tanker and was setting up for the run in toward the lighted drogue when suddenly they heard, "All units, all units, pop-up bogeys bearing zero-two-zero, two-seven-five miles bull's-eye, angels twenty, speed six-zero-zero-knots, all Aardvark units, say fuel status and stand by."

"121 flight's on the hose, ten-point-one!" Crowley shouted as he rushed toward the drogue for at least a token on-load. But the harder he tried to plug the drogue, the worse he did. He finally got the tanker to fly straight and level for longer than normal so he could plug the drogue; he took a fast five thousand pounds and cycled off. "121's clear."

"121, vector to intercept new bogey one, heading zero-five-zero, angels forty," the combat controller aboard a different E-2C Hawkeye ordered. Crowley finally realized that the new voice was from the new Hawkeye just launched to cover north of the *Lincoln* carrier group—sure enough, another Tu-22M Backfire bomber had sneaked in and was now within 250 miles of the carrier! "Go single ship, 122 will follow in trail."

"121 copies," Crowley responded, banking to the vector heading and again pushing his throttles up to military power. "Wallbanger, be advised, 121 will be bingo fuel in two-zero mike, I only got a token on-load. I'm down two Ps."

"Copy that, 121, break, Aardvark-122, top 'em off, you'll be the only north CAP when your leader bingos. Say your state."

"122 copies, I'm down two Ps also. I'm on the hose."

Crowley's RIO wasn't able to lock the second Tupolev-22M until it was within 250 miles from the carrier and just over 100 miles ahead. "Stand by for Kitchens, home plate," Crowley yelled. "Stand by!"

But the Tu-22M continued to barrel in, now traveling at well over the speed of sound. "Wallbanger, 121, do you want me on the Backfire or do you want me to wait on the Kitchens?"

"Stand by, 121 . . ."

"You better hurry with an answer, Wallbanger," Crowley said. He was now within range to fire on the Backfire bomber itself, but it had not launched a missile. "Wallbanger, let's hear it!"

Just before Crowley was in position to launch, the combat controller aboard the E-2C Hawkeye responded, "Bandit one turning . . . bandit one now heading two-seven-five, angels forty, looks like he's bugging out . . . 121, home plate says hold fire and maintain contact."

"Copy, Wallbanger. I will . . ."

"Missile launch!" Matte suddenly shouted. "The Backfire's launching missiles!"

It had happened so fast, Crowley didn't see it happening, and they were expecting another attack on the carrier, not on anything else. Before anyone could react, the Backfire bomber had launched four missiles—not at the carrier, but all of them at the third E-2C Hawkeye radar plane that had just launched from the *Lincoln.*

The missiles were new Russian Novator KS-172 Pithon "Python" air-to-air missiles, designed specifically for use against airborne radar planes and intelligence-gathering aircraft by homing in on their radars and electromagnetic emissions—they could even home in on the stray electronic emissions from computer screens leaking through the cockpit or observation windows. Flying at a speed of Mach two and fired from a distance of well over two hundred miles, the Pithon missiles were devastating weapons. Even though the E-2C shut off its radar and took evasive action, the missiles "remembered" the plane's last position and activated its on-board radar when it got within range. Then it could not miss. All four Pithon missiles plowed into the Hawkeye's twenty-foot rotodome, stripping it from the fuselage and sending the entire aircraft spinning into the sea.

Crowley could do nothing as the third Wallbanger aircraft abruptly went off the air. He immediately turned to pursue, even plugging in full afterburner to try to catch up, but he never got within Phoenix missile range of the retreating Backfire bomber, and within minutes was forced to return to the tanker.

THE WHITE HOUSE OVAL OFFICE
25 APRIL 1997, 1321 HOURS ET

"Do we know that it was an Iranian Backfire bomber?" the
President of the United States asked in a low, bitter voice.
"Positive ID . . . ?"

"We didn't get a visual ID, sir," Philip Freeman replied.
Freeman had called the President out of a Rose Garden bill-
signing ceremony, and now they were back in the Oval Office, with the President scanning a written report on the Gulf
of Oman incident. "But its size was estimated by the radar
operators, and based on the range at which it was detected,
it had to be a large aircraft. Combine its speed and altitude,
then add in the flight characteristics of the missiles it
launched—we're ninety-nine percent sure it was an Iranian
Backfire bomber."

"What in *our* inventory could do something like that?"

"The B-1B Lancer bomber has a very similar flight profile," Freeman replied. "The F-111, F-15, F-16, or F-22
fighters could mimic a Backfire's speed and performance, but
not its range or payload. We have nothing like the AS-4
Kitchen missile—all of our cruise missiles are subsonic."

"What about other countries? What about China?"

"The Chinese have a bomber, the B-6D Badger, that possibly could mimic the speed of the Backfire bomber," Freeman said. "They have one supersonic anti-ship cruise
missile, but it has a much shorter range than the AS-4
Kitchen missile—forty miles versus two hundred miles. Iraq
and Libya also fly the Backfire bomber, but none are reported
to be in serviceable condition, and neither country is known
to possess any supersonic cruise missiles. Pakistan's F-16
fighter might be able to mimic the speed and performance
of a Backfire bomber, but it could not carry any cruise missiles with the performance of an AS-4 missile.

"Russia of course still flies the Backfire and its upgraded

follow-on supersonic bomber, the Tu-145 Blackjack. Ukraine owns several Backfire and Blackjack bombers acquired from Russia, but it is uncertain if they are operational. Russia also still possesses the AS-4, a few of the AS-6, and the AS-9 supersonic anti-ship cruise missiles.''

''You're saying Russia might have done this?''

''Extremely unlikely, sir,'' Freeman said, shaking his head. ''At best, the Russians keep twenty-five percent of their supersonic bombers flyable—they were selling off their Backfire bombers to anyone in the world that might be interested, and they didn't squawk too loudly when Ukraine claimed the Blackjack bombers. Given what's happened in Iran in the past few days with the establishment of martial law and the suspension of President Nateq-Nouri by the Ayatollah Khamenei, I think Iran is the most likely culprit.'' He paused for a moment, then asked, ''Do you want us to be positive before we go further?''

''Hell no, Philip, I'm *damned* positive,'' the President said resolutely. ''I don't need a bomb to fall on me to figure out that this is Buzhazi's attempt to scare us away. But you said you're still looking for the Backfire bomber base . . . ?''

''It should be much easier to find them now, sir,'' Freeman said. ''The Navy was able to track the Backfires well inside Iran after their attack, and we've had many more surveillance assets in place looking for them. Jon Masters launched two constellations of tactical reconnaissance satellites *himself*— just gave us the satellites. Once Space Command picked out an orbit for them, Masters put them up there. He's got every airfield in Iran capable of landing a Backfire bomber under constant surveillance.''

''Good,'' the President said. ''I want to meet Masters one of these days, after this is over. Now,'' the President went on, fixing a serious gaze on his National Security Advisor, ''it's important to me to hit back without starting a huge, full-scale war in the Middle East. The allies and the oil companies are already jumpy enough—oil prices are already spiking. Now, I know it was this Intelligence Support Agency group that launched those 'screamer' missiles, but I want to start shutting down Iran's ability to make war, not just harass them. What have you got?''

''We're already sending Future Flight the entire Disruptor series of weapons,'' Freeman said. ''Brad Elliott's Disruptors don't just screw with radars and sensors—they can do a lot of damage as well.''

''I never thought I'd be saying this, Philip—it sounds like a bad movie,'' the President said, ''but it's the truth: I want this to look like an accident. When Masters finds those Back-fire bombers, I want them grounded, for good—and I want it to look like an accident. If that Iranian carrier comes any-where near the *Lincoln* or any American warship, I want it on the bottom of the Gulf—and I want it to look like an accident. If Iran even thinks about popping off any of those long-range Scuds toward Saudi or Turkey, I want a major military headquarters building in Tehran to grow a large jag-ged hole in its middle—and I want it to look like an accident. Can you do that?''

''I understand completely, sir,'' Freeman said. ''And, yes, I think we can.''

''Good. Keep me advised, day or night, before any oper-ation starts, but you've got the green light,'' the President said, straightening his tie and getting ready to head back to the reception following the Rose Garden bill-signing cere-mony. ''Get the forces moving, then brief me as soon as you can; I want to OK each mission before the B-2A crosses into hostile airspace.

''This operation is to be quiet, deniable, and squeaky clean, General, but most of all, I want Iran to pay for shoot-ing down our aircraft, the sons of bitches—attacking un-armed support aircraft is the lowest act any military man can do, and I want Buzhazi to feel it right in his damned *groin*. Get to it, Philip.''

General Philip Freeman was almost embarrassed by the enthusiasm he felt as he headed to the White House Situation Room to issue his orders to the Intelligence Support Agency. No more ''disruptions,'' no more ''screamers''—the President wanted Iran's war-making machine shut down, piece by piece, and that's exactly what was going to happen.

ANDERSEN AIR FORCE BASE, GUAM
26 APRIL 1997, 1625 HOURS LOCAL

Jon Masters didn't knock—he never knocked. He always burst into a room, day or night, and started talking as if the conversation had already started minutes before. This time, it was in the middle of a briefing being given by Colonel Dominguez on the maintenance status of the B-2A Spirit stealth bomber.

"Okay, so we got them. What we did, General," Masters said breathlessly, "was simple: we launched two NIRTSat boosters, each carrying four Pacer Sky digital photo intelligence satellites, over Iran. We targeted each and every Iranian airfield, civilian or military, longer than forty-five hundred feet long and one hundred fifty feet wide, capable of handling something like a Tu-22M Backfire bomber. We took pictures of each airfield every sixty to ninety minutes. Of course, the Iranians didn't know we launched these satellites—heck, *nobody* knew we launched them except you and me. We hit pay dirt."

Griffith and Dominguez leapt to their feet and followed Masters down the hall of the fourth floor of the Thirteenth Air Force headquarters building, which was now occupied by the members of the Air Intelligence Agency and Future Flight for the B-2A missions against Iran. When everyone was in place and the door closed and locked behind them, Masters clicked the button on his display controller. The large-screen computer monitor showed an overhead view of a very large airport. "They can run, but they couldn't hide," Masters said proudly. "Sky Masters comes through again."

Jon Masters's NIRTSats (Need it Right This Second Satellites) were small devices, smaller than a washing machine, but capable of photographing a dog from 200 miles in space clearly enough to discern the breed. Four photo-reconnaissance NIRTSats, code-named Pacer Sky, could be loaded aboard a small two-stage scissor-winged rocket booster Masters called ALARM (for Air-Launched Alert Response Missile), and two such ALARM boosters could be loaded aboard Masters's specially designed DC-10 aircraft. The DC-10 would take the ALARM boosters up to 40,000 feet, then drop them one by one. The DC-10 acted as the boosters' first-stage engine—the booster's two stages would fly the missile up as high as 400 miles in space, where the satellites would be inserted in their proper orbit. In this way, Masters could give almost any battlefield commander a complete reconnaissance, surveillance, and communications satellite network in a matter of hours.

Today, however, Masters wasn't under a government or commercial contract to launch NIRTSats over Iran—this he was doing for himself.

"Beghin Airport, near Kerman, Iran, about two hundred fifty miles north of Bandar Abbas," Masters went on. "Two hours after the attack on the *Lincoln* carrier group, we photographed this." He directed a laser-beam pointer on the screen, then clicked another button, which zoomed the image down around the laser-beam point. Magnified in the image was the unmistakable outline of a B-1B Lancer-type aircraft, with a long, pointed nose, slender body, and thin wings swept back very close to its fuselage.

"There's your Tupolev-22M bomber base, folks: Beghin Airport—at least it's one of them." Masters zoomed the image out until the entire airport could be seen. "With the wings folded, those hangars there can accommodate six Backfires, two per hangar, so we're still missing at least six more. I'm setting up round-the-clock surveillance on Beghin, and I'm still beating the bushes for the other six bombers."

"Thank you, Jon," Major General Brien Griffith, commander of the U.S. Air Force Air Intelligence Agency, said. "Good work."

"My extreme friggin' *pleasure*, sir," Masters said acidly. "The data's been relayed to McLanahan and Jamieson via

MILSTAR, fed right into their attack computers. They'll be over the target in ten hours.''

Such ferocity looked so out of place for a young-looking guy like Masters, Griffith thought, but he had undergone much in the last few days—including nearly losing his life at the hands of the Iranian navy. This young man had the technology, the money, and the desire to make Iran pay dearly for what they had done.

RIVERSIDE, CALIFORNIA
THAT SAME TIME

First Lieutenant Sheila MacNichol was just returning from her sixth trip to the ladies' room that afternoon—her sixth month of pregnancy seemed like one endless trip to the bathroom—and was returning to her desk in the 722nd Air Refueling Wing commander's office, where she was "flying a desk," grounded from her regular job as an Air Force Reserve KC-10 copilot and now acting as the wing executive officer, when she noticed the scared, almost panicked look on the face of the wing commander's civilian secretary. Instantly her throat turned dry, and the baby kicked, and she felt as if her knees were going to give way.

Even before the secretary got to her feet and headed toward her; even before she saw the door to the wing commander's office open and the general emerge, his face ashen and drawn; even before she saw the base chaplain and the squadron commander recognize her and open their mouths in surprise and dread—she knew Scotty was dead.

Sheila's husband Major Scott MacNichol was one of the best, most experienced KC-10 Extender tanker pilots in the U.S. Air Force, a veteran of over four hundred sorties, some over enemy territory, in the "tanker war" during Desert Shield and Desert Storm, a dedicated, knowledgeable flight commander and instructor pilot. No mission was too tough or impossible. The unspoken rule "never volunteer" was unheard of in Scotty's lexicon—he volunteered for everything. He enjoyed, relished, *rejoiced*, in putting his 600,000-pound tanker-transport plane in the tightest spots, the most difficult missions, the shortest runways, the most hazardous jobs.

He had been awarded the Air Medal with two oak-leaf clusters for his service in Desert Storm—very, very unusual for an aircraft that was never supposed to be in enemy territory. Scotty would go in and get his receivers if there was the slightest hint of trouble. There were only forty KC-10 tankers in the world, but as a "force multiplier," able to refuel both Air Force, Navy, Marines, and many foreign aircraft, it was worth a hundred times its number—too valuable to risk over Indian country. But Scotty went there.

Damn him, Sheila cursed silently, he did this on purpose! When the baby came, she thought, he knew he was going to be asked to give up all the TDY, all the long weeks of traveling to exotic foreign destinations, all the secret missions, the sudden midnight phone calls, the hastily packed mobility bags—packing cold-weather gear when it was ninety degrees out. She knew he wasn't going to have fun in Hawaii while she stayed home with the backaches and swollen feet and hemorrhoids. He wanted to get all his excitement, all his heroics in before he was asked to settle down and be a regular dad, a regular guy, for the first time in his life.

The wing commander motioned her inside his office and helped her sit down. Sheila knew the chaplain and the squadron commander, of course, so she got right to it: "Scotty . . . is dead?"

"His plane suffered an unknown, catastrophic failure of some kind over the Gulf of Oman," the wing commander said. "His plane was lost with all aboard. I'm so sorry, Lieutenant."

Sheila tried not to cry, but the tears came unbidden, and then the sobbing. She didn't mean to do *that*, in front of the wing king and the squadron commander and the chaplain, but it was happening, and she couldn't stop it until she heard the wing commander ask his secretary to call for an ambulance to stand by out front, and Sheila decided she wasn't going to have any of *that*, so she stopped.

"A . . . a catastrophic failure, sir? What kind? A bird strike? `Compressor failure? Fuel-system malfunction?" Everyone in this room was an experienced KC-10 driver except for the chaplain, and even *he* had a couple hundred hours in one—why was he being so obtuse? Probably because the plane had crashed in the ocean—not much chance to do an accident investigation with the pieces scattered across the seabed. The wing king was in his "comfort the grieving survivors" mode, too, so maybe he wasn't trying to be so evasive—he wasn't accustomed to talking to widows about compressor stalls, center-of-gravity violations, or inflight emergencies.

"We don't know yet, Lieutenant . . . Sheila," the general said. "An investigation is under way."

"The Gulf of Oman? Why was Scotty out there?" Sheila asked. "I heard temporary flight restrictions were in effect for all airspace within five hundred miles of Iran. What was he doing over the Gulf of Oman?"

The wing commander looked at the chaplain, who let go of Sheila's hand and stepped away. "Sheila, please, let's not focus on where Scotty's plane went down right now, all right? I just want you to know how sorry we are, and that we want to help you through this terrible tragedy."

"This has to do with Iran, doesn't it?" Sheila asked, the hurt turning into stone-cold anger. "All the things the government has been saying about how great, how wonderful everything is over in the Middle East, it's not true, is it . . . ?"

"Lieutenant . . ."

"The Iranians shot him down, didn't they, sir?" Sheila asked hotly. "The Iranians shot down my Scotty, flying in an unarmed, vulnerable tanker."

"Lieutenant, please, I know you're upset, and I'm sorry, truly sorry, but I'm asking you to keep your opinions to yourself, please!"

"I hope we went in there to bomb the *crap* out of those

rag-heads!'' Sheila cried. The paramedics were rushing into the wing commander's office with a gurney, trying to get her to relax, but Sheila's heart felt as cold, as heavy, and as still as the child in her womb did right now, and the anger she was releasing felt good, felt *right*. ''I hope my Scotty helped us get those damned Iranian terrorists, dammit. I hope they all burn in *hell*!''

FIVE

According to law, all flights landing in Iran had to be on the ground and at their arrival gate by midnight; the last flight into Beghin Regional Airport in central Iran had arrived at ten P.M., and shortly thereafter the airport was all but shut down, leaving only maintenance crews at the airport until sunrise. By two A.M. the airport appeared totally deserted . . .

. . . except at the extreme southern end of the airport, south of the 11,000-foot-long, 150-foot-wide northwest-southeast running concrete runway that had been closed to commercial and civil traffic two years earlier. Three large and rather shabby-looking hangars and several smaller buildings sat near that closed runway, in front of a large, completely deserted aircraft parking ramp. Weeds growing up through the cracks on that parking ramp suggested that the ramp had not supported an aircraft in quite some time.

This was the secret Iranian base for one squadron, six planes, of Iran's most deadly military aircraft, the Tupolev-22M bomber, NATO code-named "Backfire." The Russian-made supersonic Backfire bomber could reach any target in the Middle East within an hour or, refueled from an Iranian

C-707 aerial refueling tanker, could reach targets as far away as Italy or Germany in two hours. It carried a devastating 53,000-pound payload of gravity bombs, antiship missiles, or land or sea mines. The presence of Tu-22M Backfire bombers in the Islamic Republic of Iran's air force had been rumored since 1993, but had been constantly refuted because no Backfires had ever been spotted in Iran.

"For a secret bomber base, this place looks like shit," Tony Jamieson muttered. He and Patrick McLanahan had been orbiting over the base for twenty minutes now, "shooting" the base with the synthetic aperture radar every few minutes and comparing the SAR images with past images, trying to piece together enough information to verify that the deadly Backfire bombers were really here. They had looked at every crack in the concrete, every skid mark, every vehicle on the airport grounds—nothing. No sign of one of the world's most advanced bombers. "We've only got twenty minutes left in our orbit."

"Something will show," McLanahan said. "Jon Masters's NIRT-Sats never let us down before . . . well, maybe once before . . ."

"Great," Jamieson groused. "And I'm getting tired of always carrying these so-called non-lethal weapons on board my plane, too, McLanahan. The ragheads want to fight— let's start carrying some weapons that have a little punch. At least a couple JSOWs with high-explosive warheads would be useful—that's not too much to ask . . ."

"SAR coming on," McLanahan announced. "SAR shot, ready, ready . . . now . . . SAR in standby, antenna secure."

"Well, hot damn, there they are—a regular 'baby elephant walk,'" Jamieson exclaimed as he studied the SAR image on McLanahan's supercockpit monitor. As clear as a black-and-white photograph, the long, thin body of a Tupolev-22M Backfire bomber had appeared from one of the hangars on the south side of the airport. Another bomber was exiting the same hangar, behind and slightly to one side of the first, while a third bomber had just poked its nose outside the doors of the middle hangar, obviously waiting its turn to taxi.

By using cursor commands, McLanahan was able to electronically "twist" the SAR image until they were actually looking *inside* the hangars, as if they were standing right on the ramp, and they found all three large hangar doors open, with two Tu-22M bombers in each hangar. The rear of the hangar was open so the bombers could run their engines while inside, safely under cover. "Bingo," Jamieson said. "Shit, they *are* there!"

"And it looks like they're going hunting again," McLanahan said. "We can take care of that." And just a few moments later six AGM-154 JSOW missiles were on their way toward Beghin Airport, their autopilots programmed to fly an attack course just fifty feet over the runway.

As the JSOW missile flew toward the runway, an electronic low-light TV camera activated, sending real-time TV images back to McLanahan in the B-2A Spirit stealth bomber flying 45,000 feet overhead. McLanahan used his cursor to lock an aiming reticle on one of the bombers, and the JSOW's autopilot flew the missile to its quarry. As it passed overhead, two of its four bomb bays opened, and it ejected a sixty-pound blob of a thick, gooey substance that landed on the upper surface of the bomber. As the JSOW missile flew away, McLanahan programmed the missile to fly to a secondary target—in the first case, the airport's power-transformer substation—and drop the last two globs on that. The missile then automatically flew itself thirty miles farther west, where it crashed in the middle of the Bahlamabad Reservoir and sank quickly out of sight. One by one, each JSOW missile dropped one-half of its unidentifiable load on top of a Tu-22M bomber, then on top of another target somewhere else on the south side of the base—the regional air-traffic-control radar dome, a communications antenna farm, another power transformer farm, and three JSOWs dropped their gooey mass on the south base's POL (petroleum, oil, and lubricant) tank farm.

"Well, that was exciting," Jamieson muttered as McLanahan programmed the last of the JSOW missiles. He steered the B-2A bomber south along the Afghanistan and

Pakistan borders and out over the Gulf of Oman once again.

The air-traffic-control radar was the first to feel the effect. The two large blobs hit the thin reinforced Fiberglas radar dome and immediately burned through, then scattered on the rotating antenna and control cabin inside. Within minutes, the thin metal antenna began to twist out of shape because of the fast twelve-revolutions-per-minute speed, and the antenna quickly failed and collapsed.

The metal-eating blobs of acid that struck the first Tu-22M bomber hit squarely on the upper fuselage and on the non-swiveling outboard portion of the left wing glove; on the second bomber, they hit on the fuselage just aft of the cockpit windows and on the very upper lip of the right engine intake, spattering across the guidance and warhead sections of the AS-4 cruise missile mounted under the right wing glove. As the first two bombers taxied out onto the active runway and picked up speed for takeoff, the globs spread across the airframe, eating away inside the left wing pivot section and spreading across the fuselage fuel tanks, the upper engine compartments, the vertical and horizontal stabilizers, and the rudder.

When the acid ate through the Backfire's thin aluminum skin, the first bomber was already 3,000 feet above ground and passing through 300 miles per hour. Just as the pilot began sweeping the wings of his Backfire bomber from the twenty-degree takeoff setting to the thirty-degree cruise setting, the wing pivot mechanism failed, and the left wing uncontrollably folded all the way back to its aft-most sixty-degree setting. The bomber immediately snap-rolled to the left, quickly losing altitude.

The pilot applied hard right rudder to keep the bomber upright, and with the copilot's help he was able to keep the bomber level at 500 feet above ground and accelerate to a safe emergency cruise speed—until the acid blob finally ate through the thicker, stronger titanium lining the leading edge of the vertical stabilizer. The bomber began an uncontrolled left roll, immediately lost all lift, and plowed into the Iranian countryside just south of the city of Kerman.

The second Backfire bomber's fate was decided much quicker. The Tu-22M had just rotated and its main landing gear had just left the runway when the entire cockpit canopy failed, ripping a thirty-foot section of the fuselage directly over the crew compartment off the fuselage like an orange peel. At the same time, the electronics section of the right AS-4 Kitchen anti-ship missile sparked, ignited the acid, and detonated the missile's 2,200-pound warhead, blowing the 300,000-pound warplane into bits with a spectacular cloud of fire that illuminated the entire airport.

Luckily for the third and fourth Backfire bomber's crews, they had not yet left the runway, and the damage to their planes was localized and not so dramatic. Blobs of caustic acid burned through into fuselage fuel tanks and flight controls, starting fuselage and engine fires. Both four-man crews safely evacuated their planes and watched helplessly as their $200 million bombers burned. Soon, the lights of burning Backfire bombers were the only ones on the entire airport, for the JSOWs' deadly cargos had destroyed the main power grids . . . but those lights were soon followed by the brilliant mushroom of fire that erupted as the POL farm exploded, sending sheets of flame a thousand feet into the sky.

In minutes, one entire squadron of Iranian heavy bombers had been effectively destroyed, and their base rendered heavily damaged and unusable.

As they got closer and closer to the Gulf of Oman, the B-2A Spirit stealth bomber's threat scope became littered with dozens of Iranian threats, mostly MiG-29 and F-14 fighters—McLanahan was so concerned that he enlarged the threat display to cover almost the entire supercockpit display. The threat scope graphically depicted the position of each fighter and estimated range of each fighter's search radar; green, yellow, or red colors showed whether or not the radar was in a search, target-tracking, or missile-guidance mode. A few of the Iranian fighters' radar beams swept across the B-2A bomber, depicted in the center of the threat display, but the color of the radar cone never changed, indicating that the radar never locked on. Along with the extensive fighter

patrols, there were two Iranian A-10 Mainstay airborne warning radar aircraft in the area, plus the normal array of ground-
based radars and radar-guided antiaircraft sites.

"Jesus, there's got to be a half dozen flights of fighters
up tonight, just over this one section of Iran," McLanahan
said. "Guess they're pretty upset about what we did to Chah
Bahar the other night, huh?"

"Hey, they deserved to get their asses kicked," Jamieson
said, "and I was glad that it was *us* who helped 'em. How
long till feet-wet?"

"Fifteen minutes," McLanahan replied uneasily.

He fell silent again; Jamieson could tell that something was
bugging McLanahan. "Problem, MC?"

"Nah . . . well, it's just the arrangement of these Iranian
aircraft . . . it's changed since we went feet-dry on the bomb
run," McLanahan said, pointing at the supercockpit screen.
He expanded the ratio on the threat display until the entire
region, from Bandar Abbas to the extreme eastern part of the
Gulf of Oman, could be seen. The radar range circles from
Chah Bahar, from the carrier *Khomeini*, and from the two
Iranian A-10 airborne radar planes could be seen, forming a
"basket" all along the southern and southwestern portions
of Iran—and they were headed right for that basket. "Two
AWACS radar planes practically side by side across the Gulf
of Oman—that's weird. Everybody's clustered around each
other. Not a very efficient use of their air defense assets."

"Whoever gave the ragheads a lot of credit for smarts?"
Jamieson said. "Just keep an eye out for yellow or red—
we're clean as long as the threats stay green, right?"

Something was still nagging at McLanahan's head. This
looked too strange. The Iranians had showed much better
deployment of their forces before—even four hours earlier,
as they were heading into the target area, they had set up
their defenses very effectively. Now they were bunching up,
with many more fighters aimlessly buzzing around. Was it a
bit of confusion following the attack on Beghin Airport?
Were they a little disorganized, trying to catch a shadow and

screwing their valuable assets up even further in the process? Maybe . . .

"And look," he went on. "When the threat symbol comes up on the screen? It's not one by one—it's a flash. Look . . . *bam*, they all come up at once."

"So?"

"So, I've never seen that before," McLanahan explained. "We usually see one guy pop up, then another, then another, because their radars are different frequencies and different rpms and different timing and all that. Now, it's like all their radars are coming up exactly the same."

"That's impossible," Jamieson said. "You can't match a ground radar and an airborne radar up so they match everything like that. It's just the way the signal processor is displaying the threats, that's all. No big deal."

Yeah, no big deal. Yes, it was impossible, or at least very highly unlikely, that all of the Iranians' radars were synced up that tight . . .

. . . or maybe it wasn't. "Let's take a detour," McLanahan said. "Let's overfly Pakistan on our way out of here."

"Say *what*?"

"I know we're supposed to take pictures of Chah Bahar and the *Khomeini*, to find out how many extra fighters and ground-based air defense systems they've deployed—but I've got a bad feeling about this. It's like the Iranian air defenses are hanging around right in our flight path, daring us to drive through them. And their waves are all the same, they're too . . . similar. I wonder what they're up to."

"Well, whatever it is, they're doing it deaf, dumb, and blind," Jamieson remarked, with a satisfied smile. "They can't see us up here, MC—we've proven that without a doubt now. All they're doing is just microwaving birds and bugs. Besides, we don't have clearance to overfly Pakistan yet, and if Mr. Murphy kicks us in the butt and we're forced down over the Paks, we're really screwed. I say we follow the 'blue line' and see what happens."

McLanahan triple-checked that they were in COMBAT

mode and that all of their defensive systems were in full operation. Maybe he was being too cautious, too defensive, a little paranoid. Was it because Wendy was back on Guam, waiting for him? Probably . . . "Okay, we continue," he said. But as they flew south into the midst of the cluster of Iranian radars, he ordered the defensive systems to perform a fast self-test—no problems, everything fully functional. McLanahan then began formulating an escape plan, just in case, a . . .

But things were looking worse and worse every second.

They had been within Chah Bahar's long-range radar coverage for several minutes now, but there was absolutely no hint that they were an item of interest. As they neared the coast, flying at 50,000 feet fifty miles west of Chah Bahar, they entered the aircraft carrier *Khomeini*'s long-range radar coverage. There was still no sign of detection—both Chah Bahar and the *Khomeini*'s radars stayed in two dimensional search mode, blindly sweeping the skies in azimuth and range. The signal delta-threshold showed that the signal strength was not enough to create a return—the difference in the signal received by the threat-detection gear compared to the signal reflected back to the same source was too great. If they had been detected, one of those radars—probably the *Khomeini*'s—would switch to target-tracking mode, introducing a height-finder radar that would show up immediately. Nothing had changed . . . except . . .

"The fighters," McLanahan muttered. "The fighters disappeared."

"Say again?"

"Two fighters were right here, now they're gone," McLanahan said. "They stopped transmitting their attack radars."

"What was their range to us?"

"About sixty miles," McLanahan said. "Too far away for a missile shot . . ."

"Damned right," Jamieson said. "The AA-11 can fly for over a hundred miles, but it homes on radar, and we're not transmitting anything . . . are we . . . ?"

"No," McLanahan said—but they both quickly double-checked their switches. They were in COMBAT mode, all right—all radio transmitters were off, no synthetic aperture radars on, no Doppler radars on, no missile warning and tracking radars on, and the "cloaking device" was on—no electronic energy could leave the bomber with the electronic field activated. They were running silent. "Man, I still have a bad feeling."

"Then let's hurry up, take the SAR shot on the carrier, and let's get the hell outta Dodge," Jamieson said.

They were within SAR range of the carrier now, just sixty miles off the nose. "Okay, stand by, SAR coming on."

But just before he activated the system, which would automatically control the radar exposure as necessary to get a good picture of the carrier, McLanahan also activated the AN/ALQ-199 HAVE GLANCE system—as soon as the BEADS "cloaking device" went down, HAVE GLANCE would scan the sky all around the bomber with radar to search for nearby threats. "What's that for?"

"Precautionary," McLanahan said. "SAR exposure routine active ... in five ... four ... three ... two ... one ... SAR radiating ..."

And at the same instant, they heard a high-pitched, fast *Deedledeedledeedle!* warning tone, and a "bat-wing" fighter symbol appeared on the threat scope, just a few miles off their right rear quadrant! "Fighter, four o'clock, four miles, same altitude!" McLanahan screamed. "Descend! Accelerate! SAR down! Break, Tiger, *break right!*"

Thankfully, Jamieson didn't hesitate. He immediately rolled the big B-2A stealth bomber to 90, then 100, then 120 degrees of bank—practically *inverted!*—pulled on the control stick until it was at the forward stop, and jammed the throttles to full military power. He held the bank in until they had almost flown a 180-degree turn, facing toward the fighter, turning their hot engine exhausts away from the fighter and presenting their smallest radar and thermal cross-section.

But he wasn't fast enough. They heard a loud explosion

off to the left, the big bomber shuddered, and the ENG 1 FIRE warning light on the eyebrow panel came on. "Fire on number one!" McLanahan shouted. His supercockpit display had automatically switched over to the WCA and emergency-procedures displays so he could monitor the automatic engine shutdown, but the shaking was so rough that he couldn't read the screen. He had to trust that the computers were still functioning and they would complete the emergency shutdown checklist before the fire destroyed the aircraft.

Jamieson kept the right bank in, but now they were no longer turning—they were spinning! With no smooth airflow over the wings to create lift, the B-2A Spirit stealth bomber had stopped flying—it was in a complete stall, and with one wing low, it transitioned immediately into a "death spiral" spin. The bomber's nose was now pointed almost straight down at the ocean, and they were careening down toward the Gulf of Oman at 20,000 feet per minute.

"Recover!" McLanahan shouted. "Recover, Tiger!" McLanahan couldn't focus anymore. He had the threat display up on his supercockpit screen, with the flight instruments hidden behind it, and it was completely dark outside the cockpit windows, so he had absolutely no sense of up or down, left or right. McLanahan immediately craned his neck over to the left so he could see the pilot's artificial horizon, but moving his head like that caused the disorientation to increase a hundredfold. Jesus, they were completely out of control! They were going to hit the ocean any second!

McLanahan hit the BYPASS button on his control stick, then fumbled for the speed brake button on his throttle quadrant—normally they could not deploy speed brakes in COMBAT mode because it spoiled the bomber's stealth characteristics. He felt a rumbling in the airframe as the elevons on the bomber's wing tips split, acting as speed brakes to slow the bomber's wild, uncontrolled descent. At the same time, he held the control stick centered and full forward, then stomped on the left rudder to counteract the right spin. No good—no reaction. He tried jamming the control stick hard left, hoping that the increased elevon authority would . . .

"Let go of the controls, MC!" he heard Jamieson shout.

"I got it! I got it!" McLanahan shouted. "Let me know when!"

"I said, I got it, dammit!" Jamieson shouted back.

"No! I can pull us out! I got it! Just let me know when!"

Suddenly he felt a crushing *smack!* on his face, and the world went dark. McLanahan thought he was dead, but he wasn't . . . not yet. In a second the ocean would rush in, he'd swallow, and then . . .

But they hadn't hit the water. Jamieson had backhanded McLanahan in the face! "I said, I got it," Jamieson said calmly. Smoothly, carefully, Jamieson pulled the throttles to idle and stepped on the right rudder pedals.

The spinning was still as intense as ever. "We're still spinning!" McLanahan shouted. "Get the rudder in! Get—!"

"The plane's wings-level, Patrick," Jamieson said. "It's your damned navigator brain that's spinning." Jamieson reached up and hit a button on his top center mission display unit, and a sixteen-color, larger-than-life attitude-direction indicator appeared on McLanahan's supercockpit display. The ADI showed them slightly nose-low but, sure enough, they were wings-level. "I pulled us out of the spin, but you kept on pushing us right back into another one. That's why they call those a 'death spiral,' you know—every time you try to recover without looking at the instruments, you put yourself in another spin in the other direction. Remember to keep an ADI on your screen all the time from now on, okay?"

It took several moments for McLanahan to get his head to stop spinning and flipping upside down, but after staring at the electronic ADI on his monitor and *willing* himself to believe it was true, everything finally calmed down. McLanahan checked their status. Jamieson had them down at *100 feet* above the Gulf of Oman, at max continuous thrust, heading south toward Omani airspace—away from the *Khomeini* and those Iranian radars as fast as possible.

"You all right?" Jamieson asked.

"Yeah . . . yeah, I'm okay, thanks," McLanahan said weakly. He checked the Warnings, Cautions, and Alerts page. "Fire extinguishers fired off, so that engine is bye-bye," he said. "All number one systems down. Fuel pressure is fluctuating . . . hydraulic pressure OK . . . electrical system OK . . . fuel system is . . . wait, fuel valves three and four are still open. I'm going to MANUAL on the fuel system . . . ok, fuel shutoff valves to the number one engine are closed. All engines are feeding off the right wing tank. I'll empty that one first in case we sustained any damage." Jamieson checked the fuel panel switches, then nodded his agreement.

Iranian fighters were everywhere overhead, and the next twenty minutes was a nightmare come true. Every few minutes they would see fighters beginning to converge on them, so they would change course and edge as low as they dared to the ocean surface—at one point, they were at fifty feet, the absolute lowest they dared go without activating the radar altimeter or SAR. Even after they exited Iranian terri-torial waters, the Iranian fighters pursued. They had to fly almost all the way to the Omani coast before the Iranian fighters began to retreat. Finally they were over land, and the fighters were gone.

"Jesus, that was close. It must've been that fighter jock's lucky day, stumbling onto us like that. . . ."

"I don't think he lucked into us. Look at this," Mc-Lanahan said, motioning to his display. "We're well within radar range of Omani air defense radars and even Saudi Ara-bian F-15 fighters, but they're not coming after us. It's only the Iranians—they figured out how to track a B-2A bomber."

"*Track us?* With what? They didn't have a lock on us."

"I know, but they found us," McLanahan said. "Some-how they figured out a way to detect us well enough to vector a fighter in on us. Remember those fighters suddenly shutting down their radars, even though they didn't have a lock on us? They did that so we wouldn't find out we were being watched. It's gotta have something to do with that cluster of radars they set up."

"If that's true, then we're probably out of this fight," Jamieson said. "The whole B-2A program could be in jeop-

ardy. The Pentagon won't risk a B-2A bomber again until
they figure out how they were able to track us.''

"I don't think we'll have too much time," McLanahan
said. He began composing a report to the National Security
Agency via the Air Intelligence Agency to report on the
whole incredible, frightening incident. ''The Iranians have
the upper hand now—they might not rest until they get
everything they want.''

RESIDENCE OF THE PRESIDENT, SHAMSOL EMAREH PALACE, TEHRAN, IRAN
A SHORT TIME LATER

President of the Islamic Republic Ali Akbar Nateq-Nouri was
writing, pencil on paper, in a journal—no computer, no television, no radio in his quarters anymore—when suddenly the
door to his room burst open, and General Hesarak al-Kan
Buzhazi stormed in and strode directly up to him.

"Come in, the door is open," Nateq-Nouri deadpanned.

Buzhazi virtually dragged the President to his feet in anger. "I want the codes," he demanded.

"I am well, thank you for asking, General," the President
said. "How are you?"

"I will put a gun in your mouth and blow your addled
brain apart and make it appear as if you've killed yourself,"
Buzhazi shouted. "I want—"

"How did I get a weapon, General?"

"You took it from a guard and—"

"All of your precious Pasdaran troopers are at least eleven
kilos heavier and six centimeters taller than I," Nateq-Nouri
observed. "How can I possibly overpower one of your precious 'Guardians of Allah' after being virtually starved to
death here in my own residence?"

"I want the codes, Mr. President."

"Codes? What codes?"

Buzhazi had had enough. He clenched a fist and swung,

catching the President across the mouth. Nateq-Nouri reeled from the blow, his eyes taking several moments to clear and his head to stop spinning. "You know damned well which codes, Mr. President," the general said. "Give them to me, and I will let you live."

"I have no illusions that you will allow me to do anything of the kind for very much longer," the President said. "This proves how little you have thought about your coup d'état, General: you should have gotten the codes from me first, *then* declared martial law and had me killed. However, you still command a significant military force, so I am confused as to exactly why you need to arm a nuclear weapon. I assume you wish to arm the P-700 anti-ship missile you have on board the *Khomeini?*"

Buzhazi told himself that he should not be surprised to learn that Nateq-Nouri, who had distanced himself from the military at every turn and did everything he could to cut its size and complexity, knew about the secret nuclear missile project. It could not stay secret for very long. "Our nation is under attack, Mr. President," Buzhazi said, trying a slightly different tactic. "Beghin Airport in Kerman Province was assaulted just a few minutes ago. Two Backfire bombers were destroyed, two heavily damaged, and eight crewmen are dead, plus there are billions of rials in damage to the airport. I suspect it is the work of the United States and their stealth bomber fleet."

"Quite possible, General," Nateq-Nouri said. "You cannot hope to defeat the Americans. I suspect they have been using one aircraft, *one* stealth bomber, to conduct all these attacks—Bandar Abbas, your carrier, Chah Bahar, and now Beghin Airport. I have seen the reports, General: the American television networks have reporters at the main B-2A bomber base in the American republic of Missouri; all of the operational stealth bombers are still there. That means the Americans have one, possibly more of those infernal machines out there, being operated by some secret government agency."

"So you agree with me!" Buzhazi said, surprised. "You

agree that we are under attack by the Americans!"

"Of course we are, you idiot!" the President said. "This is all in retaliation for your flying your fighters off that carrier, sinking their spy ship, and capturing their spies."

"So you acknowledge that the Americans *were* spying on us."

"You give yourself very little credit, General—or perhaps you are even more stupid than even I gave you credit for," Nateq-Nouri said with a wry smile. "The Americans assisted the Gulf Cooperative Council in that raid against Abu Musa Island. You countered by launching that infernal carrier. The Americans respond by flying their little stealth contraption from the spy ship to spy on us—silly, really, because it would have been far simpler to go out into the Gulf of Oman with a rowboat and a radio and report on what we were doing!—and you sink their ship and capture all the spies. Sinking their ship was a colossal mistake, but the Americans would have forgotten about it if only you hadn't captured those men. After all, it was a spy ship masquerading as a civilian vessel—if America's allies in the Gulf knew that a civilian rescue vessel in their waters was really a spy ship, they would have been very upset. The United States would have gladly forfeited that ship in the hope that no one would find out it really was a spy ship.

"If you had released those men immediately, we would not be in this mess," the President went on. "We would have had an agreement in place that would have removed the threat of an American carrier invasion force sitting off our shores forever. We would have had increased foreign investment, because the military pressure would have been relieved. Instead, you started a shooting war with the Americans. You are angry about Beghin Airport and a couple of useless Backfire bombers? Wait until the cruise missiles and laser-guided bombs start falling on Tehran."

"The only way to stop that from happening, Mr. President, is force against force," Buzhazi said angrily. "Sink one of their carriers, and the American people will not allow Martindale to continue this secret bombing campaign against us.''

''You are so naive, General,'' Nateq-Nouri said sadly, shaking his head. ''All that might have been true thirty years ago, when Americans were fighting and dying in the jungles of Vietnam and the people wanted peace at any price. No longer—not with this American President. He will choose to fight. He will call for jihad against Iran, and he will rally the people and the military behind him.''

''And what about your own people, Mr. President?'' Buzhazi asked. ''If we allow the Americans to roam our skies, kill our soldiers, and destroy our bases at will, what will your people think?''

''Unlike you and the religious leaders of our country, Buzhazi, the Iranian people want peace, not war,'' Nateq-Nouri said. ''I know our people, General, you and the mullahs do not. The treaty with America and the GCC to prohibit land-attack warships and aircraft carriers from the Gulf was our best hope for peace. The American stealth bombers never would have crossed into our airspace unless that was the only hope to destroy our forces.''

''Now who is the naive one, Mr. President?'' Buzhazi interjected. ''Who is to say this is the first time the stealth bombers have been flying over Iran? Perhaps they are assisting the Kurdish rebels hiding in Iraq, or assisting the Armenians in disrupting our northern borders.''

''You may create any fantasy that your paranoid mind wishes, General, but the truth is, *our* government has influenced events around our borders and in other countries all around the world far more than the United States. Yes, we have had to deal with the American CIA in our midst for years, supporting various anti-government factions, and they have been just as disruptive as the Shah's terror squads ever were. But since the revolution, our history has been decided mostly by our own efforts, not by the United States or the Shah.

''Peace could have been ours, General. Abu Musa could have been ours to share with the United Arab Emirates—

with our oil technology and their funding, we both could have been rich. The money we have spent on that monstrosity you dared name after the Imam Khomeini and on all these Russian fighters and bombers and cruise missiles could have been used to complete the oil terminal at Chah Bahar, and we would not be at the mercy of Iraq, the GCC, or the West when we ship oil through the Shatt al Arab Waterway or the Persian Gulf. Instead, you chose war, a war we cannot win except by sacrificing ourselves. I will not assist you in following this course, General. Fight and die on your own terms."

In response, General Buzhazi pulled out an automatic pistol, cocked it, stepped around to President Nateq-Nouri's right side, and aimed it at his temple. The President of Iran closed his eyes and waited for the bullet to enter his brain. . . .

"It would be so easy, Mr. President."

"Then do it, General," Nateq-Nouri said. "If you have the courage to face the wrath of the Ayatollah Khamenei and the Leadership Council, who commanded that I be protected, do it. I am prepared to die. Are you prepared to live?"

"Prepared or not, you will be dead, and I will be alive," Buzhazi said. "You know I will get the codes to the nuclear and chemical arsenals eventually—you cannot stop it."

"It seems as if you have everything well in order," Nateq-Nouri said, with mock approval. "Carry out your plan, then. Kill me. Then explain to the Imam how all this was a suicide, or an accident. See how long you will be commanding your troops then."

Buzhazi took a deep, angry breath, leveled the pistol again . . . but did not pull the trigger. Instead, he holstered it, swore under his breath, and left the President's residence. Nateq-Nouri caught a glimpse of two Pasdaran troopers guarding the door outside as Buzhazi departed.

After what seemed like an eternity, Nateq-Nouri took a deep breath, then returned to his desk and plunked down into the chair on wobbly legs. All that bravado was a charade, he knew—he was very afraid of dying, and terrified of dying at the hands of Hesarak al-Kan Buzhazi, lying at his feet in a pool of red blood and gray brain matter. He had worked too hard to leave this life that way. He . . .

"Trouble with the staff tonight, Mr. President?" a woman's voice asked in Farsi. Nateq-Nouri turned, his heart skipping a few beats in shock. There, emerging from the curtains surrounding the bedchamber, were a man and a woman, both dressed like commandos in black skintight body suits, gloves, and boots. They were armed, but their weapons were at their sides, ready but not threatening.

When he regained his composure, the President of Iran gaily, casually waved at the strangers. "Please, come in, come in," he said effusively in Farsi. "Everyone else seems to be making themselves welcome in my residence, so why not you two? You are Arab, I am sure." Nateq-Nouri switched to almost accent-free Arabic. "Your African friend, a Libyan perhaps? Sudanese?"

"At least he's bein' sociable about this," the man said in English.

"Ah! An American!" Nateq-Nouri said, his eyes dancing. In equally good English, he said, "Welcome to my home, young man. Yes, the only luxury I have right now is to be sociable. Now, do you mind telling me why you are here? Are you here to assassinate me?"

"I *should* blow you away, motherfucker, for what you done to my homeboys!"

"Your American ghetto dialect is very difficult for me to understand, young man, but I assume you are associates of Colonel Paul White, and you are angry at me for the circumstances surrounding his capture and internment," the President of Iran said. "I have been expecting you, although I expected to see a brilliant high-tech assault on the headquarters building, beginning with some of your wonderful cruise missiles dropped by your stealth bomber, followed by your, how do you call them, your 'tilt-rotor' aircraft, with lots of well-trained, steely-eyed, square-jawed, whisky-drinking commandos jumping and sliding down ropes with guns blazing to make the heroic rescue . . . or will I not be disappointed? Is that what is happening now?''

"Tell us where Colonel White is, Mr. President, and you won't get hurt.''

"Hurt? My dear young man, I am as good as *dead* already,'' Nateq-Nouri said with a lighthearted laugh. "I assume you heard General Buzhazi. As soon as he gets the codes for the nuclear weapons aboard the carrier *Khomeini*, I will be disposed of. In his bumbling sort of way, he will try to make it look like an accident, but everyone will know, of course.''

"Just tell us where Colonel White is, Mr. President.''

"Your Colonel Paul White is being held in an interrogation center at Pasdaran headquarters," Nateq-Nouri replied, "but to tell you the truth, sir, I do not know if he is still alive.''

"We'll find out ourselves—and if he's not, we'll take the news *very* poorly," Briggs said coldly. "Can you be a little more specific about his location, Mr. President?''

"No, unfortunately not," Nateq-Nouri admitted. "I understand the Pasdaran interrogates its prisoners by administering drugs at what they call a 'medical care facility' in the basement of their headquarters—awful, brutal place, filled with evil, brutal men!—but I do not know if White has been taken there.''

"Perhaps you could inquire, Mr. President?'' Behrouzi suggested.

"I was never a favorite of the Pasdaran," Nateq-Nouri said, "but I believe there are one or two officers at headquarters that may speak to me.'' With that, Nateq-Nouri picked up a phone.

Briggs raised his Uzi. "Be careful what you ask for, Mr. President.''

"You, sir," said the President of Iran with a cold smile, "are the *least* of my worries right now.'' He dialed the phone, spoke briefly in Farsi to two different persons, then hung up. "Colonel White is indeed in the Pasdaran medical facility, headquarters building, first subfloor A, room A193. He is alive and perhaps even conscious. My friends have

arranged for the guards at the medical facility to be 'preoc-
cupied' for the next half hour. I trust you can effect some
sort of rescue in that time.''

Hal Briggs was almost too stunned for words. He
shrugged, gave Riza a confused expression, then nodded.
''Sure, Mr. President. That will be great.'' He paused for a
moment, then asked, ''Will you be safe after General Buzhazi finds out about this, sir?''

''I do not know, young man.''

''Hal. Call me Hal, Mr. President,'' Briggs interjected.
Riza looked at him in absolute surprise—Intelligence Support Agency operatives were not supposed to use their real
names—but, somehow, it fit in this very bizarre setting.
Thirty seconds ago, Briggs was ready to shoot this man between the eyes—now he was introducing himself to him,
using his *real name!*

''Thank you, Hal . . . or is it colonel, major, captain . . . ?''

''Just Hal is fine.''

''Yes. Hal it is then.'' Nateq-Nouri regarded Riza for a
moment, searched his memory; then, wagging a knowing finger at her and smiling, said, ''Ah. Now I recall. OPEC Ministers' Conference, last year, Quito, Ecuador, the reception
at Energy Minister Nazur's residence. It was hotter than
Mogadishu in the summer and the *humidity* . . . forgive me,
I do not remember your name, but I will never forget the
black dress and that delicious diamond ankle bracelet you
wore—very alluring, I must say. You accompanied Minister
Yusuf of the United Arab Emirates to the reception, but I
could not help but notice you two spent very little time together—he already had a young translator that he kept fon-
dling, as I recall—so you must have been on some sort of
secret assignment, perhaps for the Directorate of Intelligence
for the United Arab Emirates, no?''

''Your memory is quite remarkable, Mr. President,'' Behrouzi said, touched by the man's charm in the face of almost
certain disaster, ''but it would be best if your memory of me
was restricted to an ankle bracelet in Ecuador.''

"Of course," Nateq-Nouri said. "Now, you must do something for me in return."

"What's that?"

Nateq-Nouri fixed both of them with a deadly serious stare. "Destroy the aircraft carrier *Khomeini*, Hal," the President of Iran said.

"Say *what?*"

"I cannot hold out against General Buzhazi for long, Hal," Nateq-Nouri said resignedly. "He will either discover or bypass the code, or he will torture the code out of me, in a very short time—perhaps even tonight."

"Code? What code?"

"The code to arm the nuclear warhead on the carrier *Khomeini*," Nateq-Nouri said. "One of the anti-ship missiles on board that carrier has a very large nuclear warhead capable, I daresay, of sinking your *Abraham Lincoln* very efficiently."

"Holy *shit!*"

"Please, mind your sacrilegious language, young man," Nateq-Nouri scolded Briggs. His tone softened immediately, however, and he went on: "To continue: General Buzhazi has one set of codes, I have the other. I do not know how long I could hold out, but I know the general has very effective ways to get the information he desires. Then he will have both sets of codes he requires to arm the nuclear missiles. When he does, he will move the carrier and launch the P-700 missile—perhaps at Saudi Arabia, perhaps at Iraq, perhaps at your *Lincoln* carrier group. I do not know. I feel he will use that carrier, along with his other forces, to decimate the Gulf Cooperative Council military bases along the Gulf. You must stop him."

Briggs looked at Behrouzi, then slapped a fist into his other hand in frustration. "I had that sucker in my sights once, Mr. President—I'd love to get another shot at it and send it to Davy Jones's locker for real. You got a deal."

"Very good," Nateq-Nouri said. "Now, I suggest you should leave. Good luck to you." And Nateq-Nouri headed for the door to his suite, closed the door behind him and left the two commandos by themselves.

"I must be dreaming, Riza," Briggs said as they prepared to depart. "The President of fuckin' Iran is helping us spring Colonel White, and in exchange wants us to *destroy* his fuckin' . . . I mean, his friggin' carrier . . . ?"

"I am not so surprised—Ali Akbar Nateq-Nouri is truly a man of peace, a rare commodity in Iran these days," Behrouzi said with a smile. "What is even more surprising is *you* telling him your real name!"

"I felt it was a pretty safe move," Briggs said coldly. "I owed him a little sign of gratitude, of respect—and I don't think he's going to be alive very much longer to tell anybody about us, poor devil. Now let's get moving!"

• • •

The back portico of the President's residence was hidden from most of the compound because of the intricate design of the old palace; hidden sensors and surveillance cameras had effectively compensated for the shortfall, but those were easily bypassed by Madcap Magician commandos.

Chris Wohl was on the ground just below the President's apartment window, covering the primary exit, when he saw the curtain above flutter, a sliding door bang open, even heard muted voices! "Shit, Briggs, what in hell are you doing?" Wohl muttered. This exfiltration was going down the shitter real fast, he thought. He hurriedly clicked his transceiver to alert the ten other commandos in the compound to get ready to move and that they possibly had been discovered—when suddenly he heard footsteps behind him. He whirled, gun at the ready.

"Hang on, Mondo, it's me—George and Gracie." Shit, Wohl thought, it was Briggs and Behrouzi, climbing down the side of the building. "Let's get going. We know where Colonel White is, and we've got less than thirty minutes to get him."

"Briggs, what in hell are you talking about?"

"We found out where White is," Briggs said. "He's at

Pasdaran headquarters, first subfloor, room A193. He's waiting for us.''

"*Waiting* for us? Who the hell told you this?"

"Thank *him*," Briggs said. Wohl followed his pointed finger up the dark, looming walls of Shamsol Emareh Palace
and, to his continuing astonishment, saw the President of
Iran, Ali Akbar Nateq-Nouri, looking down on them from
his open fourth-floor window! "We gotta get moving,
Chris—the President has a job for us."

"The President—you mean, the President of fucking
Iran?"

"Hey, watch your sacrilegious language, young man,"
Briggs scolded Wohl. "This is serious, man—some bad shit
could be happening any hour now out in the Gulf. Nateq-
Nouri told us about it, he asked for our help, and he sprung
the colonel for us to show he's for real—he probably just
sacrificed his own life to help us. In return, he wants us to
trash Iran's aircraft carrier . . .''

"*What?*"

"Never mind now, Chris—when we get back, we'll get
hold of Future Flight and get them loaded up for bear again.
Right now, we gotta get the colonel before the Pasdaran
troopers shut the door on us for good. Let's hit it, Marine."
Briggs and Behrouzi trotted off down their preplanned exfiltration route, leaving a totally perplexed Chris Wohl and his
fellow ISA commandos shaking their heads.

THE WHITE HOUSE OVAL OFFICE, WASHINGTON, D.C.
27 APRIL 1997, 2136 HOURS LOCAL TIME

"General Buzhazi, this is President Kevin Martindale, calling from Washington, D.C. How are you this morning?"

The translator's voice responded, "Very well, thank you."
A Farsi-speaking interpreter listening in on the line made
notes on a computer terminal in front of the President, verifying the accuracy of the Iranian translator.

"I wish to speak to you about the aircraft carrier *Khomeini*, General," the President said. "My government has received disturbing news. We have learned that the carrier is carrying a cruise missile with a nuclear warhead."

There was a very long pause after the translation; then: "The Islamic Republic cannot confirm or deny the presence of any nuclear weapons that may or may not be in our possession, Mr. President."

Martindale swore under his breath, glaring angrily at the wall as Vice President Ellen Whiting, Secretary of State Jeffrey Hartman, Secretary of Defense Arthur Chastain, and National Security Advisor Philip Freeman looked on. The President recognized Buzhazi's response—it was the standard response of the U.S. military when asked that very same question about any of its bases or warships. The United States never spoke about its deployment of nuclear weapons. "I see, General," Martindale said.

"Is there anything else, Mr. President?"

"You do realize, sir, that Iran's possession of nuclear weapons and long-range maritime missile technology fitted with such warheads is in violation of the 1968 Nuclear Nonproliferation Treaty and the 1993 Missile Technology Export Treaty," the President said. "Iran signed these treaties without reservations."

"The Nuclear Nonproliferation Treaty was signed by the traitor Shah Reza Pahlavi's regime, Mr. President," Buzhazi reminded him, "not by the Islamic revolutionary government. It holds no validity for us. I am not familiar at all with the other agreement."

"Your membership in the United Nations, the World Bank, OPEC, the Seabeds Committee, and the International Civil Aeronautics Organization also predate the Islamic revolution," the President said. "Should we consider your membership in all those organizations also without validity?"

"You may do as you wish, Mr. President," Buzhazi said sternly. "In any case, all of this is of no consequence. The aircraft carrier and the destroyer *Zhanjiang* are both the property of the People's Republic of China's People's Liberation Army Navy. For a fee, Iran has been allowed to service and refurbish these vessels, and perform flight training on them. In time, they will be returned to China. Whatever weapons these vessels carry is determined by the People's Republic of China. Perhaps you should speak with Premier Jiang Zemin.'' Jiang Zemin, the successor to the powerful and popular Chinese Premier Deng Xiaoping, was a well-educated, well-spoken man—young for a top Chinese leader, at age sixty-eight—but was even more enigmatic and unpredictable than Buzhazi. Since the Chinese mini-invasion of the Philippines and the Chinese transfer of potentially devastating weapons to unstable regimes such as North Korea, Syria, Iraq, Sudan, and Iran, relations between the U.S. and China had been strained, and Martindale and Zemin did not have much to say to each other.

"Since you control the movement of the *Khomeini*, General, I'll speak to you,'' the President said sternly. "Your forces unsuccessfully attacked the U.S.S. *Abraham Lincoln* last night with long-range bombers, and now we observe your aircraft carrier sailing out of the Gulf of Oman toward our carrier group. We regard that movement as a hostile action, and we will take steps to stop it if it is not returned to port immediately.''

"Then it shall be returned to port,'' Buzhazi said. "The carrier *Khomeini* and the destroyer *Zhanjiang* will be returned to their home port . . . of Ningbo.''

"Ningbo . . . where's that?'' the President asked the room, covering the receiver. Seconds later, the information appeared on his computer screen from a military intelligence analyst: Ningbo was the Chinese Eastern Fleet headquarters, situated on the East China Sea—within easy fighter range of all of South Korea, including Seoul; the Japanese main islands of Kyushu, Shikoku, western Honshu, and all of the Ryukyu Islands, including Okinawa; and the island of Taiwan. "You're sailing a nuclear-armed aircraft carrier to the East China Sea?''

"It is what the customer ordered, President Martindale,''

Buzhazi's translator said. "We shall be conducting trials in the Arabian Sea and Indian Ocean, possibly with a cruise up the Red Sea to a port call in Libya first; then, we shall transfer the ship first to Victoria, then on to Ningbo. I trust the United States will not interfere with the transit." Victoria was to be the newest Chinese naval base—on the island of Hong Kong, about to be transferred to Chinese control.

"We strongly object to that ship carrying nuclear weapons," the President said, "and we will urge all nations through which this vessel will pass to prohibit you from entering their waters."

"And I object to the United States flying its stealth bomber across our sovereign airspace, attacking our airfields, and killing our citizens," Buzhazi interrupted hotly. "The United States has sailed nuclear-armed warships past our country for over forty years, in your 'national interest' and 'defense' interests—now we shall do the same. Is there anything further, Mr. President?"

"I should like to inquire about President Nateq-Nouri's condition and his political status," Martindale said.

"I regret to inform you, sir, that President Ali Akbar Nateq-Nouri was found dead in his home in Tehran not too long ago," Buzhazi said, completely without emotion. "He was found with a single bullet wound to the head, made by an Italian-made Beretta Model 92 handgun—I believe it is the standard issue to American military forces, is it not . . . ?"

"You son of a *bitch!*" President Martindale snapped. "You *murdered* President Nateq-Nouri!"

"An investigation is under way, but we believe the incident may have been a murder by foreign assassins," Buzhazi said matter-of-factly. "The President may have been coerced into using his office to release a foreign prisoner from a military prison facility, then killed. Such a regrettable incident. I hope Allah has no mercy to those who did such a deed."

Martindale slammed the telephone back on its cradle in absolute anger and disgust. "That *bastard!*" he shouted.

"That insane bastard! He had Nateq-Nouri killed for helping Paul White escape from Tehran!"

"I'm sorry, Mr. President," Philip Freeman said. "I'm sorry my guys got him in this predicament. I take full responsibility for Nateq-Nouri's death."

"Bullshit, Philip, it had to be Buzhazi himself who did it," Secretary of Defense Chastain said. "He was looking for a way to off the President for a long time—it's no secret that Buzhazi wanted the presidency, but he'd be completely unable to stand for an election. He's a power-crazy madman."

"And right now, he has the ear of the mullahs, including Khamenei," Secretary of State Hartman said. "If he survives the scrutiny of the Leadership Council, his power will grow exponentially—especially if he helps cement a strong relationship between Tehran and Beijing. He will be quite unstoppable then. He may gather enough strength to weaken or even topple the religious leadership."

"Our problem right now is that carrier," the President said. "I don't want it to leave the Gulf of Oman. Philip, can your boys stop that thing without starting a war in the Middle East?"

"We had trouble in our last sortie, sir," Freeman said. "The Iranians have apparently figured out a way to detect the stealth bomber."

"They *what?*" Chastain retorted. "What happened?"

"Three radar sites—land, sea, and air—perfectly synchronized," Freeman explained. "Each one receiving the other's radar signals and combing them on one display. The off-axis lobes created by the stealth design are picked up by other sites and reported to the master radar site. It's enough to get a weak return. After that, just vector a fighter close enough to that blip to get a visual or infrared signal, and he's yours. An Iranian fighter got close enough to fire a missile at our secret B-2A bomber—the missile was diverted by the bomber's active countermeasures, but one engine was shot out. Jamieson and McLanahan barely got away."

"Thank God," the President breathed. "So what's the solution?"

"The solution, sir, is to knock out the synchronized radar sites," Freeman said. "We have anti-radar missiles that can destroy the radar sites from five to ten miles out. The problem is that Iran has got every air machine they have in the air, and they're sure to intercept the missile shooters at long range. The other problem is that the only anti-radar missile shooters we have in the region right now are on the *Lincoln*—the EA-6 Prowlers, the A-6 Intruders, and the F/A-18 Hornets. It'll take just about every one of them to take out all the Iranian radars."

"And now we're talking about an invasion force," the President said, "something I want to avoid. Iran hasn't declared war on anybody—if we shoot first, we're the bad guys."

"And after all that, our chances of success will be low," Freeman admitted. "The shooters would be outnumbered ten to one by advanced Iranian fighters, and they'd be detected long before they got within firing range. And because the *Lincoln* is so far from the Gulf of Oman right now, fighter coverage would be minimal or nonexistent."

"I take it you have an alternate plan, or else you wouldn't be here right now," the President said to Freeman. "Let's have it."

"The plan involves considerable risk to Air Vehicle Eleven, the B-2A bomber Jamieson and McLanahan are flying," Freeman said. "It'll be sent in against the Iranian air defenses all by itself, armed with non-lethal weapons. It involves much more risk—not just to the crews, but to you politically as well. If it fails at a critical time, you'll be totally exposed—there'll be no doubt about what you attempted to do. If it succeeds, we'll be able to meet your original criteria: the mission will be totally deniable, it'll involve no or minimal loss of life, and it won't look like an invasion force is out to destroy Iran."

"Then let's do it," the President said. "Brief me on the plan, and let's get started."

"You should think about this for a time, Mr. President," Freeman said. "The plan involves great personal political risk."

"Philip, this job is nothing *but* a long list of great personal political risks," President Martindale said. "But I told you, I want that carrier stopped. If you got a way to do it without starting a general war in the Middle East—"

"Or Asia, sir?" Freeman interjected.

The President hesitated—Freeman and the other advisers could see the President avert his eyes, thinking hard, perhaps reconsidering . . .

"Or Asia," the President said. "Let's hear it." And with that, Philip Freeman began outlining his plan to the President and his advisers.

TEHRAN, IRAN
THAT SAME TIME

Smiling, General Buzhazi hung up the dead phone. "Your threats will do you no good, President Martindale," he said. To Air Force General Sattari, Buzhazi's acting chief of staff, he asked, "Is the mission ready to proceed, General?"

"Yes, sir," Sattari responded. "Backfire bombers from Esfahan and attack planes from Bandar Abbas will attack the United Arab Emirates' bases at Taweela, Mina Saqr, and Mina Sultan, and the Omani naval base on the Musandam Peninsula; six fighter-bombers from the *Khomeini* will attack Sib Air and Naval Base near Muscat in Oman. Six fighters from the *Khomeini* will provide primary air cover to the east, backed up by fighters from Chah Bahar; Bandar Abbas and Abu Musa will provide air-and ground-based air defense cover for the western attackers. The attack will be perfectly coordinated so that all attacks are simultaneous and that air defense fighters will launch and cover the strikers' retreat, without alerting anyone that an attack is imminent."

"And what about the Americans?" Buzhazi asked. "The

Americans patrol the Arabian Peninsula almost all the way to the Gulf of Oman.''

"We outnumber all Western and GCC aircraft by a factor of three to one," Sattari responded. "As you ordered, we shall launch six fighters for every one of theirs. The American and Saudi F-15s are respectable, but they are not a match for a locust swarm of MiG-29s and their own F-14 Tomcats.''

"Very good," Buzhazi said. "And the preparations for an attack by their stealth bombers?''

"Radar sites from Shiraz to Char Bahar are now all synchronized. We cover the entire Persian Gulf and Gulf of Oman region with radar capable of detecting the B-2A stealth bomber," Sattari replied proudly. "The network is controlled by the master combat information center aboard the *Khomeini*, but any radar facility can become the master combat center if the others should go off the line. The long-range air defense radars around Tehran have also been synchronized, and soon all of Iran's long-range radar systems will be synchronized to be able to detect stealth aircraft.''

"And what of our preparations for the follow-on attacks?''

"We are ready, sir," Sattari reported. "We have two fighter bomber and one additional fighter-interceptor teams ready to fly in follow-up sorties should the first round of attacks prove successful. The slowest element in the follow-on sorties will be the carrier-based aircraft, so we have split their force into two bomber and two fighter elements, to provide continuous air defense patrols while the bombers land and depart. The other elements from Chah Bahar and Bandar Abbas will be ready to attack the follow-on targets in Saudi Arabia, Bahrain, and Qatar immediately. In addition, other forces from Tabriz and Mahabad will be standing by to strike targets in Turkey if you so order.''

"Excellent, General, excellent," Buzhazi said. "The attack will commence tonight. May Allah be with our pilots!''

ANDERSEN AIR FORCE BASE, GUAM
28 APRIL 1997, 1551 HOURS LOCAL

Patrick McLanahan was on the third-floor catwalk of the hangar in which his B-2A Spirit stealth bomber was going through its final maintenance checks. He wore a black flight suit with no patches or insignia—it looked like mechanic's overalls—with Chinese-made flight boots, thick and woolly.

"The thousand-yard stare again," Wendy McLanahan said as she approached him. She linked her arm in his and rested her head on his right shoulder. "They did a pretty good job on it in such a short time," she said, looking at the left engine nacelles. "Can't even tell you were hit by an Iranian missile and almost blown into a thousand pieces."

"Wendy . . ."

"This is really a crazy idea," Wendy said irritably, "and I can't believe *you* thought of it, and I can't believe Freeman accepted it."

"It's the only way we can do it, Wendy," Patrick said absently, still staring at nothing, as if trying to look into the future and see if this was going to work. "If there was another way, I'm open to suggestions . . ."

"I've got one—let it be. Let the Iranian carrier be," Wendy said angrily. "No one has declared war here, Patrick. Paul White and the survivors of the *Valley Mistress* are safe, Hal got back at the Iranians for what they did—aren't we even now?"

"We were—until Buzhazi had President Nateq-Nouri killed," Patrick said. "It's obvious that he doesn't want peace. He wants to take that carrier battle group and wreak havoc in the entire region, all for the sake of glory and power for himself."

"Why risk your life for a man you didn't know—for an *Iranian*," Wendy asked incredulously. "He was just another fundamentalist Muslim looking to infect the rest of the world with his brand of Islam by whatever means he could . . ."

"Nateq-Nouri was a man who wanted peace," Patrick said. "He wasn't a Muslim fundamentalist—he was a realist. He may not have liked the United States, but he was wise enough to think of innovative ways to avoid a conflict. Buzhazi's not a fundamentalist, either—he's a homicidal psychopath. He's out there taking shots at our aircraft carriers with Backfire bombers and supersonic cruise missiles just for *fun*. What if he gets lucky and lands a one-ton warhead on the decks of the *Abraham Lincoln*, or decides to put a torpedo into one of our ships? How many Americans does he have to kill before we should go after him?" Wendy had no answer for him.

They stood together for a few minutes longer, until Patrick looked at his watch and sighed. "I've got to go," he said.

"I know," Wendy responded. He hugged Wendy closely, and she started to cry. "You know . . . you know we talked about trying to have another child," Wendy said in a tiny voice through her tears. "We should stop trying. . . ."

"What?" Patrick asked. "*Why,* Wendy? We both want one so much. Why . . . ?" He read the sorrow in her eyes, then shook his head in exasperation. "Is it because I'm with Future Flight? Dammit, Wendy, I was afraid this would happen. I never should have accepted this Future Flight assignment. I was happy working the pub in Old Sacramento—"

"No you weren't," Wendy interjected. "You wanted to come back, wanted to start flying again. When Freeman came along, it was a dream come true for you. You made a decision."

"But I love you, Wendy. I want us to be happy. I know how much you want a child, how upset you were when you lost the first one. If it means that much to you, Wendy, I'll quit . . ."

"You will? Right now? Three hours before takeoff?"

"Yes," Patrick said resolutely. "You mean more to me than this mission or Future Flight or even the damned country!"

Wendy was so surprised that she had to remember to close

her mouth. "I . . . I can't believe this . . . you'd do that for me? For us?"

"Yes."

"That's so sweet . . . I love you so much, Patrick," Wendy said. "But that's not what I meant."

"What? You don't . . . I'm confused, Wendy. What are you saying? Don't you want me to quit flying?"

"Of course not," Wendy said. "What, and watch you stare off into space and mope around the house all day and yell and scream at the employees all night? No, you're doing what you love to do, and you're the best at it, so keep doing it. I'll consult for Jon Masters, and telecommute with Sky Masters from home while I take care of our baby."

"Our . . . our *what?*"

"Our *baby,* bomber-brain—our offspring, our rug-rat, our cookie-cruncher," Wendy said. "We can stop trying to have a baby *because* we did it—I'm *pregnant.*"

"But . . . but how . . . ?"

"How? Your mom never told you the facts of life?"

"No, dammit . . . I thought you couldn't have a baby after the accident because of trauma to your follicles or something . . . I thought we had to do all that in vitro fertilization stuff, do the test tubes and the echography and follicle punctures . . . "

"Well, either it was an immaculate conception or the doctors were wrong about the old lady's plumbing, because we got pregnant the old-fashioned way—without Synarel sprays or Pergonal shots or micromanipulation," Wendy said proudly. "You're going to be a daddy after all—that is, as long as you come back to me."

"Of course I'll be back, Wendy," Patrick said. "Even if I have to walk. If I've got any skill, if I've got any luck, if I've got any brains at all, I'll use them all to come back to you."

They embraced again, tighter than ever before; and even amid the sounds of external power carts and shouting soldiers and missiles and weapons being uploaded and all the other sounds of war in that hangar, for a brief instant in time, there were only the two of them, together forever. . . .

Takeoff was shortly after darkness set in on Guam. After the area was cleared for any unidentified aircraft or vessels, Air Vehicle 011 launched from Andersen's north-south runway, instantly 500 feet above the ocean as it left the runway because the end of the runway was on a tall cliff on Guam's northernmost tip. McLanahan couldn't help but think of the last time he had taken a B-2 bomber into combat from Guam—they almost hadn't made it. But that was a lifetime ago, it seemed.

The launch brought the same thrill of fear into Tony Jamieson's heart. He remembered all too well their mission against the Chinese navy and air force over the Philippines.

And this mission was even more insane. They had planned it less, and all the planning had been done by McLanahan—a damned *civilian*, no less!—along with his computers and his buddies at Sky Masters, Inc. The enemy was more numerous, better equipped, better prepared, and they were on their home turf, defending their homeland. But Jamieson had agreed to do it—he couldn't back out now. He had to prove to himself that he really did have the right stuff to fly into combat.

Just two hours after takeoff, over the Philippine Sea between Luzon and the Batan Islands, they rendezvoused with a KC-135 tanker that had taken off before them, and they topped off their tanks—it was the loneliest feeling in the world to see that KC-135 leave. They began a step-climb to 48,000 feet, saving as much fuel as possible. Both crew members could see the lights of Manila about 300 miles to the south; 300 miles north were the lights of Taipei, and off the B-2A's curved beak nose on the horizon were the lights of Victoria and Macao. They altered course slightly to avoid overflying Hong Kong . . .

. . . but went feet-dry over the city of Zhelang, Guangdong Province, in the People's Republic of China. They were overflying China on their way to strike Iran.

"I don't friggin' believe this," Jamieson said, "but we're doing it. We've just violated China's airspace with an armed strategic bomber."

The huge naval and air base at Guangzhou was the biggest concern right now. They had picked up strong radar and air defense signals from more than 300 miles out, shortly after completing their aerial refueling. Guangzhou was alive with air defense systems—most older, ex-Soviet systems, like the Vietnam-era SA-2 long-range "flying telephone pole" missile; China was flying late-evening air patrols as well. The majority of Chinese air interceptors on patrol showed on the threat scope as MiG-21s, with a few more modern Sukhoi-27s in the mix. "Well, the Chinese air force is certainly awake tonight," Jamieson commented. "Training day, I hope."

Just then, one of the Chinese-built Xian J-7 fighters, copies of the Russian MiG-21, swept its radar beam across the B-2A stealth bomber—and the green triangle representing its search radar changed to yellow. Shit, that MiG-21 locked onto us!" Jamieson called out. "He's at eight o'clock, twenty miles!"

"If we get intercepted, our best plan is an emergency descent, then deviate southwest across Laos or Burma," McLanahan said, repeating their hastily planned escape procedures. "Range to the Laotian border is about five hundred miles. Radar coverage is almost nonexistent to the southwest."

"If he gets an eyeball on us, we'll be lucky to make it five minutes, let alone five hundred miles," Jamieson muttered. But thankfully, the fighter's radar broke lock a few moments later, and he did not reacquire. "God, that was close."

But it wasn't over yet. Several minutes later, another fighter—this one a Russian-built Sukhoi-27, a much more up-to-date fighter-bomber—started sweeping the area, searching for the B-2A bomber— and seconds later, it too showed a lock-on. "The Su-27's got us," McLanahan said. "Seven o'clock, fifteen miles."

"What in hell's going on?" Jamieson asked. "Recheck your switches." But after quickly scanning the status page of the computer readouts, they could find nothing out of place—they were in COMBAT mode, with all stealth and defensive systems on and functioning. "That's two in a row. Are we hanging something?"

"That's got to be it," McLanahan said. "Try a turn to the left." Sure enough, as soon as they turned into the fighter, the yellow target-tracking radar turned to a green search radar, and the fighter began sweeping the skies in other directions, trying to lock on. The closest he got was ten miles, well outside visual range even with night-vision optics.

"I was afraid of that," Jamieson said. "Field maintenance in a B-2A bomber is not like any other plane. The maintenance crews have to be specially trained, and the plane has to be checked to make sure its stealth characteristics weren't altered. One fastener not screwed in all the way, one seam not in perfect alignment, one ding in the skin, can destroy the stealth characteristics and increase the radar cross-section two or three times." Jamieson turned to McLanahan. "We got a decision to make, bub. The Chinese generally are known to have shitty military stuff, but their standard line aircraft got a lock-on and closed within missile range—twice. Iran's got top-of-the-line stuff; so do India and Pakistan. Burma's our last safe chance to get out."

McLanahan knew that they had no choice—the mission was in serious jeopardy. "All right," he said, "I have to agree. I think we can still make it, but the risk is too much. We'll execute the Burma escape route; once we're clear of Chinese radar coverage, I'll flash a message to Andersen to schedule a tanker." In the back of his head was Wendy's surprise message, too—he was going to be a father. He couldn't risk his first child growing up without him.

As McLanahan composed their status and abort message for satellite relay, they continued on for another hour until they were well clear of the Chinese air defense region near Chengdu, where it was safe to temporarily deactivate the AN/VUQ-13 BEADS "cloaking device," get a GPS satellite navigation fix, and activate the encoded satellite transceiver. Just as McLanahan was ready to send his message, a priority message came in.

"Shit," McLanahan said. "Iran is attacking the United Arab Emirates and Oman!"

"*What?*"

"Bomber attacks on three bases in the UAE and two bases in Oman," McLanahan read. "Iran is shutting down any Gulf Cooperative Council base that might threaten the carrier *Khomeini* while it's stationed in the Gulf of Oman. Extensive Iranian fighter coverage throughout the region, including near the *Abraham Lincoln* battle group . . . no U.S. or GCC air defense units were able to respond. The attack came out of nowhere."

"We'll get plastered," Jamieson said. "If Iran presses the attack, we could lose every usable air and naval base east of the Red Sea. We'd . . ." He knew . . . they *both* knew, what this meant—they couldn't abort their mission now. Their B-2A bomber was the only allied strike aircraft in the Gulf region ready to fight back, the only one that could shut off the Iranian surge. "What's our ETE to the area, MC?"

"About three hours," McLanahan responded.

"Well, we won't be in time to help in the first series of attacks, but we can sure as hell do some damage in the second," Jamieson said. "Let's get cloaked up again and get back on the blue line—we've got an aircraft carrier to knock out."

Once past Chengdu, all Chinese air defense activity dropped off markedly. They deactivated BEADS to get more target and status updates via satellite, activating the system once again as they neared Lhasa in southern China, then again as they approached Kathmandu in Nepal.

As they came closer to India, they studied the updated threat charts closely. "I think it's too risky," McLanahan said finally. "The original plan had us crossing northern India and Pakistan, which is the shortest track, but the radar coverage is too thick there—the border skirmishes between India and Pakistan over the Punjab and Kashmir have that area too heavily fortified. Our best bet would be to extend farther north and go through Afghanistan north of Kabul, then south to Chah Bahar."

"What's that do to our fuel status?" Jamieson asked.

"It'll add another hour to our flight time," McLanahan said. "If we assume that all our divert bases on the Arabian Peninsula and Turkey are unavailable because of Iran's attacks, that means we either hit a tanker right away over the Arabian Sea on the outbound leg, or we splash down—Diego Garcia goes away as an alternate. No other safe alternates are available."

"What's our decision point?"

"Right about now," McLanahan said. "If we decided to abort from here, we'd reverse course and bug out over Burma, head east, and pick up a tanker just east of Manila. We can probably abort later on in the sortie and bug out over India, but then we'd have to bootleg a tanker out of Diego Garcia to meet us over the Arabian Sea or Bay of Bengal. Any way you cook it, AC, we'll be skosh on gas from here on in. The last time we'll have the right amount of fuel on board is right now."

"Shit," Jamieson swore on interphone. "You know, this is exactly the situation I warned General Samson not to get into. Don't get backed into corners. Don't do stupid stunts. I guess it's true—you never learn anything new when you're yakking." He paused, then looked at McLanahan. "It's your call, mission commander. I'll drive the bus anywhere you want."

McLanahan looked at Jamieson in surprise. "First time you've said that without the words dripping in sarcasm, Tiger."

"Yeah, maybe I should check my oxygen—I might be getting hypoxic." He shrugged, then nodded. "You're a pretty good stick after all, Mack. You got us this far. Make the call."

McLanahan paused, thinking; then: "You know, I just found out I'm going to be a father. Wendy's pregnant."

"No shit? That's great. Congrats. I got three of my own. Those critters will change your life, believe me." He looked hard at McLanahan. "So you thinking about bagging this mission?"

"Couldn't think of a better reason..." He hesitated, thought for a short moment, then added, "... except there's troops on the ground counting on us. We gotta do it, Tiger. We go."

"Then we go," Jamieson agreed. "We're committed."

The trip across Afghanistan was quiet and uneventful, but things changed immediately as the Spirit approached southeastern Iran. Their original chosen flight path had them flying through the less populated parts of the provinces of northeastern Kerman and northern Baluchistan va Sistan, but the closer they got to the Iranian army air base at Zahedran, they realized they could not put the left wing toward any emitters, so they flew east of Zahedan through western Pakistan.

Before reaching the city of Zahedan, they briefly deactivated the "cloaking device" to get a last GPS satellite navigation update to the inertial navigation system, use the SAR radar to input an accurate pressure altitude into the flight computer, and to pick up any last-minute satellite intelligence and targeting data, including updates on the Iranian attacks on the United Arab Emirates and Oman. "The battle is going into phase two," McLanahan reported as he read the retrieved messages. "Kamza Omani Naval Base on Musandam in the Strait of Hormuz, destroyed. Sib Air Base in Oman, heavily damaged along with nearly all of Oman's air force. Mina Sultan Naval Base in the UAE, heavily damaged—that's where Madcap Magician was based. God, I hope they're okay."

"Your spy buddies made it this far, didn't they?"

"Yep... and I'd say they kicked some butt, too," McLanahan said with a smile. "Listen: Peninsula Shield reports a counterattack by commando forces out of Mina Sultan on the rebuilt Iranian air defense emplacements on Abu Musa Island. Some injuries, no casualties, but the Iranian defenses were destroyed—two Hawk, one Rapier SAM emplacements, the command-and-control center destroyed, and the runway cratered. That sounds like my friends, all right."

As the B-2A flew southwest past Zahedan, they picked up the first indications of the air defense radar at Chah Bahar.

"Let's head on down," McLanahan said, punching in commands to the flight-control computer. "COLA mode engaged." He configured his supercockpit display to provide a God's-eye view of the sky and terrain around the B-2A bomber.

"Ready," Jamieson said. "Deaf, dumb, and blind, we're going TFing." He engaged the autopilot to the new commands being entered into the flight-control system, and the B-2A bomber headed earthward at 15,000 feet per minute. Because the B-2A bomber used BEADS, the so-called cloaking device, it could not use a conventional terrain-following or terrain-avoidance radar system as with the B-52, F-111, F-15E, or B-1B bombers—it could not even use a radar altimeter to measure the distance below it, because BEADS would absorb all the outgoing energy.

Instead, this B-2A bomber used a system developed by the High Technology Aerospace Weapons Center called COLA, or COmputer-generated Lowest Altitude. First used on an experimental B-52H bomber nicknamed the "Megafortress"—so called because it had pioneered many of the advanced stealth and attack systems used on future war machines—the B-2A's flight computers split up the entire globe into one-mile blocks, then had the highest terrain elevation within that block programmed into it. Using its inertial navigation system, accurate to 200 to 300 feet per hour, the B-2A's flight-control system knew what terrain was coming up all along its flight path, and it would choose the lowest possible altitude while still avoiding the terrain. The flight-control computer could look "into" an upcoming turn, evaluate its airspeed, gross weight, outside air data, and flight performance, and fly as close as possible to the earth—sometimes as low as 100 feet—even though neither crew member could see out the cockpit windows! As the accuracy of the inertial navigation system degraded over time—there was no way to update the inertial navigation system with the "cloaking device" activated—COLA would select a higher altitude to provide a greater margin of safety while still flying as low as possible.

The terrain in southeastern Iran was flat, with occasional high razorback ridgelines plunging down into flat valleys, many with marshes or dry lake beds at the bottom. Fifty miles south of Zahedan, they crossed a major superhighway, the Mashhad-Chah Bahar Highway. Their flight path took them about forty miles west of it, far enough to stay away from any detection from populated areas along the highway but close enough that Jamieson could see it. "Lots of traffic out there, heading north," Jamieson said. "Good idea to get away from the coast these days."

About 180 miles north of Chah Bahar, they picked up the first threat indications from radar sites out in the Gulf of Oman. They saw a bat-wing symbol with a small circle on the apex—the symbol for an airborne early-warning radar. "There's the Iranian A-10 radar plane," McLanahan said. "About two hundred fifty miles away—seventy miles off-shore. The radar guys say that if they're going to pick us up, we'll be within one hundred twenty miles of the second site. That means we might be visible to them for seventy to one hundred miles—ten, maybe fifteen minutes."

Just then, another bat-wing symbol appeared on the scope—not an A-10 radar plane, but an Iranian F-14 Tomcat fighter. "F-14 off the nose, about one hundred miles," McLanahan said. "Not locked on yet, but he's headed right for us . . ."

"It's that loose screw or rivet or joint on the left wing," Jamieson said. "It's screwing up our stealthy stuff. And the F-14's designed to look for low-flying targets as small as a cruise missile."

"So let's start giving them something to shoot at," McLanahan said. "It's a little earlier than we wanted, but we're definitely an item of interest. I'm setting five hundred feet—stand by for missile launch." McLanahan switched the terrain-avoidance system to 500 feet, then commanded the first launch of an AGM-86C cruise missile. The subsonic AGM-86C cruise missile had a turbojet engine that flew the missile at six miles per minute for 500 miles; this one had no warhead, only radio transmitters that gave it the radar cross-section and electronic profile of a large bomber. The cruise missile made an immediate right turn and headed west toward Bandar Abbas—and the F-14 Tomcat turned west to pursue. "He took the bait," McLanahan said. "Let's make a jog east, put Iranshahr off our right wing." McLanahan reselected COLA on the terrain-avoidance computer, and they recrossed the Chah Bahar–Mashhad Highway again, heading east along the ridgelines.

"One hundred twenty miles to go," McLanahan said. "Threat scope's clear . . . got an SA-10 site at Chah Bahar searching, but so far we're . . ." And just then, the F-14 Tomcat appeared on the threat scope again.

"Shit, the F-14's back—he must've downed the cruise missile and is searching for wingmen."

"Let's give him one—this time, bugging out," McLanahan said. He commanded 500 feet on the terrain-avoidance system again and launched the second AGM-86C, this one programmed to head north, toward Beghin Airport. "Missile away, resetting COLA . . ."

Just then, they heard the computer-synthesized voice in their headphones shouting. "WARNING, MISSILE LAUNCH, WARNING, MISSILE LAUNCH!" The SA-10 Grumble surface-to-air missile site had opened fire on them—and with their bomb doors open, the B-2A bomber was a very inviting target, even at very long range. "MAWS activated!" McLanahan shouted. "Track breakers active!" But it was the wrong decision—McLanahan recognized it seconds later. "No, the SA-10 launched against the cruise missile!" But it was too late—when he activated the missile defense system and jammers, it briefly deactivated the BEADS cloaking device, and the F-14 Tomcat, which had not yet detected the decoy cruise missile, locked on to the B-2A.

"MAWS down, track breakers in standby," McLanahan reported—but they could see the F-14 barreling down on them now, coming "down the ramp" from its high-altitude combat air patrol straight at the B-2A bomber. "He's still headed for us. Stand by to . . ." Suddenly they received another "WARNING, MISSILE LAUNCH!" as the F-14 fired.

McLanahan reactivated the MAWS missile defense system, and the system immediately dumped chaff from the left ejectors as Jamieson broke hard right. "Track breakers active, MAWS tracking!" They could actually see the first missile, probably a Phoenix or air-launched Hawk missile, depicted on the threat scope, getting closer every second . . . then another "WARNING, MISSILE LAUNCH!" as a second missile was fired from long range.

The HAVE GLANCE defense system started firing its high-power laser "blinding" system only three seconds before the first missile hit—but it was enough. The Phoenix missile's active terminal radar overheated, causing a safety self-destruct. The Phoenix missile exploded less than 500 feet from the B-2A bomber. "Break left, second missile coming in!" McLanahan shouted, and Jamieson executed a hard left turn, pulling on the control stick to tighten the turn even more. The MAWS system pumped out chaff from the right ejectors in response.

The second Phoenix missile was momentarily decoyed by the chaff and by the loss of radar lock when the damaged left wing dipped from view, but reacquired a lock when the chaff cloud dissipated—however, it locked on to Kuhiri Mountain, south of Iran-shahr, not on the B-2A. Again, the second missile missed by less than 300 feet—one-tenth of a second of missile flight time!—and exploded on the barren desert highlands below.

But now the F-14 itself was moving in. "Fighter at one o'clock high, range less than three miles, closing at seven hundred knots . . . HAVE GLANCE active!"

The HAVE GLANCE system, the high-powered laser emitter married to a missile-tracking radar, had a deadly effect on delicate, sensitive combat sensors such as those found on heat-seeking missiles, passive and active radar-homing missiles—and the human eyeball. The F-14 pilot had just zoomed down the ramp through 15,000 feet and was arming up his 20-millimeter cannon when the HAVE GLANCE laser blinder locked on to his aircraft and fired.

The helium-argon laser, only the size of a large videotape

camera but just as powerful as an industrial-strength dia-
mond-cutting laser, didn't cause any pain when the orange-
blue beam hit the pilot's eyes. He saw a quick flash of dirty
blue light that temporarily obscured his vision, like a waft
of smoke or sand. He blinked—the spot was still there. He
blinked again—ah, the spot was beginning to clear, still
fuzzy but getting better. The Iranian pilot could see the radar
range click down on his heads-up display . . . 3,000 meters
to fire . . . 2,000 meters to fire . . . ready to fire . . . *now!*

But he wasn't locked on to the target anymore—like the
Phoenix missile, his fire-control radar had first locked on to
a cloud of chaff, then on a piece of terrain when the bomber
jinked away. The radar wasn't counting down to his shoot
point . . . it was counting down to when his fighter would hit
the ground. A light from a passing car near the town of Chanf
was the first indication to the pilot of how close he was to
the ground—a split second before he impacted, traveling at
almost the speed of sound straight down.

"Scope's clear," McLanahan said. "Chah Bahar's off the
nose, forty miles. We're well inside radar range of that
A-10 radar plane now."

ABOARD THE ISLAMIC REPUBLIC OF IRAN AIRCRAFT CARRIER
AYATOLLAH RUHOLLAH KHOMEINI
THAT SAME TIME

"Combined radar reports a low-flying aircraft now two hundred fifty kilometers north of our position, heading south at
very low altitude—less than two hundred meters, speed
seven hundred kilometers per hour," Brigadier General Muhammad Badi, Major Admiral Akbar Tufayli's chief of staff
aboard the carrier *Khomeini*, reported. "Chah Bahar air defense forces have engaged numerous unidentified air targets
south of Iranshahr, destroying one believed to be a decoy."

"Good," Tufayli said confidently. "This new radar system seems to be working perfectly."

"Shall we commit any of our fighters to the pursuit?"

"No, Badi, not yet," the Pasdaran naval commander replied. "We shall wait until the aircraft is over water before committing our forces." He paused to think for a moment. "The bomber is over eastern Iran now? That means it must have flown westward across Afghanistan . . . and across India and China, too, perhaps? This means that the Americans may have violated Chinese airspace to attack from the Asian side, rather than attempt another attack from overwater! I think our Chinese friends would be very interested to learn about this new development, wouldn't you say, Badi? Get me the Chinese group commander at Chah Bahar immediately."

ABOARD AIR VEHICLE-011

"It worked once before—let's see if they work again," McLanahan said. "Missile launch, ready . . . ready . . . now . . . doors open . . . one away . . . two away . . . doors closed . . ." At that instant, there was another missile launch warning from the SA-10 site—again, when the bomb doors were open, the B-2A bomber was at its most vulnerable position.

The SA-10 Grumble missile flew a high ballistic flight path over the rugged terrain of southeast Iran, flying up to 50,000 feet before starting its terminal dive into the "basket," where its quarry was supposed to fly. When it turned on its active terminal radar and flashed it into the target "basket," it acquired the B-2A bomber immediately. The SA-10 Grumble missile actually had two seeker heads—an active radar seeker in the nose and, since the missile actually flew "sideways" into a lead-computing intercept, it also had an infrared seeker head mounted in the body of the missile that looked sideways at its target as it got closer, acting as a backup and as a terminal fine-tuning device for a precision kill. With two seeker heads, the SA-10 was very difficult to decoy.

But the bomber's HAVE GLANCE laser immediately destroyed the infrared seeker, allowing the IR seeker's computers to deliver false aim-correcting data to the missile— just for about a second, but long enough to knock the missile out of its nice, smooth intercept. At the same instant that the HAVE GLANCE laser hit, Jamieson threw the bomber into another hard left break, just as McLanahan dumped chaff. The SA-10 missile wobbled, reacquired, locked on to the chaff, decided it wasn't moving fast enough and rejected that lock, reacquired the bomber—and hit the right wing, near the tip just forward of the trailing edge. The shaped-charge missile warhead punched a two-foot-wide hole in the wing, destroying the right wing ruddervators and rupturing the right wing fuel tank.

The B-2A bomber heeled sharply to the right, flipping over at nearly a ninety-degree bank, throwing the bomber nearly into a full accelerated stall. Jamieson tried to correct the turn, but had trouble controlling the aircraft. "Controls not responding!" he shouted at McLanahan. "We lost the right ruddervators . . . c'mon, dammit, give it to me, give it to me!" It took both men on the control stick, then full left rudder trim, to straighten the bomber out.

"Lost the right ruddervators," McLanahan confirmed. "Left ruddervators are deployed fifty, sixty percent. Power plants, all other systems OK. Fuel looks like it's draining out the right wing . . . right wing valves are closed, all engines feeding off the left wing, boost pumps on, system still in AUTO but I'll watch it. Hydraulics OK."

Meanwhile, the two JSOW cruise missiles were on their way, and as expected, the "screamers" did their magic once again. Two JSOW "screamers," one east and one west of Chah Bahar, created so many false targets, emergency radar locks, and close-in automatic engagements that a dozen air defense sites within twenty miles of Chah Bahar opened up all at once—and all of them shooting east or west, instead of north, toward the B-2A.

At ten miles from Chah Bahar, McLanahan and Jamieson launched the next two missiles—these were AGM-88

HARMs (High-speed Anti-Radiation Missiles), supersonic radar seekers loaded with a 150-pound conventional high-explosive warhead with tungsten alloy steel cubes embedded in the explosive to triple the warhead's destructive power. The rotary launcher ejected two HARM missiles out into the slipstream, the missiles fired ahead of the bomber, then quickly locked onto the Chah Bahar radar straight ahead and homed in. With the radar at Chah Bahar on full-cycle duty to counter the JSOW "screamers" and direct Chah Bahar's murderous antiaircraft defenses, the HARM missile had a clear shot all the way, and seconds later the search radar had been destroyed for good.

"Okay, Mack," Jamieson said. "We're at the IP. We can turn back and hightail it for the hills, and we got a pretty good chance to make it outta here. We can E and E through the Pakistani or Afghan hills, then bug out over the Gulf of Oman and catch our tanker."

"You don't want to do that, Tiger," McLanahan said. "You want to see that carrier go down. So do I."

"Yeah, you're right," Jamieson said. "Hell, I didn't want to live forever anyway. Let's take care of business and get the hell outta here." He began pushing up the throttles to full military power while McLanahan cut off the COLA terrain-avoidance system, and they started a steep climb over the Gulf of Oman toward the carrier.

ABOARD THE *KHOMEINI*
THAT SAME TIME

"The radar at Chah Bahar is down," Badi reported to Major Admiral Akbar Tufayli. "We are resynchronizing with the A-10 radar plane and our own search radar. He is repositioning his orbit fifty kilometers further north to compensate for the loss of the shore station. We have requested that another A-10 take up a position to back up our A-10 on station; his ETE is thirty minutes. . . . Stand by . . ." It took only a few moments. "We have reacquired the target, sir, bearing zero-one-five, range ninety-six kilometers, speed six hundred kilometers per hour—it appears to have slowed down considerably."

"Possibly damaged," Tufayli said. "Now may be the time to commit our forces to hunt that bomber down and destroy it forever!"

"Range ninety kilometers, speed five-ninety, altitude now reading . . . sir, altitude is increasing. He's *climbing* . . . now passing three hundred meters, four hundred . . . range eighty kilometers, passing six hundred kilometers in altitude. We have a solid lock-on, sir . . . seventy-five kilometers and closing, speed down to five hundred kilometers!"

"Engage at maximum range," Tufayli ordered. "Launch the alert fighters. Get everything we have airborne. Where is that bomber now?"

"Still climbing, sir . . . Interceptor flights Twenty and Twenty-one engaging target, range sixty kilometers and closing . . ."

"Twenty? Twenty-one? Where are those flights from?" Tufayli asked.

"Those are the air defense F-4 Phantoms from Chah Bahar, on station with the A-10." He stopped and looked at his commander. "The A-10? Could that bomber be going after the *radar plane?*"

"Get him out of there! Have him take evasive action!" But it was too late. The B-2A bomber launched two more AGM-88 HARM missiles, which homed in straight and true on the A-10 radar plane, sending it quickly spinning into the Gulf of Oman.

"He's . . . he's gone, sir, off our radar screens," Badi reported. "Interceptors have lost the target."

"No!" Tufayli shouted, slamming a fist on his seat in anger. The F-4s had poorly maintained radars, with few spare parts, and were not as reliable as the Sukhoi-33s or the MiG-29s. "Not now! We were so close! Badi, I want every fighter we have in the air right *now!* I do not care if we shoot at

every bird or every cloud in the sky that even remotely *looks* like a bomber on radar. I want it done, and I want that bomber on the bottom of the Gulf of Oman! *Now!*''

ABOARD AIR VEHICLE-011

Nose pointed down to the sea, throttles to idle to present the smallest possible thermal cross-section astern, the B-2A Spirit stealth bomber plunged down into the darkness of the Gulf of Oman. As it passed through 5,000 feet, following the computer's projected track to where it thought the carrier *Khomeini* was, McLanahan saw a tiny spot of light on the ocean—soon he saw others. ''SAR coming on . . . ,'' he announced, ''now . . . SAR standby. Got the carrier, directly ahead, fifteen miles . . . last four missiles are programmed and ready to go.''

''Punch those 'Elmers' out and let's go home,'' Jamieson said. Thirty seconds later, the last four JSOW missiles were on their way to the aircraft carrier *Khomeini*.

Following McLanahan's programmed flight plan, the four ''Elmer's'' missiles arced north of the Iranian battle group, then turned south-southeast, roughly following each other in trail 1,500 feet apart. They were just a few dozen feet above the tallest antenna on the destroyer *Zhanjiang* by the time they passed over the fleet. As they passed overhead, tiny bomb bays opened up on each missile and an invisible liquid vapor cloud sprayed over the Iranian warships. The heavy vapor droplets settled quickly in a straight sausage-shaped pattern, coating the ships with a thin, odorless, tasteless film. As the missiles completed their silent deliveries right on target, they splashed harmlessly into the Gulf of Oman, completely undetected and unrecoverable.

In seconds, exposed to air, the thin clear film that had been deposited over the two big warships began to change. . . .

"It is about cursed time!" Admiral Tufayli shouted. The first rescue helicopter was just lifting off the deck and taking position on the portside, ready to rescue any crewmen who might have to eject shortly after takeoff. It had taken more than five minutes to scramble a crew and get a helicopter airborne, and that was totally unacceptable.

The admiral turned from the helicopter deck forward to the short holdback point near the center of the carrier in front of the island superstructure, where a Sukhoi-33 fighter sat loaded with two R-73 long-range air-to-air missiles—the deck crews had managed to off-load the fighter's four Kh-25 laser-guided attack missiles, but did not have the time to replace the empty stations with more air-to-air missiles. With only a 400-kilogram payload and a partial fuel load, that Su-33 could use the shorter 100-meter takeoff run, while the heavier fighters had to use the 200-meter run along the portside of the ship. Tufayli was impatient, but he knew that night carrier operations were the most dangerous and the crews were working at their best speed. "Any radar indications on that bomber?" he asked.

"Possible unidentified target bearing zero-five-zero, range twelve miles, flying away from us," came the reply.

"That has got to be the bomber, Badi," Tufayli said. "I want it checked out immediately! And dispatch a radar helicopter to track that aircraft. If our fighters shoot it down, I want searchers to recover any bodies and as much wreckage as—"

"Sir, we have an emergency, the pilot of our rescue helicopter reports a hot hydraulic pack and wants a ready deck for an immediate precautionary landing," General Badi announced suddenly.

"Denied!" Tufayli shouted. "I want two fighters airborne before any other deck operations!"

"Sir, the Mil-8 helicopters have only a single hydraulic pack and an emergency system," Badi reminded the Pasdaran commander. "The emergency system is useful only in performing a controlled descent, not for maneuvering. Sir, no hostiles are engaging us—it is not critical to have fighter coverage airborne right away. We should bring that helicopter aboard."

"All right, Badi, but *after* the first fighter launches," Tufayli said. Relieved, Badi passed along the order.

As a second fighter was placed into the holdback position on the 600-foot launch run, the first fighter on the number two 300-foot launch track activated its afterburners, and after a few seconds to allow the thrust to stabilize, it was released and it headed for the ski jump. Acceleration looked normal, although any fighter launch off the short 100-meter run was always very tense. The fighter hit the incline bow "ski jump," sailed gracefully into the night sky, disappeared as it fell beneath the ski jump, then could be seen straight off the nose, its afterburners still on full power. "Finally!" Tufayli shouted. "Recover that helicopter, then get that second fighter airborne as soon as . . ."

"Sir, Interceptor One is reporting a flight-control malfunction!" Badi shouted. Tufayli turned his attention back to the fighter that had just taken off. It was still in max afterburner, climbing at a very steep angle. "The pilot is having great difficulty moving any flight controls, and the landing gear is stuck in an intermediate position."

"What in hell is it, Badi?" Tufayli shouted. The fighter disappeared in the night sky, its afterburners still on full. At that rate of fuel consumption, Tufayli thought, it might have time for one long-range missile shot at one of the intruders before it had to return.

"It could be contamination in the hydraulic fluid," Badi speculated. "This is a similar malfunction as the patrol helicopter. I . . ." He paused as he listened to the intercom report in his headset, then turned, ashen-faced, to Tufayli. "Sir, flight ops reports the pilot of Interceptor One was unable to maintain control of the fighter and was forced to attempt to eject.''

"Eject?" Tufayli shouted. He leapt to his feet and scanned the horizon for the plane, but saw nothing. "What happened?"

"His last report stated that his ejection system had malfunctioned," Badi reported. "The fighter has been lost on radar."

Tufayli was momentarily in shock, but his only thought was of the unidentified fighters out there. "Get Interceptor Two airborne!" he screamed. "Get it up there *now!*"

"Sir, there is something happening on the flight deck," Badi said. "I do not know if it is fuel or hydraulic fluid contamination or corrosion or some kind of maintenance error, but it may have affected the entire air wing. We should postpone all aircraft launches until the problem has been—''

"No!" Tufayli shouted. "I want air cover up immediately! We are unprotected without it! Range to the bomber?"

"Sir, the only possible target is now thirty kilometers from the carrier and increasing—it is not a threat to the group," Badi said. He touched his headset, listening carefully to the intercom reports. "Sir, combat section is reporting a possible malfunction of the radar arrays."

"What in hell is going on here?" Tufayli shouted. "Is everything breaking all at once? What sort of malfunction?"

"Problem with the antenna itself, possibly a bad bearing or problems in the gear mechanism—the radar array is not rotating properly," Badi replied. "We still have adequate radar coverage and antiaircraft capability. . . . Sir, Interceptor Two is ready for takeoff. I request permission to delay takeoff until a fast examination of the aircraft hydraulic system can be accomplished. It will only—''

"No, launch Interceptor Two immediately!" Tufayli shouted. Badi had no choice but to give the order.

The takeoff appeared normal—for only a few seconds, right at the beginning of the takeoff run. The afterburners flared, the fighter paused, the holdback bar released, the fighter leapt toward the ski jump—then seemed to actually *slow down!* Tufayli thought it was an optical illusion, but as the fighter neared the beginning of the jump, it seemed as if the pilot were braking to a halt—it *was* slowing down!

"Badi, what in God's name . . . ?"

Just as Badi was keying his mike button, ordering flight ops to order the pilot to abort the takeoff, the long twin afterburner plumes wobbled unsteadily from side to side, then suddenly pitched upward as the nose gear collapsed. Still in full afterburner power, the force of the engines snapped the Su-33 fighter in half, the fuel tanks burst open, and the fighter exploded in a huge fireball that instantly engulfed the entire flight deck. The men on the admiral's bridge dropped to the deck as the observation windows imploded, and a wall of searing heat followed the ear-shattering thunder of the explosion. Several secondary explosions rumbled around them as other fighters and helicopters up on deck caught fire and exploded.

"All stop! All stop! Damage-control report!" Tufayli was shouting. The collision and damage-control alarms were blaring as Tufayli weakly got to his feet and stared in utter amazement and horror through the shattered observation windows at the flight deck of the Middle East's first aircraft carrier. Although the foam firefighting cannons at the flight deck's edge had activated, the forward half of the flight deck was still on fire. Damage-control floodlights revealed dozens of naked, burned bodies lying all over the scorched deck.

"Badi, damn you, *report!*"

"No report from damage control yet, sir!" General Badi, his face cut up and blackened by the blast, replied. "Sir, I am receiving a report from the destroyer *Zhanjiang* . . ."

"I do not care about the destroyer, Badi. What is happening to my carrier?"

"Sir, the *Zhanjiang* is reporting a foreign substance on its decks and superstructures that is causing severe damage to all abovedecks equipment," Badi went on. "Radar, weapons, all reporting severe corrosion from a sticky substance that is preventing any movement—objects are being stuck together, as if they had been coated with a powerful liquid cement."

"*What?*"

"Yes, sir—the *Zhanjiang* cannot operate its radar or train any of its weapons, and even personnel on deck are having trouble moving around. Sir, it could be that the same substance fell on the *Khomeini*. If it got onto the fighters' landing gear, it would have prevented a normal takeoff. If it got onto the rotors or transmission of the helicopter, it could cause stress on the hydraulic system and an overheat of . . ."

"What in hell are you saying, Badi?" Tufayli shouted. "You are saying we were somehow attacked . . . by *glue?* Someone sprayed our ships with *glue* to cause such damage?"

"I do not know, sir," Badi said, placing a hand on a cut on his forehead. He listened to his intercom, then said, "Sir, the fire has spread to the hangar deck. Damage-control crews are responding. The ammunition magazines and fuel stores are in no immediate danger." He paused, then said, "Sir, you should consider evacuating the ship. You can transfer your flag to the *Sadaf.*"

"*Evacuate . . . my . . . ship?*" Tufayli muttered. "Never! I will *never*—!"

But he was interrupted by a sharp explosion and a rumble throughout the ship. He searched and found that one of the P-700 Granit anti-ship missiles, housed in vertical launch boxes on the front of the carrier near the ski jump, had exploded inside its canister, blowing huge sections of steel into the sky and gouging out large sections of the ship. Each missile weighed 11,000 pounds and carried a 2,200-pound high-explosive warhead.

"One Granit missile has exploded, sir!" Badi reported.

"I can see that, damn you, Badi!" Tufayli shouted. "Damage report!"

"Substantial damage reported on all forward decks," Badi reported. The general's battle staff was in complete disarray; reports were coming in from all corners of the ship, and he could hardly understand any of them. "Sir, you should evacuate the ship immediately. You should take the entire intelligence staff; the senior staff will remain on board. I now suggest transferring directly ashore to Chah Bahar, since it appears that the *Zhanjiang* has been damaged and cannot defend itself, and it is too dangerous to bring the *Sadaf* alongside.''

Tufayli thought for a moment, then nodded—he knew Badi was right. If just a few of the remaining P-700 cruise missiles went up, the carrier could be at the bottom of the Gulf of Oman in just a few short minutes. And if missile number seven, the nuclear-loaded missile, exploded . . . well, they would be spared the humiliation of a court-martial, at least. ''All right, General,'' Tufayli said. ''I will transfer to Chah Bahar with the intelligence staff—but the captain stays with this ship at all times, do you hear me? I want no member of the ship's complement to leave unless this ship is ready to capsize! I want the cruiser *Sadaf* to dispatch a helicopter to stand by with us at Chah Bahar, ready to take us back to the *Sadaf* to direct the remainder of the battle group in case the bomber tries to attack the fleet again.

''Badi, next, I want this ship to maneuver in the center of the international sea lane in the Gulf of Oman and remain in place,'' Tufayli continued. ''If it sinks, I want it to sink in the center of the sea lane, and I want the sea lanes blocked by all the other ships. Whoever attacked this battle group, I want it made clear that we will still close this waterway to all traffic and control its access, even if we have to use our own ship's hulk to do it!''

It took another hour to execute Admiral Tufayli's evacuation plan. Since all of the *Khomeini*'s helicopters were either destroyed, crippled by the adhesive, or under repair, a Mil-8 helicopter had to be flown out from the destroyer *Sadaf* to fetch the admiral; a simple oilcloth tarp was laid out on deck for the helicopter to land safely. While Tufayli waited for his helicopter to arrive, he had to suffer listening to the systematic destruction of Iran's fleet by Gulf Cooperative Council air attacks. One by one, the smaller ships in the *Khomeini*'s escort fleet were struck and hit by wave after wave of GCC jets and helicopters launching Harpoon, Exocet, and Sea Eagle anti-ship missiles—without forward early-warning radar coverage or air defense cover from the carrier or the Chinese cruiser *Zhanjiang*, the escorts were easy prey for GCC attackers. Twice the cruiser *Zhanjiang* was hit; three times the close-in-weapon systems on the carrier *Khomeini* came to life, destroying inbound anti-ship missiles seconds before they plowed into their prey.

When Tufayli was brought up on deck to board his helicopter, he saw the devastation in the seas around him: dotting the horizon in every direction were the bright spots of flickering red, yellow, and orange light representing burning Iranian warships. The *Zhanjiang* was still under way, and had repositioned itself between the Omani coast and the carrier, but a fire belowdecks was still not fully contained. But even worse than that sight was the look of fear, anger, and betrayal in the eyes of the Iranian sailors around him. The *Khomeini* was still afloat, crippled but still fighting—but its commander was running. Tufayli could almost hear the sailors' derisive words, calling him a coward.

It didn't matter, Tufayli thought bitterly. It was their job to fight and die for him and their country—it was *his* job to command, to lead, and he couldn't do it very well from a crippled aircraft carrier covered in contact cement, with a six-meter-wide hole yawning in its belly and a nuclear warhead threatening to blow at any second.

ABOARD THE CV-22 PAVE HAMMER TILT-ROTOR, OVER THE GULF OF OMAN
THAT SAME TIME

The CV-22 Pave Hammer tilt-rotor aircraft's refueling probe had no sooner nestled into the HC-130P Hercules tanker's lighted basket of the refueling drogue and transferred a few hundred pounds of JP-7 fuel when the navigator aboard the HC-130P Hercules called on secure interplane, "Hammer Zero-One, Peninsula Shield Skywatch is reporting a single helicopter, designate Target Seven, leaving the deck of the *Khomeini*."

"Roger," the pilot of the CV-22 responded. "Continue the transfer." He clicked open the intercom: "Right when you said he'd show, Major."

Hal Briggs punched the air with satisfaction and smiled broadly at the men of Madcap Magician surrounding him. "You were right, Paul—but we don't know Tufayli's on board that helicopter. It could be a medevac, could be anything. . . ."

"Even so, Tufayli will still be on it—no matter how many injured there might be on that carrier, I'll bet Tufayli will make room for himself." He paused, then regarded Briggs and said, "But the next step's up to you, Hal. You're in charge of this mission."

"Thanks," Briggs said. "And I say we go see who's out flying around at this time of night." He clicked open the intercom: "Greg, get a vector to Target Seven, finish your on-load, and intercept."

"Got it," the CV-22 pilot responded happily.

In less than five minutes, the HC-130P tanker had filled the CV-22's tanks. The CV-22 disconnected, turned to clear the tanker—they were flying less than *500 feet* above the Gulf of Oman, so no one dared *descend* to get separation!—and transitioned to airplane mode to pursue the Iranian helicopter. Their top speed in helicopter mode was only about 110 miles per hour, but once the CV-22 tilt-rotor's twin engine nacelles swiveled horizontally, which changed the helicopter rotors to function as aircraft propellers, the CV-22 quickly accelerated to over 360 miles an hour. Following vectors from the Saudi Arabian E-3S AWACS radar plane orbiting near the Omani border in the southeast corner of the Arabian Peninsula, the CV-22 sped northward after its quarry at low altitude.

With a nearly 200-mile-per-hour overtake, the Madcap Magician special-ops aircraft closed the distance in ten minutes, less than 100 miles from the Iranian shoreline. The Iranian Mil-8 cargo/anti-submarine warfare helicopter, a rather round, squat, bug-shaped machine with twin tails and two sets of main rotor blades counter-rotating on one rotor mast, showed up perfectly in the CV-22's imaging infrared scanner, and they maneuvered above and to the left, out of direct sight of the helicopter's pilot. The helicopter was cruising without running lights at medium altitude; its engines were brightly glowing red-hot from the engine's high-power setting. The CV-22 pilot used a small thumbwheel on the cyclic/control stick to swivel the engine nacelles up to a thirty-five-degree setting, to obtain the best combination of forward speed, maneuverability, and vertical flight capability.

"The Mil-8 is definitely not made for high-speed cruising," Briggs observed as he studied the Mil-8's image on the copilot's monitor. "Its engines will probably have to be shelled after this flight. See any door guns on that thing?"

"Negative," the pilot responded. "Nothing stopping them from sticking a rifle out the window and blowing us away, though."

"We got a few popguns of our own," Briggs said. "If you see even one pistol aimed at you, blow that bug out of the sky."

"They're going to call for help," the pilot said, "and the Iranian fighters aren't too far away. We got no comm jammers . . ."

"We'll give Tufayli the chance to surrender, or we splash him," Briggs said angrily. "I'm not letting him get away. Peace Shield Sky-watch better do their job. Let's take this bad boy down." With a touch of the power control lever, the CV-22 slipped within sight of the Mil-8's copilot, and they hit the exterior lights. . . .

•   •   •

"What in God's name . . . ?" The copilot's scream made the pilot's head snap over as if he'd been slapped. It was hard to see exactly what was out there, but in the flashing red and white lights, they saw an immense aircraft, as large as a small cargo plane but with propellers canted at an unusual angle. But there was no mistaking the black-and-green star centered between three horizontal bars—the chevrons of an American

military aircraft. The copilot could see weapons pylons with some sort of missile on it—it resembled a four-round American Hellfire anti-tank missile pod—plus a large steerable cannon on a chin turret, with the muzzle of the big Gatling gun aimed right at them! Seconds later, the American aircraft's lights winked out, plunging the horrifying scene back into total darkness. "Admiral!"

"I saw it," Major Admiral Akbar Tufayli said. "What are you waiting for? Get on the radio and get some fighters from Chah Bahar or Bandar Abbas out here to help us."

"Shall we try to lose it?"

"Don't be a fool," Tufayli said. "It found us easily, at night and at low altitude. They must be in contact with their radar planes and using infrared scanners—running will do us no—"

"Attention on the Iranian Mil-8 helicopter," came a voice in English on the international GUARD emergency frequency. "You have been intercepted. Turn left heading two-zero-zero immediately or you will be destroyed. Repeat, turn left to a heading of two-zero-zero immediately or you will be destroyed."

"Ignore them," Tufayli ordered. "Continue on your present course and speed. Any response from our fighters?"

"A flight of two Sukhoi-27 fighters, Interceptor Eleven flight, will rendezvous with us in five minutes," the copilot responded.

"Good," Tufayli said. "Then I want . . ."

Just then a brilliant flash of light and a line of bright white tracers lanced across the sky—the tracers were so close that everyone in the cockpit could hear the concussion of the shells beat on the canopy. Then they heard a voice in Farsi say, "Admiral Tufayli, you cannot escape."

"He knows you!" the pilot shouted. "He knows you are on board!"

"Colonel Paul White," Tufayli said angrily. "It is the American spy we captured. So the rumor is true: President Nateq-Nouri did conspire with the Americans to release White from prison."

"Admiral Tufayli, you have one last chance," White radioed. "Turn about now or die."

"Where are those fighters?" Tufayli shouted.

"Our fighters have the American aircraft locked on radar," the copilot shouted as he monitored the tactical frequency. "He will be in missile range in less than two minutes."

"Tell him to fly at full reheat if he has to," Tufayli shouted, "but get him in firing position *now!*"

It took a little more than one minute for the Iranian MiG-29 fighter to report that he was in radar-missile firing range . . . but: "Be advised, *Khomeini* Five, that I am painting only one radar return, repeat, one radar return. I do not see the second aircraft on my radar."

"He's flying too closely, sir," the pilot of the Mil-8 helicopter said. "Our radar images are merging."

"Tell him to close the infrared scanner range," Tufayli ordered. He knew that the MiG-29 fighter had a system called IRSTS, or Infrared Search and Track System, which could guide the fighter pilot into an intercept and kill even at night, without the use of airborne or ground-based radar. "Tell him to use his guns. The American tilt-rotor is northwest of us." The MIG-29 pilot acknowledged Tufayli's instructions.

"Admiral Tufayli, I order you to turn around and surrender," White radioed again in broken Farsi. "Your MiG-29s will not save you."

The Americans obviously had a radar plane of their own up now, Tufayli thought grimly—but it was no matter. In a matter of seconds, the tilt-rotor would fly through a hail of bullets. "Range ten kilometers," the Mil-8 pilot reported. There was no way to stop him—the Americans had no fighters up this far toward Iran close enough to help. "Eight kilometers . . ."

Suddenly everyone on the Mil-8 helicopter saw several bright flashes of light and a brief but spectacular streak of fire race through the night sky. "Missiles!" the Mil-8 pilot shouted on his interplane radio. "The Americans are launching missiles! Take evasive action!'' Although the Hellfire missile was intended as an anti-tank weapon, it was just as capable and deadly against flying targets—and evidence of that came just a few seconds later, as the Mil-8 crew saw a flash of red-and-orange light and a streak of fire arcing down into the sea.

''*Khomeini* Five, *Khomeini* Five, this is Interceptor Eleven, I have lost contact with my leader,'' a new voice on the interplane frequency said. ''What in Allah's name is that aircraft?''

''It is nothing more than a fancy helicopter, damn you!'' Tufayli shouted in response. ''Get down here and destroy them!''

The lone MiG-29 wheeled back and set up for a stern gun pass—but his fate was no different than his leader's. Seconds before flying into cannon range, the CV-22 wheeled around, locked its laser designator onto the approaching fighter, and fired another salvo of Hellfire laser-guided missiles. The MiG-29 exploded into a huge fireball long before the pilot could press his trigger. The CV-22 wheeled around again and was on the Iranian Mil-8 helicopter in less than a minute. ''You're next, Admiral,'' Paul White's voice echoed on the GUARD frequency. ''Surrender now or you'll die.''

''We have wounded sailors on board this aircraft,'' Tufayli said. ''You will not dare to harm them. That is a barbaric act of a coward!''

''Their blood will be on your hands, Admiral, not mine,'' White said. ''Surrender, and I will see to it that your wounded receive all the medical care they need and are then immediately returned to Iran.''

''Go to *hell*, filthy American terrorist pig!'' Tufayli shouted in response. ''We are in Iranian airspace, over Iranian waters. If you shoot us down, it is an act of war! You go to hell!''

''After you, Admiral Tufayli,'' White radioed—seconds before the CV-22's last two Hellfire missiles plowed into the Mil-8 helicopter, blowing it to pieces and sending it crashing into the Gulf of Oman.

"Oh, man, that looked *good*," Paul White said, uncharacteristically angry, almost bloodthirsty. "That felt *real* good."

"We'll turn you into a mad-dog killer yet, Colonel," Hal Briggs added with a wry smile. "A stone mad-dog killer."

"About as likely as you becoming a chaste monk," White shot back. "Speaking of which, where did that charming young lady of yours run off to? I'm sure she's a capable agent, and I know the United Arab Emirates must have plenty of safe houses in Tehran, but do you think it was wise for her to stay down there?"

"She's not just a capable agent—she's the best I've ever seen," Briggs said. "And as much as I want her with me, she's got a job to do. I can't wait to see her again, boss. . . ."

White noticed the unexpected intensity in Briggs's voice. "This sounds serious, Hal," he said with a smile. "Is it?"

"Could be, Colonel," Briggs said. "Could be . . ."

TEHRAN, IRAN

"Your incredible incompetence has nearly resulted in bringing this entire government down, General Buzhazi," the Faqih Ayatollah Ali Hoseini Khamenei said angrily. He and the members of the Council of Guardians, the twelve-member legal and religious tribunal that advised the Faqih on government matters, were meeting with Buzhazi in the Council's chambers. "You almost single-handedly managed to create a third world war, with the military forces of nearly the entire *planet* directed against us—only the incompetence of your military commanders on board the aircraft carrier saved the Islamic Republic from disaster. Further, you directly violated our orders that President Nateq-Nouri not be harmed. Allah and his faithful servants demand an answer. Speak, General. What have you to say for yourself?"

"Your Excellency, I demand to know why you ordered our air and naval forces to cease their operations," Hesarak al-Kan Buzhazi said in response, ignoring the Ayatollah's demand. "The aircraft carrier *Khomeini* and several vessels in the battle group sustained heavy damage, but our air forces had the upper hand . . ."

"We ordered the operations to stop because our armed forces were facing virtual *annihilation*, General," Khamenei said. "Our carrier was barely able to return to Chah Bahar, and I now understand that it is still in danger of sinking, even though several hundred workers are struggling to save it."

"Your Excellency, I was one or two days away from *completely eliminating* all foreign threats to Iran!" Buzhazi said angrily. "In just a few hours, my air forces could have destroyed or damaged every military base within fifteen hundred kilometers of our shores. With no American or foreign military forces to support them, every nation in the region would have been forced to sign non-aggression pacts with us. With this cease-fire, we allow the United States to deploy more air defense forces to Saudi Arabia, Bahrain, Turkey, Kuwait . . ."

"Several bases in the Islamic Republic, a radar plane, and our carrier battle group were attacked by the Americans— and it is said that it was a *single American bomber*," Khamenei pointed out. "Our destruction was imminent. Your failures have angered Allah, and it was his command that this senseless waste of lives and resources of the Islamic Republic stop immed—"

Buzhazi shot to his feet before the Faqih and the Council of Guardians. "Enough of this religious tripe, Khamenei," he said angrily. "My war has not ended—it is just beginning."

Every member of the Council of Guardians recoiled in horror at Buzhazi's words—everyone but Khamenei himself. "How so, General?" the Faqih asked calmly.

"Iran is suffering under men like you—small-minded men who actually believe that Allah is going to elevate this country ahead of all others simply because you invoke his name," Buzhazi said. "Iran will be powerful and take charge of the true believers around the world only if its leadership has the guts to do so—and you need a powerful military force to do it.

"My men control the government now, Khamenei," Buzhazi went on. "I control the press, the Cabinet, and all telecommunications in and out of this capital. I have a military force of two million men under arms, and I have begun the mobilization of the Basij under the direct control of my Pasdaran forces—that is another million men and women under arms. We do not believe that Allah is speaking to you, any of you. Iran is under attack, and Allah has commanded *me* to lead her, to drive the non-believers away, and to secure our borders and our future.

"I have a suggestion for all you tired, shriveled-up old men," he said as he turned to depart. "Finger your worry beads and pray in silence, or stand up and support me and your warriors. If you attempt to involve yourself in military affairs again, I will see to it that this Council is disbanded or replaced. You have been warned."

"We will discuss your suggestion—and your warning—with our military advisers," the Ayatollah Khamenei said calmly.

"Your what . . . ?"

"Our military advisers," Khamenei said, raising a hand. From a side room, several men, some in uniform, entered—including one who made Buzhazi's jaw drop in surprise. "I am sure you know the leader of our new military advisory panel: the honorable Dr. Ding Henggao, Minister of National Defense Science, Technology, and Industry of the People's Republic of China. He was kind enough to bring along General Fu Qanyou, Chief of General Logistics, and Vice Admiral Qu Zhenmou, commander of the East China Sea Fleet of the People's Liberation Army Navy. The others with him are—"

"What in God's name is this?" Buzhazi retorted. "What are they doing here? I did not request this—"

"These gentlemen are representatives of the Chinese government, come to inspect their equipment and inquire as to the status of their country's considerable investment in the Islamic Republic," Khamenei said with a satisfied smile. His smile dimmed dramatically as he went on: "They were very, very disappointed to learn of the attack and destruction on *their* aircraft carrier and their cruiser."

Buzhazi was thunderstruck. Khamenei, the man who hated all foreigners and disdained almost anything having to do with the military, had secretly called a high-level delegation of Chinese military advisers to Tehran! Next to Russia, China was Iran's largest arms supplier; most of Iran's naval and missile technology had come from China, the agreements signed by most of these gentlemen now present and delivered by these very military commanders. "I am prepared to brief these distinguished visitors from the People's Republic of China at any time on the nature of the attacks by the Americans."

"Excuse me, please," Minister Ding said in Beijing Mandarin, translated into Farsi by an Iranian linguist, "but it is quite apparent to us and to my government that any continued plans for the employment of People's Liberation Army Navy vessels and weapons by forces under your command would be foolish . . ."

"I beg your pardon, Minister Ding," Buzhazi retorted, "but Iran is the victim of American treachery. With all due respect, the Chinese government should be considering sanctions against the American government for their role in the destruction of your warships. I . . ."

"The People's Republic of China no longer has confidence in your ability to command, or any confidence in your judgment, General Buzhazi," Minister Ding said acidly. To the Ayatollah Khamenei, Ding said. "The carrier *Varyag* and the cruiser *Zhanjiang* shall be transferred to our control immediately, Your Eminence. It shall be totally disarmed and rendered completely non-operational."

"This is not possible!" Buzhazi interjected. "This cannot be done! I forbid it!"

"We would advise you not to interfere," General Fu, Chief of General Logistics, interrupted. "The People's Liberation Army Navy has already sent a contingent of soldiers to Chah Bahar to effect the turnover. These include a security detachment of two People's Liberation Army marine battalions.''

"Based in Tehran and at Bandar Abbas until the transfer is complete," Vice Admiral Qu Zhenmou, commander of the East China Sea Fleet, added. "Compliments of the Ayatollah Khamenei. This will coincide with the signing of a new friendship and cooperation treaty between China and Iran, including logistics and basing rights."

"You . . . you will allow Chinese troops to be stationed on Iranian soil?" Buzhazi asked incredulously. "It . . . it is impossible!"

"Our two countries have grown together greatly over the years," the Ayatollah Khamenei said. "We both desire expansion beyond our local regions, increased trade, fewer trading barriers, and greater technology transfer and development. Along with Afghanistan and Pakistan, China's other two allies in the Middle East, this shall be attained." He paused, fixing Buzhazi with a deadly stare, and added, "And it should prove to be a strong *stabilizing* force against foreign or domestic intrigue, wouldn't you agree, General Buzhazi?" Buzhazi's mouth went dry. He knew exactly what Khamenei meant—the Chinese troops were there to back Khamenei's government against the threat of a military coup d'etat.

"We have summoned General Hosein Esmail Akhundi to assist us in completing the transfer of the carrier and cruiser to the Chinese navy, and to help establish the People's Liberation Army's liaison offices, headquarters, and barracks in the capital," Khamenei said. Akhundi was the already-chosen replacement. Damn, Buzhazi thought, I should have had him executed when I had the *chance!* "I believe we have no further need of your services, General. There are guards outside who will *escort* you to your quarters." Khamenei said the word *escort* like a guillotine sliding down on its rails. "You are dismissed."

Several Basij paramilitary guards—Buzhazi noticed that the Pasdaran guards normally assigned to the Council chambers were already missing!—appeared out of side doors and stood ready to escort Buzhazi out. He was relieved to see that none of them were armed with rifles, only side arms—good. If he had to kill them to make his escape, he would have no trouble. "I prefer to be alone, Your Eminence," Buzhazi said. Khamenei dismissed him with a wave of his hand, and Buzhazi departed.

The hallways outside the Council chambers were empty; none of the Basij guards had followed him out. One of Buzhazi's Pasdaran bodyguards had changed positions over to the elevator down the hallway. When he saw his superior officer, the guard immediately raised his radio to his lips to alert the general's driver and other bodyguards that he was on his way downstairs. Buzhazi trotted toward the elevator, an action which only seemed to agitate the guard more. "Where is General Sattari?" Buzhazi asked.

"Waiting in your car, sir . . ."

"Good," Buzhazi said. Sattari, his air forces commander and close friend, would be vital in helping to restructure and build his opposition force—he was one of the few military commanders he could totally trust. "Radio ahead," Buzhazi told the Pasdaran guard. "Have my helicopter waiting at Doshan Tappeh ready for immediate departure. You stay here and do not allow anyone to use this elevator until you are notified that I am airborne." The guard nodded and made his radio call.

The elevator was set in "express" mode, which would take it all the way to the secure parking garage on the second subfloor of the Council building and directly to his waiting armored limousine. Finally, inside the express elevator, Buzhazi felt safe. Damn Khamenei! Buzhazi cursed. Damn his unexpected backbone. The only thing that would save him from the power and wrath of the Pasdaran was a bold, innovative move, and inviting the Chinese to establish bases in Iran was such a move. What else had Khamenei had to promise Jiang Zemin and his powerful military warlords? If it worked, Iran, its Islamic partners, and China would make a powerful Asian union, strong enough even to take on the

West and its overwhelming military superiority.

Well, this fight was not over, Buzhazi decided. Khamenei was not bulletproof, and the relations he now seemed to enjoy with China might turn sour very quickly. Both Jiang and Khamenei were ideologues, obsessed with fantasies of global domination and leadership—one Communist, the other Islamist. Buzhazi was more pragmatic. There might be others in China much like himself. The chief of the People's Liberation Army Air Force, for example: General Cao Shuangming, young, brash, opportunistic, and eager to ascend the ranks of the world's largest military force in the world's most populous state.

The elevator stopped and the doors swung open—but it had not stopped on the second subfloor security level, but on the first subfloor. There, standing before him, was a woman, dressed completely in traditional black robes and a black veil—and aiming a small submachine gun at him.

Buzhazi screamed, raised his arms to his head to cover his face, and lunged at the woman. The gun fired, spraying bullets across Buzhazi's head and left shoulder, but his sudden charge and the recoil of the weapon caused most of her bullets to pass up and over Buzhazi's left shoulder. At that same moment, General Sattari and a guard burst through the stairwell adjacent to the elevator door—they'd seen the elevator unexpectedly stop one floor above and known it had to be a setup for an assassination.

The woman whirled toward Sattari and the Pasdaran guards and fired again, but she was too late. Several guns opened up on her at once, cutting her down.

Sattari ran over to Buzhazi. His face, neck, and shoulders were masses of blood and bone, but somehow the general was still alive—the small-caliber gun of the assassin had been chosen for its small size and not necessarily for its dependable killing power. "The general is still alive," Sattari said as he began to apply pressure to the larger neck and head wounds. "Get his car up here immediately! Get a first-aid kit, and notify the headquarters doctor and emergency medical team to meet us at the general's helicopter. *Move!*"

Several guards took Sattari's place, giving Buzhazi CPR and tending to his wounds, so Sattari went over to examine the assassin. An Arab woman, young and beautiful. Her robe and veil would have assured her almost complete anonymity, and thus virtual invisibility, on the streets of the Islamic Republic's capital. Somehow she had made her way down two secure subfloors of a major government building to attempt to assassinate the chief of staff. "I want this person identified," Sattari said, "and I want it done *secretly*. No one must know of this assassination attempt."

Seconds later, Buzhazi was taken away by Sattari and his Pasdaran guards, leaving two guards to watch over the body of Riza Behrouzi until another car could come to take her away.

EPILOGUE

From the east-side patio of the high-rise condominium, Patrick McLanahan could see the beautiful skyline of San Diego, the glass towers illuminated by the first orange rays of the setting sun. He put down the phone and walked through the eleventh-floor three-bedroom condo to the west-side patio, where Wendy was waiting. He sat beside her, and they locked hands and let the sun's rays wash over them with delightful splendor.

"How is Hal?" Wendy asked quietly.

"Devastated," Patrick said. "Angry. Just what you'd expect. But he'll be all right, I think." He gazed off to the city. "You know what he told me? When ISA told him just how Riza had died, he thought . . . good for her. That's how she would have wanted it." He shook his head. "Hell of a woman."

"Hell of a warrior," said Wendy.

Patrick gave Wendy's hand a squeeze, then looked around.

"I just realized: eleventh floor, unit eleven—Air Vehicle Eleven."

"Jon Masters must be psychic—or he's got a better sense of humor than we give him credit for," Wendy said. She squeezed his hand. "I'm sure we can move if it bothers you."

"Bother me? No," Patrick said, smiling. "That thing brought me back from the brink twice. I think we'll be linked forever. Why try to fight it?" He paused for a moment, then asked, "Where is Jon, anyway?"

"He was deployed on the *Lincoln* to help keep an eye on the *Khomeini* and the *Zhanjiang* as they withdraw from the area," Wendy said. "The Navy seems very interested in his stealth drone stuff. God, I'm glad this is over. I wish Iran never had that carrier in the first place."

"Unfortunately, now we'll have to contend with it over in the East China Sea," Patrick said. "China says it's committed to refurbishing it. They're pretty angry we beat it up . . . of course, we're denying it, and it does look like an aircraft accident all the way . . ."

"A Chinese aircraft carrier," Wendy said. "Almost as ominous-sounding as an Iranian carrier. Think you might be targeting some JSOWs on that same ship in a few months?"

"God, I hope not," Patrick said. "I hope not."

OVER THE GULF OF OMAN, SIXTY MILES NORTH OF MUSCAT, OMAN
2 MAY 1997, 0817 HOURS LOCAL

"Well, there she goes," Jon Masters exclaimed happily. He was watching the damaged aircraft carrier *Mao Zedong*, formerly known as the *Khomeini*, as it cruised eastward through the middle of the Gulf of Oman. It was being towed by the Chinese destroyer *Zhanjiang*, like a daughter giving her crippled and aging mother assistance in walking home. "Good riddance to bad rubbish."

Masters was watching the progress of the warships from the comfort of the Combat Information Center on the U.S.S. *Abraham Lincoln*, stationed 200 miles east in the Arabian Sea. Masters had been allowed to deploy one of his new HEARSE stealth reconnaissance drones to the *Lincoln* to run more tests. There had been talk about deploying a number of HEARSE drones on board every American carrier and even on some smaller warships such as cruisers or destroyers.

Masters's spy plane was running perfectly after eight full hours on station—it was not programmed to be recalled for another eight hours—and the *Lincoln*'s CIC was crowded with personnel wanting to get a close look at the photographic-quality real-time radar pictures coming back from the drone. Masters caught the eye of a very pretty young female fighter pilot, pointed at the screen, and said to her: "Look, Lieutenant, here are the steel barricades the ragheads—I mean, the Iranians"—a conspiratorial chuckle all around the compartment—"put up to show that they were not going to deploy any aircraft on the carrier or launch any more Shipwreck missiles." The damaged forward part of the deck had been strewn with steel girders to show anyone who was watching that the *Khomeini* was out of action.

"See? There's where the Shipwreck missile cooked off—blew a hole big enough for four Greyhound buses to fit in," Masters went on. "The PRC kicked all the Iranians off the carrier—they have about three hundred men on board now to take it back to China. Pretty good picture, huh? I came up with this technology before I turned thirty." The lady pilot was suitably impressed, and she rested her right forearm on Masters's shoulder to admire his work, as she leaned against him for a better look. Crew members drifted in and out, looking at the images; Masters and the pilot stayed.

"So, what squadron are you with, Lieutenant?" Masters asked.

"VF-103 Sluggers," she replied. "F-14A-Plus Tomcat. I'm number two tailhooker in my squadron. I'm gunning for number one—probably get it this week, too"—she smiled mischievously—"if a certain someone would get his big toy off our deck so we can do some real flying."

"Now, now, Lieutenant," Masters said, "be nice. This is progress! This is the future of reconnaissance, maybe even of aerial combat! I'll bet you still do TARPS reconnaissance runs in your Tomcat."

"I'm not TARPS qualified yet, but I will be soon."

"God, what a waste!" Masters said with mock exasperation. "With my drones and satellites, I can get you detailed real-time pictures a hundred times better than TARPS. Check this out." Masters pointed again to the monitor as a large cargo helicopter approached the carrier. "We can even watch this helicopter come in, watch to see what they bring aboard the carrier, even count how many crew members they load or unload. Try doing *that* with TARPS. I can even . . ."

"Looks like you can't get anything," the lady pilot said. Masters looked back at the monitor—it was blank. As she left the CIC, she added with a smile, "Show's over, huh, Doc?"

"What's going on?" Masters said quickly, trying unsuccessfully to get her attention once more. "Must be a satellite relay glitch—sunspots, Martians." In his head, he was running through several dozen *real* possibilities why the picture had gone off the air. He reached for his intercom headset to his technical crew, adding, "Don't worry, it'll come back. It's very reliable . . ."

But he really wasn't that sure: on the intercom, he asked, "Engineering, this is Ops . . . dammit, Tasker, what's going on? It looks like the uplink's being jammed. Tell the carrier radar officer or whoever that their radars are jamming my microwave uplink. . . . Yes, you tell them. We can't see a damned thing until they turn off that interference . . . it's gotta be from the *Lincoln*, Tasker. Who in hell else is going to be doing it?"

ABOARD THE AIRCRAFT CARRIER *KHOMEINI*

"The microwave jammers are operational," the operations officer verified. "All communications are down."

"Very well," responded Vice Admiral Qu Zhenmou, commander of the East China Sea Fleet. Admiral Qu had taken personal command of the ex-*Khomeini*, now renamed the *Mao Zedong* for its two-month trip back to China. "Will the jammers shut down all transmissions from that American spy aircraft?"

"We believe so," said General Fu Qanyou, Chief of General Logistics, the senior officer in charge of that night's secret operation. "The Iranians gave us the data. The digital data relay between the spy aircraft and its mother ship is vulnerable to broadband microwave noise interference. If that spy plane is operating overhead tonight, it will be blind for short periods of time, until it can rechannel to another frequency. That should be long enough."

"Very well," Admiral Qu said. "We shall proceed with the transfer."

With incredible speed and precision, two dozen Chinese soldiers, sailors, and technicians streamed off the rear cargo ramp of the large Zhi-8 transport helicopter. They were followed immediately by low carts carrying several missile canisters. A section of the torn-up flight deck was removed, and several dozen sailors emerged from the hole, carried the missile canisters belowdecks, and the hole was closed. In less than three minutes, barely long enough for the rotor blades to stop turning, four carts carrying four missile canisters each had been unloaded and brought below.

"Excellent work," General Fu said. "How many does that make now, Admiral?"

"We now have a half complement, about one hundred, 9M-330 Kinzhal antiaircraft missiles aboard," Admiral Qu replied. "In ten days' time, we will rendezvous with a supply vessel to transfer the replacement P-700 Granit missiles." Admiral Qu smiled. "The carrier will have developed a serious 'trim problem' that will require the *Beiyun* large resupply vessel to assist us. The missiles will be brought aboard then."

"But how will the *Beiyun* be able to carry the missiles past customs inspectors in Singapore and Indonesia?" Fu asked. "With all the commotion, the ship is bound to be inspected."

"Six missiles will be carried by the submarine *Wuhan*, sir," Admiral Qu replied with another smile. "The *Wuhan* can bypass all unfriendly ports of call with ease—it can stay at sea for up to two months and if necessary can stay submerged for up to nine continuous days. The transfer can take place whenever the threat of a surprise inspection is over."

"Excellent, Admiral, excellent," General Fu said. "Barring any unforeseen problems, it appears that we can fully repair this carrier by the time it reaches Victoria, and perhaps even be fully operational by the time it enters the East China Sea."

"If all goes well, sir, we shall have this carrier operational *before* it reaches Hong Kong," Admiral Qu said proudly. "In the meantime, we shall continue the masquerade of making the world think this is just a useless hulk."

"And in just a few short months, we will have one of the most powerful navies in the world," said Fu.

Admiral Qu could not remember when he had seen the young, powerful commander so pleased, or for that matter, the Chinese Communist Party, the Chinese government, and the Chinese military so closely allied, its senior officers so motivated and energetic. Something was stirring, he decided, and it had to do with a lot more than just an aircraft carrier, much more than acquiring overseas bases. "And then, General . . . ?"

"And then, Admiral," General Fu Qanyou responded, "China will no longer be the sleeping dragon it has been for the past two thousand years. And any who might oppose us will feel the might of our two hundred million teeth. . . ."

NOW AVAILABLE IN HARDCOVER
JACK HIGGINS
FLIGHT OF EAGLES
PUTNAM

Now available in hardcover

W.E.B. Griffin

The SECRET Warriors

A MEN AT WAR NOVEL

Putnam